The Debt & the Doormat
By Laura Barnard

To
Shazi
so lovely to meet
you.
Love + Laughs
Laura Barnard
x x x

Published in 2013 by FeedARead.com Publishing – Arts Council funded

First Edition

This is a work of fiction. Names, characters, businesses, places, events and incidents are either the products of the author's imagination or used in a fictitious manner. Any resemblance to actual persons, living or dead, or actual events is purely coincidental.

A CIP catalogue record for this title is available from the British Library.

To my wonderful family (even the drunk and mental ones) and hilarious friends – you are my inspiration.

Chapter 1

'You're how much in debt?!' I squeal looking into my best friend's face.

'Please,' she says, throwing her hands up in defence. 'Don't over-react. It's...totally manageable.'

I roll my eyes and breathe out harshly. If I know Jazz it will be anything but manageable, or reasonable or ordinary for that matter.

'Exactly how much?' I demand, crossing my arms and trying my best to come across as intimidating.

'Well I'm not going to tell you if you're just going to scream at me!' she shouts, flicking her long blonde curls behind her and collapsing back onto the sofa.

I take a deep breath and try not to over-react. It can't be that bad. It can't be as bad as when she nearly married that Scandinavian waiter because she claimed he was the best sex she ever had even though he couldn't speak a word of English and supposedly proposed with an onion ring. I mean, how much money could she have spent? It's not like she buys that many clothes, is it? Then I notice her purple knee high boots. Are they new? I try so desperately to ignore her ridiculous wardrobe that maybe I've been blind to it. Was she really getting herself into this mess before my eyes and I was too dumb to notice?

'Ok,' I say slowly, taking a deep breath to calm myself. 'How much debt are you in?'

I do my best to smile sweetly, trying to show how reasonable I'm now feeling, pushing the strong feelings of wanting to throttle her to the back of my mind.

'Well, the truth...' she begins, her small grey eyes staring up at me sadly, 'is I don't really know. I just know that I keep getting letters and...And...' She stops to wipe a tear that's escaped from her eye.

'There's red print on them saying final demand and I thought I could handle it, but now I just seem to be drowning in red letters!' Her voice finally breaks with emotion and she grabs my silk cushion, cradling it tightly to her chest.

'Oh Hun.' I move to sit on the coffee table in front of her.

I hover my hands over her, trying to think of the best way to hug her. I've never been very good with showing physical affection to friends. Don't get me wrong – I feel like I should hug someone in these situations - but I've never been much of a hugger, having grown up with three brothers. If they wanted to show affection they'd punch me in the stomach, and I don't think that would be very helpful.

I settle with patting her on the shoulder instead. God I *really* hope she doesn't get any tears on my pillow. I can see them dripping down her sculptured cheeks, so close to the cushion that it's almost touching. Please not my beautiful cushion. My Grandma gave it to me when I moved out and sewed in a message in silver thread. Now she's gone, I love it all the more. I don't want Jazz's glitter mascara all over it.

'Here,' I say, passing her a tissue from the coffee table.

'I'm fine,' she sobs, pushing it away dramatically.

The tears are coming thick and fast now and now there's snot trickling down her chin towards my beautiful purple sequinned cushion. She's never been much of a pretty crier. *Please*, just give me the pillow. Step *away* from the pillow.

'I know!' I shout, surprising Jazz with my sudden enthusiasm. 'If you leave now and go and get the letters then I can add it all up for you and we can work out how to get you out of this mess. Yeah?'

I lightly grip the edge of the pillow. If she'd just loosen her grip slightly I could whip it away from her.

'They're in my bag,' she sniffs. 'Oh, but I can't face them!'

She turns over and presses her teary face into the pillow. Well, there goes my beautiful cushion. That's another one for the wash. I should really hide nice things when Jazz comes round. Maybe I'll turn into one of those crazy women with plastic covers for the sofas. It doesn't really sound that crazy to me, just practical. I do seem to drop a lot of stuff.

I try to pull myself together and think like a good friend. Where was I? Oh that's right – the letters. I run over to her giant pink patent bag and rummage in it to find her post. God, she's got all sorts of crap in here. A DVD, a plastic baby spoon, a miniature Hindu elephant headed God, a big pink sort of rock or stone, a banana, a pair of 3D glasses, chopsticks, some rizlas and a Swiss army knife. Jesus, she's a kook. I finally locate a stack of letters at the bottom.

'Found them,' I say, trying to sound cheery. I walk back over to her and prise her away from the sofa before she can do any more damage. 'Come on,' I say impatiently. 'We need to do this.'

'Ok, ok.' She wipes the tears from her face, smudging mascara all over her cheeks before sitting bolt upright; a sudden determined look on her face. 'But first we need some wine.' She runs out of the room, coming back two seconds later with a bottle of Pinot and two glasses.

'I still can't believe you have all of this crap in your bag,' I say, picking up the plastic baby spoon.

'It's useful actually.' she says defiantly, snatching it from my hand.

'Yeah I'm sure a baby spoon is real useful.' I snort, rolling my eyes.

'It's for really small yoghurt pots *actually.*' she says, herself like a petulant toddler.

'Ok, so explain the rest,' I challenge.

'Fine, I'll show you.' She picks up her Swiss army knife and stabs the top of the bottle with it, managing to eventually prise the cork out.

'Tah dah,' she smiles, looking very proud of herself.

'And the rest?' I ask, as she pours wine into my glass with little bits of cork floating in it.

'Easy,' she smiles. 'The DVD is one someone at work lent me, the banana for potassium, *obviously.* The chopsticks in case I have Chinese, duh. And the glasses are from a 3D movie I saw the other day.'

'And these?' I ask holding up the mini statue and rock.

'For my inner peace and wellbeing. *Obviously.*'

'Oh, of course, *obviously.*'

I laugh to myself as I root around for my calculator. When I eventually find it in the oven, which I use for storage as I have an aversion to cooking, I start adding up the totals. Jazz flicks through a magazine, seeming to have already gotten over the stress. There are at least five letters but their totals don't seem that high. She must just be being a drama queen. I'm sure it's totally fine.

The total finally flashes up on the screen and I do a double take. Oh Jesus, this can't be right.

'What? How much is it?' Jazz asks, pouting her lips from behind the magazine; still barely showing any concern.

I open my mouth to speak, but nothing comes out. What can I say? This is definitely not going to make her feel better.

'Chick, you're worrying me now. Please just tell me. How much?'

She stares at me for a moment and her expression quickly changes when I can't meet her eye. She takes a large gulp of wine, her hands trembling.

'I must have added up wrong.' I touch my temples, which have started to throb. I press clear and start to add them up again.

'How fucking much?' she demands impatiently.

I take a gulp of wine myself for courage. 'Five thousand.'

Jazz sits silently for a moment, her pretty features contorted in shock and horror. She slowly puts her glass down onto the coffee table, still completely bewildered. She grabs the bottle of wine and begins urgently chugging on it. She stops when she's out of breath and looks up at me, her eyes scared and vulnerable.

'Fuck.'

'Yeah, fuck indeed.'

There's an awkward silence while I desperately try to think of something to do or say to make her feel better. There must be *something*, right? I'm sure if I watched more Jeremy Kyle I'd be better equipped to deal with situations like this.

'There's only one thing we can do in a situation like this,' she announces, standing up.

I don't believe it. In this moment of madness she has a plan. For once, my 'go with the flow' friend has a plan. Everything is going to be ok, thank God.

'Yes?' I ask, trying to hide how impressed I am. The feeling of sickening panic starts to drain out of my stomach.

'Get totally fucked.' she nods.

She grabs hold of my arm and drags me into my kitchen before I can show my disapproval. The tequila bottle is grabbed out of the cupboard and before I can protest she's forced me to do five shots. The picture on my fridge of the two of us in Ibiza with traffic cones on our heads reminds me of the last time I drank tequila. She helps me out of the kitchen with another bottle of wine in her hand, turning the stereo on full blast.

'Get serious for a second!' I shout over my Abba CD. It's this carefree attitude that's got her into this mess.

'Ok,' she says, sighing heavily as she begrudgingly turns the music down slightly.

'You need to start paying this off. How did you even get yourself in this mess anyway? I thought your Mum paid your credit card bill?' The tequila fog is starting to cloud over me. I fight it, desperate to sort this out.

'She's cut me off. Edward's persuaded her that I should *grow up* and *act my age*. Can you believe that prick?'

'He's probably right,' I reason, already slurring my words.

'How can you say that? She already gave me the budget of a poor person! You know how I hate him.' She juts her jaw out, beginning to sulk.

Edward is her Mum's current husband. I say current because he's her fourth. She first married Jazz's Dad when she was 22 and he was 80 with a heart complaint. He owned a porn empire and was worth an absolute mint. She obviously thought he'd die very quickly, but the old bastard ended up living for another ten years to the grand old age of 90. When he died he left them very rich. *Very* rich.

Carol didn't need to marry again. She could have quite happily lived off that money for the rest of her life, but she was quick to give her heart away again. She fell in love with Harry, a playboy that she travelled the world with while Jazz was expelled from several boarding schools. That quickly ended when she discovered his affair with the maid.

Then came Raul, their Spanish villa's pool boy. She was completely convinced that it was the true thing and insisted he wasn't after her

8

money. She moved over there and lived happily for a while, drinking Sangria and dancing to Salsa. It only took her a year to realise it was pure lust and he *was* in fact after her money. She agreed a settlement; small compared to the money she still possessed, and he was on his way.

And now she has Edward. A stern skinny man, who never smiles and lives in a suit. I actually like his dry sense of humour and the way that he makes Carol happy. Since meeting him they'd moved from Chelsea to the Sussex countryside where they bought a fabulous Grade II listed farmhouse. They now spend their days looking after horses and protecting chickens from fox attacks.

'Look, I'm sorry. But if you ever want to start paying this off you'll have to start living frugally for a while. A long while actually. I need to just totally take over your life and sort you out.'

'Oh thanks! If you had your way I'd be living like you, bored and lonely in a flat all on my own.'

'Hey!' I say, hurt by her sudden outburst. 'I'm not bored and lonely. I'm totally happy with my life, thank you very much!'

Since when did she think I was such a loser?

'Oh *purlease!* How can you be? You spend most evenings alone. You never want to do anything since you broke up with Stuart and that was nearly a year ago.'

I wince at the mention of his name. She knows the rules – we don't talk about him.

'That's not true! I wanted to wear my dressing gown all day and eat Jaffa cakes for lunch. I wanted to start drinking in the morning. Don't say that I don't have goals!'

She ignores my attempt at humour and looks at me seriously.

'You need to start being a bit free. Start living for the moment.'

'Yeah and you need to start being a bit more trapped in for a while! Stop wasting money. I mean, how did you even get in this mess?' I pick up one of the many statements and scan it. '£89 in Bar Res, £60 in Monsoon, £110 in Threshers. Jazz, most of this is just on clothes and going out getting trashed.'

'It's called living,' she says, looking at me as if I were pathetic not to do this sort of thing.

Well *sorry* for being responsible.

'It's called five grand in debt,' I snap.

We both shudder from the sound of that number again.

'Ok, well maybe I'll start being better with money if you start being worse with it,' she says, a mischievous glint in her eye.

'Why would that be of any benefit to me?' I say smugly, feeling sorry for my clueless friend.

'Pops, what happened last Saturday night on CSI?'

'Ok, well Catherine and Nick found a body in an alley and......Alright, I get your point.'

'Look, the only way I'm going to change is if you promise to as well,' she says, running her hands through her knotted hair. I suddenly feel un-nerved. 'You're throwing your life away, sitting around waiting for Mr Right to come crashing through your living room on a white horse.'

White horse, how dramatic. And I'd much prefer a Porsche.

'Ok...what would I have to do?' I ask, my stomach fluttering with sudden fear.

'Easy. We swap lives.'

'We swap lives?' I say, displeasure showing in my voice.

'Yep. We swap houses and start living each other's lives. Each of us can't make a single decision without asking the other first what we should do. And we have to do what the other says, regardless of whether we like it or not.' She leans back and smiles triumphantly as if this is the best idea she's ever had.

'So wait a minute. If I say that you have to stay in and watch DVD's for a whole week you would?'

'Absolutely,' she nods. 'Just like if I said you needed to go out and get drunk every night you would.'

'Why the hell would I need to go out and get drunk every night?'

'Chick, it's time,' she says, smiling sympathetically. 'You need to get back to the old you.'

'What do you mean, the old me? I'm the same person.' I cross my arms.

'Come on chick. Before...him, well you were so much fun. You were a force to be reckoned with. It's like you were a hurricane and now you're just a gust of wind.'

'Thanks for the imagery,' I say sarcastically, smiling despite myself.

'Seriously though chick. You've become a shadow of yourself. Stu...I mean...he was too busy keeping you down. He took over. Before you met him you used to rule your own world and you were great at it.'

'I'm fine,' I snap sharply, wishing she'd just shut up. She's the one with the problem.

Yet she starts me thinking. I mean she's totally getting the raw end of the deal. I'm going to be so tight with her money she'll have that debt paid off in no time and in return I just have to go on a few nights out. I can just go along with it and pretend to her it's a project for me if it makes her happy.

And maybe I could do with a change. I think about my current evenings spent slobbing in my gravy stained velour tracksuit bottoms while I eat a family sized Dairy Milk and consume at least one bottle of wine. Some evenings I even finish it off with a shot of Night Nurse just so that I'll be able to get to sleep through the pathetic tears.

'Ok, it's a deal.'

'Deal.' She shakes my hand with a wide smile on her face.

I shiver as I suddenly feel I may have made a big mistake....

Chapter 2

The bright sun wakes me up, a dazzling white ball shining brightly through the window. I scrunch my eyes up trying to block out the pain from my banging head. It's as if an angry obese elf is sat on it, bitch slapping me repeatedly. My mouth is as dry as a Nun's vagina, yet I seem to still have dribbled all over my purple silk cushion. Well, if it wasn't ruined before now it definitely is. I sit up and wince from the pain in my lower back. How did I end up on the sitting room floor?

'Morning buttercup,' Jazz sings bounding into the room holding two mugs of tea.

Why is she shouting? Or talking to me at all? She knows the rules in the mornings. I open my mouth to speak but my mouth is so dry nothing really comes out apart from a croak better suited to a frog. I feel just as green and slimy.

'Here.' She hands a mug over to me.

Thank God. I drink it quickly, burning my tongue but not stopping. I hope the sugar will wake me up and stop me feeling like I want to hug the toilet bowl for the rest of the morning. I try to ignore the fact that its not in my normal china tea cup, which I see on the coffee table full of wine.

'How are you walking and talking?' I ask in a gravelly voice, noticing her sparkling skin and bright eyes.

'You know me. I'm out a bit more than you, my little hermit friend.' She pats me on the head like a dog. 'You just can't handle it anymore.' She throws her head back and laughs.

I grunt in response. Talking is too much effort at the moment. I think I'm going to crawl into bed and stay there for the rest of the day. Thank God it's Sunday.

'So anyway, I've packed a bag for you. There's all of your toiletries, bras, knickers, make up and all that. But I've decided that you have to wear my clothes and shoes.'

I stare at her in disbelief, rubbing my forehead as if that will help me gather my thoughts.

'What the hell are you talking about?'

She must have lost her mind. I suppose too much Tequila can do that to someone.

'The deal, remember?' She looks back at me as if I'm mentally retarded.

I close my eyes and try to trace back my mind. I can remember drinking wine and singing I Will Survive at the top of our lungs, but then it all goes a bit hazy and then nothing. Actually, now I remember her saying something about debt. Yes, she's in some debt. And she said we should swap lives. Yes that's it. I said I would if it made her feel better.

'Now I remember. But remind me...what exactly are the terms?'

'Well, I've written a list.' She holds up my notepad and moves discarded naan bread from the sofa so she can sit down.

Eugh. We got another Indian. I'm seriously gonna have to tell Raj to stop delivering to me. Yet I'm impressed by Jazz; she's already becoming so responsible. I don't think I've ever seen her write a list, apart from that time she wrote top ten celebrities she'd like to shag.

'We swap homes. I get this place and you move into the house. Then basically any decision we have to make we should consult the other. And we have to do what they say,' she adds, looking at me sternly.

'Why do we have to swap homes?' I look towards my bedroom where I know my duvet is all snuggly and warm.

'Because otherwise I'll be too tempted to go out. My housemates are quite persuasive,' she smiles. 'And anyway, it'll work out perfectly. You'll practically halve your commute.'

'Ok. But you don't need a list for that.' I lie down on the sofa, having decided that sitting up really is too much effort.

'Oh, but I do! I've written everything that I want you to do,' she says, smiling mischievously.

My stomach tenses as I see her flicking through the pages, all scrawled with biro.

'Can't we just start with the basics?' I beg. 'I really don't feel like hearing loads of stuff right now.'

'Oh muffin, you do look rough. Ok fine. Well, like I said, I've packed you a bag, but I want you to wear my clothes and – '

'But I won't fit your clothes! You're miles taller than me! And thinner!' I wince from the pain. Why did I shout? It's like my head has an echo.

'Ok, calm down drama queen,' she says, putting her hands up defensively. 'Most things will fit. We're roughly the same size and I'm only a few inches taller than you.'

I look up at her slim model like 5 foot 8 stance and laugh at how she expects my 5 foot 4 height to carry her clothes off. They'll drown me.

'So anyway, I thought to make it more fun that we wouldn't tell my housemates the truth.'

'What do you mean?' I ask, my pounding head taking over. Why tequila?

'I mean you should make up a story. Come up with some funny story about who you are and why you're there.'

'This is ridiculous. Why would I bother lying?'

Why does she always have to be so childish? It's so irritating. And, why is she shouting everything?!

'Because your own life is so boring! I thought I'd give you an opportunity to start again. Start an adventure for once!'

'Ok whatever.' I say, choosing to ignore the insult, my eyelids feeling heavy. 'What happened last night anyway? I barely remember anything.'

She pouts her lips and sips her tea, as she always does when she's playing for time. A smile spreads across my face as I realise.

'You don't remember either!' I accuse, a smile spreading on my face. Jeez, my face is sore.

'Yes I do!' she retorts quickly. Her face is plastered with a smile she seems to be desperate to hide.

'Ok. What happened then?' I challenge.

'Well...what's the last thing you remember?' she asks, clearly trying to get some clues herself.

But I do want to remember. I try to trace my mind back and concentrate. It's all so hazy, as if we were dancing around in a bubble machine.

'Ok. I remember dancing around the sitting room...but...nothing else. Did we just dance and then pass out?'

'Um...yes. Yes, that's it. We just went to bed.' She sips more tea.

'You liar!'

Oh God. Don't shout Poppy. Deep breaths, deep breaths.

'I'm not lying!' she says boldly. 'Anyway, chop chop. You best get going. I'll stop by tomorrow and pick up my stuff. Oh and I want you to go out tonight.'

'Fine! Well...I want you to stay in and be miserable!' I growl.

'Of course I'll be miserable,' she says, smiling widely. 'We have swapped lives remember.'

She thrusts my sports bag into my hands and pushes me towards the door. I struggle to walk, each step feeling like I'm on a boat, sea sickness taking over. I swing open the door to find Raj, the owner of the curry house underneath my flat, looking awkward. Suffice to say, we know each other more than most people know their local delivery boy.

'Raj! Hi.'

'Hi Poppy darling,' he says, in this thick Indian accent. He looks at us both a little nervously. 'So...what happened last night?'

I stare back at him, my mind spinning with confusion. What is he talking about? Oh my God, were we so loud that we disturbed them last night?

'She just said exactly the same thing,' Jazz laughs wickedly.

'Sorry Raj. Were we loud last night?'

He stares back at us perplexed, as if we're winding him up.

'You don't remember last night?' He looks between me and Jazz.

I turn to stare at Jazz. She must remember something. Yet she just looks back at me blankly.

'To be honest....I don't really remember anything about last night. Did we see you?' I ask, taking a deep breath and praying that the sick feeling leaves my body soon.

15

'Err, yes. You...honestly don't remember anything?' he asks, half smiling as if we're joking.

'Raj, I told you! Seriously, nothing. Unless...Jazz does?' I turn to her.

'Well...no,' she admits sheepishly.

'Well, yes, you saw me. I came up after the fire,' he smirks.

'The fire?'

'Yeah, what the fuck?' Jazz shouts alarmed.

'You...really don't remember the fire?' He puts his hand up to his head in confusion.

'No! What fire?' I look around the flat for any sign of a fire damage. I knew it would only be a matter of time until I started a fire cooking drunk. But there's nothing burnt.

'Maybe I should come in?' he offers, shuffling his feet awkwardly, still on the door step.

We sit around the coffee table with more tea and some chocolate biscuits. God knows I need the sugar.

'Ok, well we were in the middle of a busy Saturday night and all of a sudden we see you both walk out into the street with a load of paper. You put it in the bin outside the restaurant and set it on fire.'

Oh. My. God.

'Please tell me you're joking,' I say grimacing from behind my hands.

'Nope. I ran outside and tried to put it out. I tried to ask you both why you did it but you just couldn't stop laughing and saying you were wetting yourself.'

That would be me and my weak bladder.

'Oh my God,' Jazz says, cradling her head in her hands. 'I remember.'

'Remember what? What the hell did we set on fire?' I plead.

I can't believe this. I'm a vandal! I'm a mindless thug you see on the TV. I might get an ASBO.

'My bills,' Jazz says, shaking her head ashamed. 'We thought it'd be funny to set my bills on fire.'

'What! That's madness!' I shout, getting more distressed by the second.

'Well if I recall, we weren't actually thinking that clearly at the time,' she retorts sharply.

'Oh God. Was the fire bad? Did you put it out easily?' I ask, looking between Raj and Jazz.

'Not exactly,' Jazz says, avoiding my gaze.

'The fire brigade had to come,' Raj adds.

'Oh my Jesus. And did they want to speak to us?'

Maybe we already have an ASBO? Maybe we're due in court today. We could go to prison. I'll have to be someone's bitch.

'They were a bit suspicious and did ask lots of questions,' Raj says, sighing heavily and taking a biscuit.

'AND??' I ask, losing my mind.

'Well...' He looks at the floor. 'We just told them that some kids did it. But...you did kind of kiss the fireman.'

'Jazz! You can't go around doing that!' I shout, turning to berate her and then back to Raj. 'She can be such a hussy when she's pissed.'

'Actually...' he says shyly. 'It wasn't Jazz. It was you.'

'What?'

Oh my God. I kissed a man and I don't remember. I'm the hussy, not Jazz. But wait, he was a fireman. Maybe he was gorgeous. Maybe we'll end up getting married at the fire station surrounded by Dalmatians in fire hats.

'What was he like?' I ask trying not to show how intrigued I am.

'Well, he was pretty old.' He smiles from ear to ear. 'I think he actually knows your Dad.'

Oh my God. How did I get so drunk that I ended up kissing a middle aged fireman? I mean, I only had a bit of wine and tequila. Didn't I?

'Oh my God. That is too funny!' Jazz giggles, doubling over in hysterics.

'Jazz! It's not funny!'

'I'm sorry, but it so is!' she spits, snorting tea out of her nostrils.

'This is all your fault Jazz!' I shout, mortification taking over my body. How could I have been so reckless!

'How is it my fault?' she asks offended.

'You forced me to drink loads!'

'Er, sorry, but at no point did I hold you down and force the drink down your neck.'

'Actually at one point I'm pretty sure you did.' Flashbacks of Jazz pouring wine into my mouth while I lay on the sofa come into my mind. She was singing Dancing Queen at the top of her lungs.

'Anyway,' Raj says, grabbing our attention again. 'So I take it you don't remember anything about me?'

Jazz looks at me with the same confused expression on her face as mine.

'Did we...,' God I'm really clutching at straws here, 'plan to meet you somewhere?'

He lets out a big sigh. 'No. I suppose if you don't remember that, you won't remember the rest.'

'There's more?' I don't even want to look at him.

'Well, we took you girls into the restaurant to try and sober you up for a bit, but you were adamant on coming back up here. You made us promise that we'd come up after closing.'

'And you did?'

How could I not remember four Indian geezers in my flat? Maybe I've got Alzheimer's.

'Yes. We brought up some left overs.' He looks disapprovingly at the naan breads strewn on the sofa beside him. 'You insisted that we have a few drinks and...'

'And what?' I ask, on the edge of my seat.

He squirms in his chair a little uncomfortably. 'Well, you made us watch your performance of Spice Girls Wannabe.'

'Ha!' Jazz rolls over to her side in hysterics, clapping to herself.

'We...' I swallow hard. 'We made you watch us dance...to the Spice Girls?'

I don't know why I'm asking. I don't want to know the answer.

'And sing,' he nods.

'Oh. My. God.'

'Oh chill out Pops,' Jazz says, lighting up a fag. 'It's funny. We always revert back to Spice Girls when we're really pissed.' She turns to Raj. 'We did a talent show in Uni as the Spice Girls for a laugh and for some insane reason when we get really trashed we want to relive it.'

18

'I understand,' he nods. 'Anyway, we all ended up getting pretty drunk. I don't remember leaving or getting home, but all I know that is my wife told me she found me outside our flat in the rain with blood everywhere and she had to put me to bed.'

'Blood?' I recoil.

Oh my God. How the hell did he get blood on him? Did we sacrifice someone last night? I knew we'd watched The Craft one too many times.

'Did you kill somebody?' Jazz whispers, her eyes wide. 'Don't worry, if anyone asks we were with you all night.'

'Of course he didn't kill someone!' I shout in irritation. Jazz can be so ridiculous. 'You didn't...Did you?'

'Of course I didn't! That's what I was trying to figure out. Look.' He pulls back his bushy black hair to reveal a massive cut on his forehead and some grazes on his forearms.

'Oh my God Raj,' Jazz says, considering touching it and then deciding not to.

'Do you know anything more than that? Did your wife see anything?'

'No. She just found me covered in blood, apparently totally incoherent. She cleaned me up and put me to bed. I'm really freaking out. I've never been so drunk that I completely black out. Anything could have happened.'

'Raj, I'm so sorry.'

'It's ok,' he smiles. 'But damn, you white girls can drink!'

'Oh thanks.' I roll my eyes, but then realise it's too difficult at the moment. 'That's the British binge drinking culture for you.'

'Well, we Indian boys clearly aren't used to it. I've already had two call in sick. Jazz, how on earth do you look ok?'

'Thank you! I've been saying the same thing to her. She says it's just because I'm a hermit.'

'Look, I'm sorry if you're a bunch of wooses, but some of us know how to drink.' She flicks her hair back smugly.

'I thought you said you didn't remember anything either?' Raj challenges, winking at me.

'Look, we got trashed. It's no big deal,' she shrugs, looking peeved.

'No big deal!' I practically scream. 'Jazz, we started a fire, kissed a fireman and nearly killed Raj.'

'*You* kissed a fireman and he may have nearly killed *himself.*' She looks accusingly at Raj.

'Either way. I wouldn't say it was one of the best evenings.'

'Look, thanks Raj for popping in, but Poppy was just leaving.' Jazz gets to her feet and folds her arms crossly.

'Yeah, Jazz is throwing me out,' I grunt looking at her resentfully.

'I'm gonna be your new neighbour,' Jazz smiles wildly at Raj.

'Ah yes! The life swap thing. You told us about that last night. Good luck,' he says unconvincingly.

*   *   *

Before I know it she's pushed us both out of the door and I'm on the train to her house, in the same clothes as yesterday. I would have taken the car but I don't think I'm sober enough yet. I keep laughing at squirrels, which I think is evidence of this. I sit down, careful to avoid everyone's eye contact. Everyone knows London is full of nutters and I do not intend on being murdered by one.

I catch my reflection in the window and recoil in horror. My hair is lank, my eyes blood shot and puffy, and my chin is red and angry looking. Beautiful. I pull some sunglasses out of my bag and put them on over my naked face. A few teenage boys giggle at me but I quickly look away. They're either laughing at what a twat I am, fancying myself a celebrity, or planning my rape and murder. Either way, I'm not taking the chance. I slink lower in my seat, wishing I could hide away from everyone. And get a giant McDonald's Chicken sandwich.

I wonder what the house will be like. I've never actually been inside it before. Jazz has always been too embarrassed to bring me in, saying I'm a total snob and would never recover. She assures me it's worse than the studio in Balham she rented a couple of years ago and that had rats. Although her Mum's always given her a gigantic monthly budget, she's always preferred to 'keep it real' and 'live with the real

20

people' as she says. That, and I think it allowed her to spend more money on shoes and getting trashed. We tend to hang out at my flat, especially as she has three housemates. I don't even know their names. I really should listen more.

I get off the train and struggle along the platform, wondering if I could just go and move into my Mum's house instead. Would Jazz even notice? Someone's embarrassing ring tone stops my thoughts as my head starts to quake in misery. I think it's *Oops up Side Your Head*. What kind of mental case has that as their ring tone? Poor bastard. Like I said, London is full of head cases.

I wonder what her housemate's names are – I think maybe Tilly? I know it's one guy and two girls. He's probably gay. I've always wanted a gay best friend.'

God, I really can't concentrate with that ringtone making my head rattle. And it seems to be following me. It must be someone around me. I survey the crowds carefully but they all seem a bit too grown up for such a ridiculous ring tone. Maybe it's one of those people that wear dull grey during the week and swing at weekends.

'Excuse me,' a man with red hair and piercing green eyes says to me.

'Yes?' I smile, suddenly aware that I haven't even brushed my teeth today.

Surely he's too good looking to be distracting me while his friend robs my bag? Maybe I should watch a little less Hustle. Maybe I'm one of those people you hear about that meets their husband randomly on a train platform. I mean, I never thought I'd marry a ginger, but you can't choose these things can you. Sometimes fate is just mapped out for you.

'Err, I think your phone is ringing.' He gestures at my bag.

The ringtone is still going and he's looking at me strangely, amusement on his face.

'No, no. It's not mine,' I protest, digging my phone from my bag to prove it to him. But it is mine. The phone is lit up, flashing urgently 'Home'.

'Oh.'

'Have a good day,' he says, rushing off chuckling to himself.

'Hello,' I almost shout down the phone in frustration.

'Darling! What took you so long?' my mother screeches in her usual high pitched tones.

'I was just being whisked off my feet by a gorgeous man.'

'Really?' she says, excitement showing in her voice.

'Of course not. This is me, remember.'

'Oh. Well, that's what I'm ringing about. Have you got a date for the wedding yet?'

'Oh, I'm just on the final round of selection. I just need to see the final five's party tricks before I make a final decision.' I can't help but be sarcastic around my mother.

'Is that a joke darling?'

'Of course it's a joke.' God, I worry about her sometimes.

'Oh. Ha ha. Anyway, you really must work on it darling. The girls at pottery class are starting to talk about you. They keep asking me when you're going to get married.'

'Yes, well unless you have a crystal ball, I don't know.'

'Oh please stop being so sarcastic darling. It's this sarcasm which makes me wonder if you'll ever meet someone.'

'Oh thanks for the confidence,' I snort.

'I'm your mother darling. It's only right that I worry about you.'

'Yeah. Well I have to go mum. Bye.'

I hang up before she can make me feel any worse about myself and stare at the phone. My screensaver has been changed to the picture of Jazz holding up two shot glasses for her eyes. I should have known she'd be behind this.

I have five weeks to get a date before the wedding. Totally achievable. *Totally.*

'Taxi!'

*　　　　　*　　　　　*

I get out of the taxi and stare up at the slim terrace house. I'd never realised before how run down it looks compared to the other houses. It's the only one on the street that doesn't have double glazing, and the red paint on the door and window frames is chipped. All of the other houses have been painted pastel colours and have hanging baskets full of busy lizzies. This one has cracked pebble dashing and over flowing rubbish bins. It hardly looks welcoming, barely habitable to be honest, but I have to think of Jazz. This is what's best for her and if that means I have to live in a crumby house for a while then fine. Maybe it'll be an adventure.

I go to the door and put the key in nervously, unsure as to whether I should knock first. But then everyone else might be asleep still and their first impression of me would be that I'm the bitch that woke them up. Maybe they're all in bed together and Jazz forgot to mention that they're a sex colony. No Poppy, you're getting ahead of yourself.

I take a deep breath and walk in, the smell of damp hitting me hard in the face. The swirly flower wallpaper in the hallway looks a hundred years old; making my head spin and the carpet is covered in brown and red stains. Someone must have died in this house. I look around, hoping it's not haunted.

I walk straight ahead into what smells like the kitchen, not from fresh bread being cooked or sausages and bacon, but from coffee and cigarettes. I dump my bag on top of the aged brown worktop and let out a big sigh. This is my new home I suppose.

'Err, hello?' a voice says from behind me, making me jump out of my skin.

I turn around, my heart racing, to find a man with brown messy hair sat at the kitchen table in a grey dressing gown. His dirty bare feet are resting on the other chair. God I hate other peoples feet. Don't get me wrong, mine are nothing to write home about either. In fact I could probably read a newspaper with my gangly toes. But still. I shudder at the sight of them in a kitchen. Milk from his porridge drips sloppily down his chin into his heavy dark stubble.

'Hi!' I say feeling instantly uncomfortable.

'So...who are you then?' he asks narrowing his eyes at me, as if he's considering calling the police.

'Oh...of course. You must be wondering who I am, of course!' I laugh awkwardly. 'I'm Poppy. I...'

But then I remember that Jazz said I have to lie. Have to make my life sound more exciting. I look around the house for inspiration, but all I can see is a toaster and a kettle. Then I spot a sombrero hanging up against the door. Perfect.

'I'm Poppy, Jazz's cousin from Spain. I'm staying here for a while and she's gone to stay with a friend.'

'Really? You don't look Spanish?' He eyes me suspiciously, whilst still managing to wolf down his porridge.

I try and stop my face retracting in disgust. I still feel a bit woozy and the smell of milk isn't helping to settle my stomach.

'Well, obviously I'm not actually Spanish. I've lived there for a few years and now I'm back.' Yes that sounds viable, doesn't it?

'How long have you lived in Spain? You don't look very tanned,' he questions, his face unfriendly and his voice deeply sceptical. His eyes look over my pale face and body. I should have put some fake tan on; really committed to it.

'Did I say years? I meant months!' I say in unnaturally high tones. 'I was only over there to...' I search desperately round the room and spot some handbags. 'To design handbags…for Jessica Simpson,' I add, looking at the Simpsons advent calendar. Hang on, advent? Christmas was six months ago.

I stare at him a little discomfited. He stares back, seeming to study me. Maybe I went a bit too far with the Jessica Simpson thing.

'Oh, well that's random.' he finally says, seeming no friendlier. He tips the bowl up to slurp the last remains of the milk.

Hold onto your stomach Poppy. Do not vomit.

'Morning!' a girl sings, skipping into the room.

She's shorter than me, probably only about 5 foot 2, but her limbs are long and tanned. Her brown wavy hair has honey highlights through it. It hangs down to her bum, swishing as she moves. She's wearing pink tracksuit bottoms with a white vest top that shows off her tan. Now, *she* looks like she could have lived in Spain and designed handbags for Jessica Simpson.

'Oh, I didn't know we had company,' she says, seeming taken aback. She looks back accusingly at the guy. 'I can't keep up with all of Ryan's lady friends.' She smiles and winks.

'Oh – I'm not....I mean, I'm not here for...'

'She's not here visiting me.' he grunts. 'But if she were you'd have been totally rude. Thanks for that.' he says, with another flash of irritation. He turns to face me, still not smiling. 'This is Poppy. She's Jazz's cousin from Spain. She was there designing handbags for Jessica Simpson.' he explains.

Did I notice sarcasm in his voice? Does he know I'm lying? Am I that transparent?

'Oh my God! How cool is that! Did you get to meet her? Could you design me a bag?' she squeals in excitement, her big brown eyes nearly popping out of her head. Well, she clearly believes me.

'I...err...'

'Jesus, Izzy, give her a second! She's barely walked in the door and you're harassing her.'

'Oh shut up. She's probably dying to tell someone all the gossip, aren't you Poppy?' she says, grinning broadly.

'Actually, I am kind of knackered. Probably jet lag, you know.' Hopefully now she'll leave me alone.

I notice Ryan smirk out of the corner of my eye. Oh, come to think of it, I probably wouldn't have jet lag from a two and a half hour flight. What an idiot.

'Well, I'm Izzy,' she sings. 'Let me show you to Jazz's room.'

She picks my bag up and dances out of the kitchen. Ryan gives me a vicious stare and I stare right back. Who does he think he is anyway? I follow her, not wanting to be left in the same room as that arrogant prick who is clearly not going to be my new best friend.

'Here we go,' she smiles opening the door next to the kitchen.

I stare back at her. She must be confused. Surely that's the sitting room. My bedroom must be upstairs, no? She opens the door and I quickly realise this is my room. Jazz's crap is thrown all over the room, barely leaving any floor space, and every surface is covered with make-up. I kick away some jeans so that I can make a path towards the double bed.

'Well thanks.' I flop onto the bed, hoping she will leave me alone. She smiles and hops out of the room. Christ, she's like a ballerina the way she dances around everywhere.

I stare at the ceiling while loud music starts playing through the walls and my stomach contracts with nerves. I'm living in a strange house, with strange people, telling them random lies about designing handbags. Why on earth did I ever agree to go along with this?

Chapter 3

'Poppy!'

The sound of my name being called wakes me up. I sit upright and look at my watch. Its 7pm – I must have slept for hours.

'Poppy!' the screech comes again.

It sounds like that Izzy girl and she seems quite persistent. I get up and walk into the kitchen in my crumpled clothes, removing the sleep from my eyes.

'Ah, there you are. We were thinking about going out for a few drinkies. Are you up for it?' she asks as enthusiastic as ever.

'Sorry, but who is she?' a loud husky female voice asks.

I turn around to follow the voice and find a gorgeous woman in just her bra and knickers. She walks into the kitchen and takes a seat next to Izzy at the kitchen table.

Wow. She's so breathtakingly beautiful I can't help but stare. Her long black hair is tousled, as if she's been having sex all afternoon. She has cheekbones you could sharpen your knives on and eyes so dark brown that they're almost black. She's got dark olive skin, possibly Cuban, but I really can't work it out. Her pale pink lace bra shows of her amazing boobs, which I'm not sure are real. Her waist is tiny but her hips and butt are curvy. Her figure is probably better suited to FHM than this grubby kitchen. She takes a cigarette out of the packet on the table and lights it, leaning back casually, surveying me disapprovingly.

'Poppy,' Izzy says, miffed, as if she'd already told her twice.

'Poppy?' she smiles. 'What, were you born on Remembrance Day or something?' She laughs, her voice raspy, as she looks at me up and down.

'Err...no,' I laugh awkwardly. 'My Mum just liked it I guess.'

'How amusing.' Her full dewy lips turn into a wide smirk.

I hate her.

'Gracie! You should really try and be friendlier. You come across as such a bitch sometimes.'

27

'Sorry, but we can't all be miss sunshine 24 hours a day like you,' she roars. 'Anyway, I'm Grace. It's nice to meet you Poppy.'

She extends her hand and shakes mine formally. Her hand is so cold that it sets the hairs on the back of my neck up. Her black painted nails press into my skin as she squeezes it tightly. What is with this chick? She reminds me of the beautiful bitches at school, always waiting to trip you up. Her face does mesmerise me though; it really is enticing. She could be a model. Maybe she is. Maybe I'm now living with a house full of models. Sure fire route to suicide... or at least bulimia.

'So, are you up for coming out then Poppy?' Izzy asks, smiling hopefully.

'Um...yeah, ok.' I try to sound half as upbeat as her.

'Sweet!' She jumps up and down, catching me off guard by hugging me. God, she clearly has no problem with physical contact. She swivels round. 'Ryan! Are you coming too?'

I look around a wall and find a tiny two seater sofa with a TV in front of it. Ryan is sprawled out over it, still in his dressing gown, his long hairy legs dangling over the edge.

'Yeah cool,' he grunts barely looking up.

Great. He's going to ruin my evening.

'Super-duper,' she beams. 'We'll leave at about 8, ok?'

'Yeah sure,' I say, exhausted at the thought of it. God, I wish I could just stay in and watch a DVD. I barely feel like I've had any sleep at all. I pull out my phone and text Jazz as I walk back to the bedroom.

'Going out as you wish. Remember to stay in and watch a film. There's food in the fridge. Do not get a take-away! Even if you think you can sweet talk Raj for a freebie! Do not spend money!xxx'

I go into the room and open her wardrobe. What on earth am I going to wear? As if reading my thoughts I get a text back from her.

'Great – wear my yellow one-shoulder dress with the pink shoes. I will be miss boring tonight. But remember you have to be naughty! Flirt, laugh and get drunk! Xxx'

Responsible as ever I see.

*　　　　　*　　　　　*

When the taxi pulls ups I look outside the window at the queue of young girls in sequins, all seeming desperate to get into what looks like the door of a grotty garage. I take a deep breath to try and calm the butterflies in my stomach. It's been ages since I've been on a proper big night out and I'm not sure I'll fit in. I mean, what if everything is different now? What if there's a whole new ritual and it doesn't involve dancing around like a twat?

Plus, it doesn't help that I'm going out with three models. I haven't actually found out what they really do – they could be important accountants for all I know – but for now, in my head, they are models. I'm not used to hanging around with such gorgeous people. I mean Jazz, of course, is gorgeous, but even she has slight imperfections, like her almost invisible upper lip and scar above her left eyebrow from trying to pierce it herself. But these people, they're like aliens. It makes me feel sick every time I look at them. Especially when I compare it to my own average complexion in the taxi window. I feel such an ugly duckling. Especially with half a can of dry shampoo in my hair.

'Come on,' Izzy sings. She smiles widely and takes my hand to help me out of the taxi.

I'm glad for the help. These ridiculous shoes that Jazz has made me wear make me feel like I'm wearing stilts. Plus, I'm wearing so much make-up I could possibly enrol in the circus as Bobo the Clown. Note to self: must Google how to apply eye shadow. Or stop attempting. Jazz's yellow dress is so florescent I could pass as a street cleaner on first glance. And it barely covers my arse. Great – a mix between a street cleaner and a high end prostitute. I was seriously considering changing but then Izzy bounded in telling me the taxi was outside.

Izzy has on a leopard print boob tube dress which makes her look like Gisele, but has teamed it with casual converses. She looks so cute and sexy at the same time it makes me sick. If I tried to wear that outfit I'd look like a stuffed sausage.

Grace has on a stunning black bondage dress. It's basically ripped and completely see-through everywhere, apart from a tiny patch by her vagina, ass and her boobs. She can't be wearing any underwear. It shows off how slim her tiny waist is and her long brown legs seem to go on forever. Her hair is tied into a pony with a backcombed quiff at the front. Her eyeliner is heavily applied, done to make her eyes feline like a cat. She's basically dressed as intimidating as her personality. Ryan on the other hand is wearing a pair of dark denim jeans and a v necked black t-shirt. The only effort it seems he's made is to have a shower. This guy clearly thinks he's too cool for school. What a knob.

We get straight in, avoiding the long queue of people, as apparently Grace 'knows' the bouncer. More like used to shag him; she practically licked his ear when she said thank you. What a giant slag. After walking through a long corridor, we enter a dark room with a high ceiling and massive glass windows showing the night stars. The bar is lit up with purple and green lighting and bar men are throwing bottles back and forth to each other while the DJ plays funky jazz.

I try not to gasp. I look at the others expecting to find their mouths ajar too, but they seem totally unimpressed. Jesus, if this is the place they come for a Sunday night drink I dread to think where they go when they want to create real carnage.

'Shots please!' Izzy yells to the barman.

'Oh thanks, but I'm off shots,' I shout over the music.

They all stare back at me, making me feel like the new girl at school. They look at each other amused and then burst into fits of giggles. Sorry, am I missing something?

'What?' I say, feeling the blood rushing to my cheeks. Please don't blush.

'You don't do shots? Where do you come from, outer space?' Grace says condescendingly. Her eyes narrow and something inside me shivers, as if she's penetrating my soul. My throat chokes up and I pray I won't burst into tears. I use all of my mental strength to lose her gaze.

'I'm still a bit rough from last night. But...ok, I suppose one can't do any harm can it?'

Within an hour I'm terribly drunk. Izzy's been pouring vodka into our lemonades all night, saving me from having to take out a personal loan. I nearly passed out when I saw the drinks menu. I'm grateful to Izzy for sneaking the bottle in her handbag, but it means I've lost track of how many drinks I've had.

Izzy is my new best friend. Sure, she may have been really hyper and annoying at the start, but now she's a riot! At least she wants to dance. Ryan and Grace are just being weird and boring, sipping their drinks and shooting me the occasional dirty look. What is their problem?

I feel nice and floaty, a drunken buzz taking over my body, which means maybe I've had...four drinks? Five? Oh God, all I can think about is it being a Sunday. I have work in the morning and my boss will have me running around all day. How am I going to do this?

'Come on – let's dance!' Izzy shouts, her hand motions getting bigger by the second. 'I love this song!' She takes my hands and pulls me towards the giant dance floor, alive with beautiful people pouting and pretending to enjoy themselves.

Maybe it's not the drink. Maybe it's hanging around with Disco Barbie Izzy that's making me so happy and outgoing. I mean, I am dressed like a Barbie doll, so maybe this is how I'm expected to act. I start shaking my moves to the beat; ignoring the strange looks I get from some blonde girls as they basically dry hump each other. What is it with girls like that? They're always too busy checking who's looking at them to really have a good time. They need to let loose like me. I'm pretty sure I could currently have Shakira in a dance off.

I'm so into the music that I barely notice when someone's hands appear on my waist. I turn around, assuming that it must be Grace or Ryan but I instead find a gorgeous man with olive skin and dark hair. He smiles and licks his lips suggestively. I almost lose my footing. He's so ravishing I think I might faint. He must be a male model. And he's dancing with me!

I look back at Izzy who's now dancing with Grace and she smiles back, giving me the thumbs up. Grace, on the other hand, looks like she's about to spit with jealousy. Imagine this – another girl jealous of me! I'm so flattered that I barely notice her shooting daggers at me from all directions.

His hands grip tighter on my hips, pulling me closer to him. A quiver of excitement shoots through my body. I sway along to the music feeling a bit uncomfortable and strange. He hasn't even said hello. Is this how it works these days? I've been out of the dating game for so long I'm really not sure.

He moves his head towards me as if to engage in conversation, but instead he catches me off guard by pushing his lips against mine, pulling me hungrily into him. He quickly plunges his tongue into my mouth and I'm over-whelmed by the forwardness. I mean, whatever happened to someone buying you a drink first? I push him off and try to take a breath, but he pushes himself onto me again, his hands suddenly everywhere. Wow, this is a bit much. I know he's handsome but he's quite forceful and I'm feeling a bit too drunk to be into anything like this. I just want to dance to Beyoncé.

I try to push him away again, but feel weak against his strength. Damn those shots. Ok, don't panic. He'll eventually have to breathe and then I can run. I relax my mouth and start counting to pass the time. One, two, three, four. His weight is suddenly off me, so quickly that I almost lose my balance. Thank God, he's got the hint. I look up, relieved, to see Ryan holding him back by his shoulder.

'Are you bothering her?' he shouts aggressively over the music. His eyes are almost black with anger.

Mr Hotty looks at him horrified.

'No,' I shout. 'He wasn't bothering me. I swear!' I put my hands up in defence, scared that Ryan is going to murder him right here on the dance floor. Mr Hotty stares at Ryan with his mouth open, his eyes wide with horror.

'Oh. Ok, sorry.' Ryan releases his grip on him, glances at me, as if to double check I'm ok and then stomps off.

I watch him, my mouth still gaping open, as he walks away. So that must be why they keep him around. He's handy in an emergency. Mr Hotty looks at me, still seemingly in shock. What should I do? Should I just walk off?

'Can I have your number?' he shouts in my ear.

Oh, ok – that sounds fairly normal. He hands over his phone and I type in my number, sure he'll never contact me again. I hand it back to him and walk off to find the girls. I notice Ryan from the corner of my eye glaring at me. What the hell is his problem?

*   *   *

My body aches as I turn my alarm off at 7am the next morning. It's been a long time since I've danced all night, especially in five inch heels. As I switch it off I discover a text from Jazz.

'Task for today – ditch work.xxx'

I sigh heavily, too tired to argue. I mean, is she crazy? I can't just ditch work. Even though my feet are heavily blistered and the thought of me squashed between hot bodies on the tube repulses me, I can't let my boss down. I haven't had a sick day in four years and I'm not about to start now.

'Ok. You need to go to agencies and get a job. Any job – but a full time perm one – no more of this temp business. And u need to ring your credit card & bank people & tell them you're getting yourself sorted – they just need to give you some more time.'

I get an instant reply.

'Ok, but wear something yellow ☺ xxx'

Wear something yellow? Is she serious? Is that all she can say to the list of demands I've given her? I drag myself out of bed, my feet crying from the bruises and blisters, and start rifling through her wardrobe. Amongst the tutu's, sexy nurse's outfit and zebra printed jacket, I find a pair of plain black trousers and a white t-shirt. They seem to be the only things that aren't every colour of the rainbow. I cover it with the grey cardigan that I wore here and place a yellow Alice band on my head. That should do. This way I'm not *actually* breaking the promise.

That's all I'm doing. My feet are too raw to even consider wearing high heels. I slip on my old faithful black ballet pumps. I'm definitely not going to ditch work. I know I'm supposed to be doing what she

33

says, but I can't be totally irresponsible. What would it solve, me getting sacked? She's hardly one to be giving out advice anyway.

I go into the kitchen and try not to retch from the cigarette stubs in the ashtray. I vaguely remember getting in last night and trying to cook eggs on toast. The fire alarm is still hanging open from where I hit it with the broom. How embarrassing. What a first impression. I get out some cereal, not caring that it's not mine. I mean, this whole life swap thing is really just to help her anyway. My life's fine. Totally fine.

'How're you feeling?' I jump round, heart racing to see Ryan in his same position as yesterday.

'Jesus, scare the crap out of me why don't you,' I snap, startled.

'You're a ray of sunshine this morning,' he laughs, leaning back cockily in his chair.

I'm in no mood for this arsehole.

'Whatever. I don't have time for this.'

I throw my cereal bowl in the sink and flinch when it cracks in half. Shit. I planned to bolt out of the door, making a triumphant moody exit, but now I should clean it up. I walk over to it, then decide I should still go. Or should I? I hover over it for a second, thinking over my options as I feel my cheeks redden. Ryan looks up from his cereal.

'I thought you didn't have time for this?' he smirks.

I feel my temper flare up, all the more because of the hangover I'm nursing. I glare at him quickly before making the triumphant moody exit I planned. Well, apart from the small trip. I really wish I hadn't tripped.

*   *   *

I get off the tube and spot a familiar flash of bright red hair in the crowd. Lilly from work is one of my best friends. We're both PA's at the same firm that sells head lice treatments for kids (possibly the most boring and un-sexy place to work ever), so have spent many a late evening ordering pizza while we work on presentations for the next morning.

We used to just be work colleagues, but our friendship was finally cemented when she tried some diet pills and ended up farting and accidentally shitting herself at work one day. She said the way I locked her in the toilets and rushed out to buy her new tights and a skirt made her realise I was a friend to keep. That and I'm sure she was terrified I'd tell anyone.

That night she invited me round her flat and we watched her favourite all time film, Thelma & Louise, to make her feel better. I don't really get it to be honest. Sure, Brad Pitt's in it and its fun, but then they kill themselves. I guess I just don't really see that as a happy ending. That night we ate so much pizza, ice cream and, ok, a bit of white wine, I ended up vomiting on her carpet. We knew we had to be friends after that. However, I still think it was cruel to post the picture on Facebook.

'Thelma!' I shout over what seems like hundreds of commuters.

'Hey baby-doll,' she smiles, waving. Her bracelets jangle loudly as she weaves her way through the crowds.

Her round chubby face is plastered in its usual fake tan. She's got fake eyelashes on, which frame her wide set blue eyes and so much bright red glossy lip gloss on her lips that they're practically dripping. Her un-natural red hair is blow dried perfectly with lots of volume and massive diamante earrings dangle from her ears. She's wearing a tight fitting burnt orange crochet dress, which is high necked and goes just below the knee. To say it's slightly too much is an understatement.

'I really don't feel like work today,' she shrugs.

'I know, me too.'

'What do you say? Run away from our lives and drive off a cliff in a convertible?' she grins.

Jazz's text flashes into my head. 'We could always just ditch it.'

She looks at me in complete confusion.

'Ditch? You mean, do a sickie or something?' she asks, her eyes widening with interest.

'Yeah. I can't promise any wild adventures, but I've got tea and biscuits?

'Tea and biscuits! Why the hell didn't you say! Let's go!' She breaks into her deep, husky laugh. 'But seriously, since when did you become so reckless?' Her face twists into a confused smile.

'It's a long story. So are you in?'

'Yeah, why not.'

We go into the station toilets and take it in turns to call into Mandy the receptionist. I feel my heart in my throat as the phone rings in my ear.

'Good morning, Nits R the Pits. How can I help you?' Mandy drawls, sounding half asleep.

'Hi, it's Poppy,' I croak. 'I'm so sorry but I just feel really, really ill. I don't think I can make it in today. I need to be close to a loo....but, oh God, I've got so much work to do. Maybe you could...bike my computer and desk over to me? I don't know,' I say, my voice fading. 'Ring me or text me....about anything. I'll keep the phone by the bed.'

'Nah don't worry Poppy, I'll tell Victor. Feel better.'

I let out one more moan before hanging up.

'We did it!' Lilly exclaims, shocked by our own excellence.

We skip onto the tube, giggling like school girls. I feel so naughty, as if I'm bunking school. I can't help looking over my shoulder all the way home to check that I don't see anyone from my work.

We go back to the new house and I flick the kettle on, glad that Ryan seems to have moved from his eternal chair. I start opening cupboards, searching for biscuits.

'So, what are the new housemates like?' she asks as she perches on the kitchen table, having been filled in by me on the ride back.

'Ugh!' I sigh. 'One of the girls seems sweet, but the other ones a right bitch and there's a guy.'

'A guy?' Her eyes light up with interest.

'Yeah, a *guy*,' I drool sarcastically. 'He's a bit of an idiot though.'

'Yeah, but is he fit?' she asks searching around, as if I've hidden him under the sofa.

'I suppose in some way. Not my type. All shaggy hair and attitude.'

'Mmm, sounds yummy,' she licks her lips.

'He's not a dessert,' I laugh, putting tea bags in the mugs. 'And by the look of things we're not even having biscuits.'

'Don't they have any?' She starts rifling through their cupboards. Victor suddenly flashes through my mind and an urgent flicker of panic goes through my body, starting in my stomach and ending up buzzing in my brain. What have I done? He's going to find out I'm lying. How could I be so irresponsible? He's got two meetings today. Who will he ask to make drinks? Maybe Cheryl. But what if Cheryl's better at my job and they decide to get rid of me completely? Oh God, what have I done!?

'I'm going back,' I declare.

'What?' she yells, sticking her head out of the cupboard, completely surprised.

'I'm going back. I'm sorry Lil, but I just can't bear it. We're going to get found out. I just know it!' I edge towards the door as panic starts to rise in my throat. He's going to fire me.

'No! You can't go back. If you go in after you called in sick they're gonna know that you were faking. And they'll know we did it together! They'll put two and two together and we'll both get fired!' she screams, shaking my shoulders with desperation.

I'm getting hysterical now, imagining Victor's face as he sacks me tomorrow. God, I can't bear it. My stomach weighs with worry and dread. Why did I ever think this would be a good idea? Victor's going to go mad. He might even smack me round the face. I think I'm going to be sick.

'I don't care! I have to go!' I shout, throwing her hands off me and running for the door.

'No! Please!' she begs, pulling on my arm like a child.

I break free again and run towards the door, struggling with the door handle, not used to its ancient lock. She grabs my arm again, this time twisting it back in agony. She throws me face down onto the smelly carpet and climbs on top of me, locking both hands behind my back. I try to wriggle free but my head only gets pushed harder into the carpet. How can she be so strong? I knew I should have done that Body

Combat class with her. I feel her tie some sort of fabric around my hands, restraining them in place.

'What the hell are you doing?' I yell, with a mouth full of carpet fluff. She lifts me up and drags me towards the banister. I shake my body violently, trying to release myself as she pulls tighter on the fabric, almost cutting off circulation in my hands. After a few seconds she stands back and blows a strand of hair off her face. I try to move towards her but I'm attached. There's no getting loose.

'Lilly! Please don't tell me you just tied me to the banister!'

'Ok I won't,' she smiles sweetly.

'Lilly! Let me go!'

'Can you promise not to leave?'

'No! I'm going straight back to work.'

'Well then I'm sorry.' She grabs her purple tote bag and leaves.

Chapter 4

A clicking sound pulls me out of my deep trance. I stare at the door, never in my life being so pleased to hear a key in the lock. Please say it's Izzy. *Please* be Izzy. But of course, it's Ryan.

I tried to get loose, I really did. I tried everything! First I tried to undo the several knots she'd created, but that bitch must have been a girl guide or something. There was no way I was getting through that. Then I tried to kick the banisters apart, which you'd think from how old they look would be an easy task, but all I got from that was a throbbing leg. My last resort was to try and chew my way out. Suffice to say, I'm still here.

I'm actually so hungry that I almost ate a bit of fluff on the stairs, sure that it was a chocolate covered raisin. I still have the taste of dirt in my mouth. If I were at work I'd have had a full lunch and about ten Jaffa cakes. Lilly and I normally celebrate Monday's with a Cornish pasty and some chips. But instead, I've been trapped here, bursting for the loo and planning how I'm going to kill Lilly once I'm free. I'm torn between strangling her with my bare hands and battering her to death with my keyboard.

Ryan stands still, staring at me, his mouth ajar. I try to ignore the fact that I must look like a monster and concentrate.

'Ryan! Thank God. Please un-tie me,' I plead, feeling utterly ridiculous, but past caring. He and I aren't going to be friends anyway, so who cares?

His face is unreadable as he stands there, looking me up and down. God, if he laughs I think I will punch him in the face. Well, as soon as he unties me. I start to clench my fists in preparation, my jaw hardening. Who the hell does he think he is? But then his features re-arrange themselves to a look of concern.

'Who the hell did this to you? Are you ok?' He hurries over and struggles with the knots.

'I'm fine. It's...a bit of a long story. It was my friend Lilly.'

'Your *friend* did this to you?' he asks, puzzled. 'Wow, I'd hate to see what your enemies do.'

'Ha ha bloody ha. Just un-tie me will you,' I snap. I'm so sick of his wise cracks. He's such a smarty pants.

He continues to struggle with the knots in silence and then looks at me, frowning thoughtfully.

'Quite a few knots,' he nods.

'Yes. Thank-you for the clarification,' I bark. He ignores me and carries on trying to un-tangle them.

'There you go princess.' he snarls sarcastically as he finally releases me.

I resist the strong urge to punch him in the stomach and run to the toilet before I wet myself, already feeling it releasing from my bladder. Thank God he didn't actually find me having soiled myself. That really would have been something.

I walk back down the stairs feeling about a stone lighter. He's still in the hallway waiting for me, a blank expression on his face. He probably just wants to swim in my embarrassment. I walk down the stairs, tensing my body, ready to tell him to get lost. He smiles crookedly and catches me off guard by grabbing my hand.

'What are you doing?' I shout, throwing his hand off.

He turns round in disbelief, his forehead wrinkled in anger and confusion as I glare at him. He grabs my hand again, roughly this time and practically drags me down the hallway into the kitchen.

'Get off me!' I shout, wriggling to get loose. I've had enough of being dragged around today.

'Just sit down here will you,' he says, almost throwing me on one of the kitchen chairs.

I hold my hand protectively and look down to see that it's red.

'You've bloody bruised me, you idiot!'

'Oh *please.*' He rolls his eyes. 'Anyway, omelette, fried or scrambled?' He holds up two eggs from the fridge, smiling angelically.

'What?'

What is with this erratic behaviour?

'I'm offering to cook you some food. Do you want some or not?' he asks slowly as if he were speaking to a toddler.

'Oh, um...yes.'

Why the sudden kind gesture? Maybe he's a manic depressive who has different personalities. Maybe I met Ryan yesterday but now I'm speaking to Freddie.

'Which? Omelette, fried or scrambled?' he asks again, sighing heavily, as if to portray what a massive inconvenience I am to him.

'Oh, um...scrambled would...be perfection,' I blurt out, my tongue almost shaking with nerves.

Scrambled eggs would be *perfection*? I could have said 'yes, I'll have scrambled eggs please,' or 'whichever you prefer,' but no-no-no-no-no. For me, scrambled egg is *perfection*. I loathe myself.

'Do you want a tea?' he asks, flicking the kettle on as he smiles to himself. Smiling at what an idiot I am.

'Yes please,' I say cautiously, watching him carefully. I'm totally un-nerved by how nice he's being.

'Do you take sugar?'

'Yeah, four please,' I say absentmindedly as I carry on surveying my sore wrist.

'Four sugars? Fuck. No wonder,' he snorts.

'No wonder what?' I demand.

Freddie has left the building. What is his problem? If I wasn't so starving I'd tell him to stick his food up his arse. He mutters something under his breath and, although I can't hear it, I'm sure it's not something complimentary.

I sit in awkward silence watching him whip up scrambled eggs on toast for both of us. He places it in front of me and, although I'm terribly fussy, I actually approve of them. People tend to either do them for too long, letting it go rock hard or not enough and serving yellow snot. But his are perfect.

'Do you...' I stop myself, wondering if he'd take the piss out of me if I asked for ketchup.

'Do I what?' He gets ketchup out of the cupboard and squirts it all over his eggs.

Oh my God. I don't know anyone else that does that. He looks at me confused, and I realise I must look like a social retard.

'Oh...nothing,' I say trying to sound in control. I squirt the ketchup all over my eggs and then tuck in, feeling like I haven't eaten in days.

'So…' he says, suddenly serious, 'I guess Jazz told you that I've had previous things with Izzy and Grace?'

Things with Izzy and Grace? What does he mean by that?

'But I just wanted to let you know that you're safe,' he winks, his mouth full of eggs.

Oh. Oh, I see. Jazz never told me I was moving in with a man whore.

'Oh thanks,' I say sarcastically, trying not to gag from the way he eats. Where was he raised, the zoo?

But wait, did he mean I was safe because he wasn't attracted to me? Obviously, I don't care, but am I that ugly that there would never be any attraction? That he would laugh about how ridiculous the idea would be? Well that's a bit mean isn't it? Besides, I'm shocked he's managed to sleep with them. He's a total slob. What on earth did they see in him?

'So...do you not work?' I enquire, breaking the awkward silence.

'Not at the moment. I'm looking into a few things, but nothing solid.'

'So, how do you live here? Are you on the dole? Or do Mummy and Daddy pay the rent?' I add bitchily.

'Neither actually,' he replies scathingly.

Neither? How does he pay the rent?

'Do you work?' he asks. 'What am I *saying*! Of course you work, that's where you stormed off to this morning,' he says, clicking his tongue.

'Well...I'm not very good in the mornings.' I suddenly feel ashamed at what a bitch I must come across as.

'Well that's clear.' He smiles amused. 'But then, if you work why did I find you chained to our banister?'

'Well...it's a bit of a long story.'

He smiles at me, exposing perfect white teeth and I'm suddenly aware of every muscle in my body and how close he is to me. The atmosphere quickly turns awkward and a stupid grin takes over my face. I bite my tongue, trying to remove it, sure he must think I'm a window licker. It's almost like when I was at school and the popular boy talked to me. No. I'm wrong. This is completely different. It's just that he's a weirdo. He finds it amusing to watch people squirm. 'I have time. Like you said, I'm not working or anything,' he sneers. I look down at my eggs, embarrassed at being such a judgemental bitch. Maybe I am turning into my mother.

'That was a quick job you managed to get,' he continues. 'Especially when you've just moved from Spain'. He raises an eyebrow, a tight smile on his lips.

I take it back. He's a smug bastard.

'Ha ha, bloody ha. You know I didn't come from Spain.'

'*No*!' He puts his hand up to his mouth in mock shock. 'You're not from Spain? I feel totally cheated.'

'Was I that much of a bad actress?' I ask, a tiny laugh escaping despite myself.

'That...and I know Jazz's best friend is called Poppy. She talks about you enough.'

'Oh, right.'

I wonder what she says about me.

'She...talks about me? What does she say?' I ask, intrigued.

'Not much. But she never mentioned anything about you moving to Spain to design handbags for Jessica Simpson.'

Not much? Why does he have to be so mysterious? I stare at my tea wondering if it's because there's not much to tell about me. I'm such a bore since he left.

I glance back up to find him watching me intensely. He looks hard at my face, starting with my mouth, slowly moving up to look into my eyes. I feel my body freeze and shut down; my mouth suddenly dry. He doesn't seem embarrassed to be lingering, but the goose pimples on my arms tell me I'm not comfortable with this. His eyes are dark brown, I notice, the colour of Bourneville chocolate. And when he doesn't have food in his mouth I suppose he could pass as not completely ugly.

'Your eyes are really green,' he says, holding my gaze.

'Oh....thanks...I guess.' I try to look coy and cute, but instead I snort and spill my tea.

'It's strange against your black hair.'

Then without another word he turns and walks upstairs. Well, that was weird.

*   *   *

When I un-lock my flat door I feel a massive relief. Finally I'm safe. The smells of my perfume greets me instead of dry rot and damp. An enormous urge to run to my bedroom and jump into bed takes over me. I'd happily never resurface from the layers of warm duvet.

'Pops?' Jazz's voice bellows from the sitting room.

'Yeah, it's me,' I say, suddenly excited to see her.

I almost run into the sitting room with my arms open. It feels like years since I've seen her.

Jazz's panicked face greets me as I turn the corner, her normally loose curls pulled up into a rough bun. She's wearing dungarees with a bikini underneath. She keeps looking down at her feet and back at my face. Why is she looking so worried?

'I wanted to wait until it was finished before I showed you,' she says, smiling warily.

'What?' But before the word is even out of my mouth I realise. I look around the room, my mouth on the floor. Dust sheets are on everything, newspaper on the carpet. There's a paintbrush in her hand. The walls are red. Red! Post box red. My gorgeous magnolia walls are gone.

'Oh my God,' I gasp, suddenly out of breath from the shock.

'Please don't over-react,' she pleads. 'It's not finished yet and when it is it will look fab. I promise you.'

I sigh heavily and collapse onto the sofa, the dust sheet crumpling underneath me. 'Didn't you think to ask?' I sigh again, exhausted from her un-predictable behaviour.

'It wouldn't be a surprise then, would it!' she laughs, carefree as always.

'Oh, whatever.'

There's no point in arguing with her when she's like this. She'll get her own way in the end anyway, a product of parents that spoilt her rotten. I look at the tins of paint, trying to work out if she's planning on painting the entire room this colour. I'm hoping it's just a feature wall. Then it dawns on me that she must have spent a fortune on it. She's not supposed to be spending!

'How did you pay for this? And don't tell me, you've been so busy doing this you haven't had a chance to go to the agencies or ring your credit card people? Bloody typical.'

'Are you quite finished?' she asks, smiling smugly. 'Because I have been to the agencies. Not only have I been, but I've had an interview...' her smile brightens, 'and I've got a job!'

'What?' I shout excitedly. 'You've got a job already?'

'I know! It's fab isn't it. I thought I'd be searching for ages, but they sent me straight to this interview and offered it to me on the spot. They seemed a bit desperate, but who cares, right? I got it, that's the main thing.'

'Totally! I just can't believe how lucky you've been.' Only Jazz could be this lucky. 'What's it doing?'

'Well, it's only a shitty marketing assistant role and the money's rubbish, but its full time. Like you said, it's regular money isn't it. I start tomorrow!'

'Exactly!' I exclaim, still shocked.

Wow – she really is listening to me. I can't actually believe she's been so easy to crack.

'So, did you ring the credit card companies?'

'Yeah, but they weren't really helpful. They just said that I still need to make my minimum payment each month or else they'll take further action.'

'Oh, well I was thinking anyway. You need to transfer all of those debts onto an interest free credit card. That way you'll only pay off the debt.'

'I know,' she nods, 'that's what your Dad said. I've sent off to Virgin and they've accepted it in principle. They're sending me through my details and then I can make all of the transfers.'

'Sorry? Did you just say my Dad?'

'Yep. He rang last night and we had a long chat. Good old Douggie,' she smiles affectionately. 'I told him everything and he said it'd be the best thing to do. He was really helpful. I think he was just glad to have someone that would listen to him, you know?'

Unfortunately I do know what she means. My Mum, although I love her to bits, is a nightmare to live with. She's so busy keeping up with the Jones's and re-decorating every room in the house, that she doesn't realise she's spending the whole time driving everyone else around her mad.

'But he was worried you'd get yourself into trouble. You know how he worries about you.'

Oh great, so now I'm going to have more lectures from him about being safe in London and carrying my rape alarm. When will he realise that I'm not going to die just because I'm on my own? I mean, I may be a bit accident prone, but still. The truth is that the amount of stories he's told me over the years have terrified me so much I'm scared to go almost anywhere. And I'm sure that's why I trip.

'Did he say what he was ringing about?'

'Yeah, it was to chat about your brother's wedding. And your Mum shouted something in the background about you only having a month now to lose the puppy fat.' She turns quickly to paint the wall, trying desperately to hide her giggles.

Like I could forget. Mum's been ringing me practically every day to remind me that I need to look fabulous, and boring me with all of the preparation details. She even 'accidentally' e-mailed me a link to a plastic surgery clinic advertising boob jobs.

'So anyway,' I try to shake the thought of her out of my head. 'Did you spend money on the paint?'

'No, even better. I was walking past this house down the road which is having loads of work done and I got chatting to the builders. They said the woman was being a nightmare and saying they'd bought the

46

wrong shade of red. Anyway, long story short, this gorgeous builder said I could have the paint and some brushes if I agreed to go out on a date with him. It's win, win!'

'Oh my God! You've pimped yourself out just to get some paint.' Images of Jazz walking past in stripper heels and leopard print flash through my mind. Mainly because I know she owns those clothes.

'Didn't you hear me – he's gorgeous! Quite magnificent actually.'

'Really,' I say sarcastically.

'Totally! Did you ever see Titanic?' she swoons.

'Oh yeah,' I say, brightening up at the thought of Leonardo Di Caprio. He must be hot.

'Well he's kind of like the guy I went to see that with.'

'Oh.'

She makes no sense.

'I can't wait. He's already called and we're going out tonight.'

'Jesus, he's keen! But wait, I thought we said any decisions had to be passed through the other one? And how are you going to afford it?'

'Chill out Grandma!' she giggles. 'Its only pizza express and hopefully he'll be a gentleman and pay.'

'Whatever,' I retort. I hate when she calls me Grandma.

'Oh and your brother popped round.'

'Which one?'

'Ollie. I filled him in on our little arrangement.'

'Oh great. So he's gonna rip the piss out of me next time I see him.' She giggles again, seeming desperate not to openly laugh in my face.

'Anyway, I've told you about my day. What happened with you?'

I fill her in with the excruciating details. It really does amaze me how she can be so lucky and me so the complete opposite. In one day she's managed to get a job, start to deal with her debt, paint my sitting room a God awful colour and get a date. What have I done? I've been chained to a banister. She really is like a cat, always landing on her feet. I'm more like a dog with a missing leg and one eye, that people feel sorry for but are too horrified to take home.

'Wow chick, it sounds like you've had a right adventure,' she laughs, as if she's not surprised. 'So, what do you think of the guys in the house?'

I roll my eyes with contempt.

She raises her eyebrows. 'That bad?'

'Well, Izzy's lovely obviously, even if she is like a puppy on speed.' Jazz lets out a giggle and I can tell the feeling is mutual.

'But Grace is a total bitch and that Ryan's a complete weirdo.'

'Don't be so judgemental! Once you get to know them they're fab. You just have to know how to handle them,' she winks.

Know how to handle them? What, shag Ryan like Grace and Izzy? I don't think so. He did never say that Jazz had got with him, but it does make me wonder. Wonder whether she ever did fancy him.

'I suppose.' I say, already deciding to ignore her advice. 'Jesus, your rooms a bloody mess by the way. I was trying to sort it out a bit and I found loads of old letters. Even the one you made me write to Him!'

'Oh my God! I'd completely forgotten about that!' she giggles.

'Exactly. That's how much your room is a shit tip.'

'Oh well. I'll just have to hope the world doesn't end from this catastrophe.' She rolls her eyes and flicks me with some paint.

'Stop!' I exclaim, ducking out of the way just in time for it to get the other wall.

I can't stop wondering if Jazz ever had a crush on Ryan. Whether it's a house curse.

'Anyway....can I ask a weird question?' I already feel my cheeks reddening.

'Yeah, but it's not more questions about money is it? You're boring me to death with all of this crap.'

'No...It's...well...'

'Jesus, just spit it out!'

'Ok.' I take a deep breath, wondering if I'm being ridiculous to even ask this. 'Have you ever...slept with Ryan?' I look at the floor, not wanting to look her in the eye.

The sound of hysterical laughing makes me look up. Her face is bright red with hysterics, her eyes watering and she's holding her crotch with her hand, as if to stop her peeing her pants.

'What's so funny about that?' I ask, my cheeks burning. I wish I'd never asked.

'Sorry, it's just...' She barely finishes her sentence before she's collapsed over again in a big head of hysterics.

'It's not that funny! He has slept with the other two,' I say defensively crossing my arms.

I haven't seen her laughing this hard since our Ireland trip when we got so drunk I was convinced the cows were staring at me. My stomach muscles ached for days. I wish she'd stop laughing. The longer it goes on the longer I'm contemplating throwing myself out of the window.

'Stop!' I demand, my face now puce.

'Sorry, sorry.' She straightens herself up and seems to pull herself together.

'Well, is that a no?'

'Yes,' she laughs. She quickly turns her face into a stern one, probably sensing my mood. 'I've never slept with Ryan. I mean, God! He's more like an older brother or something. I really don't even really see him that way. In a nice way obviously, but no. I can honestly say I've never felt attracted to him.'

'Oh, ok.'

'I don't really get it to be honest. Everyone seems to just swoon at his feet and he doesn't even seem to try. I mean obviously he is gorgeous but I don't see what the big deal is. Yet girls are constantly coming out of his bedroom in the morning. It's weird.'

'Great, so I'm living with a man whore.'

'Why do you ask anyway?' Her expression quickly changes to excitement. 'Oh my God, don't tell me you've fallen for his charms too?'

'Don't be ridiculous!' I snap, feeling myself redden again. 'I just wondered that's all.'

'Good,' she nods warningly. 'Don't go falling for him. He's a player. Doesn't keep a girl for more than a night. In fact Grace is constantly trying to re-bed him. You should see her when she's got a drink in her, all over him like a bad rash. But I don't think he's interested in her, which probably infuriates her.'

I can't really imagine a man being able to turn Grace down. Even though she's a massive bitch, she's a force to be reckoned with, what with her amazing figure and chiselled cheekbones.

'Anyway, now it's my turn,' Jazz declares.

I look at her confused. What can she question me on?

'You honestly think that by wearing a yellow hair band, that's taking my orders? When I say yellow I mean wear fucking yellow. Not some pathetic attempt.'

I touch the hair band and feel my cheeks burn. I do feel a bit awful. I mean, here she is going above and beyond and I can't even wear yellow.

'And you're in flat shoes! And I bet your underwear is gross, all grey and baggy?'

How does she know this?

'A general tip babe; if your underwear is older than the pizza delivery boy it's time to get some new ones.'

'Oh shut up. It's totally pink and pretty actually,' I say hoping she'll drop it.

'*Really*?' she taunts, jumping over to me and tugging at my trousers.

'Jazz! Get off me, you bloody lesbian!'

'I vanna see your knickers!' she shouts in a loud German accent, giggling.

'Get off!' I screech, as she wrestles me to the floor.

My phone beeping stops her. She runs off and gets it from my bag.

'Oh my God,' she says, her eyes lighting up as she reads it. 'Did you meet someone last night?'

Meet someone? Crap, could it be the sexy stranger? I was sure that Ryan would have scared him off.

'Why? What does it say?'

'Wouldn't you like to know,' she teases, stalking round the sofa slowly.

'Just tell me for God's sake.'

'Ok, it says, "Hey sexy, it's Hugh from last night. Fancy a bite to eat tonight? Kiss kiss."' She grins widely at me, her eyes lit up with intrigue. 'Tell me EVERYTHING!'

'Oh, he's just some guy from last night. I didn't even know his name until now. He was good looking I suppose, but...he was kinda pushy.'

'Kinda pushy is what you want! I love a man that takes charge.'

'I'm sure you do.' I sigh heavily, sure she's not going to drop this.

'Well! I'm going to text back and say you'd love to.' She starts texting away and I instantly panic, my sweat glands going into overdrive.

'No, Jazz don't! I can't!'

I jump up to wrestle her to the ground, trying to pry my phone from her fingers, but my God she's strong.

'I know nothing about him, apart from the fact he likes tongue kissing strangers on the dance floor. Hardly a glowing reputation. I mean, does he even know my name?'

'Who fucking cares! You just want a good shag, no?' She kicks me away.

'No! And what if he's a total nutter out to murder me?'

'Jeez, constantly with the drama. You've been watching too much Crimewatch; I blame your mother.'

'Just give me the fucking phone!' I scream, straddling her with my legs and pushing her hands over her head, her delicate fingers still prised protectively around the phone.

'Hello? Girls?'

I turn my head in shock to see Raj walking into the sitting room. What is he doing here?

'Ha ha! I pressed send,' Jazz laughs.

I grunt in frustration and fall to the floor.

'What? Raj, what are you doing here?'

'Sorry girls,' he says, cowering shyly. 'The door was open. I just wondered if you wanted some onion bhajee's? They went off yesterday but there's nothing wrong with them.'

'No thanks,' Jazz announces proudly, her face red from the wrestling. 'We've got dinner dates.'

Chapter 5

I take a deep breath as I walk into the restaurant. This is going to be fine. No – better than fine. It's going to be a fantastic evening. It doesn't matter that this is your first date since Him. Of course not. I'm sure it will be fine; no, amazing! I take my time to walk down the steps, all too aware of Jazz's six inch heels that are already digging into my ankles.

I scan the room, trying to find him or Jazz. I decided to meet him in the same Pizza Express so I could use Jazz for moral support. Maybe he's stood me up. Maybe he's had a better offer. Maybe Jazz has set me up and didn't plan on coming here at all.

'Hey sexy,' a male voice whispers in my ear, appearing out of nowhere.

'Fuck!' I shout, alarmed, jerking my head round in shock.

The whole restaurant turns round to stare at me. Perhaps I was a teeny tiny bit loud.

'Shall we go to our table?' he asks ignoring my crazy behaviour.

I feel his long strong hands on my neck and I flinch, before I realise he's taking my coat off me. It feels strange to have someone taking off my coat, almost intimate really. But I have to pull myself together. It's just been so long since anyone has touched me. At all. His eyes are everywhere, admiring Jazz's purple dress that she'd squeezed me into. It's so tight I can barely breathe, but Jazz reassures me that's how I'm supposed to feel.

We take our seats at a quiet table in the corner, next to a giant painting of a naked fat woman. It strikes me as strange as to why a restaurant would put a painting like that up. Any woman looking at it would immediately fear of ordering a side of dough balls, seeing her potential near future. As I sit down, Jazz's familiar cackle echoes against the walls. I discreetly follow the sound and manage to spot her at the other side of the restaurant, talking with lots of hand motions to some guy. I can't see him, but the back of his head looks nice.

The meal goes fine, but I barely say a word. He spends the whole time talking about himself; about his job, his boat, his big house. He really does seem like a self-obsessed prick if I'm honest, but I have to remind myself that he's gorgeous, if nothing else. And that this is a massive step for me – my first date since Him. It's really an achievement if nothing else. I stare into my wine glass, wondering if I'd look like an alcoholic if I ordered another bottle.

'And that was the year we went to St Tropez. Have you ever been? Oh you should, the beaches are amazing and last year we saw Brad...'

The table trembles and I grab my wine glass to stop it from falling over. I look up to see that Jazz has thrown herself against the table. What is she doing?

'Oh my God, I'm so sorry! I'm such a klutz!' she apologises to Hugh. She turns to face me in sudden recognition. 'Oh my God...Poppy? Is that you? It's been years!'

Oh God, her acting really is so transparent. It's embarrassing. He really can't be buying this.

'Come to the ladies with me and we can have a catch up, hmm?' she says, in her ridiculous posh accent that she puts on whenever she's lying. Anyone would think she went to Oxford instead of Leeds.

None the less, I smile politely and follow her into the toilets.

'Nice acting,' I say sarcastically as soon as the door is shut.

'Thanks. I'm thinking about my Oscar speech,' she jokes as she pulls up her sky blue dress and yanks down her knickers, plonking herself on the toilet and not bothering to shut the door.

I swear I've seen this woman's vagina more times than I've seen my own. She really does have no boundaries.

'So, what's he like?' she shouts, even though she's barely a foot away from me.

'To be honest, he's a bit of a douche. He won't stop talking about himself.'

'Yeah, but Pops have you seen him? He's fucking gorgeous; who cares if he's boring.'

'Well it's not going to go anywhere.' I look in the mirror and re-apply the near purple lipstick that Jazz forced me to wear. I'm sure it makes me look like a super hero.

'Jeez, I'm not asking you to marry the guy! Why don't you just have a one nighter with him?'

She says it like it's the most normal ordinary thing to do in the world. Just like saying 'why don't you buy butter instead of margarine'. The thought of a near stranger touching my bare skin makes me shiver in disgust.

'Because I'm not a whore! I can't just give myself to a practical stranger.' She really doesn't know me at all.

'Give yourself?' She yanks up her knickers and comes out of the cubicle. 'Next you'll be talking about your special flower.'

I narrow my eyes at her, trying to show my irritation.

'I just think you should have a one night stand with him. I do it all the time, it's great. Pure, hot, indulgent sex and no strings attached. You really can't go through life without doing it at least once.'

'Oh really, and you're such a good example are you? Where have all the one night stands got you?' I ask bitchily. Her face drops and I immediately feel awful.

'Hey, I've had loads of hot sex actually,' she says defensively.

'Which is more than I can say about you. How many men have you slept with? Was it three?' she mocks.

Well now I practically feel like a virgin.

'I'm sorry,' I sigh. 'I didn't mean to be a bitch. It's just....I'm scared. I don't know if I can get naked in front of someone I don't see a future with.'

'God, you're practically a nun!' She turns to face me, placing her hands on my shoulders. 'Look, I know it'll be the first time since...Him. But, remember that you can be anything you want to be. For all he knows you're some vamp who eats men for breakfast. Just think of it as a performance.'

I think about it for a moment and try not to allow my stomach to curl up in fear. Maybe this would be good for me. Help me move on completely. It would be nice to get my number up to four.

'The only way you're going to completely get over him is to get *under* someone else.'

'Jazz!' I exclaim. She can be so crass.

'Whatever, virgin,' she jokes, a comical look on her face.

I think about her poor date. He has no idea what he's let himself in for. She'll eat him alive. An idea pops into my head.

'Ok. I'll do it. But only if you don't sleep with your man tonight,' I challenge.

'What? Why do I have to suffer?' she asks dramatically pouting her lips.

'I'm doing this for your own good. You seem to like this guy, so why ruin it by jumping into bed with him? Make him wait a while and it will be even better.'

She ponders over this for a while as she puts on more neon pink lipstick and puffs up her long tangled hair.

'Ok it's a deal. But remember – think Madonna in her slutty days.'

*　　　　　*　　　　　*

As I put the key into the unfamiliar door, I notice my hands are shaking. I'm really going through with this. Is it too late to change my mind? I mean, I have made him travel all the way to the house, insistent that I didn't want to go to his bachelor pad. And he did pay for the taxi. It'd probably be unreasonable to change my mind now. I tip toe into the house, glad to find it in darkness. They must be in bed, or maybe they're still out. I open the door to my bedroom and push the clothes from the floor with my foot to make a path. I really should tidy up this pig sty.

I turn to him and swallow hard, desperately trying to think of something sexy to say. There's no need as he plunges his lips onto mine. I kiss him back and try to think vamp as he claws at my dress. Fight every natural urge in your body to run away and commit to this. It's really no big deal.

*　　　　　*　　　　　*

56

Well that was different. That really was something. I was an *animal*!
Jazz was so right, once I got into character, I was on fire. To think at
the start I was actually worried I wouldn't know what I was doing.
But it's just like riding a bike. And boy, oh boy, did I just get back on
that saddle.

My fears of bats flying loose from my vagina as my knickers were torn
off are over. I was fine. Actually I was better than fine. I was
throwing moves I never even knew I had. I threw him all round that
bedroom. I think I even slapped him in the face at one point. It was
crazy. Just for that night I was someone else. I *was* Madonna.

I creep out of bed, scared to death of waking him, and put on Jazz's
pink fluffy dressing gown. Suddenly I'm terrified that he'll expect a
repeat performance. My whole body aches as it is, I'd probably just
have a heart attack and die if I went through it again. No matter how
good it was, I'm still pleased it's over. I can just move on now.

I skip into the kitchen, thinking what a seductive vamp I am while I
flick the kettle on.

'Morning.'

I jump and turn round, with my heart still in my throat, to find Ryan.
He's in his usual spot, reading a paper and drinking a cup of tea.

'Oh hi,' I say, quickly checking that I don't have mascara gunk in my
eye. 'You'd think I'd get used to that,' I mutter under my breath.

I hear him snort a laugh. Whoops. I hope he didn't hear me.

'Right...I'll be off then,' my one night stand says, suddenly walking
into the kitchen. He's only half dressed, pulling on his shirt. Oh my
God. What's his name? I can't remember his name!

'Yeah, bye.' I smile awkwardly, wishing he would leave quicker.

He leaves and I breathe a breath of relief. Damn, I was wishing I
could have snuck him out before anyone else was awake. I glance up
quickly to see Ryan smiling. Sudden irrational anger takes over me.
Why the hell does Ryan get up so early if he doesn't work? It's
unnatural, and confirms to me he is definitely a freak. I turn back to
the kettle and try to think cooling thoughts; ice cubes, polar bears.
Anything to stop the fire in my cheeks.

'So, you had fun last night then?' Ryan asks cockily from above his paper.

'Hey don't judge me, man whore,' I snap, feeling my lip curl, ready for a fight.

'Man whore?' He puts his paper down and stares at me.

Wow – I've really got his attention. I can't back down now.

'Yes, you heard me. I've heard all about your reputation. And for your information that was the first one night stand I've ever had. So don't think *you* can judge *me*.'

Yeah, that told him.

'Hey, I believe you. Millions wouldn't, but I do,' he says sarcastically, as he takes a sip of tea.

God, he's so infuriating. I want to throw his tea all over him. Who does he think he is judging me? He doesn't know me and he never will if I have anything to do with it.

'Tell me,' he raises his eyebrows, 'What was his name?'

'It's....it's....none of your business,' I stay stiffly.

I storm out of the room, trying to ignore him smiling happily away. What a smug bastard. I want to just punch him hard in the face. That would soon take that smirk off his stupid face.

I get changed as quickly as possible, putting on Jazz's pink and blue wrap dress and black court shoes, as ordered by her last night. Well actually, at first she wanted me to wear her jungle dress which looks like it's made from leaves and trails on the floor after her as she walks. This was a compromise.

I try to forget all about Ryan, only next door. I mean, who the hell is he to judge me? He probably doesn't even know how many people he's slept with, let alone their names. He's probably riddled with crabs and he doesn't even know. Yes, crabs, I've decided. The thought of him with crabs makes me smile. He can be a smug bastard all he likes, but he'll still have crabs, in my head.

The house phone rings, shaking me out of my thoughts. I open my door in case it's Jazz for me.

'Ryan!' Izzy shouts down the stairs. 'It's for you.'

'Thanks,' he shouts back.

58

Who would want to call that jackass? Especially at this hour. I take my cup out to the kitchen and put it into the sink. Some unnatural urge makes me want to eavesdrop on his conversation. Probably some tart. Probably a booty call. I fuss around, pretending to look for something in the cupboard, while all the time trying to tune my ears into what he's saying.

'Yeah, you're right...I know....I'll come see you soon...yeah, I miss you too...ok, love you.'

Love you? God, he really is a player if he's telling them he loves them. What a bastard. I doubt Jazz has it all wrong and he's actually got himself a girlfriend. I can't imagine anyone wanting to spend more than an hour with him. He looks up and catches me staring at him. Shit. I snap myself out of it and turn, quickly trying to leave the room.

'Ow!' I yelp, banging my leg on the kitchen table. Why can I never just make a dignified exit?

'Are you ok?' he laughs.

'Yes, of course!' I shriek unnaturally. 'I was just, um...'

QUICKLY! Think of *something*.

'Eavesdropping?' he accuses with a smug smile.

'No!' I say far too quickly. God, he's so self-obsessed. 'But I couldn't help over-hearing. And *you're* judging me for having a one night stand. Going around telling every girl you meet that you love them, that's far worse!' My voice is shrill, and I swallow, trying to get my normal voice back.

'Sorry, but I thought you were just having a go at me for being judgemental? Pot calling kettle if you ask me,' he snorts.

'Ha! How bloody dare you!' As soon as I say it I feel like I've over-reacted.

'Whatever.' He rolls his eyes and stomps out of the room.

* * *

Lilly greets me at my desk, dressed in a bright peach dress which makes her tan look amazing. I wish I had natural fashion flare. I once tried to wear a gorgeous black and white dress, but I spilled strawberry milkshake down it within half an hour. I would normally gush over her outfit, telling her how pretty she looks, but today I hold back. I'm still furious with her for yesterday. I tense my face, looking as stern as possible.

'Hey, I love your dress,' Lilly says admiringly, seeming to ignore my cold reception.

'I'm not talking to you,' I say stiffly, sounding like a child in the playground.

'Oh *please!*' she begs. 'I'm sorry. It just got a bit out of hand. I was just so scared you'd end up getting us both in trouble. I mean really, I was kind of saving you?'

I look up and her pathetic face wins me over. Her large blue eyes seem to have a power over people.

'Ok. I forgive you.'

'Thank God,' she says, as if the whole incident had been a massive inconvenience.

'God, you're annoying.'

'Love you too Pops.' She smiles and punches me on the shoulder.

'What have you two crazy cats been up to?' Cheryl asks from the next desk, her obnoxious condescending face making me want to immediately punch her.

'No, nothing for you to worry about,' Lilly smiles politely.

'Oooh, it must be interesting then. I do love your little stories; they remind me of my single days before I settled down and got real.'

'Well thanks for the advice,' Lilly snaps, rolling her eyes at me.

I quickly grab a post it and write on it 'I HAD SEX LAST NIGHT!'

'No!' Lilly shouts, clapping her hands together. Her bracelets jingle together, as if a bell is being rung.

'What's going on?' Cheryl asks.

I glare at Lilly, pleading with her not to say anything.

'Oh, nothing. I just broke a nail,' she says, sucking her finger dramatically. She smiles back at me, while giving me a warning look which I think translates as "you must tell me everything later".

'Poppy! Ah, there you are,' sighs Victor, coming out of his office, his normal olive skin red and flustered.

Lilly immediately runs towards her desk. Everyone here is terrified of Victor. He's the CEO, and although only five foot tall, everyone runs in fear of him. He's taken turns in humiliating every member of staff publicly over the years. Lilly's incident involved a report and a banana. It still gives me chills just thinking about it.

'Morning.' I smile and quickly grab a post it and pen.

'Glad to see you're feeling better,' he says formally, brushing a bit of dandruff from his shoulder. 'Could I see you in my office for a moment?'

'Yes, of course.' I take a deep breath as I run there. I hope he's not going to give me a lecture on being reliable. One bloody sick day in four years!

'I've got the chairman, Mrs Dewitt, in today. She's in the boardroom now, as you were late.' He looks at his watch and then at me disapprovingly.

Late by two minutes. Definitely a sackable offence.

'If you could sort out drinks and make sure she feels as comfortable as possible.'

'Of course,' I smile.

'It's a B-I-G meeting today,' he says, stretching out the word 'big' for emphasis. He stares at me, willing me to ask him to elaborate.

'Oh really, why?' I ask, un-interested.

'Well, Poppy as you know, business has not been going very well this past year.' He pauses for a second and looks over my shoulder. 'Shut the door.'

I quickly close it, sudden nerves pulsating through me.

'Business has not been good and I'm afraid...I'm afraid we're going to have to make redundancies.'

'Redundancies?' I blurt out.

My stomach curdles at the thought and I suddenly feel ill with panic.

'Yes. Strictly confidential, you understand.' He lowers his bushy grey eyebrows on me in a threatening manner.

I nod, unable to speak.

'This is the final sign off and we'll be making them by the end of the month.'

'This month?'

My hands are clammy now.

'Yes,' he nods.

'Do they have to be made? These redundancies. Isn't there...another solution?'

'Poppy, this is a recession,' he says, sighing heavily.

'Yes, but...'

'But what Poppy?' he shouts, his face getting red as he loses what little patience he had.

I was going to say that surely kids still get nits, even in a recession.

'Nothing,' I say instead, hating myself. Why can't I be like the women in those films that stands up to her boss and instead manages to get a promotion?

'Good. Now you are to say nothing about this, understood?'

I nod and follow Victor into the boardroom. I watch him numbly as he starts his usual middle classed babble of ridiculous chat with the Chairman. How can this be happening?

'Have you seen any of that big fat gypsy wedding?' Mrs Dewitt says to him from across the boardroom table. 'Oh Victor, it was such fun!'

'Oh, yes!' Victor nods. 'Poppy here is Irish. Tell us Poppy, are any of your family in it?'

I look over my shoulder, sure he must be talking to another Poppy. Is he serious? Is he seriously calling me a gypsy?

'Um...no. Not all Irish people are gypsies and it's only on my Mother's side.' Why did I feel the need to tell him that? I'm not embarrassed.

'They're a funny bunch, aren't they,' Victor says, ignoring me completely. 'The outfits they wear! I mean, my goodness!'

I look down at Mrs Dewitt's outfit, consisting of an orange mini skirt with fish net tights and a purple shirt which looks like it's going to burst open at any moment.

'Tea or coffee?' I offer, not sure how they're managing to have normal care free conversation when they're about to talk redundancies.

They're going to ruin some people's lives.

'Oh, but I do love the Irish,' Mrs Dewitt says. 'Went to Dublin a few years back. Wonderful people.'

'Oh yes. Well, like I said we have our very own little leprechaun to bring us good luck,' Victor laughs.

I wonder who's safe and who's not. Paul the salesman has just bought a new house and Jeremy's wife has just had twins.

'I know!' Victor exclaims, pulling me out of my thoughts. His eyes grow wide as he stares at me.

'Tea? Coffee?' I offer again, my smile strained.

'Why don't you give us a little Irish jig?' Victor suggests, his eyes dancing at the idea.

Irish jig? Is he *serious*?

'Oh yes! Goody. I do like a show,' Mrs Dewitt says, clapping her hands together.

'I...I can't,' I stammer, my legs going wobbly at the thought.

'Of course you can Poppy,' Victor says, smiling with his mouth, but warning with his eyes.

Please don't make me, I try to communicate back.

'Have you got enough room?' Mrs Dewitt asks, pulling her chair out of the way.

'I...I...'

I can't speak! I cannot do this! I cannot dance around the room like an idiot.

'Take your shoes off Poppy,' Victor instructs.

Why don't I just take off all of my clothes and have an *actual* nightmare? Mrs Dewitt bends over and starts pulling at my shoes. I'm tempted to kick her in the face and run for the hills.

'My goodness, what small feet you have!' she shouts, as she prises my un-willing feet out of them. 'What size are you?'

'I'm a five.'

'My goodness - so small!'

Size five is average actually. Not like your size 9 clown feet.

'Let me Google a tune for you,' Victor says, already on his iPhone.

This can't be happening. This *cannot* be happening.

'Here we go!' Victor says happily, as the rooms fills with a tune. It reminds me of my childhood in Irish bars drinking red lemonade and eating Tato crisps.

'Go Poppy!' Victor shouts, clapping his hands together.

'But....I'm really not – '

'Go! I said GO!'

His snarl is enough to pull my body into action. I jump to my tip toes immediately and try to forget about them staring at me. I jig around, quickly remembering the steps, flinging my legs in the air, all the time wishing I was dead.

'Brilliant Poppy!' Victor shouts, encouragingly.

I smile back, the old steps becoming clearer with each one I take.

Why should I even be embarrassed? I'm good at Irish dancing! I won loads of medals when I was younger. I mean, granted, I was seven at the time, but still!

'Yes, thank-you Poppy,' Victor says abruptly, his playful mood over. 'Two coffees.'

I stop abruptly, panting, out of breath. Well, he changes his mind bloody quickly. Just when I was getting into my stride. I pick my shoes up and walk out of the meeting room, heading for the kitchen.

'Oh, Poppy thank God!' Lilly says, rushing towards me. 'I have an important message for you.'

'Really? What?'

The worst thoughts go running through my head. My Mum, my Dad; are they ok?

'Michael Flatley called. He wants his moves back. Something about you stealing them?'

My face freezes in embarrassment.

'Oh ha bloody ha,' I say hitting her on the shoulder. 'You saw then?'

'Not just me! Victor e-mailed a video of it to everyone in the company.'

My stomach hits the floor and I can suddenly hear my heart thumping hard.

'Please, *please* tell me you're joking,' I plead. I need to run away and escape.

'I wish I was.' She eyes me sympathetically. 'Yeah, good luck with the rest of the day.' She smiles wickedly, walking away.

I make the coffees, my hands still shaking and take them towards the meeting room.

'Top of the morning to ya!' Jeremy says, as he walks past.

'Oh, fuck off.'

*   *   *

The minute I get back to the house I throw my shoes at the wall and lie on the lumpy sofa. Those damn fucking shoes! They've given me angry, vicious looking blisters at the back of my foot where they've rubbed. The last ten minutes of my walk home I had to rip them off and go barefoot. Jazz keeps telling me off for doing that.

'Hey Pops. Bad day?' Izzy asks coming into the room wearing nothing but a towel.

'Yeah. Understatement of the year actually,' I answer, feeling very sorry for myself.

She begins towel drying her hair and I can't stop noticing what an amazing body she has. Don't get me wrong – I'm no lesbian, but her legs are so toned and tanned. Her whole body looks like it should belong in a high gloss magazine, not in this grotty sitting room in Shepherd's Bush. In fact, if there were a girl to turn me it would probably be her.

'Poppy? I said what happened?'

I pull myself back into the room, telling myself off for daydreaming again.

'Oh, sorry. It's a bit of a long story actually.'

'Oh, well to be honest,' she says, scrunching her face up in regret, 'I haven't got too much time on my hands. Me and Gracie have got dates.'

'Oh really, that's great. Anyone special?' I ask, pleased that the conversation has turned back to her.

'No. Just some guys from her office. Probably bores, but you never know.' She winks at me.

'Oh, well have a great time.'

'Thanks. And I *will* chat to you about this, I promise. Why don't we go for brekkie tomorrow before work?'

'Oh.' I'm genuinely surprised at the offer of real friendship. It's been so long since I made a new friend. 'Yeah that would be great.' I try to smile half as widely as her, while pretending I will be fine to get up at a ridiculous hour.

'Awesome. Well I'm gonna go blow dry my hair, but I'll wake you in the morning, ok?'

'Yeah, cool.'

*   *   *

When she's gone I make a big bowl of spaghetti bolognaise. If there's one thing I'm sure will always cheer me up, it's a plate load of carbs and it's easy enough for even me to make. I always end up making enough to last me the week. Then I usually eat most of it in one sitting, spending the rest of the night crying, disgusted at what a beast I am. I really must ask Izzy what the deal is with buying food and stop stealing theirs in the hope that they won't notice.

I've just put the garlic bread in the oven when my mobile rings. I run to get it and my spirit picks up when I see that it's Jazz. I've got so much to tell her.

'Hiya love,' I sing down the phone.

'Disaster! I need your help urgently. Can you come round?' Her serious tone shocks me.

'Yeah, but why? What's wrong?'

'Oh Pops,' she says, her voice breaking slightly.

She's been in a car crash. No, worse, she's set my flat on fire.

'What??'

I hear her take a deep breath.

'I need to get the morning after pill.'

'I'll be there as soon as I can.'

Chapter 6

The tube is a nightmare. Trust Jazz to have an emergency at rush hour. And trust me to always find the sweatiest, most obese people to be squeezed between. When I finally get to the flat I find her sitting at the kitchen table in my track suit bottoms, a half empty bottle of wine beside her. This must be bad. She never wears tracksuit bottoms.

'Tell me everything.' I demand as soon as I take my coat off.

'Oh it's such a fucking mess.' She drains her glass. There's smudged mascara under her red rimmed eyes, indicating she's been crying.

'Have you got trainers on?' she asks, suddenly staring disapprovingly at my feet.

'Yes, but TELL me. What happened?'

'They look terrible. I thought I told you to wear the shoes today?'

How can she pick on my shoes in the middle of an emergency?

'I did and they gave me fucking blisters! Now tell me what the fuck happened?'

'Ok, ok,' she waves her hands in the air. She takes a deep breath. 'I slept with Jake. You know, the builder from last night,' she explains while pouring herself another glass.

'Against my orders,' I say, my jaw clenching in anger. If she would have just listened to me she wouldn't be in this mess.

'Anyway, it split and I told him no worries as I'd get the morning after pill. But then I overslept and had to get to work. I was still half an hour late on my first day and they told me I'd have to work through my lunch to make up the time. So I didn't have a chance.'

'I'm surprised they didn't fire you on the spot! But what about after work? Why didn't you just go straight to a chemist on the way home?'

'I did. I went into one and ended up buying loads of random crap, but I just couldn't work up the courage to ask for it.'

'Work up the courage? You're a grown woman for God's sake!'

'*Exactly*. That's exactly my point. If I was a stupid teenager then it would be better, but I'm a grown woman. I should have known better and I know that's what they'll say to me. Plus all the women in there are always bitches.'

'They're not bitches.' But I know what she means. They do seem to cast their eyes over your purchases and judge you. God forbid I buy thrush cream.

'It's fine anyway,' I say, trying to remain calm. 'It might have only split when he pulled out. You may be ok, but either way we're better setting off now for a chemist.'

I glance nervously at my watch as Jazz bites her lip, a big fat tear trickling down her face. I know that look. She needs to tell me something but she's afraid of how I'll react. We really don't have time for her to be keeping secrets.

I sigh heavily and look her straight in the eye.

'Just tell me.'

'Ok,' she gulps. 'I lied. It didn't split. We just didn't have any condoms and got caught up in the moment.'

'What? And this is the guy you were supposed to be resisting on my orders?' I can't help but add.

'See, right there! That's why I almost didn't tell you. You always go into this judgemental, I told you so, attitude. For once, could you just not ask any questions and help me?'

Now I feel awful. Maybe I am a massive judgemental bitch and I don't even realise it. It must be years of my mum doing it to me. God, please don't say I'm turning into her.

'Ok, I'm sorry.' I wipe a tear away from her face.

'It's fine. I know you don't mean it. It's just that....well, I feel like such a massive failure already. I just don't need my best friend thinking that of me too.'

'I know I'm a bitch, but I don't think you're a failure!' I bring her into an awkward half hug. 'Anyway, come on, get your coat. It's 6.30. We need to find a chemist that's still open.'

'Ok.' She smiles and drains her glass.

'I wouldn't worry too much anyway. I mean, it would be just plain luck to get pregnant from one time, even for you.'

'Actually...it was three times.'

Ok, three times makes it a bit scarier. We walk quickly to the local chemist, all the while my blisters still stinging like hell. I spot the neon OPEN light glowing through the window and feel myself start to relax. Thank God.

'We're just closing up girls,' the lady behind the till yells as we enter.

'Ok, we just need one thing,' I shout back smiling insistently.

'Poppy? Is that you?'

I turn around to find my Mum's friend Helen grinning at me with lipstick on her teeth.

'Helen! Hi!' I exclaim, not quite believing our bad luck.

'How are you? Your Mum says you're keeping well and still have that great job in the City.'

Typical mum, talking me up. I wouldn't be surprised if she told her I was the CEO, not his assistant.

'Yeah, all good thanks, but we really must get going. You can go first,' I offer, watching Jazz's anxious expression.

'Oh no dear, after you. I know what you busy City girls are like.'

'No, no, I insist. Please, after you.' I almost push her forward with my arms.

'Now listen here love,' she says insistently, 'I couldn't possibly take your place. Like I said, I know how busy you are.' She looks at me expectantly and I realise I'd look crazy if I refused again.

I exchange a glance with Jazz, it now obvious we can't ask for the morning after pill with her here. At the very least my Mum would know and at worse so would the whole of St Albans.

She smiles wildly, still insistent that I take her up on her offer.

'Ok thanks,' I say through gritted teeth. I walk slowly to the woman behind the till who looks annoyed that we're taking so long to leave her shop.

'What can I get you?' she asks eagerly looking from my face to Jazz's.

'Um...just some...aspirin please.'

*   *   *

As we walk through the high street nothing but closed signs greet us. We instinctively walk towards the tube station, the nerves taking hold of both of us. Jazz has started chewing her nails and my own hands are shaking as I twirl my hair frantically. Always a bad sign. I twirled it so much during my Uni exams that I almost got a bald patch on one side and my hairdresser told me I'd have to stop or I'd go completely bald.

Ok, don't panic – it's only ten to seven. We still have plenty of time. I take a slow deep breath and try and get my nerves under control. I'm sure that loads of chemists are still open.

'Where are we going?' Jazz asks stopping in her tracks.

'I don't know. Let's just get the train back towards the house and I'm sure we'll find one near there. The closer into London I think. You know what they say, the City that never sleeps.' I laugh nervously.

'Do you actually *know* one there?' she asks narrowing her eyes at me.

'Yeah, of course,' I say avoiding her gaze as I feel my insides clenching.

*　　　　　*　　　　　*

As we walk up Shepherd's Bush high street I'm feeling a little more optimistic. We're going to find a chemist and this silly nightmare will be over. We'll laugh about this soon enough. I notice a neon green cross in the distance and smile, now calm and confident that we'll get this sorted. We head towards it, but soon our fast walking turns into a light run and before we know it we're sprinting at full speed. Perhaps I'm not as confident as I'm telling myself.

We collapse over once we're outside, panting and sweating like athletic runners. We really should take an aerobics class.

'Thank God,' Jazz says to me, between breaths.

'I know.' I pant back. 'Come on.' I grab her hand and open the door. As we walk in the lights suddenly flick off and a young girl comes barging into us.

70

'Sorry ladies, but the shop is now closed.' She puts her arms up wide and pushes us out.

'No! We just need one thing.' I try to push against her with all of my strength.

'I'm afraid not. We will however be back open tomorrow morning at 09.00.'

'*Please*,' Jazz begs putting on her best puppy eyes.

But the woman doesn't care. Before we know it we're back on the street and she's locking up the doors.

'Please,' Jazz pleads. 'You don't understand, this is life or death.'

'I'm sure it is madam, but I'm afraid that's not my problem,' she says with a snarl. I can't believe the rudeness.

'Well, I'll be writing to your supervisor,' I say to her back as she walks off. She really doesn't care. 'Minimum wage bitch!' I shout out, despite myself.

A few people on the street turn back to stare at me disgusted, but not her. She's already getting on a bus and going home.

'Oh my God,' Jazz says, bursting into hysterical tears. 'It's hopeless. I'm going to be a single mum and I'll have to live in a crumby flat and live on benefits. My life is over.'

She slumps against the shop window and sits down on the floor with her head in her hands. I open my mouth to tell her that she's over-reacting, that it'll all work out perfectly, but the truth is that I don't know if it will. I start racking my brains but I can't think of one chemist open past seven o'clock on a Tuesday night. What the hell are we going to do?

'Drink?'

I drag her to the nearest pub and plonk her down on a tired looking bar stool.

'Two beers please,' I tell the heavily tattooed barman.

What the hell is this place? The barman looks like he just escaped from prison, but the only few customers in here seem to be old men nursing a bitter and playing dominoes. The place stinks of smoke, and I wonder if this is the kind of place where they make their own rules. Maybe this is one of those pubs you hear about on programmes like

'Britain's Worst Pubs' where they have boxing matches and fight dogs.

'Is your friend alright, love?' the barman asks, breaking me from my thoughts.

'Yeah, why?' I ask, turning round to see what he's talking about.

Oh dear. Jazz is crying hysterically, seeming to be telling a balding man next to her everything. I swoop back and try to disengage her from the conversation as he offers her a dirty old handkerchief.

'Sorry. She's fine, honestly,' I say turning my back on him.

'Well, there is that Boots chemist down by Pearl Cross. I'm pretty sure that's a 24 hour one. Because of the area, you see. Full of druggies and hookers,' her bald man says.

'Oh my God, really?' I shout as I turn round to face him, as excited as a school girl.

'Yeah, last time I checked.'

*   *   *

We run from the tube onto Pearl Cross high street, but stop dead in our tracks when we take in the view. Wow, that guy was right. This place is a shit hole. Boarded up warehouses line the streets, as do hookers dressed in PVC. The air stinks of sewage. A quick stab of fear hits my chest. I grab hold of Jazz's hand to slow her down, and clutch on a bit tighter to my handbag.

'Oh my God, this place is scary.' I whisper to her as we pass a crowd of guys with their hoods up. I mean, why would they have their hoods up unless they wanted to mug us?

'It's fine,' she says confidently, but her eyes say she's just as scared as me.

'Where is this bloody chemist?' I hiss at her.

'I don't know. Let's ask her.' Before I can stop her she walks over to a woman wearing a short strappy leopard print dress and red knee high PVC boots.

'No! Jazz!' I whisper running after her, scared to be left alone for a second. It seems to be getting darker.

'Excuse me, but do you know where the all night chemist is?'
The woman smiles, exposing buck teeth with red lipstick on.
'Yeah, it's down this road. Just keep goin' for 'bout another mile. But be careful. You girls look classy and that means money round 'ere. Jus' keep your wits about ya.'
My stomach curdles at the thought and I'm suddenly ill with panic.
'Ok thanks,' I smile. Who'd have known it, a nice hooker.
'See,' Jazz whispers proudly.
We carry on down the street as instructed; trying to ignore the odd looks we're receiving. I take to looking down at the pavement, counting each pave block to try and take my mind off the danger surrounding us. Any minute now I'm expecting to be held up at gun point.
When we finally get to the chemist (83 steps later), we're relieved to find it wasn't a lie and it is open. There's a little hatch where you can ask for things, like in a petrol station. Jazz runs over and practically shouts that she wants the morning after pill, all previous embarrassment gone. The man behind the counter doesn't seem to flinch, clearly used to this kind of erratic behaviour. He gives her two pills; one to be taken now and one to be taken tomorrow. She swallows it down without water.
'Well thank God that's over.' she says, the colour already back in her face as we step back onto the street.
'Yeah, let's just get the hell out of here.'
The sky is suddenly pitch black, only moonlight and the occasional working street light guiding us along.
Jazz zips up her hooded tracksuit top and holds my hand as we begin to walk hurriedly along, keeping close to the street lights. Just keep walking, I will myself. Everything is going to be fine. We just need to get on that train and we'll be fine. Yet my stomach is not one to be reasoned with and churns with nerves. My face aches from the tension in it and I have to let go of Jazz's hand every so often so that I can wipe the sweat from them on my dress. It's so hard to avoid everyone's gazes as we walk past them. I'm sure that if we catch their gaze they'll turn on us like wild animals.

We turn the corner and I spot the tube station sign, my body starting to release in relief. Thank God. Jazz beams at me, clearly as relieved as me. We start to almost skip towards it, like school girls, the stress of the day leaving our bodies.

We're almost at the entrance when I lose my balance and feel myself falling forward. I push my hands out in front of myself and scrunch my eyes up, knowing it's going to hurt. I open my eyes a second later, feeling bruised and disorientated, to see that I've fallen face down on the pavement. I try to pull myself up, but find my hands are grazed quite badly where I've tried to break my fall.

Oh well, at least they did seem to break my fall; this could have been my face. Yet at that moment they start to sting fiercely. Probably already full of pavement dirt and rat's faeces. I'll probably get the plague. Maybe I should have a tetanus? God it stings.

I look up to Jazz but she's nowhere to be seen.

'Jazz?' I ask, pulling myself slowly up.

Shit, where is she? Where the hell is she? I look around, spinning in a circle, but I can't see anyone. She wouldn't have got the train back without me, would she? She wouldn't have left me completely in the dark in a shit hole like this, would she? A figure suddenly appears running round the corner and I tense my body, ready for attack. That is until I realise it's Jazz. Where did she go?

'I tried to,' she says, doubling over, completely out of breath. 'I tried to chase him, but...wow, I'm really out of breath. But he was too fast for me.'

'Chase who?' I ask confused. I study her face, trying to read it. 'Am I missing something?

'The bastard that stole your bag.'

I look down and sure enough my bag is no-where to be seen.

'I...I was mugged?' I ask totally dazed.

*   *   *

When we're back at the flat, Jazz forces me to have a brandy from the bottle Dad left here two Christmas's ago.

'It's what they do in films isn't it? Have brandies when they're in shock,' she assures me.

I roll my eyes, but decide to knock it back regardless, the heat stinging the back of my throat. I run my grazed hands under the tap, hoping Jazz won't find the savlon she's gone looking for. I just want to go back to the house and get into bed.

'Well, I better be off then,' I shout through to the bedroom where I can hear her rifling through my drawers.

'Are you crazy?' she says, sticking her head out of the door. 'You're too shaken up. Why don't you just stay here?'

'No, I'm fine. I just want to go home.' I try to look brave and muster up the courage of leaving here alone.

'But this is your home,' she says, her eyes widening, looking at me like I'm crazy.

'Oh yeah, I forgot.'

'I think you're concussed.' She puts her hand to my forehead.

'No, I'm fine.' I hit her hand away. 'I just want to get back and pretend this never happened.'

'But this did happen. You need to come to terms with it.'

'Jazz, please just stop fussing will you? You've been watching too much TV. I'm totally fine.'

'But why do you feel the need to go home tonight? Why not stay?'

'Because I have the feeling that if I don't go now I'll turn into one of those crazy women that never leaves the house again.'

She looks at me unconvinced and goes into the bathroom sulking.

'Ok, but please get a taxi back?' she shouts out. 'If just for my peace of mind?'

'Ok fine, although there really would be nothing left to rob me of.'

'Found it!' she shouts, excited. I turn to see her bounding out towards me. She pulls my hands out towards her and sprays the savlon over them.

My hands tingle at first, turning quickly into an intense angry burning. I think I'm imagining it at first, but within a few seconds a fire is ablaze, my hands shaking. I look down at them in horror to see that they're more inflamed than before. I go to speak, but the pain is taking over me, cursing over me in waves, leaving me helpless.

'H...H..Help!' I stutter. 'Burning! Burning!' I scream. I push her out of the way and run them under the tap, the water cooling it instantly.

'Whoops,' I hear Jazz say behind me. She walks over to the sink slowly. 'It wasn't savlon. It was mosquito spray. My bad.'

*   *   *

As the cab driver pulls up at the house I feel sudden relief. I feel so fed up I just want to be by myself and sulk in my bedroom. But first I want a chocolate biscuit. I open the door and head straight for the sofa. Ryan is stood in the kitchen on the phone, his other hand in his hair, pacing back and forth looking anxious.

'There you are,' he says when he sees me. 'Don't worry Jazz, she's here now,' he says into the phone before hanging up.

'Hi,' I mumble, exhaustion taking over my body, making my eyelids heavy. I don't know if I can make it to the biscuit tin.

'Where the hell have you been?' he shouts, shocking me out of my trance. 'I called Jazz but she's making no sense, just blabbing on about some guy she met.'

Ah, she was obviously trying to tell him the whole story. His eyebrows narrow down on me, making me feel like a naughty child.

'Sorry, but it's a long story. Can I tell you later?' I collapse onto the sofa. God, this lumpy sofa never felt so good. Now I just need to try and peel off these trainers.

'Tell me later? I've been going out of my fucking mind! I get home to black smoke and – '

'Black smoke?' My eyes widen in confusion.

'Yeah; you'd left garlic bread in the oven,' he says, with a blank, scary expression.

'Oh. Whoops,' I say, disbelief colouring my tone as I remember.

'So I get home to an almost house fire and see a half made dinner and you nowhere to be seen. I don't have a number for you, so can't call you, and I can't get hold of Jazz either. I thought you'd been abducted or something!' his voice erupts in an angry growl.

'Oh Jesus, you're a drama queen,' I say flatly, too exhausted to muster any emotion in my voice. 'Plus there really is no need to shout. I'm sorry about the dinner but there was an emergency.'

'What emergency?' he asks, still sounding more pissed off than concerned.

I stare back at him, struggling to think clearly, to find some way to explain. As I search for the right words I can see him getting impatient, frustrated by my silence. He starts to scowl.

'I...I can't really tell you.'

He slams his hand down hard on the kitchen counter, making me jump, his brown eyes growing sharp. What is his problem?

'Chill out, ok.' I hold my hands up to him defensively, terrified that I'm living with a psychopath.

I discreetly start searching the kitchen for a weapon. The hairs standing up on the back of my neck tell me to be on guard, that this man cannot be trusted. But then his expression quickly changes to one of worry.

'Shit. What happened to your hands?' he asks in a softer voice. He comes forward and grabs my wrists, bringing them closer to him to inspect.

'Oh, I got mugged.' He really is quite rough. Doesn't he realise I'm a girl?

'You got mugged? Where?' His eyes are wide with alarm.

'At Pearl Cross. I didn't really notice until I got back up. Jazz tried to run after him.'

'Jesus, what the hell were you both doing there? It's the end of the world.'

'I know. I found out the hard way.' I pull my hands away and attempt a laugh to lighten the mood. It doesn't seem to work.

He stares back at me, analysing, searching, and attempting to find out what's wrong with me.

'God, you really do have a way of getting yourself into trouble don't you.' he says, more as a statement than a question.

'Well I'm very sorry that I'm such a bother to you. I don't know why you care anyway. I'm a grown woman, I can look after myself.'

He snorts. 'Yeah looks like it.'

My lip curls up in anger.

'Why don't you just fuck off and mind your own business. I don't need someone playing older brother to me; I have three of my own thanks.'

'Well fine. If you wanna be a bitch about it then I won't bother next time.'

'Fine!' I snarl.

'Fine!' he shouts.

My fists clench and I turn on my heel stomping off to bed, ignoring my hungry, growling stomach.

*   *   *

Ryan sneaks into my bedroom, a regretful pained expression on his face.

'Poppy, I'm sorry.'

I look up to him and our eyes lock. He looks at my face and moves to sit on the bed, close enough for me to hear his breath. He takes my face in his hands and pushes his warm lips against mine. I melt, pushing back the covers to invite him in. He climbs in, his lips not moving from mine. He reaches under my night shirt, searching hungrily for my breasts. I begin to unbutton his shirt, feeling his toned stomach as my hand reaches to undo his belt.

Chapter 7

I wake up from the dream trembling. What on earth was that all about? I suppose I could blame it on that crazy day, but it doesn't stop the disturbed thoughts running through my head, again and again. I get up, wiping the sticky sweat from my forehead and check my watch. 5.30 Am. Well, at least I have a few more hours sleep before I have to face the day. I just hope I can dream about something else. I throw the duvet over my head and breathe in Jazz's familiar floral perfume.

'Poppy?'

I must be losing my mind. Now I'm hearing voices. I keep my head under the duvet, half scared that it's a ghost Jazz forgot to mention. Maybe that's why she was so eager to swap homes. This room is haunted by an old woman who likes to give you disturbed dreams and pester you at half five in the morning.

'Poppy? It's me, Izzy,' she whispers.

I throw the duvet back in disbelief. She's leaning over me dressed in pink jogging bottoms and a sports bra. She can't seriously want to grab breakfast at 5.30 in the morning. I mean, is she crazy?

'Izzy – what the? I mean...what is it?' I ask, irritation showing in my voice.

'You said to wake you in the morning remember?' she whispers encouragingly.

'Yeah, but you said for breakfast. So I assumed it would be at least 7 or something?' I check my watch again.

'Yeah I know, that was the plan. But then I thought why bother sitting around doing bugger all when instead we could go for a refreshing power walk?' She smiles enthusiastically.

'Power walk?' I laugh. But then I realise she's serious. She's wearing jogging bottoms and holding a water bottle. She's actually serious.

'So...I'll give you about five minutes to get ready.' She smiles and pulls the curtains back exposing me to the early morning sunshine streaming in. I feel like a witch who might melt under it. The birds are tweeting loudly.

I stare at her, still half expecting her to laugh and tell me she's only joking. But underneath that smiley, petite face she looks kind of stern. I realise she means business and there's no way I'm getting out of this.

It can't be that bad, I think to myself as we leave the house. I just hope I don't sweat all over my borrowed sports clothes. It's only a walk. I mean, how bad can it be?

It turns out pretty bad.

'So, what do you do then Izzy?' I ask her, hoping she'll slow down to answer.

'I'm a personal trainer,' she smiles. 'Come on, keep up.'

Well that figures.

'I'm...trying' I say in between breaths.

God, my chest is tight and my shins are starting to ache. I've only been walking five minutes.

'So, how long have you been a personal trainer?'

'About two years now. I love exercise. I'm just so happy that I can do it for a career.'

'How can you love exercise?' I ask panting. How could anyone possibly love this?

'The endorphins it releases are like magic. It gives me so much more energy,' she beams. 'I always feel super-duper after a workout.'

Why would she want more energy? She's like an excitable puppy as it is.

'So...do you work at a gym or anything?'

'I actually do a mix of both. I do personal training at a gym, but also have my own private clients. I like the mix, but I think that if I get a lot more private clients then I'll go totally freelance. I can set my own hours then. I could make you an exercise plan if you like?' she suggests barely out of breath.

'Um...maybe.'

'Yes! That's what I'll do,' she says, her face lighting up. 'So anyway, what happened yesterday at work?'

I fill her in on all of the details and she happily laughs along.

'Do you ever get any fit clients?'

'Yep,' she laughs. 'It's funny because sometimes the biggest fatties are hiding stunning faces. Once they shed the weight it's really hard not to start fancying them!'

'Yeah, it must be hard.'

Ryan pops into my head and I can't help but ask her about him.

'So, what's the deal with Ryan?'

'What do you mean?' she asks, taken aback, but not meeting my eye.

'I mean, he seems such an arrogant prick. He obviously thinks the whole world is in love with him.'

'He's really not that bad,' she says, quickly and curtly.

Whoops, I think I've offended her.

'Sorry. I didn't mean to be horrible or anything.'

'No, its fine,' she smiles, all signs of a bad mood gone. 'It's just that Ryan puts on this act for the world, but he's actually been through a lot.'

'Really? I ask, intrigued. 'Like what?'

'Anyway, we're back on our road now Pops. I want us to run all the way to the door, ok?'

'What?'

She's grabbed my arm and is dragging me down the street before I have time to even realise what she wants. We're actually moving so fast that I'm scared I'm going to fall flat on my face. It's like we're flying, except my legs are thudding against the pavement, my blisters screaming in protest as they take the full weight of my thunder thighs.

'You can have a shower first. I'm gonna make myself a smoothie,' she says, smiling at me as she opens the door.

I stand there, panting and sweating profusely.

'Tha – tha – thanks,' I finally manage. I'm so out of breath I honestly think I might die.

I grab my shower bag and walk up the stairs to the bathroom, my legs feeling like weights. I long so badly for the heat of the water on my tight muscles, but the sound of running water stops me in my tracks. Damn, somebody beat me to it. I sigh in annoyance, turn round and begin to walk down the stairs when the door abruptly opens.

I turn round to face Ryan standing in the doorway holding a loose white towel around his waist, dripping wet. His hair is curly from the moisture and I notice one particular drop of water trickle down his chest, past his belly button to beneath the towel.

'Morning,' he says, giving me a strange sideways glance. Maybe I'm staring, whoops.

I meet his eyes and feel my cheeks burning. The last time I saw him was in my dreams, when his hands were under my night dress. My back arches as I remember the pleasure. When I was touching what lies underneath that small little towel.

'Poppy, are you ok?' he asks, studying my face, seeming to be frustrated by my irrational behaviour. 'You seem kind of...ill?'

'Yeah...I'm just...having a shower, you know,' I mumble like an idiot.

'O...kay,' he smiles tightly.

I hate this. It's like he knows I had the dream and it amuses him. My mouth keeps twitching, wanting to break into a big hysterical smile, but I keep biting my tongue to stop it. I will not let him know what I'm thinking. I will not give him any kind of satisfaction. And definitely not the kind of satisfaction I dreamt about last night.

'Anyway,' he says, his voice formal. 'I was thinking about last night and...I think an apology is in order.'

'Oh yeah, I agree,' I say in surprise.

We both stare at each other expectantly.

'Well...' He looks me dead in the eye. 'Go on then.'

I stare back at him bewildered.

'What? Wait...you want me to apologise TO YOU!?'

Surprise flashes across his face.

'Yes. Like I said, I think you need to apologise.'

'I only agreed because I thought *you* were going to apologise. Why would I apologise? I've got nothing to apologise for,' I shout, shocked by the loudness of my own voice.

'Really?' He narrows his eyes. 'So, nearly setting the house on fire doesn't count then?'

'Oh, whatever. You were just a drama queen.'

We scowl at each other in silence. I decide after a few awkward moments that I should be the first to speak. I try to keep myself focused. I'm in danger of being distracted by his livid, gorgeous face. It's like trying to stare down a sexual God. How can one dream make me suddenly like his face when in reality the only time he looks at me is to shoot me an evil look?

'Now, out of my way. I need a shower,' I say icily, all politeness gone.

'Yeah, that's clear,' he says, looking at my sweaty appearance. 'It's all yours.' He steps to the side and gestures with his hand while the other one clings onto the tiny towel.

'Thanks,' I say through gritted teeth. I walk very slowly past him. It's taking all of my mental energy not to trip up or look at how loosely he is holding that towel. It really could just drop any minute and he doesn't seem bothered. His fresh scent follows me as I turn and lock the door.

I shower quickly, trying to rinse away my thoughts. My head feels like a whirlpool of confusion. Why do I let him bother me so much? Why did I have that crazy dream? That's the last thing I need in my life at the moment - another complication. Oh well, I only have to put up with him for a few weeks. It's not like I don't have enough to worry about. I've got another full day ahead with Venomous Victor. And I need to cancel my debit cards. And I still don't know who's being made redundant.

When I'm finished I wrap myself in a towel and walk down the stairs towards my bedroom, already making a mental to do list for the day. I turn the corner at the banisters and almost bump right into Ryan, still holding his tiny towel. Why can't he just get dressed?

'Oh, sorry,' I say, clinging onto my towel, suddenly aware of how nearly naked I am.

'Yep,' he says, ducking to the left. I go the same way, and then we both go right.

He looks me dead in the eyes and the tip of his tongue pokes out, covering his upper lip. Could someone like him ever get nervous? His eyes hypnotise me, drawing me in. I want to look away, I really do. But it's like his eyes won't release me.

He puts both his hands on my waist and I take an involuntary sharp intake of breath. He clasps on harder and pushes me away to the right. His hands linger for a second too long and then he walks away calmly as if nothing has occurred.

Am I imagining the whole thing? Maybe I do have concussion. I stand there, panting from the wanting in my body. How does he manage to do that? Is he magic or something? I feel a bit sick, like I might pass out and I steady myself against the wall. I try to pull myself together and remind myself that I'm a grown up. I'm far too old to be acting like a teenager, crazy hormones racing through my veins. It was just a dream. You should never think of it again.

*　　　　*　　　　*

'Morning Pops,' Lilly says, perched on my desk, her long orange legs dangling off the side.

'Hiya.' I throw off my jacket and hand her one of the teas I've bought, while immediately pouring mine into my own china tea cup. I just cant drink out of cardboard. 'Oh, and this is funny. Whose bright idea was it?' I ask pointing towards my desk.

It's covered in shamrock confetti, leprechaun teddies and a trophy which has a post it attached saying 'International Irish Dancing Champion.' Ha ha bloody ha.

'Don't know,' she smirks. 'And no thanks, I'm off caffeine.' She hands me her tea back, sticking her nose up to it.

'Off caffeine? Not another one. My new housemate is trying to make me give it up.'

Izzy decided to give me a lecture on healthy eating before I left this morning.

'I'm on a detox. No more cellulite for me. All the celebs are doing it. You should do it with me!' She eyes up my arse as if I were twenty stone.

'Oh thanks! Nice to know you can count on your friends to make you feel better.'

'Morning Poppy,' Neville says, as he walks past in another frightening cartoon tie. Bless him.

'Morning Nev. You look good today. New tie?'

He looks delighted and glances down at the tie, as if trying to remember when he bought it.

'This old thing? I've had it years!'

I actually know this. He's actually worn that tie nearly every week for the past year, but still. It's nice to be nice isn't it?

'Well it looks good.'

Lilly shoots me another warning look. She hates me being nice to Neville. Keeps telling me I'm leading the poor boy on and that he'll get the wrong idea, but Neville knows it's just friendship between us. Plus it's handy having someone you know in accounts when you need to get Victor's expenses paid immediately or he won't be able to attend the Grand Prix.

'Have you girls checked out those new hand dryers in the bathroom?' he asks excitedly.

'I thought that was just a rumour!' Lilly shouts in fake enthusiasm.

I cringe as Neville looks at Lilly, trying to work out if she's serious or not.

'Ignore her Neville.' I shoot her a look. She really needs to stop being so mean.

'Poppy!' Victor yells.

Neville and Lilly jump. God, he never fails to catch us off guard and send me into a panic spiral. I run to his door, notebook and coffee in hand.

As I turn the corner I see a male figure sat across from his desk through the blinds. I hate when he has early morning meetings that he doesn't bother putting in the diary. It completely throws me off. He'll probably want me to go to Starbucks and get them both breakfast.

Victor sits on his desk in front of his guest. His pot belly is pressing against his too tight green shirt. Any minute now I'm sure a button's going to ping off and blind me.

'Poppy, I'd like you to meet someone.'

I plaster my usual polite smile across my face and reach down to shake the man's hand and introduce myself. Only the face that greets me is a familiar face. Oh my God. Fear completely takes over my body and I freeze, trying to remain on my feet, the room moving around me.

It can't be. My bad luck can't have reached a new level already. I got mugged last night for God's sakes.

Staring back at me is what's-his-face from the other night.

'Poppy, this is my Son Hugh.'

His SON?

'Actually Dad, we've already been introduced.' Hugh smiles wickedly and licks his lips.

'Oh really?' Victor enquires, cocking his head up in interest.

Hugh smiles at me, enjoying my humiliation. I feel my insides turn to liquid. I need to be sick. God, I can't believe I ever thought I could sleep with a creep like this and get away un-scathed. I mean, who do I think I am? I am NOT Madonna.

'Just through a friend,' he answers coolly.

Thank God he didn't tell him. My body starts to de-clench slightly. But then, how would he? Oh yeah Dad, we actually had wild sex the other night.

'Actually, how is that friend of yours?' Hugh asks me, cocking his head to the side. 'I heard she got a right roasting from some fella she met.'

'Hugh! Don't use that kind of language around Poppy!' Victor shouts at him, seeming horrified by his son's behaviour.

God, he really would be horrified if he knew what kind of language he used the other night.

'I'm sure she can take it.' He locks eyes with me, as images of him taking my bra off with his teeth flash through my mind. I look down, completely ashamed. Why did I ever listen to Jazz!

'Well anyway,' Victor says, clearing his throat. 'Hugh has just re-located here with his wife and children and–'

'Sorry, what?' I blurt out, hoping I've heard wrong.

Wife and children? Please don't tell me I slept with a married man. I try to remember his hands. I was sure there was no wedding ring.

'Poppy, are you unwell?' Victor asks, seeming more annoyed than worried. 'You seem to be acting a bit strange.'

'Oh, do I? No...I'm fine. Absolutely...fine.' I clear my throat uncomfortably.

I wish I could just run out of the office.

'So anyway. As I was saying.' He looks at me as if warning me to not interrupt again. 'Hugh has relocated and is going to be taking the new position of HR Director. He's going to help out with the redundancies. From now on, you'll also be Personal Assistant to him. I hope that's ok.'

I go to open my mouth, but quickly shut it when I realise it was a rhetorical question.

This is going to be a nightmare.

*   *   *

I try to hide at my desk the rest of the day, but Victor calls me in again after lunch.

'Poppy, Hugh's new office is down the corridor. John's old room. I suggest you go and get yourself used to him.'

Get used to him? If only he knew how familiar we were.

'Of course.' I force a smile and hand over his coffee. He doesn't even look up, already dismissing me.

I walk up the long corridor towards John's old office, feeling my heart beat fasten. Calm down. You're a grown woman. He's probably just as embarrassed as you are. Yet all I can think of is the thudding fear growing inside me.

I open the door to find him sitting with his feet up on the desk, a cappuccino in one hand and a paper in the other.

'Hello Hugh.' I smile politely. 'Is there anything I can get you? Stationary? Maybe another drink?'

He looks up and smirks.

'Hi. Sorry, what was your name again?' he asks.

Is he serious?

'Poppy,' I say through gritted teeth. Resist the strong urge to throw his coffee over him.

'Ah, yes that's it. Actually, you could help me with my computer. There seems to be a problem with it.' He stands up, offering me his seat.

'Sure.'

Maybe he won't mention it at all. Maybe that's why he asked my name. He's trying to pretend the whole incident never happened, if only for his wife and kids. I walk round the desk and sit down looking at the blank screen.

'So, what seems to be the problem then?' I sense him close behind me and shift uncomfortably in my seat, my body clenching up.

'Open up word and I'll show you,' he says, his voice low and sultry close to my ear.

I do as he says, staring straight ahead waiting for more orders. I will not turn round to face him.

'That's it,' he whispers into my ear. When the hell did he get so close? I literally feel my vagina tighten with fear and embarrassment. 'Open up a document called finance team,' he whispers. 'Nearly there.'

He puts his hand on my shoulder and I swallow hard. Please don't touch me. His finger begins tracing a pattern on my skin. I feel my insides turn to ice. I stare ahead at the computer helplessly, feeling sick with fright. I daren't move a muscle.

His hand quickly slips down underneath my dress to my breasts. It shocks me into action.

'Get off me!' I yelp, turning and hitting him in the chest.

'Ooh, feisty. Not just in the bedroom but the office too,' he winks.

I glare at him; feeling totally violated. I stand up and fold my hands defensively over my chest.

'Look, you better back off. I'm still reeling from the fact that you're married with kids.'

'Don't let that put you off,' he says, pushing me against the filing cabinet. 'You can always be my mistress.'

'Get off me!' I shout, trying to push him off with both hands, but all strength seeming to have left my body. He keeps pushing me against it, his hands suddenly everywhere. Panic takes hold of me. What if he doesn't take no for an answer?

I retract my arm and slap him hard round the face, stepping into it, using my whole body for power. It makes a loud whooping sound. He stares back at me shocked.

'Poppy?' I whip my head round to see Victor at the door. 'Did you just hit my son?'

'Um....'

'You better have a God damn good explanation!'

*   *   *

As I walk home from the tube that evening I'm contemplating killing myself. I mean, how on earth do I manage to get myself in these stupid arsed situations? Do I have a serious debilitating condition that means everything I touch turns to shit? I barely escaped that situation pretending that there was a bee in the room I was trying to squat. I obviously didn't expect Victor to freak out as much as he did, jumping on the desk and screaming 'I'm allergic to bees!' I do personally think calling Bee Specialists in to check that we haven't got a nest was slightly over dramatic.

Plus my bank tells me that it'll take at least a week for new cards to be sent out. Luckily they haven't been used. They must have just taken the cash. All twenty pounds of it. Bastard. And my phone company won't send out a new phone for a couple of days.

Izzy smiles at me from in front of the sofa, where she's doing squats. Does she never rest?

'Hey Pops. Have a good day?'

'Yeah, bit of a random one really.' I avoid eye contact, not wanting to explain the saga that is my life.

I pour myself a much deserved glass of wine, hoping Izzy won't tell me off for stealing again.

'Anyway, I've got a surprise for you!' she sings, clapping her hands together.

'Really?' I ask wearily, wishing she wouldn't get so excited over everything.

'Follow me!' She grabs my hand and leads me into my bedroom.

When I turn the corner my room is unrecognisable. Where there were once piles of clothes on the floor I can now see carpet. I mean, it is awful red and brown swirly carpet, but still! My bedside table, once full of makeup and jewellery is now completely clear. It's sparkling. The furniture's even been moved around.

'So, you like?' she asks, seeming as if she might burst from excitement.

'Oh, I love,' I say, still staring in awe. 'Thank-you so much.'

I try not to let the disappointment show. Is it sad that I kind of liked the way Jazz's make up was sprawled all over her dressing table? I kind of enjoyed the mess. It's so different from my flat.

'It's totally Feng shui now. You'll have much better harmony.'

'Oh...great,' I say with as much enthusiasm as I can muster.

'I've been trying to get Jazz to clean her room for ages,' Izzy continues. 'It's really been stressing me out for ages.'

Stressing her out? She must be a massive control freak. Well, this house must well and truly freak her out. I glance around the room and feel my stomach unsettle itself as I remember the letter to Him which was on the bedside table.

'Um...Izzy, there were a letter on the side. Do you know where you've it?'

Don't panic. I'm sure it's just safely put away in a drawer somewhere.

'Oh yeah, don't worry. I posted it for you.' She smiles as she stretches, pushing her boobs in my face.

'Posted it?' I ask carefully, not wanting to let the words sink in.

'Yep, posted it,' she repeats as if I'm mentally retarded.

'Did you...' I swallow, my mouth dry. 'Did you notice one with a North London address on it?' I feel my throat tighten.

'Yeah I think so. Was it in a pale pink envelope?' She sticks her leg up on the dressing table and leans into it like a ballerina.

'Yes! You definitely sent that one?' I ask, wiping the sweat from my sticky forehead.

'Yep. Why, was it important or something? I only posted it at the box at the end of the road.'

'No, no. Don't worry, its fine,' I say as the room starts to spin around me.

Ok, don't panic. Don't panic. The post doesn't get picked up till 6pm and it's only...ok, it's 5.58pm! I dash out of the door, slamming it behind me. When I reach the street I begin running blindly as fast as I can, aware of nothing but the seeds of panic already sprouting inside my mind.

The post man isn't there yet and I'm not sure if it's a good sign or a bad one. I mean, what if he's already been and got the letter? What if it's already on the way?

When I reach it I attempt to stick my hand through the tiny hole, in the hope that it'll shrink and I'll be able to pick it out. No such luck. I think I'm going to be sick.

'Poppy?' a voice calls, breaking me from my panicked thoughts. I look around and see Ryan leaning out of his car window. 'You alright?' He looks at me strangely.

'Yeah...just waiting for the post man.' I smile politely and turn away from him. Please leave me alone.

'Why?' he asks. I turn round begrudgingly to see him still stationary in his car, staring at me.

'Don't worry about it. Just go and park.' I wave him off.

He parks right next to where I'm standing and gets out, intent on ruining my evening completely.

'Seriously,' he says, standing next to me. 'What are you doing? Should I be concerned and call the loony bin to cart you off?'

'Oh shut up will you,' I say shortly. I really don't have time for his attempt at humour. 'It's just...Izzy's posted something she shouldn't have and I'm waiting for the post man to come.'

'But, it's 6 o'clock,' he says, looking at his watch. 'You must have missed him.'

'No, I'm sure he'll be here any minute,' I say trying to feel as positive as I sound.

'Really? I think maybe you should just give up. What's in this letter that's so important anyway?' he asks raising his eyebrows at me. Why is he so nosey!

'Um...' I look around, desperate not to have to tell him. 'Oh my God, there he is!' I point at the post van coming round the corner. 'I told you,' I add smugly.

He looks at me unimpressed as the van pulls up on the curb.

'You can go now,' I say, trying to push him away. I really don't want him to have to see me beg this man for my letter back.

'No, it's ok. I'll wait with you,' he says, smiling knowingly. He knows I'm going to embarrass myself and he wants to watch. What a sadistic arsehole.

An old postman with greying hair gets out of his van, wearing blue shorts and a red hat. I smile and brace myself.

'Hi Mr Postman.'

He looks at me questionably, as if he's wondering whether I'm taking the piss. He turns and opens the post box.

'I actually need a letter back that I posted by accident,' I say as sweetly as I can. He ignores me and takes out the grey bag. 'So if I could just get it.'

'Afraid not love. Once it's posted it's posted.'

'Sorry? What do you mean; once it's posted it's posted? It hasn't been posted. It's just been put in the red box and I want it back. So I think, you know as the customer, you should give it back to me.' My voice is raising in panic. Try to remain calm.

'Sorry love, but its policy. Once it's in our hands it's ours.'

'But you've only literally just put it in your hands! Can't you just turn a blind eye this once?' I ask trying to dazzle him with my smile.

92

'Well...' he looks at me questionably. 'If you show me some ID then...well, maybe I'd think about it.'

'Great!' I exclaim, already starting to calm down. I reach into Jazz's patent bag for my purse. A sinking feeling starts to take over my stomach. I don't have my purse. That bastard thief has it.

'I....I don't actually have any ID. I got mugged last night. But, is there anything you could do anyway?' I smile as brightly as I can.

'Well then, like I said, there's nothing I can do.'

I knew I should have had my teeth whitened. And maybe a boob job.

'Surely you can try and help us out?' Ryan asks, reminding me that he's still here.

I turn to stare at him, shocked that he wants to help. Or maybe he just wants me to embarrass myself more and is setting me up.

'Like I told your lady. It's no good. It's now Royal Mail property. Have a good evening.' He loads the sack in the back of the van and starts up his engine. I stare helplessly from the pavement.

'Well....I'm calling your supervisor!' I shout at him.

He ignores me and starts indicating to pull out.

A helpless feeling, threatening to give me a heart attack starts spreading over my body. What the hell am I going to do? I can't let that letter get to Him. The thought of him reading it makes me feel sick. He'll think I'm crazy and any last shred of dignity I had will be washed away forever.

'Quickly, give me your keys!' I shout to Ryan.

'What?' he asks, his eyes narrowing in confusion.

'Just give me your fucking keys! I need to follow him,' I shout impatiently.

'No way am I letting you drive,' he snorts.

'Please!' I beg, jumping up and down like a spoilt child. 'I'm desperate!'

He looks at me, seeming to be considering if this is a good idea.

'Come on,' he says, opening the car and getting in. 'I'll drive you.'

'Great.' I jump into the small ford fiesta. 'Follow that van! I've always wanted to say that,' I giggle.

He rolls his eyes, but smiles.

'So...what's so important about getting this letter back anyway?'

'It's...it's a long story. Let's just say that.'

'Come on. I'm following a post van. The least you can do is tell me why?' he asks, a comical look on his face.

'It's private, ok'. I cross my arms defensively.

'Ok.' He rolls his eyes. 'Always a drama,' I hear him mutter under his breath.

'Here! He's pulling over,' I screech, watching as the postman pulls over next to another red post box.

Ryan pulls over a little behind him.

'What do we do now?' he asks, yawning as if to show how bored he is.

'Sssh! I'm thinking.' I watch the postman get out of the van and head towards the post box. He seems to decide to walk to the end of the street to get the other post box and I grab my chance.

'Stay here,' I instruct Ryan.

I get out of the car and sneak over to the back of the van, which he's left open. I look inside and see at least ten identical grey sacks. Shit. I start rifling through one of them, desperate to find the pink envelope but there must be a hundred letters in this sack alone.

'What are we looking for?' Ryan says, suddenly at my side.

'A pink envelope,' I say not stopping for a moment.

'Shit, he's coming,' he whispers, grabbing my arm, trying to pull me away.

'But I need to find this letter!' I persist.

'Come on!' He begins to pull me away, more forcibly this time.

'No! I need this,' I wail, throwing him off me. 'You don't understand'.

Before I can think rationally I climb into the back of the van.

'Poppy! Get the fuck out! He's coming,' Ryan whispers angrily, his face scrunched up in impatience.

'Just go. I'll be fine,' I whisper.

He looks around, clearly considering his options. He lets out a big sigh and then jumps in too.

'For fucks sake,' he sighs, crawling to the back of the van. 'Quickly, hide!'

We sink down behind the sacks so we're not seen just in time for him to arrive at the back of the van whistling. We look at each other nervously, hoping he won't notice us. I'm trying so hard to be quiet, but even my breathing sounds heavy. The postman calmly goes round to the front and turns the engine on, loud trance music blasting out of the stereo. What kind of old dude listens to trance?

'Quick,' I whisper. 'You take that sack. It's a pink envelope.' I riffle through, but all I see is stacks and stacks of white letters.

'Is this it?' Ryan asks holding up my pale pink letter.

'Oh my God, I could kiss you!' I say, massive relief taking over me. He smiles awkwardly and I quickly feel embarrassed as I realise what I've said. What if he thinks I'm after him now?

'Now how the fuck are we gonna get out of here?' he asks, his voice low and serious.

'Um...I didn't really think that through,' I admit reluctantly.

'Yeah, that much is obvious,' he snorts.

'I say we just make a run for it,' I shrug.

'Are you serious?' he asks, completely horrified.

'Yes. Now shush!' I put my hand over his mouth and listen as the van grinds to a halt.

I feel his warm breath on my hand and try not to think how it's giving me goose pimples. This is neither the time nor the place. We listen as the doors open and sunlight streams through the sacks. Footsteps go away from the van, probably to collect some more post.

'Go!' I whisper pushing the sacks out of the way. Ryan looks at me in disbelief, but follows me as we both jump out and run as fast as we can down the road.

'You two! Come back here!' we hear him shout after us.

I look back for a second and to my horror he's actually running after us. Oh my God. And he's actually quite fast for an old man.

'Run faster,' Ryan shouts. He grabs my arm and practically drags me along the street.

I run as fast as my legs can take me, but they feel like lead weights, probably still exhausted from Izzy's workout. If he catches me will he call the police? Will I go to prison for stealing post?

After we've turned into the next street and run to the end of that one we finally stop, both completely out of breath. I've got a stitch on my right side, doubling me over in pain. I consider demanding he carry me the rest of the way, but I don't know if that would just play into his whole princess idea of me.

'Where are we?' I ask him, not recognising any of the houses around us.

'I think we're on Evelyn Street. We need to walk another three roads before we get back to my car.'

'Oh crap,' I say, the soles of my feet burning. 'Wait. I just need to take these shoes off.' I bend over and release the straps of my flats. I press my feet onto the pavement and moan with pleasure.

He smirks at me, but quickly looks away when I catch him.

'Anyway, are you ever going to tell me what the letter was about?' he presses.

'It was...it's really embarrassing.' I look at the pavement and my feet, covered in blister plasters. What a mess I must look like. Since I've met him I've lied about being Jazz's cousin, been tied to a banister, had a one night stand, nearly started a house fire, been mugged and now chased after a post man. He must think I'm a raving lunatic.

'It sounds funny. Come on...tell me.' He smiles encouragingly. 'If the police come knocking on the door for stolen post I want to know what I'm going down for.'

I look back at him, feeling warm from his humour. When he's nice he can be quite cute.

'I doubt you'd go to prison for stolen post,' I retort, blushing despite myself.

'You don't know how serious this is. A proper brush with the law I'd say,' he says playfully.

'Ok! If you stop winding me up I'll tell you.'

'I can't promise anything,' he says, his eyes smiling.

'Ok, it was a letter I'd written to my ex just after we'd broke up.'

'Oh. And what? You never got round to posting it?'

'No. I never meant to post it. Jazz made me write it; said it was good therapy or something. Read it in some magazine of hers and then she took it away so I couldn't actually post it.'

'And then Izzy found it?'

'Yep.'

'She's always tidying things away. I can't tell you the amount of stuff I've lost because of her incessant cleaning.'

'Yeah, well she meant well,' I say, suddenly feeling bad for talking about her.

Ryan's phone starts buzzing and he takes it out of his pocket. 'Jazz,' he explains to me.

'Hey Jazz, what's up?' he says into the phone. 'Um, yeah, sure. She's just here with me.' He hands over the phone to me and I look back at him confused. 'She wants to talk to you.'

'Hey hun.'

'Um...hi,' she says, sounding weird. Her voice is clipped and high pitched.

'Jazz? Are you ok?'

'Um....yeah. I just....' she trails off and I hear her gulp heavily. This must be bad.

'What is it?'

Ryan looks up, his face full of concern. 'What?' he mouths to me.

'Um....the police are here,' she says, her voice quavering.

'The police?'

Ryan's eyes widen in confusion.

'They say I need to go down the station with them.'

'What? Why? What did you do? Oh Jazz, I really do wish you'd stop getting yourself into trouble.'

'Actually,' she says, a bit defensively, 'that's why I'm calling. They want you to meet us there.'

'Where?'

'St Albans police station. They're arresting us. Apparently....something to do with a...fire.'

Chapter 8

An hour later, Ryan and I are walking into St Albans police station.
I've explained everything to him and although he's horrified, he hasn't
told me off, which if I'm honest is what I thought he'd do. I assumed
he'd be the first to rub it in. How I'm a raving criminal.

I walk up to the little glass window with a woman sat behind it. She's
got grey hair and a stern long face. She instantly reminds me of my
old headmistress.

'Um...' I clear my throat. 'My name's Poppy Windsor. I've been
asked to come down. My friend Jasmine Green has also been
arrested.'

She looks back at me with disgust and I retract, my stomach bubbling
with nerves.

'I'll call someone. Please take a seat.' She gestures to some red
plastic chairs.

I go to sit down, my entire body now shaking. Ryan smiles weakly at
me as if to try and reassure me.

'Don't worry,' he says. 'I won't let them keep you for long. I'm sure
they have no evidence anyway.'

I smile, my mouth now so dry I can barely swallow. I look down at
the cracked tiles and start counting the corners to try and calm my
mind.

'Miss Windsor?' a butch policewoman says, towering over me. She's
got a heavy black moustache that she should really bleach and her
brown hair is tied back tightly into a boring low pony tail.

'Y-y-yes,' I stammer.

'I'm DI Darcy. I'm arresting you for the criminal damage caused to St
Bernard's Street in St Albans.'

I stare back at her, my heart sinking. In spite of myself, I'd still
harboured a secret, tiny belief that it would all be ok. That they'd
apologise and say it was all a big mistake. I mean, I didn't actually
think they'd properly arrest me.

'You'll have to be kept in a cell for a short while, during which we'll conduct an interview with Miss Green. You can have one phone call if needed and we can arrange for you to have free legal advice. Will that be required?'

I open my mouth to try and respond but Ryan stands up.

'I'll be representing Miss Windsor and Miss Green,' he says, puffing his chest out proudly.

What the hell is he doing? He can't pretend to be a solicitor. They'll figure it out.

'Oh really?' the policewoman says to him in amusement. 'And can I ask who you are?' She raises her eyebrows at him as she surveys his tracksuit bottoms and white t-shirt.

'I'm Ryan Davis, her Solicitor. Previously of Hanson & Estuary law firm.'

'Oh,' she says, taken aback. 'Well fine. We'll get her checked in. If you could wait here and we'll call you when we're conducting the interviews.'

'Fine,' he says, with a stern face. 'Please ensure my clients aren't held for any more time than needed.'

She nods and blushes. Wow, he's so strong and powerful looking.

'Miss Windsor, if you could come with me please,' DI Darcy says, her stern voice back.

I look up at her, still in my seat. My insides are turning to jelly. I look at her and then Ryan helplessly, feeling sick with fright, not daring to move a muscle.

Ryan offers me his hand. I take it and slowly get to my feet, taking deep breaths to try and calm myself. I swallow hard, my eyes pricking with tears. Ryan puts his hand on my lower back, guiding me towards her.

'Don't worry Pops,' he whispers in my ear. 'It'll all be fine.'

I smile back gratefully as I'm herded away. I'm taken to a ginger policeman who takes my fingerprints and then takes my handbag, mobile phone and shoe laces from my trainers. I mean, shoelaces? What the hell do they think I'm going to do, hang myself on them?

I'm led into a large hallway with doors all the way down it. People are shouting and I flinch nervously. At least the ginger policeman didn't put me in handcuffs. He leads me into a tiny blue room without a window. There's a tiny bed big enough for a midget and a heavily stained smelly toilet. The walls are covered in penned graffiti. How did they manage to get a pen in here when I'm not even allowed shoe laces?

'We'll come to collect you for interviewing as soon as we can.'

I nod nervously. He smiles back briefly, clearly feeling slightly sorry for me. Then he slams the door and locks it. I sit on the bed, scared of what disease I might be contracting doing it and start to cry. How could I have gotten myself into this mess? This isn't Jazz's fault. This is all of my own doing. I'm so *so* stupid.

I get up and walk to the door, opening the little hatch and stare outside. There's still a lot of shouting going on and I listen to what they're shouting about. The closest voice I hear sounds familiar.

'Jazz?' I call out sheepishly.

'Pops?' she bellows back.

'Yeah, it's me,' I say, rubbing the tears from my face. 'You OK?'

'As OK as I can be. I'd be better if these *fucking pigs would let me go!*' she screams, her voice suddenly picking up. I forgot what she's like about authority.

'Jazz, shut up! You'll get us in more trouble!'

'Whatever!' she shouts. 'Do you know they took my heels from me? My fucking *Prada*! They're pigs. *Heartless pigs,*' she screams, her voice breaking from emotion. That's Jazz – she could be arrested fine, but take away her shoes and she'll cry like a baby.

'Don't worry hun. I'm sure we'll be out of here soon. Ryan's being our solicitor.'

'Well thank fuck for that. I tried calling the family solicitor Reggie but it went to voicemail and the fucking arseholes said I'd had my one phone call and they could offer free legal advice! Free legal advice! Some idiot that got their degree at a local college? How ludicrous.'

'Shut up you stupid bitches!' a voice suddenly barks towards us. I peer out of the latch trying to work out who said that, as a swoop of fear takes hold of me.

'Why don't *you* fucking shut up!' Jazz shouts. 'Or I'll give you something to fucking shout about!'

There's silence as I wait for my life to end.

'Jazz!' I whisper, completely horrified. I've never seen Jazz like this. 'You're really scary in prison.'

'I know,' she giggles. 'Thank God I watched so much Bad Girls years ago.'

Heavy footsteps echo along the hallway and we both freeze as we watch a policeman round the corner. He walks towards Jazz's cell.

'Miss Green. DI Darcy is ready for you.'

She's taken out of her cell and as she's led past my cell she smiles at me. Yet I can see that behind that bravado she's as terrified as me.

Half an hour later she's back, her hair frazzled and her eyes droopy. Before I can ask how it's gone, the policeman opens my cell door.

'Miss Windsor. DI Darcy is waiting for you.'

I swallow hard and let him lead me into the grey interview room. Ryan is already sat there, with the butch policewoman on the other side of the desk. He doesn't smile at me. He actually looks a bit worried.

I sit down next to him, feeling completely hopeless. I'm going to prison. I'm going to have to eat Spam to survive and I'll probably end up being someone's bitch. And I'll get tattoos and probably contract HIV from the needles. My whole prison life flashes before me.

Ryan clasps my hand under the table, making me jump. He squeezes it reassuringly and I try to smile back, but my face is frozen in fear.

Butch policewoman DI Darcy presses a button on her tape recorder and turns to look at me.

'Interview with Miss Poppy Windsor, conducted on June 10th at 19.37.' She leans back in her chair. 'Miss Windsor, you do not have to say anything. However, it may harm your defence if you do not mention when questioned something which you later rely on in court.

Anything you do say may be given in evidence. Do you understand or would you like me to explain further?'

'No, that's fine' I nod. 'I've seen a lot of CSI.'

Ryan puts his hand up to his mouth to stifle a giggle. I don't see how laughing at me is helping me.

'Miss Windsor, we have sufficient evidence to believe that you and your friend Miss Green set a public bin on fire in St Bernard's Drive in St Albans. What do you say to that claim?'

'I say it's all lies! I'm innocent, I tell you! Totally innocent. I've never had anything like this before. Well, OK, so I did once return my library books late when I was fifteen and I got a fine, but Greg Carlson was fighting Tim Kevinson and I totally forgot all about it!

She stares back at me blankly. Maybe I'm starting to ramble.

'Right. Can you tell me what happened on the night of Saturday 1st?'

'Nothing! Me and Jazz just had a few drinks and kind of passed out. I don't actually remember anything.'

'So you *could* have done this and just been too drunk to remember?'

'Please don't put words into my client's mouth,' Ryan protests, his face blank and scary.

'So you have no idea how the fire got started?' she asks, licking her lips and leaning in towards me.

'No! No idea whatsoever. I didn't even go near it.'

'Really?' She smiles, as if she's caught me out. 'Because your friend Miss Green says, that you did see the fire being lit and you just tried to put it out. Is that not what happened?'

'Um...' I look at Ryan trying to understand what to say, but his expression is blank. 'Yes...that's what happened. I'd...forgotten about that.'

'Really?' she enquires. 'So you both saw a group of gay French tourists dance down the street juggling fire and accidentally setting the bin alight?'

My mouth spreads into a smile, despite myself. How can Jazz be so ridiculous? I quickly frown and bite my tongue to cover it.

'Err...yes, that's it. French gay tourists. That's what happened,' I nod.

102

'And can you describe these French gay tourists?' she asks, leaning back in amusement.

'Um...well, they had on tight t-shirts and spoke in French accents. That's all I can really tell you.'

'That's all? Because Miss Green told us one had pink hair and they all wore stripy shirts with berets and were talking in English about cooking frogs legs when they got home and how they hated the English.'

Oh for goodness sakes Jazz.

'Oh yes. I....forgot about that,' I grimace.

'You seem to forget a lot Miss Windsor. Do you suffer from a memory disorder?'

'No,' I say, my cheeks flushing. She knows I'm lying.

'The thing is that I want to believe you. In fact, I have more reason to believe you rather than Miss Green. You've got a clear criminal record, but I can't say the same for Miss Green'. She consults a file and starts running her finger down it. 'We've got her being arrested in 1999 for shop lifting. Then there's the drunken and disorderly in 2001. Plus the protesting that got out of hand in 2006. She's got quite a record.' She leans back in her chair and tutts.

'Well I'm sure she wasn't charged for any of them, so she was obviously innocent,' I protest, one blush blending into the other.

'Was she innocent? Or was there just not enough evidence? Or did Mummy and Daddy's lawyer help her out?'

'Excuse me,' Ryan pipes up. 'But I fail to see how Miss Green's past record has anything to do with my client.'

DI Darcy stares back at him, grimacing. She's obviously been caught out.

'Can we please cut to the chase?' Ryan asks. 'What actual evidence do you have of my clients?'

She glares back at him. She gets a laptop out of the top draw and turns it on, all the time smiling smugly back at him.

'I'm now showing Miss Windsor exhibit A. The recording acquired from St Albans council showing activity on St Bernard's Drive on the night in question'. She turns to look at me, raising her eyebrow.

'Miss Windsor, are you saying that this is not you?'

I watch the patchy black and white recording of the corner outside my flat. After a few seconds you see two women walking out and, although grainy, it's clear to see it's me and Jazz. We stumble out of the door with pieces of paper in our hands. We throw them in the bin and Jazz gets some matches out of her pocket. She lights it and throws it in, small flames glowing in the night. We high five and hold hands, dancing around it like school children. Jazz stops for a second to vomit in the street. Raj comes running out with a wet towel, trying to put out the fire. He calls for help and two other men come to carry us away while they battle with the fire.

DI Darcy turns it off and stares at me, the silence in the room deafening. I recoil in my seat, not daring to look anyone in the eye. How the *hell* am I going to get out of this one? I glance up from behind my hair to see Ryan's expression. His mouth is still open and he's staring at the screen, his face drained of all colour.

I'm going to prison.

'So Miss Windsor. Do you still claim that isn't you?' DI Darcy asks, smiling smugly.

I feel my chest tightening and my throat closing. I burst into angry sobs before I can attempt to pull myself together.

'Miss Windsor, I need a yes or a no,' she presses. 'Obviously if you were to say no we'd have to look into this further. Waste more police time and interview a Raj Mohamed. He could be charged with withholding evidence.'

'No!' I wail. 'I did it ok! Please just don't involve Raj in this. He's got a family, it's not his fault. It was me, all me. I'm so sorry! I just got so drunk and...And....I don't know what I was thinking. I'm so sorry.'

I cover my face in my hands and tell myself to be stronger. I'll have to get tough before I go to prison. Oh God, and even worse, how am I going to tell my Mum?

Ryan places his hand on my shoulder.

'What's going to happen? Surely just a caution will be sufficient?' he enquires.

'We will be issuing a caution to both Miss Windsor and Miss Green. But I warn you Miss Windsor. If I catch you doing anything like this ever again, I will make sure you are charged.'

I look up and she stares back at me, with the smallest bit of amusement in the corners of her mouth.

'A caution? Am I...free to go?' I whisper, not daring to believe it.

'Yes,' she says. 'I'll just arrange the paperwork.' She leaves the room, slamming the door loudly. I burst into more angry sobs.

'Pops, don't worry. It's only a caution,' Ryan tries to reason. 'You're fine.'

'But...I still got in trouble! Don't you get it, I feel sick. I hate being in trouble.'

'You are funny,' he laughs.

I look up to see him smiling at me warmly.

'Funny? How the fuck is any of this funny?'

'Trust me, you'll look back at this and smile,' he assures confidently.

'I doubt it.'

Within twenty minutes I've signed a notice to say that I accept a caution and I'm in the reception area waiting for Jazz. She comes running out dramatically, still screaming.

'You wait! I'll be back,' she screams at the policemen as she puts her shoes on. 'Taking my shoes, it's fucking police brutality if you ask me!'

'Jazz shut up,' I snap, grabbing her and pulling her out before she can get arrested again.

'Well it's ludicrous,' she shrieks, flicking her hair as she gets into Ryan's car.

'No, what's ludicrous is your French gay tourists,' I snap.

Ryan chuckles and looks back at the both of us.

'You two really are different.'

Me and Jazz look at each other confused. I glance back at him to see him studying me with curious eyes.

'What do you mean by that?' I ask.

'I just assumed that you'd be like Jazz is all. But you're really not'. He stares ahead at the road leaving me wondering what he meant by that.

'I need a fucking drink,' Jazz proclaims. 'Who's up for a cocktail bar?'

'You've got to be joking,' Ryan laughs.

'Actually...I could do with a drink,' I say before I can help it.

*   *   *

Two hours later we're in a cocktail bar in St Albans called 'Mine's a Mojito'. It's decorated like a Hawaiian hut with wood cladding and deck chairs darted around. They've even made us wear flower necklaces. I'm a little bit drunk, but I mean, after the shock that I've had that's to be expected, right?

Jazz and Ryan are talking about the letter I wrote to Him.

'I can't believe you made her write a letter,' Ryan snorts. 'It's such a stupid girl thing to do.'

'No it's not!' she retorts. 'I read it in Cosmo!'

'You're kind of proving his point there Jazz,' I say, finishing off my Sex on the Beach.

'I'm not!' she exclaims, her face getting red. 'You should have seen her. She was a right mess. All panda eyes and tracksuits.'

Ryan laughs while he orders us another round.

'It's not that funny! It was actually a really bad time for me,' I say, feeling giddy.

'Oh, I think it is,' he chuckles darkly.

'I'm glad my personal misery brings you so much amusement. Shall I really make you laugh and read some for you?' I ask pleased by his attention.

'Yeah, go on then,' he says, flashing his lovely straight teeth.

'Ok.' I take it out of my bag and rip it open. I clear my throat and sit up straight, taking my cocktail from him as I open it up. I go to read the first line, but it looks different. This is black biro and I could have sworn I wrote it with blue. I never write with black, it's too depressing. I clutch my stomach as realisation comes flooding into my brain. This isn't my letter. This is an old lady's letter to her friend Anne.

'What's wrong?' Jazz asks, smiling.

'It's....it's....um, not the letter.'

'What?' Her face drops and she grabs the letter from me, reading it.

'Shit. Does this mean the letter really is on the way to him?'

'Yeah-huh,' I mumble.

I can just imagine him getting the post, maybe even Claudine getting it. Opening it and reading all of that crap I wrote. Oh my God, he's going to think I wrote it recently and that I'm still in love with him or something!

'Is it really that bad? Ryan asks, sipping his mojito.

'It's...' I gulp, remembering the words.

'It's bad,' Jazz interjects. 'We called him a shit head.'

'And....an interfering old man twat,' I say, my body still feeling like a zombie's.

'Ok. Well, at least it's straight to the point,' he smiles.

'God, he was a cock,' Jazz says remembering.

'Oh God,' I grimace. 'And I insulted his hair.'

'In her defence, I did make her drink Sambuca before she wrote it,' Jazz explains.

'Ah, is that another reason you don't do shots anymore?' he smiles playfully.

I can suddenly remember it off by heart. The pain resurfaces for a second before I push it back down and lock it away, where it belongs. 'I heard about your new girlfriend. Funny coz you didn't mention it when you broke my heart,' I say out loud. Ryan looks up at me as if he's not sure whether to leave. Jazz grimaces and downs her Pina Colada. I smile and take another gulp of my cocktail.

There's silence as they both look at me, their faces full of awkward pity. The atmosphere has quickly changed and I'm now aware of how pathetic I look.

'It's...funny really,' I say wanting to diffuse the atmosphere. I want it to be back to us laughing again.

'Really? Because it sounds kind of...awful,' he says, his eyes sympathetic.

Jazz orders another round of cocktails even though I'm nowhere near finishing mine.

'No, honestly I'm fine,' I say, surprised at the sudden moistness at my eyes. Why the hell do I feel like I'm going to burst into tears? I'm well over this. It's the damn drink. Why do I keep drinking!?

'Come on. Tell me.' He puts his warm hand on mine, sending shivers down my spine.

'Don't push her,' Jazz warns, shooting him a sharp look.

'It's just...it's just that I really didn't see it coming. I thought he was going to propose and instead I got dumped,' I blurt out, the words almost choking me.

'Oh,' he says, biting his lip. 'I...don't really know what to say.'

'I told you not to push her dickhead!' Jazz shouts, shoving him.

'No, it's cool. I'm over it now. It was ages ago. I don't really like to think about it.'

He stares at me, trying to figure something out. 'You really didn't see it coming?'

'What the fuck did I just tell you!?' Jazz shouts, banging her fist on the table.

'No, Jazz its fine.' I take a deep breath. 'I thought we were happy. But then he suddenly decided that he didn't want the boring life of a couple. And I mean, I can't really blame him. We were so young when we got together. I just...'

'What?' he encourages, seeming completely intrigued by my pathetic little life.

I can't remember the last time someone, anyone, took this much interest in me.

'I just wish I'd listened to everyone when they'd told me I was too young to be settling down with someone and I should have been out partying.'

'Yeah you should,' Jazz says under her breath.

'So you've been making up for it ever since?' he asks, his cheeky smile returning.

'Not exactly,' I laugh.

'I keep moaning on at her that she lives like an old granny; staying in and being boring,' Jazz explains. 'So now I've made her move in with you guys and start to try new things.'

'Oh, so that's why,' he says, seeming to be putting the pieces together in his head.

I suppose it isn't every day that a complete nutcase moves into your house.

'And how's it going? Trying new things I mean.' he asks.

'Awful,' I laugh. 'Everything I do seems to turn into a disaster.'

'You can say that again,' he winks, staring at me intently with his big brown eyes.

I take another gulp of drink, feeling myself blush. Maybe it won't be that bad to fancy someone a little bit. It might actually be good for me. He might be like medicine to me, a bit of a remedy. I just hope he doesn't turn out to be poison.

*   *   *

In the morning there's a note from him left on the kitchen table.

'Poppy,

My number is 07836 784 893. Please put it in your phone. It will stop me worrying so much.

Ryan'

Chapter 9

Imagine writing me a note. I don't know whether to be seriously offended or pleased that he seems to care about me. And why does he seem to worry about me? It's weird. Why do I even care? It's just nice that someone does. And maybe it helps that *the* someone in question has a jawline that I can't stop imagining touching.

'Poppy,' Hugh says, suddenly at my desk. 'Can I see you in my office for a moment please?'

My stomach drops and my body starts to tremble. I get up from my desk as calmly as possible and follow him into the small room at the end of the corridor. I should have bought a rape alarm.

'Please take a seat,' he says professionally.

Maybe he's changed. Maybe yesterday has shown him that I'm not interested and that we can only have a professional relationship.

'Poppy, I was very upset by your behaviour yesterday,' he says, while he squeezes a stress ball menacingly.

'Well actually Hugh, I was very upset by your behaviour,' I say, my teeth almost clattering from nerves.

'Oh really?' he says, shocked. 'Well then maybe you shouldn't dress so provocatively around the office. You'll give all of us men the wrong impression,' he smiles insincerely.

'Wrong impression?' I ask puzzled.

'Yes. That you're up for it.' He narrows his eyes at me like I'm some slut from the street.

I swallow hard, feeling the strong urge to burst into tears.

'Up for it? I was wearing a wrap dress for Christ's sake!'

'Exactly,' he nods. 'Anyway.' He gets up and moves to sit on the desk directly in front of me. 'I feel like you and I have got off on the wrong foot.'

God, his crotch is so close to my face. This is awful. How the hell did I get myself into this situation?

'Ok,' I say carefully, shifting uncomfortably in my chair. Where is this leading?

'I'm your boss. My Father has agreed for me to set your KPI's and objectives and I do hope that I'm not unhappy with you. It would be really awful for you to lose your job.'

'Sorry? Are you...threatening me?' I swallow hard and take a deep breath, praying the tears stinging at my eyes don't escape.

Please tell me this isn't happening. This sort of thing doesn't happen in real life does it? This is the kind of crap you see on soap operas.

'Of course not Poppy. I'm merely advising you to keep me happy,' he says, with a bloodcurdling grin.

My body shakes all the more violently as his stare moves to my boobs and he licks his lips.

'And right now I need these people's personnel files.' He hands me over a sheet of paper scribbled with people's names. He sits back and smiles, as if the previous conversation didn't just happen. 'That's all.'

I run from his office straight to the toilets, tears already starting to fall down my face. How can this be happening to me!? I have to leave; I can't work here anymore under him. He's going to make my life hell. Absolute hell on earth.

I burst through the toilet door and jump when I see a familiar body shape standing by the sink crying. She instantly straightens herself up and wipes the tears from her face.

'Cheryl? Are you ok?'

'Oh yes. I'm fine,' she says, wiping a tear from her red blotchy face.

'Well you obviously aren't. What's wrong?' I ask, quickly cleaning up my own tears.

'It's nothing, honestly. I just...I don't want to talk about it.' She turns to look back at the mirror, removing the mascara smudges from under her eyes.

Ok. Well maybe she does just want to be left alone. She's upset as it is now, let alone if I start pestering her for information. Even though I'm seriously curious, I must remember that this isn't gossip. This is her life.

'Ok. Well if you need anything.' I open the door to leave.

'He's having an affair,' she blurts out.

I let go of the door and stare back at her in disbelief.

'What? Who's having an affair?'

'Well my husband, obviously,' she snaps, her face hard.

I must remember that she's in emotional pain. Try not to let the fact that she's an obnoxious bitch play a part in how I react.

'Are you sure?' I say carefully.

'Of course I am,' she growls as another tear escapes. 'Well at least...I think I am.'

'Well, you don't sound very sure,' I challenge.

'Look all I know,' she says, her voice breaking and her chin beginning to quiver 'is that he's lost all interest in me since I've had Matilda.'

'But that might just be – '

'I'm not finished,' she bawls, shooting me an irritated stare. Don't hold it against her. Just smile.

'Then a few things have made me wonder. He's suddenly in a really good mood all the time and buying me presents.'

'But that's good isn't it? Maybe he's making an effort?'

'Poppy. I'm still not finished,' she says sharply. 'If you'd just stop interrupting like this I could have already told the story.'

Maybe he is cheating. I can't imagine being excited to come home to this bitch.

'Anyway,' she says, jutting out her jaw and turning back to face the mirror. 'Every woman knows that a man only buys presents when he's feeling guilty.'

I consider interrupting to tell her she's just being paranoid, that maybe he loves her. But I bite my tongue, remembering her strict orders.

'So last night I went through his phone. I didn't see it at first. There were loads of texts from a friend called Chad. There were so many that I thought maybe I'd go into one message to see what on earth they were talking about. I mean, I'd never heard him even mention a Chad.' She stops for a minute to take a deep breath, her words seeming to drudge up painful memories. She closes her eyes. 'Then I saw it.' She opens her eyes. 'It said 'can't you make an excuse?'

I stare at her expectantly as she pauses dramatically.

'So I went through the rest and I realised that Chad is a cover name for some woman he's seeing. She wants him to come up with an excuse so that she can see him tonight after work.'

'Are you sure...' I don't know quite how to say this. 'Are you sure Chad is a woman?'

'What?' she yells turning to face me. 'Now you think my husband is a faggot?'

'No! And Cheryl, no-one says faggot.'

'Well I'm *very* sorry for being so politically incorrect!' she snaps, waving her hands dramatically.

'Look, I'm sorry but you still might be wrong.'

'Well he just text me and said that he had a last minute client after work and so won't be home until later.'

'Oh,' is all I can muster. 'But, I mean, he could be telling the truth.'

'He's a personal trainer Poppy. How can you just suddenly need a last minute appointment? What, you suddenly eat a doughnut and need to urgently work it off,' she rolls her eyes.

'Maybe. Oh, I don't know.' I rest myself against the sink. This is just too much to take in. 'So what are you going to do?'

'No idea. I love him Poppy,' she says, fresh tears escaping as her voice breaks. 'I really do.'

This is probably the first time I've seen her vulnerable. I have to just forget about the past and see her as a woman. A woman heartbroken over her husband's cheating.

'Maybe you should go and spy on him. You know, just to check. I still think you could be wrong,' I offer.

'Oh my goodness, you're right! That's what we'll do,' she says, her face lighting up with sudden excitement.

'What do you mean – what *we'll* do?'

'Me and you. We're going to follow him after work and see if it is an affair,' she says determinedly.

'Oh. I don't actually know if I'm free after work...,' I say hoping she'll let me off the hook.

'Of course you are, silly. You're the one that came up with the idea.' She turns to walk out, a new spring in her step. She turns back to face me smiling. 'Thanks Poppy. You're a good friend. I'll meet you in reception at five.'

Oh crap.

When I get back to my desk I take the piece of paper Hugh gave me out of my pocket and scan the list of names. He wants their personnel files, which can only mean one thing. They're the people going to be made redundant.

I go through the names, feeling sick as I see Jeremy's name, then Paul in accounts. But then I freeze and close my eyes, wishing I haven't seen it. That I'm wrong.

Because the name I'm looking at is Lilly Evans.

*   *   *

By quarter to six Cheryl and I are walking towards a park that she says she knows her husband often takes his clients to. My stomach starts churning, telling me this is a terrible idea. Either that or I need a cookie. I mean, hopefully we'll just find him with an old man called Chad doing chin ups, but a terrible feeling in my gut tells me that we're going to find what we're looking for.

How will she react? Will she want to run over and confront him? And if she does what should I do? Should I just walk away and leave them to it or try and calm her down. And what if she attacks the woman? What if this is a trick and she's planned for this? What if she's currently carrying a knife in her bag and just wants a witness to the murder she plans to commit?

Ok, calm down Poppy. Don't let your imagination run wild.

'There he is!' she says, grabbing me and pulling me down behind a bush. I part the bushes in front of me to try and spot him, but I can't see him anywhere.

'Shush!' she snarls to me.

'I didn't say anything!'

'You just did!'

'I can't see him. Are you sure you saw him?' I ask, thinking her poor fragile mind must be playing tricks on her.

'Look. Over there.' I follow her pointed manicured finger and see him in his sports gear with a woman whose back is turned towards us. She's got medium length brown hair and a great arse. Maybe I should let Izzy train me if you get an arse like that. I try to analyse their body language for any signs of an affair but they're just talking.

'See,' I say to Cheryl smugly. 'They're just talking.'

'You don't see it?' she asks, her face crumpled in agony. 'That's his flirty face.' She points towards him again.

I try to focus in on his face and it looks anything but flirty. If anything it looks contorted, like he's in some sort of pain.

'That's his flirty face? Are you sure?'

'Completely positive,' she nods.

God, I'd hate to think of his orgasm face. Images of this flash through my head and I try with all my might to get them out. If I don't I might not be able to sleep tonight. Or ever again.

He smiles at the brunette and closes the gap between them with one step. He leans in towards her and I hold my breath in anticipation. Please no. Don't do it. It's like a car crash – I can't help but look.

He kisses her. Oh my God. We can only see the back of her head, but I'm sure it was a kiss.

'Oh my God,' Cheryl says, clutching onto my arm as if she's just been punched in the stomach.

I watch her as she struggles to breathe, her face drained of all colour. The worst thing is that I know there's nothing I can say to make this better. Instead I grab her shaking hand and squeeze it. She looks up to me and smiles gratefully between tears. Poor Cheryl.

'Maybe we should go?' I offer, hoping she won't want to confront him.

'No. I want to see what else they do,' she says, determined.

Does she really want to torture herself? We both turn back to them as they stroll hand in hand to the ice cream van parked on the green. He buys an ice cream and licks it, offering it to her. She licks it too. My stomach turns. This is too much. Poor, poor Cheryl.

They turn to walk towards us and I do a double take, feeling the blood draining from my face. My breath gets caught in my throat and I physically shake my head, hoping my vision has blurred over and I'm wrong.

Because the woman he's with is Annabel. Richard's Annabel. My brother's wife Annabel.

Oh. My. God.

*   *   *

When I get home I head straight for my bedroom, not wanting to face anyone. How could this be happening? Why Annabel? I'm not going to lie and say I'm shocked and that she's a lovely girl and a close friend. The truth is that I've never really liked her. We've never seen eye to eye. We're different breeds.

She was always the girl at school that everyone wanted to be. Popular, beautiful, clever. But in reality she was a bitch who'd trip you up as soon as look at you. I'm sure Richard would agree if he wasn't the complete male version of her. They're the annoying perfect couple that everyone secretly hates. I swear, even my Dad seems to find them annoying.

But I was sure that they loved each other. They'd been together forever. Since they were fourteen. Everyone called them the perfect couple. Richard will be devastated.

But then, how would he ever find out unless I told him? Should I tell him? Would he thank me for ruining his marriage? I doubt it. He'd probably just tell me I was lying, like the time I told him Henry had crashed his bicycle when it was actually me. But I was only twelve and surely I can't just let him continue on in ignorance. What if someone else saw them? What if all his friends know and they're laughing at him behind his back? I might not be best friends with him. Hell, I might not even like him very much, but he doesn't deserve that. Some deep down sisterly instinct wants me to protect him.

The house phone rings and a few seconds later Izzy knocks on my door. She pokes her head around the corner, the cordless phone in her hand.

'It's for you,' she says, holding her hand over the receiver. 'Some Lilly?'

Lilly. Another dilemma. I consider telling Izzy to say I'm not here, but then she'd only keep ringing. She hates being ignored. I once found my phone to have 15 missed calls and three furious voicemails. I can't imagine how poor Alex copes with her sometimes.

I thank Izzy and take the phone.

'Hey Lil,' I say as cheery as I can.

'Hey bitch. You're not answering your phone. So where the hell did you go with Cheryl?'

I thought she'd notice us leave together. Nothing much gets past Lilly.

'Oh, just a bar for a chat.' I can't tell her the truth. Not only would that be completely unfair to Cheryl, but I don't want anyone knowing what a cheating bitch of a wife my sister in law is.

'A chat? What about? All she ever rabbits on about is her bloody child.'

'Yeah, well that was it. She was upset...by something the child-minder had done and she wanted my advice.'

'Really?' she says, sounding suspicious. 'Why did she want your advice?'

'Oh, I don't know. To be honest I don't actually think she has many friends.'

'Yeah, there's a reason for that. The woman's a fucking monster.'

'Lilly! She's not that bad.'

'Ok, whatever,' she says, sounding peeved.

'Are you...are you jealous?' I ask, feeling stupid at having to even ask the question.

'No!' she retorts a little too quickly.

'Are you sure?' I'm feeling an intense urge to giggle.

'Ok, well maybe I felt a little left out. I just don't want you turning into a boring bitch like her.'

'Ah, Lil! I didn't know you cared,' I say jokingly.

'Oh shut-up.' She sounds embarrassed.

'Well I don't think I'll be hanging out with her too much. Plus, you'll always be my number one workmate.'

'Workmate? Try number one work best friend. That sounds a lot better.'

'Ok fine. But please don't bring in friendship necklaces tomorrow or anything, ok? I think that would be *slightly* too much.'

'Really? Ok. I guess I could cancel the order.' She bursts out laughing.

I laugh too and feel my body release into the chuckles. I've been holding so much tension in it since I saw Annabel.

'But seriously. I think we should be a bit nicer to Cheryl. She's nice underneath it all.'

'Really? You mean underneath all of that self-righteous, judgemental bitchy persona, she's actually someone we should invite to our sleepovers?' she mocks.

'Yes. I know she comes across as a total obnoxious bitch sometimes, but she's just a woman at the end of the day. She has feelings too.'

'Oh spare me the crap, Oprah. Anyway, tomorrow I want a proper catch up. I wanna find out properly about your new housemates. No interruptions this time! Ok?'

God, she's going to drag it all out of me whether I like it or not.

'Um...ok.'

'Anyway, Alex has just got in so I've gotta go. Laters bitch.'

'Bye.'

When I hang up, the anxious feeling bubbles back up again. What am I going to do about Lilly? Should I tell her they plan to make her redundant so she can get a heads up with finding another job? But then that'd be unfair to all of the other people. Plus if work ever found out I'd get sacked for sure. I'm not sure if I could trust Lilly to keep quiet about it. She's hardly the most tactful person I've ever met. But when she is told she'll know I've known and not told her. Oh God, it's lose lose.

And what am I going to do about Annabel? I look around my very clean room for some kind of distraction. Maybe some kind of book I could read, but the only ones I manage to find are 'The Complete Idiot's Guide to Tantric Sex' and 'The Odd Squad Little Book of Sex'. Jazz is far too sexed up. I do consider flicking through for a moment, but as images of Jazz performing barely legal sex acts on strange men flash through my mind I decide against it.

I unpack some of my things and find some bikini wax strips in her knickers drawer. Jazz is always going on about how I need to wax. How hard can it be?

I go into the kitchen and pour myself a glass of wine as I read the instructions.

'You want some dinner?' Ryan asks, popping his head round from the sofa area.

I quickly shove the instructions in my pocket and try desperately not to get lost in his athletic body leaning casually against my door frame, his muscular arms folded against his chest.

'Um....no, I'm fine thanks,' I lie. I've got too much confusion whizzing through my head at the moment and I don't think I could add him to the equation.

'Ok,' he shrugs.

I quickly go into my room before I can look into those eyes and change my mind. I get a wax strip out and warm it up between my hands as it says. I peel one side away and smooth it against my bikini line. While I'm at it I pull them all off and cover my whole bikini line with them.

I wait a minute for the hairs to attach to it properly. The user guide says to pull the strip back quickly against the direction of hair growth to reveal silky smooth skin for up to four weeks. That sounds easy. Right. Here we go. I grab a corner of the first one and hold my skin taut as I quickly attempt to whip it off.

HOLY FUUUUUUUUUUUUUUUUCK!

I clench my fist from the earth shattering pain that goes throbbing through my body, starting at my vagina. I'm frozen from the pain, not able to make a sound, the intensity too strong. When it submerges enough for me to start breathing again I look down. I've only managed to remove half of it! You've got to be joking me! I down the rest of my glass of wine and brace myself.

'FUCK!' I shout as it's released from my skin.

119

I glance down to check that my skin's still attached. It is, but stares back at me, red and furious.

'Poppy?' Ryan says, knocking at my door. 'Are you ok in there?'

Oh my God. He can't come in; I'm naked apart from my bra and bikini wax strips.

'I'm fine thanks! Just...saw a spider. All fine now.'

'Ok,' he says, his voice deeply sceptical.

What the hell am I going to do! I can't take the rest of these off. I don't have the guts. I grab the phone and call Jazz.

'Hey buttercup, you ok?'

'No! You have to come round NOW.'

'Why? What's wrong?'

'I...well....it's kind of ridiculous.'

'Just tell me,' she laughs.

'Ok. I'm covered in bikini wax strips and I can't get them off.'

There's an awkward pause and I wonder if she's going to laugh down the phone at me.

'I'll be right round.'

I try to take deep breaths. Everything is going to be fine. Absolutely fine. Jazz will come round and she'll know a way to take them off without hurting me. She'll have some sort of lotion or something. Actually, maybe she has something here. I start rifling through her drawers in desperation.

A knock on my door sends me into a spiral of panic. Go away Ryan! Why won't he just leave me alone!

'Poppy? It's Izzy. Can I come in?'

Shit.

'Um...I was just...sleeping'. It's only 7.30pm, I remind myself. 'Can you come back later?'

'Really? Jazz just called me.'

Oh crap. I grab Jazz's dressing gown and let her in, feeling like a prize idiot.

'I come bearing gifts.' She hands over a bottle of wine.

'Well then you're welcome,' I say, a reluctant smile breaking on my face.

'Poppy?' Ryan says, knocking on the door. 'Jazz is here for you.'

'Yes, she knows I'm coming idiot,' Jazz says, as she barges through the door.

Ryan strains his neck, trying to get a glimpse of what's happening in here, but Jazz slams it quickly in his face. She looks at me and then stares at Izzy dead in the eye.

'Izzy, please tell me you haven't just spent the last 45 minutes getting her pissed?'

'I'm fwine,' I slur. Hmm, maybe I am a bit drunk.

'I'm just trying to numb the pain,' Izzy protests. 'She won't let me near them.'

'Jesus Pops. How the hell did you think you were gonna do this on your own?'

'I just...oh I don't know. Stop judging me! Now, have you brought the cream that takes this wax off or not?'

'Cream?' she laughs, raising her eyebrows.

'Yeah.' I'm confused. 'You know, the cream that's going to take this off.'

'Chick, the only way that's coming off you is us pulling it off.'

'What? Are you serious?' I ask, my voice sharp with nerves. But her expression says it all. I suddenly feel very sober.

I turn to Izzy. 'Please tell me that you know a way to get this off?'

'Sorry Poppy. I don't get waxes. I find them too painful,' she squirms.

'Where the hell were you an hour ago when I got this stupid idea!'

'Don't blame Izzy,' Jazz says. 'It's not her fault you're the only twenty five year old that has never been waxed. Jesus, I had my first bikini wax at school.'

'Yeah, well you probably had your own beautician,' I growl.

'Do you want my help or not?' she snaps, tapping her foot impatiently on the floor.

'Yes,' I say, exhaling a big breath. I haven't got much choice now.

'Ok. First things first. I brought pain relief.' She goes to her bag and takes out a bottle of wine, a box of paracetamol, a cigarette packet and a joint.

'I told you I've given up smoking,' I snap. 'I have done for nearly a year.'

'They're for me you idiot,' she says, taking a fag out and lighting it.

'Right. Take these.'

She hands over the paracetamol and I take two while she opens the new bottle of wine and takes a swig of it. Izzy has some after her and then it's given to me.

'Ok,' Jazz says determined, taking a puff of her cigarette and looking at Izzy. 'Izzy, are you strong enough to hold her down?'

'Hold me down? What the-'

Before I can even finish my sentence Izzy throws me back on the bed and restrains me by my wrists.

'Izzy! This is totally unnecessary!' I shriek.

'Here we go!' Jazz sings, her fag still in her mouth. She rips open my dressing gown, exposing not just the wax strips, but also the rest of the vagina.

'Don't look Izzy! I don't want you to see me like this,' I shriek, cringing.

'Don't worry. You've seen one vagina, you've seen them all,' she laughs, still restraining me heavily.

How is she so strong? She's only little. Jazz clasps onto one strip and flicks it back quickly. I scream in agony.

'Jazz! Fuck!' I scream.

'What? This is what I'm here for remember,' she says, rolling her eyes.

Izzy loosens her grip for a second to get the bottle of wine for me. She puts it into my mouth and I start glugging. The second strip getting removed is more painful than the two others put together.

'FUCK!' I shout, trying to throw them off.

'Stop kicking!' Jazz giggles.

'Is everything ok in there?' Ryan shouts at the door.

'Yep, it's all cool,' Jazz shouts giggling. She turns to me. 'Do you want the spliff?'

'No! You know I don't do drugs. And neither should you!'

She ignores me and turns to Izzy. 'Izzy, get ready,' she gestures to her with the fag in her hand.

'Ok! Maybe I'll have a fag to steady my nerves,' I say, giving in.

The next two minutes are the most painful I've ever experienced. Jazz continued to attack the strips, while Izzy at first calmly fed me wine and puffs of the fag. By the end she just clamped her hand over my mouth so that Ryan couldn't hear the screams.

'Good as new,' Jazz beams when they're all off.

'Never again,' I stammer, my whole body still trembling.

'You're welcome,' they both say at the same time.

'Well, I think it's pretty clear that I'll never be able to give birth.'

'Why the hell would you want to?' Jazz says. 'So anyway, have you decided what you want to do for your birthday yet?'

'What?' I groan, the stinging still not dying down. 'How many damn times do I have to tell – '

'Ok! Jesus,' she says, putting her hand up in defence.

'When's it your birthday Pops?' Izzy asks, obviously already having fantasies about pink bouncy castles.

'It's next Saturday,' Jazz informs her. 'But she hates celebrating it because she always has bad luck.'

'Really?' Izzy giggles. 'Worse than normal?'

'Yes, but I'd rather not talk about it,' I snap, the memories still raw.

'Well I still think you should do something. Actually, Jake and I are going to some festival next Friday night with a few of his friends. Why don't we all go? It can be your half arsed birthday celebration.'

'Yay! Let's do it!' Izzy squeals.

'Festival?' Images of mud, baked beans and peeing in bushes flash through my head.

'Yes, f-e-s-t-i-v-a-l,' she says, slowly as if I'm retarded. 'Apparently they go every year and they've got a few spare tickets.'

'Oh, you're really selling it to me. Sounds *well* popular.'

'Stop rolling your eyes, it'll be fun! And I'm taking that as a yes,' Jazz confirms.

'Do I even have a choice?'

'God, you're so dramatic. Of course you don't have a choice. You wanna come shopping with me to get some camping gear?'

'Camping gear? What the hell do we need? Plus, I thought you weren't supposed to be spending money!'

'Oh yeah, but if it's a necessity.'

She's a nightmare.

'Are you girls OK in there?' Ryan asks, knocking on the door again.

'You can come in now,' Jazz announces. I quickly make sure my dressing gown is done up.

He pops his head round the door. 'You want some chips?'

'Only if you can feed all of us,' Jazz challenges.

'Of course,' he laughs.

I quickly slip on some tracksuit bottoms and a vest top, before following them into the kitchen. He places down onto the table a massive tray of chips and some bread and butter.

'Did you know we were coming?' Jazz asks.

'Let's just say that I had a hunch you'd want feeding,' he laughs.

'You mean you thought Jazz would be getting high?' I ask.

He raises his eyebrows but doesn't answer.

'Jazz, when the hell are you gonna stop smoking that crap?'

'Maybe you should start,' she says, ignoring my gaze like a sulky teenager.

'Tell me when,' he says, as he spoons chips onto my plate. He keeps pausing after each spoonful, but there's hardly any chips on my plate.

'Keep going,' I say, irritated at his slow pace.

'I like a girl who eats,' he says grinning.

'From what I hear you like all girls,' I say before I can stop myself, my mouth half full with bread.

Jazz and Izzy chuckle. Oh great Poppy. Why did I say that? It makes me sound like a jealous pratt.

'Well, the ones I know normally don't eat,' he says, smiling.

'Especially not to *this* extent.'

I roll my eyes. 'Well I grew up with three brothers. I've learnt to eat while I can.'

Jazz winks at me.

'So anyway, how is that creep from work?' Jazz asks as she refuses a second spoonful from Ryan.

'What creep at work?' Ryan asks with a mouthful of bread.

'Oh...it's nothing,' I shrug, trying to kick Jazz under the table.

'It's hardly nothing,' Jazz exclaims. 'She found out her one night lover is her boss's son and now he's touching her up.'

'You are joking?' he says, his tone slow and serious.

'It's no big deal,' I shrug. My eyes sting with sudden urgent tears. Do NOT cry in front of him. It must be the wine. 'I got myself in this mess by being a reckless little slut.' My chin wobbles with the threat of bursting into sobs.

'Oh, Pops. Don't get upset. It'll be ok,' Izzy says, resting her hand on my shoulder.

'Our Poppy likes to be a bit dramatic,' Jazz laughs.

'I only bloody did it because you told me to!' I shout, unable to stop myself breaking into a light sob, my nose suddenly full of snot. Why couldn't I be a pretty crier?

'Sorry? Jazz is pimping you out now?' Ryan asks darting his eyes between us both.

I stuff a mouthful of my chip butty into my mouth and hope this will stop me from having to answer. Yet when I look up he's still staring, analysing, searching for some kind of explanation. Didn't anyone ever teach him it's rude to stare?

'You know I'm in control of Poppy's life at the moment,'' Jazz says, leaning back, leaving her food and lighting up another cigarette.

'Sorry? So you decided that she should sleep with him?'

I don't like how they're talking like I'm not here.

'Well...yes. And I mean, at the time, she didn't really put up that much of a struggle, let me tell you.' She winks at me.

I glare at her as I drop a bit of ketchup onto the table. Damn it! Why am I such a klutz? And why am I allowing them to discuss my sex life? Ryan hands me a tea towel and I snatch it off him, annoyed at myself.

'I was just glad to remember how to do it!' I laugh, suddenly feeling the effects of the wine again.

'Remember it? Why? How long have you not had sex for?' Ryan asks, his eyes penetrating me in disbelief.

'Um...'

'Ryan!' Izzy shouts. 'That's rude to ask her!'

'She'd practically gone back in time and become a virgin again,' Jazz chuckles.

'Thanks Jazz!' I shout, kicking her under the table.

'Wow,' he breathes, completely shell shocked.

'I'm sure that the concept of no sex for a slut like you seems ridiculous but I don't make a habit of sleeping around,' I bark.

'And I do?' he says, taken aback.

'Well...that's what I've heard anyway.' I risk a look at Izzy who avoids my gaze. I take a large glug of wine, needing it's calming reassurance.

'I can't believe this guy at work though. I think someone needs to have a word with him.' His eyes turn fiercely protective.

'Don't worry. I can handle myself,' I say, suddenly worried that he's going to hunt him down.

'Well, I'm not so sure about that.' He smiles and points to a bit of ketchup that's stained my top.

'Why are you so worried anyway?' Izzy asks, intrigued, as I struggle to remove the stain with a bit of kitchen roll.

'Am I?' he asks vaguely.

'Well...you just seem kind of...worried about her,' Izzy says, her voice full of hidden questions.

I drop my eyes immediately in a flush of embarrassment.

'Well, from what she's proved so far, I'd say it's a normal reaction from anyone around her,' he smirks.

'Oh thanks!' I kick him hard under the table.

His eyes flick up at me from under his lashes, the hint of a smirk on his face. He stares, his eyes hypnotising me, enveloping me, putting me under his spell. My breathing starts to quicken and I remind myself not to lean in.

I break away from him and notice Jazz smiling at me suspiciously. A sickening feeling creeps into my stomach, the tension growing by the second.

'Well...I better go to bed.'

My body feels tingly all over and a stupid grin threatens to break across my face. The same grin I used to get when I fancied boys at school. Why does he make me feel like a teenager? Jazz keeps looking at me, a hundred questions on her face. I avoid her.

'It's early,' Izzy protests. 'Why don't you chill for a bit longer?'

'No thanks. I'm tired. Tonight was enough excitement.' I smile knowingly at both of them.

Ryan looks at all of us suspiciously.

'I should get to bed too. Got an interview tomorrow,' Ryan says, getting up as I do. 'You girls can wash up, right?' He walks quickly behind me before they can protest.

'Well, goodnight,' he says, once I'm outside my door.

I stupidly get the feeling that I'm on a date and he's dropping me home. I look up to him, his gaze mesmerising me. He puts his hand up as if to touch my face, hovers it for a second and then tucks a strand of my hair behind my ear, sending shivers up the back of my neck. I hope he didn't notice.

'See you tomorrow,' he says, his face serious, towering over me.

My breathing gets faster and faster, but I'm frozen. I literally cannot move a muscle.

'Yem,' I mumble.

Fuck, did I just say yem? I'm literally losing the skill of speech.

He turns and bounds up the stairs, an amused expression on his face. I go into my room before Jazz can assault me with questions and throw myself under the duvet. I lay there, still trembling and panting, not sure if I want to get sick or have another dream about him. Ok, now I get it. I'm suddenly aware of how he pulls so many women.

Chapter 10

'I'm afraid that we've had a complaint about Hugh,' Victor says the next day.

'What?' I ask, totally thrown. Where did this come from? I haven't said anything.

'Yes,' he says, biting his thumb nail. 'HR received a phone call this morning from a solicitor, warning that he had a client willing to take the company to a tribunal for sexual harassment.'

'You're joking?' I ask, trying desperately to keep a straight face and seem shocked.

'I'm afraid not Poppy. Dreadful business. I'm also afraid that this isn't the first time I've had such a complaint about him.'

'Really?'

Victor exhales sharply. 'He was previously working at the Hertford office, but I had to move him when I received another complaint much like this one.'

Oh my God. I slept with a sex pervert. I shudder at the thought of it. Note to self: ring Jazz and tell her I'm never listening to her advice again.

'But obviously, this must remain between us. We can't let such a scandal get out; it could ruin me.'

'No, of course not.' I nod professionally. 'What are you going to do?'

'I really don't know. I'll have to speak to him, obviously, but I just hope his wife will be so forgiving. She was furious that they had to move because of his behaviour. This might really be the end for them and to be frank I couldn't blame her.'

'That's terrible.' I purse my lips together sympathetically and try not to smile.

*   *   *

As soon as I'm back at my desk I whip my temporary phone out of my bag. Izzy gave me an old phone the weight of a brick.

'Was that you? Were you the solicitor?' I text him.

I drum my fingers on the desk impatiently waiting for a reply.

BEEP BEEP.

I nearly drop the phone in excitement.

'Maybe'

Is that all he can reply? God, you have to seriously drag information out of him.

'Ok, well thanks. Good luck 2day in your interview'

That's not too desperate, right? I mean, maybe I should have been totally indifferent and not bothered texting back. Left him wanting more or something? When it beeps again I notice Cheryl eyeing me suspiciously.

'Lots of beeping going on over there. Got a fancy man, have you?' she asks, smiling smugly.

You'd think that finding out your husband is shagging someone else would make you reflect on yourself for a while. But no. I haven't even had a chance to ask her if she's OK and already she's acting as if nothing happened last night.

'No, no, just a friend thanks.' I smile politely through gritted teeth.

'Thanks. I'll prob be knackered after so can't be bothered to cook. You want to catch dinner?'

I nearly pass out in excitement. He wants to take me out to dinner! Why am I getting so excited? Calm down Poppy, get a hold of yourself. A friend is asking you to dinner. You don't get this excited when Jazz asks you out to Pizza hut.

'Oh, you young ones. Carefree and single; I remember the days,' Cheryl says, smiling off into the distance.

'Actually Cheryl, you're only a year older than me.'

'I know sweetheart, and look at the difference between us.' She smiles sympathetically. 'I'm married with a gorgeous baby at home and you're still...painting the town red.'

Sorry? Your husband is cheating on you? And gorgeous baby? Shrek called - he wants his baby back. But I obviously can't say this to her. She must be in severe denial.

'Yes, well. We have very different lives,' I retort. Why can't she leave me alone so I can just text him back in peace?

129

'And such a shame. You were so close to getting it all with Stuart.'

God, his name hits me like a dart to the heart every time I hear it.

'Yeah thanks for the reminder. Now, if you don't mind, I'm actually really busy.'

'Ok cool' I text back, my fingers shaking with excitement.

'I'll book a table and text you details later'

I'm going to dinner with Ryan! How exciting! I turn my attention back to Cheryl.

'How are you anyway, Cheryl? You know, since last night?'

'Last night?' She flutters some papers around her desk as if she's very busy.

'Yes, last night. You know...' I lower my voice to a whisper 'when we *saw* them.'

'Actually Poppy, I'd appreciate it if you kept out of my marriage. It really is none of your business.'

'Wow. You were the one dragging me along yesterday,' I say defensively.

'I'm afraid I'm very busy.' She turns away from me, already typing an e-mail.

I hope it's to your divorce lawyer, you horrible bitch.

*   *   *

My good mood is short lived when Victor tells me to sort out the bad smell coming from the kitchen. After thirty minutes of investigation, Lilly and I have finally decided the stench is coming from the back of the fridge.

'So, they're alright. Just alright? I need a bit more information than that please,' Lilly begs as she pulls the fridge out from under the worktop.

A fresh bout of potent smell wafts through the air, so strong that my nostrils burn and my stomach clenches in disgust. I swallow convulsively, my stomach heaving.

'Oh shit, that's fucking vile,' Lilly coughs, covering her mouth and nose with her hand.

I nod, trying to think calming thoughts, but the smell keeps creeping into my mouth, trying to gag me. I look behind the fridge, sure to find a skunk covered in his own vomit, wearing a smelly sock. But there's nothing there.

'What is it?' I say in an in-breath, desperate not to consume any of the air.

'I don't know,' she says, clearly a lot stronger than me. She grabs a bottle of Cif and starts attacking the area. 'So come on, what are they like?'

'Who?'

'Your housemates! What are they like?' She pulls out the fridge a bit further and starts inspecting the back of it.

'Izzy's a girlie fitness instructor. Grace is a big breasted bitch of a beautiful model. And then there's just Ryan.'

'Ryan?' she asks quizzically as she puts on some yellow marigolds. 'Ah yes, the beautiful man! What's he like?' she probes, her eyes widening excitedly.

'Stop making me talk! I'm gonna be sick!' I wail.

'Just tell me!' she snaps, not bothering to look at me. 'Anything to take my mind off this.'

I honest to God don't know how she is so close to the smell. Victor gave me this job, but I've been pretty useless; just gagging occasionally and running to the sink because I think I'm going to vomit. Lilly is going to make a great Mum one day. Things like this never faze her.

'He's ok. Nice...I guess.'

God, I really can't think with this smell. Is something dead?

'Oh my God,' she says, leaning away from the back of the fridge with a serious face.

'What? What!?'

She's found a dead rat, I just know it. I start backing away into a corner. I can't see it. I'll drop dead in shock. I'll never recover. My dreams will be invaded by rats and I'll wake up screaming. I'll imagine them following me down the road. People will call me 'that rat woman'. I'll have to have years of therapy.

She leans in and studies me seriously.   I stare back at her in confusion.

'What?'

She smiles wickedly. 'You *like* him.'

'No I don't!' I shout, inhaling some stench in the process. I gag and drop my eyes in a flush of embarrassment. Perhaps I was a bit too dramatic.

She raises her eyebrows. 'The lady doth protest too much me thinks.' I feel my cheeks redden and I pray they'll stop.

'Oh shut up. He's just a horrible boy, a player actually. I'm really, really not interested. Now, where's the smell coming from?'

'Oh please! You've gone all red. You really need to learn how to lie better. Either that or stop bothering.'

'I'm not lying! Now what is the smell?' I shout, starting to lose my temper. I still can't believe we're even doing this. What other PA's have to do this sort of thing? It's ridiculous.

'Found it!' she shouts in triumph. She pulls out a tray from the back of the fridge and presents it to me. It looks like some milk has leaked into it and slowly rotted away, it now black and mouldy.

My stomach flips and I swallow back my convulsion. She looks at the tray and then back at me. What is she up to? She smiles before thrusting the tray under my nose.

'Oh my God!' I scream, pushing it away from me.

'You tell the truth and I'll sort this out for you. You continue to lie and I leave you here to sort this mess out yourself.'

Is she serious? She can't honestly think I could clean this up myself? It's beyond gross.

'It's up to you'. She edges forward, the tray closer to me. I'm backing away in horror, realising I don't have any options.

'Ok! I'll tell you!'

'That's my girl. Spill.' She throws the tray in the sink, covering it in fairy liquid and hot water. She rubs her hands together like a witch. 'So?'

'Ok, well I suppose he is totally gorgeous. But in an arrogant, I'm God's gift to women kind of way. I never really know where I stand with him. I'm sure he's not interested in me.'

'Err, why the hell wouldn't he be? The fool would be lucky to have you.'

'You have to say that because you're my friend. I don't know if it's worth the bother anyway. I act all stupid around him, like a teenage crush or something. Jazz has warned me off him too.'

'Why?' she asks, her playful face changed to one of worry.

'Because she says he's a player.'

'Oh.' She looks a bit deflated. 'Well maybe if Jazz is warning you off him...maybe you should listen. She normally likes them like that.'

'Yeah I know,' I say feebly. 'Oh just shut up and clean, wench.'

*   *   *

'Good evening. Have you booked a table?' the glamorous looking lady behind the desk asks me.

'Um, yes. My friend booked it. It's under Ryan...' Oh my God, I don't know his surname!

'Sorry? Ryan...is there a surname?' she asks, narrowing her false eyelash coated eyes at me.

'I...I don't know it,' I admit.

'Don't worry,' she smiles kindly. 'I know what these blind dates are like.' She glances down at the list.

Blind date? Do I look that desperate? I'm only wearing tight black jeans and one of Jazz's green tops with heels, not wanting to be over dressed. Surely I don't look that desperate? I spent ages trying to deliberately look not desperate. Maybe I should go home and change? Would I make it home and back again in time? But then what would I wear? This isn't exactly the place for baggy jeans. Calm down, you're getting hysterical.

'Here we go. There's a Ryan Davis for two people.'

Davis. What a beautiful surname. Poppy Davis. I now pronounce you Poppy Davis. Mrs Davis, your table is ready. No! Stop it!

'Yes, that must be it.'

'Well, the table's just finishing up. But you could wait in the bar area.' She smiles, already dismissing me.

I walk over to the red and black bar and sit on one of the white leather bar stools. I order myself a vodka, lime and soda and sip it; the bubbles instantly making me feel a bit giddy. I scan the room feeling a bit self-conscious to be alone. I purse my lips together and lick them, my usual nervous habit. I pick up a strand of hair to twirl, but stop myself. The restaurant is packed with smartly dressed people laughing about their day, happy for the weekend to have begun. So am I. Thank God I won't have to deal with Hugh anymore.

As I scan the room further, I notice that most women are in little dresses. Actually I'm the only woman in jeans. Maybe there's a strict dress code and everyone is actually laughing at me, thinking what a tramp I am. Maybe I should go home and change.

Then I spot another woman in smart jeans. I smile over at her warmly and she responds by looking away alarmed. Great. She probably thinks I'm a lesbian trying to come on to her.

I look around some more, annoyed that Ryan's making me wait. I mean, what time is it anyway? I've been waiting here forever. I glance at my watch and realise he's only two minutes late. Nothing to be alarmed about.

I continue scanning the room, making up life stories for the people. The bald man in the corner is shagging his secretary and is trying to persuade her friend to join in. The woman in her forties is working out a way to tell her husband she's leaving him for another woman. He's working out when to surprise her with the plane tickets to the Bahamas. The group of men drinking bottled beers work in the gherkin and have a secret. They're in a love cult together.

A strange sense of recognition goes through me when I look at the back of a man's head. It looks so familiar. Could I actually recognise someone from the back of their head? But a niggling feeling in my stomach tells me I do. The ears, his neck, they look so familiar. Oh my God.

I know where I know that neck from. Images of me kissing it flash though my head. It's him. Stuart. My ex-boyfriend Stuart. Just thinking his name gives me a dart to the heart.

Oh my God. I quickly look away into the opposite direction and grab a cocktail menu from the bar, hiding my face behind it, my breathing suddenly erratic. Please let this be a dream. Please don't let him be here. I'm hot, suddenly very hot. I can feel every sweat gland in my body waking up and going into over-drive.

I need to get out of here. I clench my fingers tightly round the plastic cocktail menu, feeling bubbles of panic rising inside me. I don't want to see him. I just want to run away like a child and block him from my mind forever. Where are my nearest exits? Could I make a run for it and just ditch Ryan?

'Poppy?' his familiar voice calls.

My stomach jumps and begins convulsing. His voice. His beautiful voice. Memories of our relationship flash through my head. Memories I've locked away for a long time. Us sitting on the sofa laughing over some film. Him making me pancakes with strawberries and whipped cream. Us talking about baby names.

My heart starts beating faster and faster. So fast it feels like it's going to jump out and hit the barman in the face. Just ignore it. Don't look up. Just pretend you haven't heard it and you're someone else.

'Poppy?' A hand is on my cocktail menu and it's pushed down to expose me. 'It *is* you.'

I carry on looking down, thudding fear growing inside me. I have to look up at him. He knows it's me. There's no escaping this. I slowly look up at him. I look into his deep blue eyes and feel a sharp stab in my chest. Those eyes that I woke up to every morning. My stomach drops as it does when you're on a rollercoaster. Memories of the day he left come flooding back, suffocating me.

You're too boring. I've started to resent you.

The scars, which I thought were healed, now feel like they've been ripped open with a razor blade. We were so close to our happy ending. *So* close. More memories come flooding into my head, whizzing round like a blender. Us on Brighton pier in the rain, eating soggy

135

chips. Us dressed up as Fred and Wilma from The Flintstones for a fancy dress party. Him touching my belly and saying 'I'm gonna put a baby in there someday'. I start gasping for breath, like I'm drowning. I gave him everything; my heart and soul and he decided to stamp on it.

I open my mouth to speak, but it's so dry I can barely get any words out. Stuart looks at me strangely, clearly wondering if I've lost my mind. I cough, trying to release the lump in my throat.

'Oh, hi! What a coincidence!' I squeak, my voice unnaturally high pitched.

The letter. Dear God, the letter.

'How've you been?' He smiles; that same pearly smile which used to make me go weak at the knees. 'Oh, this is my girlfriend, Claudine.' The same Claudine that I'd heard he'd started dating two weeks after he left. It's funny because when he said 'I want to be single, I want to be free' I didn't see him settling down with someone else two weeks later. I suppose she gave him things I couldn't give him. Like she took it up the arse. What a whore.

Her hair is dark red, almost the colour of purple and is curled, heavily hair sprayed to stay in place, making it look like straw. Her face is thin, almost gaunt, but she has massive collagen filled lips that are coated with so much red lip gloss I'm sure it'll drip onto the floor any minute. Her fake eyelashes frame her tiny blue eyes, making it look like butterflies have landed on them.

'Hi! Nice to meet you!' God, I really can't stop squealing. What is wrong with me?

I'll always love you in some way. But right now you need to let me go. His last words read through my head. I wince my eyes trying to block them out, the room going blurry. The worst possible words a female can hear from her boyfriend. I gave him the space so that he could breathe, sure that if I kept my distance for a few weeks he'd realise he'd made a massive mistake and come running back to me. But he never did.

In hindsight, I do wish I hadn't cried, begged and rang him every night for two weeks drunk and demanding to know why he didn't love me.

'Poppy!' Ryan's silky voice calls from behind me.

I turn around, glad for the distraction, feeling sick from all of the raw emotion in my head. I look around desperate to see his dreamy face but I can't see him. Did I imagine it?

I see someone weaving through the crowds, but it's not Ryan. He's quite dishy actually, but where is Ryan?

Oh. My. God.

That is Ryan. He's waving and smiling, apologising to people as he squeezes past them. Except he's in a smart black suit with a pale green shirt and tie! He looks so different. So...well, sexy. Sexy isn't even the word. How can someone manage to look even more devastatingly handsome just by throwing on a suit?

Every woman in the restaurant is turning to look at him and even I feel myself swooning, forgetting for an instant that Stuart is even here.

He kisses me on the cheek. 'Hey, sorry I'm late.

'H...Hi,' I stammer. I actually feel weak at the knees.

'So, who're your friends?' he asks turning to Stuart and Claudine. He wrinkles his forehead in confusion from the clearly noticeable atmosphere.

Stuart leans in, puffing his chest out. He extends his tanned hand to him.

'I'm Stuart. I'm Poppy's ex-boyfriend.'

God he's a smarmy creep. But I knew that when we were together, and I still loved him. He must have got my letter by now. How mortifying.

'Hi,' Ryan smiles. He turns to look at me as if he's trying to read my expression. He turns back to face Stuart and extends his arm out to shake it.

'I'm Ryan. I'm Poppy's *current* boyfriend.'

What? My mouth practically drops onto the floor. As does Stuart's. Ryan turns and winks at me before wrapping his arm tightly round my waist. His warm hands send tingles up my spine. I try not to look as shocked as I feel and play along, but it's hard for me to imagine having a boyfriend this stunning. Surely Stuart won't believe anything so ridiculous.

Both couples stare at each other, awkward silence filling the air.

'So,' I say turning to Ryan, having remembered his interview. 'How did it go?'

His face lights up into a wide smile.

'I got it,' he says coolly.

'Oh my God!' I exclaim, throwing my arms around him. 'Congratulations!'

He squeezes me tightly and I'm sure it's for Stuart's benefit. God, he smells incredible too.

'Excuse me, but your table's are ready,' the hostess says. She signals to both couples, but gestures in separate directions.

Thank God. My body starts to release itself. It's over.

'That is unless you'd like to eat together?' she offers.

I open my mouth to thank her, but tell her there is no way that is happening but Stuart jumps in before me.

'Yes,' Stuart says. 'Why don't you join us?' He looks at me and Ryan. He seems very intrigued by my new relationship.

'Oh, I'm not sure-'

'We'd love to,' Ryan interjects. He takes my hand and leads me towards their table. I try to pull back in protest, but he ignores me, striding forward.

What is he doing? Why is he making me live out this misery? I try to catch his eye to show my annoyance but he seems to be deliberately ignoring me.

When we're seated Stuart starts with all of the questions.

'So, how did you guys meet?'

'It was through Jazz actually,' I say, taking the first easy lie as I munch on a breadstick. I avoid his gaze, unable to look him in the eye. Every time I look at him I feel so stupid. Like a stupid child.

'Oh, good old Jasmine! How is she? Still causing trouble?' he grins. I hate how he talks about her. He always thought she was a no good tart.

'She's great actually. Just got an amazing new job and is seeing a really nice guy.' As long as I don't elaborate then I'm not actually lying. Don't elaborate and don't look at him.

'Shall we order champagne?' Stuart says, looking around for a waiter.

'Yes, excuse me, can we have two bottles of champagne please.'

He's so pompous. I can't believe I ever loved this man. I think I'm going to need the alcohol.

It's only taken me a year, but I can finally sit back and see him crystal clear. See him for the dickhead he always was. I can't believe that for months I tortured myself, worried that I hadn't given my all. That I hadn't tried my best. The truth was that I'd given him everything I had and it wasn't my fault. We weren't meant for each other. But that doesn't make it hurt any less.

'So, how serious are you guys?' Stuart asks. He stares at Ryan who has pulled his chair up close to me. His arm is round my waist again. Ryan begins to finger a pattern into the side of my stomach, making my mouth go numb in response. Try to play it cool. He smiles affectionately at me.

'Well, we live together so I'd say pretty serious.'

I smile back, feeling myself blush. I know this is only a lie, but he's so believable I find myself going along with it happily. His jaw line is so strong. I'm so tempted to reach out and touch it.

'Starters?' the waiter asks all of a sudden.

'I'll have the Calamari and Claudine will have some olives,' Stuart says.

I used to hate how he'd order for me. We once had the biggest argument at his Mum's retirement dinner because of it. Again, in hindsight I wish I wouldn't have been so drunk. And I wish I hadn't fallen over, taking a dinner cloth and his Grandmother down with me, but hey ho, you can't plan these things can you? And I hear she's got a perfectly good hip now, since the operation.

Ryan chuckles and looks sympathetically at Claudine.

'I didn't realise she couldn't talk for herself.'

Stuart glares back, his face like thunder.

'I'll have the Bruschetta. And Poppy, what would you like?' Ryan asks, turning and winking at me.

'I'll have the garlic bread please.'

'Oh, bless you Pops!' Stuart smirks. 'Always going with the safe boring option as usual.'

I feel so exposed, like I'm still going out with him. He always had the ability to make me feel stupid. Why doesn't he talk to his own girlfriend? She's just sitting there knocking back the champagne with a sour expression on her face. What an airhead. I down my own glass, dribbling some down my chin. Very attractive.

'Actually I love how Poppy's never afraid to be honest and ask for what she wants,' Ryan says, bringing his face closer to mine, smirking cheekily. 'Even in bed.'

Oh my God – did he just actually say that? I choke slightly on my drink.

Stuart stares at Ryan dumbfounded.

'Well, it seems you really have changed Poppy.'

I just nod in response and fill another glass with champagne, downing it immediately. If I'd have told Stuart what I wanted in bed I'd have mentioned how it freaked me out when he'd shout out 'Attack! Attack! Aliens have landed' every time he'd come.

'So Brian, what do you do?' Stuart asks leaning back into his chair, clutching his champagne as if he owns the restaurant.

'It's Ryan,' I correct him, through gritted teeth. Fury starts building in my body. He knows his name is Ryan. Who does he think he is? Luckily Ryan just looks back at him, amused.

'Oh, of course! Sorry,' Stuart says insincerely. 'Are you an actor? Or a model?'

A model? Is he trying to insinuate that Ryan is some dumb pretty boy?

'No,' Ryan laughs. 'I'm actually a lawyer.'

Stuart stares back, flummoxed, his mouth actually hanging open. Well that shut him up.

'What about you Stuart?' Ryan asks him, smiling angelically.

'I'm in marketing. Just made Marketing Director.'

'Oh congratulations,' Ryan says insincerely.

I pour myself another glass of champagne, but spill most of it on the table cloth.

'Whoops.'

'So...what do you think of Poppy's accident prone behaviour then? Does it get on your nerves?' Stuart laughs as he sips his champagne. What a bastard. I feel my temper flare as I glare back at him, my lip already curling up in anger.

'Actually, I find it really endearing,' Ryan answers. He cups my face with his hands and plants a quick kiss on my lips. Wow – he's so believable. His lips are so warm. It takes all my strength just to breathe.

He turns back to look at Stuart and for a second their eyes lock. I wonder if they'll offer each other an arm wrestle. The atmosphere is so tense you could cut it with a knife. I take a large gulp of champagne. Gradually the alcohol seems to be dulling my nerves, the adrenalin pounding round my body starting to slow. My legs have actually stopped shaking.

Stuart smiles cockily.

'Maybe you're like that now. But I'm sure it'll eventually grate on you. Poppy, do you remember when you fell over at Ethan's wedding? God, I still laugh about it.' He starts chuckling.

'Yes, thanks for the reminder,' I say slowly, trying to control my anger.

'Do you remember my little nickname for you?'

I glare back at him, all previous feelings of love a distant memory.

'Of course I do.'

Ryan looks between us both confused. Stuart seems pleased with himself, as if having this over Ryan makes him the winner.

'I used to call her Humpty Dumpty,' he declares proudly.

'Humpty Dumpty?' Ryan repeats, horrified.

'Because I always had great big falls,' I clarify, wanting the ground to swallow me up.

Ryan gives me a look which I think means 'what an arsehole.'

Our starters arrive and I'm pleased for the distraction. The waiter places down my garlic bread and I start tucking in. I shove a big bit of garlic bread in my mouth, wanting this evening to be over as soon as possible. Its garlic butter melts on my tongue. God, it's delicious. I swallow it quickly, eager to eat more, but it gets caught in my throat. I cough to get it out.

I try to cough discreetly, but no noise comes out. That's strange. I try to breathe through my nose, but I can't do that either. I try to cough again, louder now, desperate to dislodge it. But it's moulded together to completely lodge my throat. I try to speak, to say help, but nothing comes out. It dawns on me – I'm choking.

I grab a glass of champagne and neck it back, but the liquid just sits on top of the garlic bread, not having any impact.

Ok, now I'm starting to panic. I turn to Ryan and start pointing to my throat with my mouth open. All I get back is a confused face, obviously wondering why I'm being so weird.

I stand up, suddenly so hot I feel I might burst. I'm going to die. I'm going to die.

'Is she choking?' Claudine asks calmly, still sipping on her champagne.

I nod my head like a lunatic, trying to plead with my eyes for help.

'Shit, she's choking,' Ryan says, jumping to his feet.

He throws the chairs out of the way and starts tapping me on the back of my neck. But it's no use; he's patting me instead of hitting me and it's making no impact. Pressure starts to build in my chest and I start to panic, my body going into full on spasm. My throat burns as I slowly suffocate.

Ryan begins hitting me hard on the back, now seeming desperate, but it's not working. Nothing is working. The ache's getting worse. Ryan's still hitting me harder and harder. A small crowd begins to form around us. I can hear people shouting for an ambulance. Things are starting to go a bit hazy around the edges.

I want Ryan to stop hitting me now. It's so hard and if I'm going to die I want to die in peace. My eyes are getting heavy. I just want to give up and die. It's really not worth it. He's saying something like 'come on' over and over again. I close my eyes trying to think of happy thoughts.

I think of Jazz. Us going to a Garage night at Uni. Us stealing her boyfriend's car so that we can drive to Sheffield to pick up a trumpet she bought on e-bay. Us dancing to the Spice Girls and me falling off stage while doing my zig a zig ah.

Ryan grabs my floppy body, now seeming desperate and puts one arm around my stomach. He bends me over slightly and starts whacking me harder on the back. But it's useless. I'm running out of time.

I keep my eyes closed and try again to think of happy thoughts. I try to ignore the intense pain I'm feeling against my chest. I think about the garlic bread and how I could be the only person in the world so ridiculous as to choke to death on a lousy piece of garlic bread. How amazing to think that you can live for twenty five years and then within two minutes your life can be over forever.

I think I imagine it slowly begin to dislodge, a tiny air hole formed. I pray that it isn't my imagination playing tricks on me. It seems to move slowly, too slowly. I think this is actually worse than choking, just waiting and hoping for it to move. Hoping I'm not dead by then. This is slower, more painful. Bit by bit it starts to move. Eventually it slips down my throat.

One giant gasp of air escapes from my mouth, burning my throat. I feel my body completely give way. Ryan clutches hold of me as I fall floppy to the floor.

I open my eyes to see that I'm still on the floor and my wish of having passed out hasn't been granted. Ryan's touching my face and calling my name, but I can't hear him properly. It's like the volume has been turned down. I close my eyes, trying to hear through the ringing in my ears.

Suddenly I can hear. EVERYTHING. It's mega loud, like the volume had been turned up full blast. I turn my face away from the noise. I can hear everyone in the restaurant talking about me, asking if I'm OK. Loudest of all I can hear Ryan shouting my name as he slaps my cheeks hard.

'Alright,' I croak in a weak voice, my throat still burning. 'There's no need to shout. I can hear you.'

He smiles and looks extremely relieved, but still cautious.

'Can you walk?' he asks, his brown eyes narrowing on me.

'Yeah.' I try to get up, but the room is still spinning slightly.

'Right.' He tucks his arms underneath my neck and knees, scooping me up in one swift movement. I open my mouth to protest, but reconsider.

He walks towards the door. The rocking movement of his walk isn't helping my nausea. I close my eyes and pull my head into his chest, trying to shield myself from all of the staring faces. God, why did this have to happen to me? Mortification floods over me. I wish I had died.

'We're leaving,' Ryan shouts back to Stuart and Claudine.

'Yeah of course, but do you want any help?'

But Ryan's already half way out of the restaurant. The door slams and I feel the cold fresh air on my skin. I struggle to get free and stand on my own.

'I'm fine now,' I protest, completely humiliated.

'Are you sure?' he asks, a hand still around my waist.

'Yeah, honestly I'm fine.'

I steady myself against a shop window. I take another deep breath, fighting the nausea with all of my strength. I can't believe I choked in front of him. He's never going to find me remotely attractive if I keep behaving like such a retard around him.

'Well, I've known some excuses for getting out of dinner, but that was crazy.'

I laugh weakly, just wanting to get home and hide under my duvet.

'You scared me for a minute there,' he admits after a pause. His tone makes it sound like he's confessing to a humiliating weakness.

'Thanks,' I smile gratefully. Maybe I should just get a red nose and enrol in the circus.

He puts his hand out into the street for a black cab and one pulls up immediately.

'A cab? I thought we'd just get the tube?'

'After that drama, I think you deserve a taxi.' He opens the door for me. 'After you, princess.'

He *has* to stop calling me princess.

'Thanks,' I say once we're in. 'Thanks for everything. *Obviously* saving my life, but also lying to him about being my boyfriend. I couldn't believe it when you said it.' I smile at the memory of his shocked face.

'Yeah, well I guessed it was your ex from the way you were acting. You looked all flustered and panicky.'

'Oh, I didn't hide it that well then,' I laugh.

'Not really. But shush, just rest yourself for a little while.' He pulls my head into his chest. 'You did nearly just choke to death.'

His body is so warm and strong. I feel myself relaxing as I listen to his heartbeat. I could happily stay here forever. I'm already afraid of when I'll have to leave him. It's actually like a slow form of torture. I'm just beginning to drift off when I hear him speak to the cab driver.

'If you could just pull over here for a minute. I'll be back in a sec.' He gently removes me from his chest and leans me against the seat, disappearing. I look out of the window to see where he's going. I nearly cry with relief when I see him go into an Indian take away. He's a mind reader. I'm sure that stress makes me hungry and at the moment I am positively starving.

I watch him order, charming the girl behind the desk, who's completely taken by him; twirling her hair and sticking her chest out. He seems completely unaware of the effect he has on people. He leans against the wall reading a paper while the girl flutters her eyelashes nearby and tries to engage him in conversation. He eventually walks back towards the cab holding a brown paper bag.

God, he's so sexy. Just watching him walk makes me want to rip his clothes off. I really can't believe how a suit can change someone so much. I thought he was gorgeous before, but now he's like an Adonis. He climbs into the cab, holding up the brown bag.

'Dinner.' He pulls some naan bread out and tears it, handing some over to me.

'You read my mind.' I stuff it into my mouth.

'Chew slowly now, remember,' he teases.

*   *   *

When the cab pulls up outside the house he insists on paying. I flick the lights on, glad to find the house in darkness. This must mean that Izzy and Grace are out. We have the place to ourselves. I grab some plates and cutlery while he grabs a bottle of wine and some glasses. We settle down on the floor in front of the TV and begin un-wrapping the contents of the bag.

'I didn't know what you liked, so I got you a chicken korma. Is that ok?'

'Am I that predictable?' I laugh, remembering Stuart's cruel words.

'No, trust me, you're *anything* but predictable.' He stares at me, serious for a second.

I blush heavily. What does he mean by that? Does he mean I'm a nightmare?

'So anyway,' I must change the subject. 'You got the job! Tell me about it.' I start picking peas out of my rice.

'Well, it's with a firm called Swift and Taylor. I actually had a job offer from them before I went travelling.'

'Really? And you still went travelling?' I ask, wanting him to tell me his entire life story. From the day he was born, until now, not leaving out a single detail. 'Did you just get bored of work or something?'

I spoon a bit of my korma onto my plate and manage to spill a bit on the carpet. I quickly cover it with my hand hoping he hasn't noticed.

'Yeah pretty much.' He hands me a tea towel to clean up my mess. Damn it.

'Did you go with anyone?' I ask wondering if he ever had a proper relationship. He seems to know everything about me and my past, but I know nothing about him.

'Nope. Just me,' he says, his voice shockingly vulnerable.

'Really? And you liked it?'

'It was unbelievable. Obviously, I wouldn't recommend it for you; you'd probably end up being eaten by a shark or something, but I loved it.'

'Ha ha!' I slap him hard on his strong chest.

'So then I came back here and I heard they were looking again.'

It's funny how he's not the complete layabout I first thought he was.

146

'That's great. Do you get to say 'I object' and all that?'

'No, it's a different kind of lawyer to that,' he says amused. 'I'm a family lawyer, so it's mainly divorces, child custody battles, the occasional domestic violence, that kind of thing.'

'Oh,' I say, disappointed. 'That doesn't sound too good.'

'It's not as boring as you'd think. The firm is actually a really good one to get in with. They're well known for being very good at promoting people internally.'

It always makes me want to laugh when people say 'promoting people internally'. It just makes me think of the insides of people's bodies.

'No, I didn't think it was boring. I just think it's a bit sad, that's all.'

'Sad? Why?' He frowns, seeming genuinely confused.

'Well, seeing relationships break up every day. That must get you down, no?'

Note to self: don't talk with a mouth full of naan bread.

'Not really,' he shrugs. 'It's just part of life isn't it? You know, they say now that one in two couples will divorce.'

'What? That's rubbish!'

'Is it?'

'Yes!' I protest, waving my hands in the air. 'How can you think that? Look at all the couples out there in love!'

'I'm not saying they're not in love. I'm just saying relationships never last.'

'That's bullshit,' I say, losing my temper slightly.

He looks taken back.

'Really? Because you and Stuart ended so well?'

'Don't talk about him!' I say, my voice scored with hurt. 'We obviously weren't meant to be. I'm sure there's someone out there for me.'

And I hope it's you.

'Maybe. Maybe not.'

'Oh my God! Don't say that, you'll make a girl kill herself!'

'Sorry,' he laughs, leaning back. 'I am trying to listen to you actually. You know, be a bit more optimistic.'

'Really?' I say, amazed that he's listening to me.

147

I've had an effect on him! My God, if he only knew of the effect he's currently having on me.

'Yeah. In fact...I actually met someone.'

My face drops and I let out a tiny pathetic sound as if I've been kicked in the stomach. Met someone? I try to quickly compose myself and act casual, but it's hard when all you want to do is burst into tears.

'Met someone? Who?' I say through the ringing in my ears.

'A woman in the office,' he smiles.

Wow. So he's met someone he likes. He doesn't like me. Why did I even think that for a second?

'Oh...great!' I'm trying my best to sound pleased for him, but I want to run and hide under my duvet and listen to my Adele album.

'Yeah. Normally I would have just brought her back here straight away, but all I could hear was you calling me a man whore.' He gives a short laugh. 'So instead I'm taking her out tomorrow.'

'Oh.'

'And it's all thanks to you. You calling me a man whore made me think maybe I should try and have a relationship again.'

What an idiot I am. I feel so stupid for even having a flicker of hope that he might find me remotely attractive. And even if I ever had a chance, it's because of me that he's planning to have a relationship with someone else. What is wrong with me?

But then, did he kind of lead me on? I just felt like there was something between us. I must just be so emotionally starved of affection that for someone to even show me the slightest bit of friendship I think they're in love with me. What an imbecile.

'That's...great,' I force myself to say.

'I know. I'm taking her out tomorrow night,' he beams.

'Oh. Well my advice would be to wait...you know...to sleep with her.'

'Really? Why?' he asks puzzled, eyeing me suspiciously.

'Oh yeah! There is really nothing sexier than a man that doesn't want to have sex.'

'Really?' He scratches his head.

'Oh totally! I don't care if she begs for it. Even if...if she threatens to sleep with another man. You just hold it back. She'll want you all the more.'

'And you're sure this works for women?'

'Oh yeah! Trust me. If you really like her then take my advice.'

'Oh, ok. Well maybe I should.' He smiles, but still seems suspicious. I'm going straight to hell.

Chapter 11

Don't ask me how, but somehow yet again I'm on a power walk at 6 in the morning. It turns out Izzy can be very persuasive. Don't let that smiley persona get to you. Underneath that smile she's an army Major. Not one to be messed with.

'You'll get better the more we go,' she says to me as we enter the house.

'More we go?' I ask, hoping she isn't going to make me do this again.

'I thought we could make this a regular thing. Well, as long as I don't have client appointments.' She walks towards the kitchen. 'You know, like we talked about.'

'Oh...do you think I need it?' I follow her towards the sink, desperate for water.

'Yes,' she says bluntly. 'Don't get me wrong, you're tiny, but you just need to tighten up a bit.' She crushes her hands together in a menacing way. 'And remember what I said about giving up caffeine and sugar.'

'Morning,' Ryan says, making us both jump.

'God, you scared us,' Izzy says, as she stretches out her legs.

'Morning,' I say, conscious of my sweaty forehead. I avoid eye contact, the same humiliation from last night taking over my body.

'So I probably won't see you guys tonight. I'm at my Grandma's today helping her with some gardening and then I'll probably go straight from there to my date.'

'Oh yeah, I forgot about your date,' Izzy says. 'You must like her. Normally you'd just bring her back here for a quick shag. Is she *special*?' she teases.

'Shut up,' he snaps, rolling his eyes.

'Going anywhere nice?' I enquire, trying to sound casual.

'Not sure yet,' he says, blasé as usual.

As I pour myself a glass of water I notice a card for the new Italian restaurant Delanios round the corner on the worktop. Ah, so that's where he's going.

*　　　*　　　*

'Hello?' Jazz croaks down the phone.

'Hey Jazz, how are you?'

'Jesus, what time is it?'

'Early.'

'It is Saturday right? I haven't slept in for work?'

'No, no, it's Saturday. How is work anyway?'

'It's OK, boring as fuck, but it's work. I just can't wait for my first pay cheque.'

'Well, I've decided that I'm going to take you out tonight. Treat you for being so good and frugal.'

'Oh my God – fab! Where do you wanna go?' she squeals.

'I was thinking Delanios.'

*   *   *

When we arrive at the restaurant that night I'm tingling with excitement. Obviously, if I were to bump into him I would say hi, but it's really not about him at all. I'm looking forward to catching up with Jazz and trying out the new food.

Plus, I look totally amazing, if I do say so myself. I've got on Jazz's skin tight jeans, which I'm not sure are supposed to be this skin tight. I've got a black lacy top which actually manages to make my boobs look big. I've teamed it with killer black heels, sure that Jazz would moan if I didn't and my makeup is done to perfection.

The short Italian waiter shows us to a small table in a corner. It's quite dark, the only glow from the red tea lights which sit on each table. The walls are painted to look like we're in the middle of an Italian market and there's a female singer in a red dress singing in the corner.

'So, I haven't had a chance to chat to you properly since we swapped lives. How are you finding it at the house?' she asks while scanning the menu.

'Oh, yeah great.' I'm barely listening to her. I'm desperately craning my neck to see if he's here.

'And? Have you got to know the girls and Ryan better?'

'Yeah. They're great actually. Although Izzy's on my case to shape up.'

'I knew she would! She loves a challenge,' she giggles.

'Challenge? Well thanks! So have you seen anymore of lover boy?'

'Actually, I have. And his *name* is Jake. You should meet him, his body is amazing, totally ripped. He's taking me out again tomorrow.'

'And, will he bring condoms this time?' I whisper over the table.

'Yes, thank-you Grandma. I learnt my lesson the first time.'

'If you'd learnt it the first time I wouldn't have had to do the same thing the first week of uni.'

'Why do you always have to drag things up?' She narrows her eyes at me.

'I know, sorry. I'm turning into my mother, I just know it!' I wail.

'Never even joke about that!'

We collapse into giggles and can barely keep a straight face long enough to order our meals. The waiter looks frustrated as we attempt to pronounce the food. I'm sure right now he's on the phone to the local loony bin, asking if anyone has escaped.

I fill in Jazz on bumping into Stuart and she's naturally horrified. She also seems interested in why Ryan pretended to be my boyfriend.

'I wonder why he did that?' she asks, picking the nail varnish off her fingers.

'Your guess is as good as mine,' I say, feeling flushed.

Remember – you are just a joke to him. I quickly scan the room again. Where is he? We're halfway through our meal now and I can't see him anywhere.

'Are you ok muffin? You seem kind of distracted.'

'Do I?' I say absentmindedly. Where the hell is he!? I knock back another glass of wine.

'Yeah. Are you looking for someone?'

'No! Of course not!' I shriek. Perhaps a little dramatically.

'Ok, calm down!' She looks at me strangely.

'Actually...If I tell you something do you promise not to tell anyone?' Her eyes light up with intrigue. 'Yeah of course.'

'I mean no-one. Not a living soul.'

152

'Yes! Just bloody tell me!'

'Ok.' I lean across the table and double check that no-one I know is in the restaurant.

I'm ready to confess to her my feelings for Ryan but as I open my mouth I chicken out. I can't tell her. She's already warned me off him, telling me he's a player. She'll just get mad and tell me I'm making a mistake. The truth is maybe I want to make a mistake. A very delicious one. I desperately search for something else to say.

'Richard's wife is having an affair,' I blurt out before I change my mind.

'What? Annabel?'

'Yep.'

'Are you sure?'

'Of course I'm sure! I did this stake out with Cheryl from work and she's cheating with her husband.'

'Oh my God! I just...I just didn't think she was the type, you know.'

'Trust me, I know! I can't believe she'd betray him like that.'

'I know! I thought they were the perfect couple.'

'Me too! It's weird. So...do you think I should tell him?'

'Who? Richard?'

God, she can be dense sometimes.

'No. The tramp that lives in the park. Of course Richard!'

'Ok! Jeez! Chill out.'

'Well? I have to tell him don't I?'

'Well, I wouldn't,' she says seriously.

'You wouldn't? Why not?'

'Because it's their business. Their marriage. If you tell him he probably won't even believe you.'

'Yeah, I did think of that actually.'

'Trust me. Just forget it. Just pretend you never saw it.'

'Maybe you're right.'

'I definitely am,' she nods confidently.

*   *   *

After the dessert I realise I'm not going to see Ryan. I mean, what was I planning on doing anyway? Jumping into his arms and forcing him to want me? We sink another bottle of wine before we eventually get the bill. Fuck. £90! This having a social life thing is making me skint. I'm starting to realise how Jazz got herself in this mess to begin with.

We call a cab and Jazz drops me off outside the door.

'Your half is eighteen pound,' the taxi driver says to me.

'She'll give you a fiver and a blow job,' Jazz announces before bursting into hysterics.

The cab driver looks back at her, horrified. I try to apologise, but all that comes out is a slur and a bit of dribble. I throw a twenty pound note at Jazz and stumble out.

When the fresh air hits me I realise that I'm quite drunk. My legs feel like jelly and it's actually a bit of an effort to even put one foot in front of the other. Come on Poppy, make it to the front door. I trip on the front door step and land on my knees. I laugh at myself. What a dunce. I turn to wave at Jazz who waves back, giggling like a lunatic as the cab pulls off.

Damn. I need to get up, but everything's a bit spinny. Every time I try to clutch onto the door handle to pull myself up I seem to be slipping and falling hard on my arse again. And giggling. Ok, one more time. Grab the door handle and try and pull yourself up, you retard! I grab hold and am just raising myself up when the door gives way. I fall backwards onto the stained carpet, giggling.

I look up to see Ryan's frowning forehead. I love those little wrinkles. I want to touch them.

'Poppy, are you OK?' he asks, looking very concerned.

'Hmm, you're pretty.'

Then everything goes black.

*   *   *

When I wake up I can barely open my eyes for the pain. That angry obese elf is back sitting on my head again, except this time he's thumping it with a large brick. Breathe, just breathe! The pain will stop eventually. Either that or I will die.

I turn over to my side, squinting my eyes from the amount of effort I have to put into it. My stomach churns and makes me immediately wish I hadn't. I must just freeze and not move again. I open my eyes when the feelings of nausea have started to calm down. Ryan's face is on the pillow next to me.

What the hell is he doing here? I look around, very slowly, to see that I'm in my bedroom. I didn't sleep walk in the middle of the night and crawl into his bed, thank God. But what is he doing here? Oh no. Please don't tell me we slept together? If I've slept with him and can't remember it I'll never be able to live with myself.

I try to sense my body. Am I dressed? But it all just feels numb. Numb apart from the crushing pain in my head. I daren't look down. Moving my head is too much right now. I slowly move my hand under the duvet covers and feel around. My top is off but my bra is on. I reach down and thank God my jeans are still on. What the hell happened? Did we start making out and then I threw up on him? Please God, no.

I look at his peaceful angelic face. He's like a dream when he's sleeping. He stirs slightly and then slowly opens his eyes. I smile weakly but he looks a little freaked out. God, was I staring at him while he was sleeping? I must look like a loon.

'Oh, sorry,' I say, the words echoing through my brain. Keep v-e-r-y still Poppy.

'Are you OK?' he asks wrinkling his forehead. I must look a right mess. If I look even half as bad as I feel I must be like a dragon.

'Yeah I'm OK,' I whisper, my throat feeling like a group of teenagers have skateboarded down it. 'But why are you here? We didn't...you know?'

He bursts into loud laughing and my head rattles. OK, it's not that funny.

'No, you're safe. I like my victims to be conscious.'

Well it's nice that he seems to have some standards. But why is he shouting? Every word he says is hurting my eye sockets, as if he were punching me in the face.

'You were just in such a state that I was scared to leave you in case you choked on your own vomit.'

I start a smile, thinking he's joking, but then his serious expression tells me that he is in fact serious. Shit, how bad was I when I got home? I barely remember getting the bill.

'Thanks,' I say. I meant it to come out as sarcastic but it instead came out plain and un-interested.

He smiles kindly. God, he's amazing.

My stomach suddenly feels very tight and I freeze completely, hoping that it will stop what I know is coming. I feel breathless, but I try to take a discreet deep breath. I don't want to exert myself. It only seems to make it worse. Shit, its coming. It's coming now.

I jump out of bed, but the room is still spinning. I end up falling on my side. Shit, this is hard work. Maybe I'm still drunk. I get up again, holding onto the bedside table and run out of the door.

'Poppy! Are you ok?' Ryan calls behind me.

But I don't answer him. I'm too busy running for the kitchen sink, sure there's no way I'll make it up to the bathroom. I reach it just in time and thank God it's not filled with dirty dishes. I vomit so heavily and strongly that it's like my body is possessed.

I flinch when I feel someone's cold hands on my shoulders. I know that it's Ryan, but I can't turn and look at him. He grabs hold of my hair and holds it back for me as I continue to chuck my guts up, my whole body shaking from the motion.

God, I'm dying. I'm actually dying. The tears are coming thick and fast. Why do I always have to cry when I'm sick!? I stop for a second and look up into the dirty garden, the bushes seeming to be laughing at me.

'Jesus, Poppy! Are you ok?'

I turn my head to follow the voice and to my horror Izzy and Grace are sitting at the breakfast table. Grace looks totally disgusted and pushes her toast away from her. Oh my God. The humiliation is too much to bear.

'I'm...I'm sorry,' I cry before dramatically running from the room. I run up to the bathroom, tripping on a step on the way. I park myself down on the bathroom floor, hugging the toilet bowl. The cold tiles feel nice against my hot sweaty skin. I hear footsteps and wish whoever it was would just leave me alone.

'Do you want a drink of water or something?' Ryan asks me.

'No. I'm fine than-'

But the vomit train is passing through again. He sits behind me again. He pulls my hair back and rubs my back.

'Please just leave me,' I cry in agony. 'I don't want you to see me like this.'

'Just shut up.' He ignores me and rubs my back.

I pray to God to just let me die quickly.

*   *   *

About an hour later I'm better enough to be lying on the sofa with a cold flannel on my head. Thankfully Grace and Izzy have gone out, probably disgusted from the smell of vomit wafting through the house.

'How are you feeling?' Ryan asks.

'Well, I don't think the restaurant is there anymore, because I drank it.'

'Do you want me to put a film on for you, or something?' He hands me a cup of tea.

'Yes please,' I say pathetically.

'What do you wanna watch?' he asks, scanning the small DVD collection in the TV cabinet.

'I know I sound really gay, but do either of the girls have Singing in the Rain?'

He smiles. 'You're into old films like that?'

'Yeah...I know it's weird, but they always make me feel better.'

There's no need for me to be embarrassed – he's seen me vomit. There are officially no more barriers between us. And it could be worse, I remind myself. It's not like I danced to Simply the Best and then showed him my fanny. This was not prom.

'Well the bad news is that neither Grace nor Izzy have anything like that.'

Oh God, I'm gonna end up watching Die Hard.

'But the good news is that I have it.'

'What?' I sit up in shock and immediately wish I hadn't. My head is still so sore. 'You own them?'

He's not gay is he? Is my gay-dar working?

'Well, I don't actually own it. It's my Grandma's birthday soon and I've got DVD versions of all of her favourites. I got her a DVD player for Christmas but she hates how she can't watch any of her old movies on it.'

That's so nice of him. Maybe I could just handcuff him, drag him to Gretna Green and force him to marry me.

'Which films have you got?'

'Come and see.' He smiles and offers me his hand.

I take it, revelling in its warmth. He leads me slowly up the stairs while I try and push my headache out of my head. We walk into one of the double bedrooms. It's clean, if not a little impersonal. The walls are painted magnolia and he has matching light coloured furniture. But his walls don't have any pictures on them and I can't see any photo frames anywhere.

It still feels strangely intimate for me to be in his room. I sit on his brown and cream patterned bed spread and check for mirrors on the ceiling. I wonder how many women have been in this room. I discreetly look at his bedpost in case there are actual notches on there.

'Here they are.' He takes a box out of the cupboard and places it on the bed.

I crouch over it and flick through them, my eyes lighting up like a child on Christmas morning. All of my favourites are in here. Casablanca, Brief Encounter, It happened one night, Gone with the wind.

'You like them, then I take it?' He sits down next to me, his smell waking my nostrils. How can he smell that beautiful after just waking up?

'I love them. Your Grandma really has good taste.'

'Yeah, she's great. You should meet her some time. You kind of remind me of her in a small way.'

I blush, but then realise that he's comparing me to an old woman. Probably not the best compliment I've ever had.

'So, you and her are close then?' I ask, trying to sound casual, when really I'm completely intrigued.

'Real close. She raised me actually.'

'Really? Where were your mum and dad?' As soon as I've said it I wished I hadn't.

His smiling face turns sad. Oh God, what happened?

'My Mum had me when she was 19. She was a drug addict and couldn't even stay off them when she was pregnant with me. My Grandma took me off her as soon as I was born and she died a few years later from an overdose.'

'Oh my God,' I blurt out. Well, that's hardly helpful Poppy. 'And what about your Dad?'

'I never knew him. He could be anyone. Apparently she was sleeping around at the time, desperate for a hit.'

Does that mean she was a hooker?

'My Grandma tried everything to get her off them. She even locked her away in her room, but she'd escape. It just turns out that she loved the drugs more than anything or anyone.' He smiles as he pretends to look out of the window but I can see sadness clouding his eyes.

'God, I'm so sorry.' I wish I'd never brought it up.

'Don't worry. People always say that, I'm sorry. It makes me laugh to be honest. It's not anyone's actual fault. It's just life. But...I don't really make a habit of telling people. The girls don't know and if it's ok with you I'd prefer to keep it that way?'

'Yeah, of c-c-course,' I stutter, falling over my words.

'It's just that its no-one else's business and I don't want pity from anyone.'

159

'Oh no, I totally understand.'

'Thanks. That's why I could tell you' he smiles. 'I knew you're not the sort to judge someone on their past. Even if you do keep calling me a man whore,' he winks.

'Well, you are a man whore, but of course I won't tell anyone. If I pity anyone right now, it's me. I just spent half the morning vomiting in front of you in my bra. I'm totally mortified.'

He laughs and I'm glad my joke has broken the tension.

'By the way, how come I was in my bra? Did I get sick on my top last night or something?'

'No...Actually,' an amused smile spreads on his lips. 'You kind of took it off yourself.'

'What?' Oh God, the horror.

'Yeah, you just kind of threw it off and started saying how pretty my hair was.'

'OH MY GOD!' I actually want to die.

'Don't worry about it. You were drunk and I do have incredibly pretty hair.'

I cover my face with my hands, wishing I could be someone else. Some classy woman that didn't do ridiculous things like this.

'So anyway, which one do you want to watch?'

'I think I'll go with my old classic, Singing in the Rain.' I smile at the memory of the film and already I'm feeling its calming effects.

'Cool, that's one of my favourites too. But...don't tell anyone that or they'll think I'm gay.'

*   *   *

We spend the next few hours on the sofa watching it. He insists on me lying down and so sits with my legs on top of his lap. I do wish I was in something sexier than my pink fleece pyjamas and slipper socks. Even if he doesn't fancy me, it's nice to just have a friend to enjoy this with. Even if every time he moves it sends tingles down my spine. Jazz has never shared my taste in old films; in films at all to be honest.

She's says there's no point staying in and watching someone live their life when you can be out living your own.

In fact, I've decided. I'm going to let go of these foolish fantasies where we ride off bare back into the sunset and instead focus on being a good friend. What more could I ask for? A big hunky friend. Like a gay best friend, but smouldering with sexiness.

A knock on the door makes us both jump.

'Are you expecting anyone?' he asks.

'No,' I say, annoyed that someone has interrupted the film.

He jumps up to answer the door and I turn down the volume so I can hear who it is.

'Oh, hi. I wasn't expecting you today. Or...did we arrange something?'

'No, I just thought I'd surprise you. Are you pleased?' a loud squeaky female voice says.

'Um, yeah of course. I just didn't expect it is all.'

'Well, are you going to let me in?'

'Oh yeah, of course, come through.'

I quickly sit up right on the sofa and turn the volume back up to the normal number. I try to straighten my knotted hair down. He comes through the opening grimacing and mouthing 'sorry'.

'Oh hi! I didn't know you had company,' a big breasted blonde asks him, eyeing me suspiciously.

She looks almost identical to Claudine. All fake hair extensions, breasts and nails.

'This is just my housemate Poppy.'

Just my housemate. Nice. My boobs suddenly feel like fried eggs.

'Well it's nice to meet you Poppy,' she says insincerely. 'I'm Tabitha.' She quickly turns back to him. 'Ryan, it's so strange to see you without a suit. You look so scruffy.' She eyes up his tracksuit bottoms and t-shirt.

He smiles, but it doesn't meet his eyes.

'So, do you fancy going out for a drink or a bite to eat?' she asks, touching his arm possessively.

The mention of drink makes my stomach churn in protest.

'We have wine here,' he says, going towards the kitchen.

'No. I wanted to go out,' she says sternly.

God, she's demanding. I look over at him. He catches my eye and smiles. He must be thinking the same thing.

'Ok.' He turns to me apologetically. 'Pops, do you mind if I leave you?'

'No, of course not! You go and have fun,' I say as brightly as I can. In reality I want to burst into tears.

'Sure?' he asks, his forehead full of concern wrinkles.

'Yeah. Go.' Go have fun with your cheap slut of a girlfriend.

'Ok. Feel better.' He smiles kindly towards me and pats me on the head. Like a dog.

'Yes, do feel better,' the bitch says, smiling with her lips, but warning with her eyes.

Chapter 12

When I open my flat door on Monday night, giggles peal over into the hallway.

'Jazz?'

More giggling. It's definitely Jazz and someone else.

'Ssshh!' I hear her say.

Oh my God, who has she got here? I walk very slowly into the living room, worried I'll find her in a newly installed sex swing. Instead I find her and my brother Oliver on the sofa. They've got tight smiles on their faces and wide black pupils.

'Hey Po Po,' Oliver slurs, his eyes blood shot. Smoke dances up from behind him.

'Ollie, is your arse smoking?'

'Oh, um...no. It's just...I'm hot stuff. I'm actually smoking hot.'

Jazz explodes over in fresh giggles. Ollie pulls the joint that he's been hiding from behind him and takes another deep drag.

'I can't believe you two have been getting stoned! I told you no drugs in my flat!'

'Oh chill out Pops,' Jazz laughs. She gets up and tries to hug me, but misses me completely, falling flat on the carpet. She looks up disorientated, only to throw her head back laughing.

What the hell are these two doing together anyway? They don't normally hang out.

'You ready to go?' Ollie asks me, standing up and wobbling a little.

'Yeah, although I really don't feel up to it. You know Mum called just now and reminded me not to wear my hair up. Did you know that my ears are my worst feature?'

He smiles at me. 'Sometimes it's all I can think about.'

I slap him on the shoulder and take a good look at him.

'Jesus Ollie, your eyes are so blood shot. How are you gonna hide this from Mum?'

'She'll be too pissed to notice anyway,' he laughs. 'Right, come on then.' He turns to wink at Jazz 'Bye cheeky.'

Jazz winks back, a tight smile on her face. What the hell is going on between them?

'What are you two doing hanging out together anyway?' I ask, not able to help myself.

Awkward silence fills the air and I wish I'd just kept my big mouth shut.

'I think he fancies me,' Jazz jokes. 'I can't blame him really. I mean, look at this.' She points over her body, pushing her boobs out.

'Yeah right!' he snorts, playfully hitting her on the shoulder. 'Other way round maybe.'

This flirting is outrageous. I can't believe my eyes.

'Look,' Ollie says to Jazz. 'If you wanna fuck me, you know where I live.' He blows a kiss as he dances away.

Jesus. What a tool.

'Bye Romeo,' Jazz sings after him. I shoot her a warning look and follow him out.

'Jesus Ollie, are you wearing Timberland boots in June?'

'Yeah, so what?' he says, attempting to look at me, but instead getting distracted by a pigeon.

'So, who do you think you are, P Diddy?'

'I'm telling you, the only difference is I'm not black.'

'Yep, only difference,' I drool sarcastically.

We drive around to Mum's house, whilst listening to Ollie's Dubstep album, which he's insisted on playing. We're going round for our weekly Sunday roast, which for some bizarre reason we always have on a Monday. I haven't been in a while but I know I'll just get another whinging phone call if I don't, and it's really not worth it.

'Oh, hi my little darlings,' Mum sings from the kitchen. 'Come and give Mummy a hug.' She puts down her glass of wine and heads towards us.

Her style has never changed over the years, preferring to emulate a Barbie doll than a human being. Her blonde hair is scooped up into a hair clip, her sculpted cheeks painted with blusher and her thin lips glossed with the brightest neon pink. Except tonight it's smudged.

Ollie heads straight for the back door and lights up a fag while Mum squeezes me so hard I'm sure all of my secrets are going to fall out. Richard and Henry wave politely as they walk into the dining room. All three brothers share Mum's gorgeous gene pool, the same blonde hair and piercing blue eyes. It's only me and Dad that are the ugly ducklings.

'Hi Poppy Poppet,' Dad says, as he comes out of the dining room. His pale milky skin is unusually flushed. He pulls me into a tight bear hug. 'It's nearly ready.'

Dad always has to take over Mum's cooking attempts. She's always the first to offer to cook massive complicated meals, but then when the first item burns she decides to crack open the wine and let Dad save the day. That's what happens when you insist on drinking two bottles of wine while you cook.

'Did you hear that everyone?' Mum shouts. 'It's nearly ready. Everyone in the dining room and remember, no-one is allowed in the sitting room!'

'More wine Meryl!' Auntie Beryl shouts, sticking her head out briefly from the dining room. 'Hi Poppy darling,' she smiles. Mum grabs another bottle and runs in.

I follow Dad into the kitchen and steal a roast potato, throwing it from hand to hand when I realise how piping hot it is.

'Why aren't we allowed in the sitting room?' I ask Dad.

He sighs heavily and rolls his eyes.

'She's re-decorating it again. Doesn't want anyone to see the new theme.'

'*Another* theme?'

'Yep.' He hands me the spoon and indicates for me to continue stirring the gravy.

'Dad, why don't you stop her? She only decorated that room three years ago.' It always gets to me how she bosses him around and doesn't let him have a say in anything.

'You know her, love. Wild horses couldn't stop her.'

I help Dad carry the plates into the dining room. I look around at the 'tropical' themed dining room and shudder. I remember when she unveiled this one. The mural walls of a Caribbean island, the giant fish tanks on either side of the room with tropical fish, the bamboo table and chairs. When it was originally unveiled she'd actually got sand imported, much to mine and Ollie's delight. We spent the entire evening making sand castles, but she wasn't happy when Ollie got drunk and peed on it and then dragged it all around the house on his shoes.

I've just got to get through this one meal. And hope Ollie doesn't look suspicious.

'So Richard, how are you and Annabel?' I ask, not being able to fully look him in the eye.

'Fine thanks,' he smiles, beaming brightly. 'Well actually, really good. We're actually going to start trying for a baby.'

WHAT?

'Oh darling!' Mum sings. 'I'm so happy for you both!'

'A baby!' Auntie Beryl screams. 'Fantastic news!'

Trying for a baby? Is he mad? She's cheating on you, I want to scream! But how could I do that? What the hell is Annabel playing at? What if she's off the pill and gets pregnant by Cheryl's husband and Richard ends up raising it, wondering why the baby looks nothing like him.

'That's a bit rushed isn't it?' I blurt out, without thinking it through properly.

'Rushed?' he asks, turning to face me, puzzled.

'Yes darling, what do you mean?' Mum asks. 'He and Annabel have been together forever. It's a natural normal step.'

'A baby?' Ollie asks, giggling. 'Babies are silly.' God, he's stoned.

'Oh, yeah...I know that. I just wanted to make sure you were sure,' I mumble.

'They've got like really small feet,' Ollie continues 'and like really, really small hands.'

Mum looks at him strangely.

'Yes darling. Babies are *generally* small.'

'I think someone might be a little jealous, hmm?' Auntie Beryl says, smiling knowingly at Mum as she tops up their wine glasses.

166

'No! Of course I'm not jealous,' I retort.

They all smile knowingly and start different conversations. I can't believe this. Do they all think I'm madly jealous of happy couples or something? I'm just trying to stop him from making a huge mistake with a woman that's cheating on him. God, if only they knew.

Two hours later I decide to swap seats with Ollie (who, thank God, has calmed down a bit now) so that I can sit next to Richard.

'So Rich,' I say as casually as I can. 'How is Annabel?'

'Yeah, good thanks,' he nods politely. This is what I hate about my two older brothers. They always talk to me like I'm some office acquaintance, not their baby sister. I want to be someone that they can confide in.

'Oh, good good. Good, good good.'

I think that may be a little too many 'goods'. He stares back at me as if I'm doing a Britney Spears, crashing his car with an umbrella, only moments away from shaving my head. Perhaps I should have tried this before I sunk a bottle of wine.

'So, how long have you guys been together? God, it's been years, hasn't it? And still.....good.'

'Yes Poppy,' he says very slowly, as if speaking to a toddler. 'It's been twenty years and still going strong.'

'Fuck!' I shout, spitting out a bit of my wine. 'Twenty years?'

'Yep. We got together when we were fourteen and now we're thirty four'. He smiles to himself. 'Time flies when you're having fun.'

My poor clueless sap of a brother. He has no idea what an evil conniving bitch his wife is.

'Yeah,' I nod. 'And you are still having....fun? You know, date nights and stuff to spice it up?'

His mouth drops open slightly and his eyes boggle out of his head.

'Are you....'

Oh my God, I've said too much. He's figured it out. He knows she's having an affair. He's had his suspicions before tonight and now he's put it all together like at the end of those murder mysteries.

'Are you....asking me,' he lowers his voice to a whisper, 'about my sex life?'

This time I definitely spit out my wine. It sprays in several directions and manages to get Auntie Beryl on the face. She looks horrified and starts cleaning herself off with a napkin.

'No! Not sex! Just, you know....date nights and stuff.'

'Oh Pops,' he says, resting his hand on my shoulder. 'I think I know what this is about.'

Finally!

'Don't beat yourself up. It's not your fault,' he says kindly, smiling weakly.

Huh?

'I know it's not my fault?'

'Stuart just didn't want to go out with you anymore. It wasn't because you didn't do enough date nights or anything like that. He just wanted to invest in himself, do something on his own for once.'

Is this guy for real? He looks at me, his face pained from how apparently pathetic I am to him. I open my mouth to reply, but no sound comes out.

'Annabel and I make time for ourselves. It's like at the moment, she's doing this writing course. It's two nights a week, every Tuesday and Thursday and I let her get on with it.'

'Mmmhmmm,' I just about manage.

'I try to get her to read some out to me, but bless her, she's so shy.' He smiles fondly.

Writing course, my fucking arse! Those are obviously her booty nights. I know I should feel really sorry for him at the moment but I can't help but want to punch him in the face. How can he be so condescending to me?

'But don't worry Pops. It will happen for you. One day you'll be as happy as me and Annabel. I'm...almost sure of it.'

I nod, the skill of speech seeming to have escaped me. I look away from him, desperate for some kind of distraction. Does my own brother honestly think I am this pathetic?

I look over at Mum, desperate for her to behave like a Mum for once. For her to notice just by looking at me that I'm upset. To take me into the front room, put a blanket over me and make me some hot chocolate while I tell her all about it. Instead I notice her and Auntie Beryl swapping insults, swaying from side to side on their chairs. Why can these two never handle their wine? You'd think with twenty years' experience they'd have it down to a tee.

'Well, it's like I've always said, you can't buy class,' Mum snorts, eyeing her disapprovingly.

'And what on earth is that supposed to mean?' Auntie Beryl slurs. She attempts to smooth her hair back, only making it stand more on end.

'It means that you've got no class,' Mum retorts.

'Mum!' I shout.

'Oh, back out Poppy. This is between me and her.'

'Don't get angry with Poppy. You've never been a good mother!' Auntie Beryl slurs back, spilling her wine on the table.

'A good mother? How *dare* you! You don't even talk to Carolyn anymore.'

Auntie Beryl gasps and freezes in horror. Carolyn is my cousin, who was always a goody two shoes. She was always the golden girl in the family, until she announced on her twenty first birthday that she was a lesbian. Well actually, I think her exact words in her speech were 'massive muff muncher and if you don't love me you can go fuck yourself mum'. It was one of those excruciating embarrassing family events that we all pretend never happened. Shortly after, she moved to India to teach English and we haven't talked about her since.

'Well, I did a damn site better job than you,' Auntie Beryl slurs, tears in her eyes.

'Oh really? And so now you think my children are delinquents?'

'Mum, she didn't say that,' I try and interrupt.

'Jesus, Meryl!' Dad shouts.

'Don't you get involved Douglas!' she shouts, waving her hands frantically.

Ollie gets up. 'I'm going for a fag.' He gives me a look which says 'run while you can'.

'If you'd have been a better mother maybe Oliver wouldn't still be living at home smoking like a chimney.'

'Hey, don't get me involved!' he shouts looking hurt.

'Don't start picking on my son! Maybe if you were a better mother, Carolyn wouldn't be licking vaginas in India right now!'

'Mum!' I shout, horrified.

'Poppy, for Christ's sake! Do something!' Dad shouts, a helpless exhausted expression on his face.

Why does Dad always think that I can control them? A riot squad of policemen couldn't control these two.

'I...I...listen to me!' I try, desperate to get their attention.

'If you think for one moment, I'm going to stay here and let you insult me,' Auntie Beryl says, swaying heavily in her seat.

'Go! No-one's holding a gun to your head Beryl,' Mum barks, crossing her arms.

'Listen to me!' I shout. I look around desperately at Richard and Henry who are looking at their watches and clearly wondering if they can make a run for it.

'What? What are you going to do about it? Hit me Meryl? Because I still have the scar from the last time you lost your temper!'

'Don't fucking tempt me Beryl!'

'Just listen!' I shout, standing up.

'I'm not afraid of you. Come on! Let's go.' Auntie Beryl stands up and puts her fists up to her face.

'Stop this!' Dad shouts.

'Listen!' I stand between them.

'Do something!' Dad shouts at me.

What the hell can I say to stop this? Think. Think of something that would shock them. Anything!

'I've got a boyfriend!' I shout.

A sharp silence fills the air. Five gawping faces stare back at me. Oh dear. What the hell have I done?

'Sorry?' Mum says, speaking very slowly, as if I'm a bird that she doesn't want to startle in case I fly away. 'You've got a....a boyfriend?'

'Um...yes.'

'A real one?' Auntie Beryl asks, pulling her head to the side.

'Well of course a real one!' Mum says, clicking her tongue.

'Stuart mentioned you were with someone new,' Henry adds. 'Ryan, isn't it?'

'Why the hell do you still hang out with Stuart? I've told you it makes me feel uncomfortable.'

'He's in my rugby team and I don't see why I should stop hanging out with him just because you guys broke up.'

'Um, let me think. Because he dumped me, because you're loyal to your sister?' He looks back at me like I'm some deranged nutter.

'Darling,' Mum says, her face lighting up, 'you have to tell us *everything*!'

*   *   *

When I get in I head straight for my bed, my temples pounding. How the hell do I get myself into these messes? Never have I been so accepted by my family. Anyone would think I'd cured cancer tonight, not just announced that I'm seeing someone. I now have an imaginary boyfriend called Ryan.

How the hell do I do it?

Chapter 13

Not to worry. No need to panic. Although my life does seem to be getting more ridiculous and unpredictable by the second, there's one thing I can always count on. A tea and a cupcake.

As I walk into the bakery the smell of freshly baked bread invades my nostrils. I take a deep breath and already feel calmer. Thank God for bread. The owner Glenda greets me with a smile. The moody goth girl with the black hair and lip piercing is helping out again, but she doesn't acknowledge me.

'Morning,' I say to goth girl.

She does her usual grunt of response. Glenda looks up at me from serving a nearby table and smiles as if to say 'when will she cheer up, eh?' Seriously, why is this bitch always so miserable? It's not like she can say she's tired – she's surrounded by unlimited coffee!

Beep beep. It's a text from Jazz.

Today's challenge – make a new friend to bring to Nobo 2mo nite. Don't worry Grandma, free entry and complimentary drinks xxx

Oh great. Another night out. Just what I need. Who the hell am I going to be able to befriend before tomorrow night? I don't have the time and to be honest I can't be bloody bothered.

I look behind the glass counter at the lines and lines of cupcakes. There's sunflower cupcakes, chocolate orange cupcakes, cupcakes that look like shuttlecocks, cupcakes with chocolate buttons and balls on top, cupcakes with strawberry slices coated in chocolate. Everywhere I look there's sprinkles, flakes, butterflies.

'I'll have a tea and one of those cupcakes please.'

The cupcake I'm pointing to is only the most beautiful cupcake every created in the world. It's got yellow and blue swirls, with a glittery flower in the middle of it.

Goth girl grunts and presses the buttons on the machine. You'd think she'd make a bit of an effort. I do come in here most mornings. And lunchtimes. And occasionally after work. OK, so I'm basically here all the time. All the more reason for her to make an effort. Yet each time she just grunts and throws my tea at me. Maybe it's me. Maybe she could be my friend for tomorrow night. That way I wouldn't have to bother running around desperately after work.

Ok, think friendly.

'Has it been a busy morning?' I ask, trying to sound bright and perky.

She nods. Ok, well that's put an end to that conversation. Think Poppy, think.

'Do you...like working here?'

She turns from the very loud machine to stare at me as if I'm crazy.

'Do I like working here? Are you mad?' She narrows her eyes at me suspiciously.

'No. I just wondered. Trying to...make conversation, you know.' I wish I hadn't bothered.

'You don't have to bother,' she shrugs.

She is SO rude!

'Well it's better than the awkward silence while the machine spurts all over the place,' I snap.

She turns to look me square in the eye, as if she's sussing me out. Then she relents.

'I hate it. Glenda bosses me around all day and makes me work weekends and I stink of coffee.'

'Oh. Well...at least...you're providing a service to people. You know...people without tea or coffee, they'd be nightmares. And people love cakes. You're probably saving loads of people from grumpy bosses. Take mine for example. He's a right misery most of the time but the quick half hour after he's had his coffee he's like a different person.' I realise I'm speaking really fast, but I can't help it, the nerves are spurring me on.

'Really? Your boss is a nightmare too?'

'Oh totally! He's the fucking devil incarnate, in truth.'

'Well...I suppose that makes me feel a bit better.' She smiles slightly.

'Exactly! We're all in the same boat.'

'Here you go.' She hands over the beautiful cupcake and tea. I give her my money before I drool over it.

Through all of her piercings she has a pretty face with clear blue eyes. I've already laid the groundwork. I just need the guts to ask her.

'Actually,' I say, stalling. 'I...I was wondering if you fancied going out tomorrow night. A few friends of mine are going to Nobo in Soho and it's gonna be a laugh. It might cheer you up?'

'I'm not sure.' She wrinkles her face up.

God the rejection is hard. This is why I don't ask guy's out.

'Go on. You deserve to let your hair down.' I smile desperately.

'No it's not that,' she says, looking everywhere apart from me. 'It's just...well...'

'What?'

'I don't play on your team,' she blurts out, suddenly red all over.

Same team? What team? Does she mean netball?

'You...you think I'm a lesbian?!' I shriek.

A few people sitting down with their coffees turn to look at me. Maybe I was a bit loud.

'Yes. I mean...weren't you trying to chat me up?'

'No! Jesus, I was just trying to be friendly. I won't bloody bother next time!' I grab my tea and cupcake, getting ready to run, wondering if I'll ever be able to show my face in here again.

'No! Please! Honestly, I'm so sorry. I didn't mean to piss you off. It's just...'

'It's just you thought I was a massive lesbian. Why the hell would you think that? Do I give off a massive lesbian vibe or something?'

'No. But....you know. The way you dress and stuff, I did wonder. And then with you asking all of those questions – I just put two and two together.'

'Yeah and got a hundred and twenty-five!' I shout, feeling flushed.

Do I dress like a lesbian and not realise it? Maybe when everyone moans at me to dress more feminine it's actually because they think I look like a complete fanny muncher. Don't get me wrong, I've got nothing against lesbians. My Cousin Carolyn's one. To be honest I totally get it. Men are baboons. But me? I thought lesbians were butch, with boy haircuts and they wore work boots and listened to indie music?

'I'm really sorry. I didn't mean to offend you.'

'No it's fine. I've gotta go.' I turn, my cheeks hot from humiliation.

'No please! I will come out with you. 8pm at Nobo right? I'll be there!'

'Whatever.' I just want to get the hell out of here. I walk quickly to the door and then I drop my cupcake.

*   *   *

I still can't stop thinking about it. Not the cupcake, I got over that about an hour ago. Do I look like a lesbian? Is that why Ryan isn't showing any interest in me? Does he think I'm a lesbian? Do I need to send out a newsletter or something?

'Poppy, you've got a visitor downstairs,' Gavin says, breaking me from my thoughts.

'Oh yeah, who is it?' I say shortly, glaring at him. 'Michael Flatley? Louis Walsh? I've had enough of the Irish jokes, ok!'

'Wow! Chill!' he says, his hands up in defence. 'It's your Mum.'

'My Mum?' I ask, puzzled.

'Yep. She's downstairs.'

Oh great.

'Really? She didn't tell me she was coming.'

I wander down the stairs into reception and there she is. She's wearing a zebra print suit with an orange t-shirt. Her hair is scooped up into its usual clip.

'Hi Mum.' I quickly look around, eager for no-one to see her.

'Hi darling! I can't believe I've never been to your offices before. They're really...' she trails off as she looks around at the cracked plaster and Suzanne the receptionist picking her teeth.

'Yes, well anyway. What are you doing here?'

'I'm meeting you for lunch darling.' She looks at me as if I'm mad.

'Did you send me an e-mail or something?' I sigh, trying not to show how frustrated with her I am.

'No. I just thought I'd pop along. You're not busy are you?'

'Um, actually. I'm not sure. I have got loads on,' I stall.

175

'Oh. Well remember darling, I have trekked all the way here from home. To London, crime capital of England. I can't believe I'm still alive to be honest with you. It'd be an awful shame for me to have to go back hungry.'

God – always with the guilt trip.

'Ok. I'll just grab my bag.' I walk back to my desk cursing under my breath. It's so typical for her to just turn up and expect me to drop everything.

'Guess what!' Lilly shouts, running up to me with flushed cheeks.

'What?' I ask, my voice flat and uninterested.

'Me and Alex have just put an offer in on a flat. And it's been accepted!'

Oh my God.

'Isn't that amazing!' she shrieks, dancing up and down, her boobs nearly falling out of her top.

She can't be buying a flat. She's about to get made redundant.

'I...' I clear my throat uncomfortably. 'I didn't even know you were looking?'

'I know. That's Alex; he was all like don't tell anyone until we've found a place, we'll just jinx it. Bless him,' she giggles.

'Are you sure...I mean, do you think it's a good time for you to buy?'

'Yeah of course. We're both in stable jobs, we've got a deposit and been accepted for a mortgage. Why wouldn't we?' She narrows her eyes at me accusingly. 'Why, is there something you know that I don't?'

You're going to be made redundant and be stuck with a flat that you'll probably have to have repossessed.

'No!' I shriek unnaturally.

'Because if you know something I don't, you should tell me'. She's looking at me really upset now, her big eyes boring into mine.

'Because if Alex is having an affair, I want to know now!'

'Affair?'

'Yes! If you know he's having an affair I should know now! So is he? Yes or no?'

'No! Of course it's a no! I'm sorry.' I pull myself desperately together. 'I just worry about you stretching yourself too thin with money and stuff.'

'Ah Pops,' she beams at me. 'I love how you worry about me, but don't worry. That's what we got a financial advisor for.'

'Ok,' I say, unconvinced. 'I've gotta go to lunch with my mum anyway.'

'Good luck,' she laughs, already running off to tell everyone else.

When I walk back down the stairs Mum's telling Suzanne about how wonderful dry shampoo is and how she should use it to stop her hair being greasy.

'Come on Mum.' I drag her away, smiling apologetically at Suzanne.

'Oh, lovely girl that Suzanne. Just a bloody shame about the greasy hair.'

'Mum! We haven't even left the reception yet,' I whisper.

'Well some people need to be told,' she scoffs, completely unembarrassed.

'Ok whatever. Anyway, where do you want to go for lunch? There's a nice little Italian a few roads away from here.'

'Not sure about that. I'm off the carbs now. Auntie Beryl's got me on another diet.'

'When will you stop with these crazy diets!'

'They're not crazy sweetheart. Maybe you should try one sometime. It wouldn't kill you.' She looks me up and down disapprovingly.

Great. Now I've been called both a lesbian and fat in the same day. A fat lesbian.

'Anyway, where do you want to go then?' I ask through gritted teeth.

'Wherever Ryan wants to take us,' she smiles.

'Sorry? Ryan?'

Oh my God. My imaginary boyfriend Ryan.

'Yes. You should always let the man decide on where to eat. Makes them feel superior,' she nods knowingly.

'But...we haven't invited Ryan.'

'Well we can invite him now!' She shakes her head as if I'm retarded.
'Mum, he's very busy. I doubt he'll have time,' I say playing for time. Think Poppy, think of an action plan.
'Well you won't know until you ask.'
Oh my God. What the hell am I going to do? She stares back at me expectantly. I know she won't drop this.
'Actually Mum, I'll just call him.'
I grab my phone out of my handbag and realise I probably won't get away with pretending to call someone. With my luck it would call while I was faking. I'll call Jazz.
'Hey babe, you ok?' Jazz says down the phone. I've just got to hope that she realises what I'm doing.
'Hi R-y-a-n,' I say, pronouncing his name very slowly.
'Ryan? Babe you've called the wrong number. It's me.'
'Yes, R-y-a-n. My mum's in London and she wondered if you wanted to have lunch?'
'Ryan? You're taking Ryan for lunch with your Mum?'
Jesus. She really doesn't get it does she.
'What's he saying?' Mum says, trying to grab the phone off me.
'Oh no! What a shame,' I say hitting her hand away. 'Well don't worry, we'll organise something soon.'
'Oh I get it. Is this something for your mum?' Jazz finally clocks.
'Yes, yes. OK bye, love you.' I hang up. Shit. Why did I say love you? I'm so used to saying it to Jazz.
'Darling, you didn't tell me you were at the stage where you've told each other you love one another?'
'Oh...didn't I?'
Shit shit shit.
'No! I'm pretty sure I'd remember that darling. My little girls in love,' she beams, her eyes crazy wide.
'Anyway, he can't meet.' I pull a disappointed face. 'He says he's very sorry but he's got loads on and simply can't leave the office.'
'Oh, what a shame. Well, I'll tell you what. If he can't leave the office then we'll go to him.'
'What?'

'Yes. We'll give him a little picnic. Come on, we'll go to Marks and Spencer's.' She grabs hold of my arm and starts pulling me along.

'No, you don't understand. He's very busy. He won't have time,' I try and protest.

'Well, he'll have time to see us for two seconds won't he?'

'No! You don't understand. He's very important and can't be interrupted.'

Before I know it I'm leaving Marks and Spencer's with a full picnic and Mum's talking about when he might propose. How the hell do I get myself in these situations!

'Right. Which building does he work at?'

'Um. I can't remember,' I say playing for time. There has to be a way to get her to drop this.

'What was the name of the bank where he works again?' she asks.

'Um...I can't remember that either.'

'Jesus darling! How can you forget this kind of stuff? Wait a minute.' She starts rubbing her forehead. 'Barclays! That's it, I remember.'

How can she remember that! How can she remember my false story?

'Ok, but we still don't know where his office is. Why don't we just go for a nice picnic, just us?'

'Don't be ridiculous. We've bought far too much food for just us. I'm not supposed to be eating half this stuff anyway. Auntie Beryl would go mad at me if she found out.'

'Ok, but – '

'Excuse me.' She grabs a stranger's arm. 'Do you know where Barclays head office is?'

'Oh yes. It's two streets away.'

Two streets? Why couldn't it be the other side of London? The whole of fucking London and its two streets away.

'Great thanks.' She turns back to me, seeming very pleased with herself. 'See darling! If you use your initiative you can do anything.' As we begin walking down the street I start to sweat. What the hell am I going to do? I can't hold her back. Dear God, wild boars couldn't hold her back! And what am I going to do when she asks for Ryan and they tell her he doesn't work there. She'll have me committed.

Just think! Oh my God, I've got it! I'll go along with this and when they say he doesn't work there I can act all dramatic and cry and say that it's over. Perfect. I can stop this whole charade before it gets out of hand.

As she pulls me into the building I'm feeling better about the whole situation. It'll be over in two minutes.

'Excuse me,' she says, dragging me to the reception desk. 'Could you please call Ryan and tell him that we're here to see him.'

'Sorry...Ryan...? What's his surname?' the receptionist asks, looking Mum up and down in alarm.

Trust my mother to think that only one Ryan works here.

'Poppy, what's his surname?'

'Um...it's...Smith.' I start psyching myself up for the tears.

'And your names are?'

'My daughter is Poppy Windsor and I'm – '

'Sorry,' I interrupt. 'But are you telling me that there is a Ryan Smith?'

'Yes.' She looks at me strangely.

'Don't interrupt me Poppy, it's very rude,' Mum snaps. 'I'm Meryl Windsor, her mother.'

'Ok, I'll just ring up.'

Oh my God. Oh my fucking God. What the hell am I going to do now? I need to get her out of here.

'Mum, I feel sick. Let's go and we'll get him another time.'

'Don't be silly. She's called up for him now.' She shakes her head at me, annoyed.

I watch the receptionist on the phone, talking away. He's probably saying 'who the hell are these people?'

'Yes but...I think I...may have come on my period. I need to get a change of clothes.'

'A change of clothes darling? How heavy could you be?' She starts staring at my crotch. 'I don't see anything.'

'Very heavy. Come on, we need to go.' I grab her arm.

'Auntie Beryl used to be the same. Used to go through everything she wore. I couldn't lend her anything. She ruined two of my favourite white trousers. Had to have her womb microwaved in the end.'

'Sorry, but Ryan's not expecting you,' the receptionist says, holding a hand over her receiver.

'Oh, he won't be darling. It's a surprise.' She looks back at me excited. 'Where was I anyway? Yes, she had to get her womb microwaved. Terrible business.'

'He's coming down now,' the receptionist says, still suspicious.

Oh my God. Oh my God. I need to get out of here.

'Mum, we need to go! Now!' I scream. I'm sweating. My neck is hot.

'He's your boyfriend Poppy. You're already telling each other you're in love. I'm sure he's not going to be bothered by a bit of blood.'

'But he will! You don't know him. He's...he's allergic to blood,' I stammer, my insides churning. How could I have got myself in this mess!

'Allergic to blood? What the hell are you talking about Poppy?'

I look up as the lift pings and a man in his late forties walks out looking around. Oh my God, that must be him. What the fuck? What the fuck!

There's only one option left. I pretend to pass out.

I try to relax my eyes as I lay on the floor with them shut. Mum is fussing over me.

'Oh my God! Poppy! Someone call an ambulance!' she shouts.

'Is she ok?' a male voice asks. Obviously Ryan Smith.

'I don't know,' Mum says. 'She was fine a minute ago. I don't hear anyone calling that ambulance!'

'It's on its way,' the receptionist shouts.

Oh my God. An ambulance is coming. This is fraud. I can't do this. What if the ambulance doesn't go to an old man having a heart attack because it was busy coming for me and he died? I'd never be able to live with myself.

I open my eyes and take a deep breath.

'Poppy darling! She's alive!' Mum cheers.

I sit up and shake my head.

'That was strange. But I feel fine now. Come on Mum, let's go home. If you could please cancel the ambulance,' I say to the receptionist clutching my head dramatically.

'Don't be ridiculous! You still need an ambulance. Normal healthy people don't just pass out, do they Ryan?' She turns expectantly to him.

'Um...how do you know my name?' he asks looking at her as if she's mad. 'Have I scheduled a meeting with you?'

'I'm Poppy's mum.' She gestures at me.

'Mum I need to go now. Sorry Ryan.' I quickly try to drag her out with all of the strength left in my body.

She resists but I still run out of the office and breathe in the fresh air. I hear Mum's footsteps running out after me. How the hell am I going to explain this one?

'Poppy darling, why are you running away from Ryan? And why did he just ask me who you were?'

I look into her face and instead of suspicion I see genuine concern. Oh God, now I really feel terrible. I should just tell the truth. She deserves that.

'He's...got amnesia,' I say before I can stop myself. I stare at her, waiting for her to tell me I'm ridiculous and realise I'm lying. I watch her face as she seems to consider this.

'Amnesia? What happened to him?' she asks intrigued, as if it were her daily soap instead of my life.

'Um...he fell down the stairs,' I say quickly, avoiding her suspicious gaze.

'Oh what a poor love!'

Why the hell is she believing this crap? It's almost as if she's so desperate for me to have a boyfriend – any boyfriend – that she's willing to ignore rationality.

'So he doesn't remember anything?'

'No. Not a thing.' I frown, pretending to be upset.

'Oh, don't worry darling, I'm sure he'll remember. But I still think you should see a doctor. You can't just faint and then forget about it. Unless...' she trails off, her mouth gaping open and her eyes widening. 'Oh my Jesus. I can't believe I didn't realise immediately. You're pregnant! My baby's pregnant!' She wraps her arms around me and starts rocking from side to side.

Oh my God.

'No! Mum, I'm not pregnant!'

But it's as if she hasn't heard me. Already planning the nursery in her head.

'Of course! I fainted during all four pregnancies. You obviously get that from me. But don't worry darling, we're going to get through this together. Ryan will remember soon and then we'll all be a happy family.' She stares at my stomach excitedly.

'No. You don't understand,' I protest.

'I thought you'd put on a bit of weight.' She pats my stomach.

'Mum! Listen to me! I am NOT pregnant!'

'Ok darling.' She winks at me. 'I get it. You don't want to tell anyone until after the twelve week scan. Totally understandable.'

'Listen to me.' I grab her face with both my hands and speak extra slow. 'I. Am. Not. Pregnant.'

She looks at me, still in my hands and smiles.

'There really is no need to be embarrassed darling. Plenty of people have children out of wedlock these days. But we can get you married in an instant.' She takes a notebook out of her bag. 'We'll have to get you married as soon as possible. I'll call Father Trevor and – '

'We're not getting married!'

'Not this second darling, but soon he'll get his memory back.'

'No! I...I don't want to marry him! I might actually dump him.'

Yes that's a good way to get out of this.

'Dump him? But why would you do that darling? He needs you now more than ever.'

'Well...' I rack my brain trying to think. 'Don't you think he's a bit old for me?' I remember his appearance. He was easily late forties, if not early fifties.

'Age is just a number darling.'

'Well I'm afraid that I've made my decision,' I say firmly. 'You can tell everyone that it's over.'

'But he's not that old sweetheart and you *are* carrying his baby.'

'Yes he is Mum!' I say losing my temper. 'He's an old man with a wrinkly cock!'

Oh my God. Why the fuck did I say that?

'Oh!' she says, seeming taken back. 'Well...I understand.'

Is she talking about my Dad's penis? Please God, don't say she is. Block out the thoughts of your Dad's penis! Throw yourself off a bridge if you have to!

'Thank you for understanding. I have to go.'

And then I run.

Chapter 14

I can't stop thinking about Annabel and what a poisonous witch she is. It's helping me get over the shock of yesterday. Anything to block that out. I couldn't even confide in Lily when I got back to the office, as I'm too embarrassed to admit I have an imaginary boyfriend. That and she was busy showing me pictures of the flat she's buying that only I know she can't afford. That and I haven't had a chance to interrogate Ryan on his feelings for Tabitha. Big Tits Tabitha.

How could she do this to Richard? How can she be feeding him some line about trying for a baby while all the time shagging someone else? I've come to the conclusion that I must have been wrong. I just *must* be. It was a very trying day and I was probably exhausted. My brain showed me some kind of old image of Annabel. I'd probably see her again and laugh at how unlike Annabel she is. She'll probably have bright blonde hair and a broken leg and I'll say 'my God, how could I have been so wrong!?'

I hope. But just in case, I've decided to do some investigating. Richard says that she does her 'writing course' on a Thursday night so here I am. I'm waiting in my car outside their house. I've parked a bit down the road and am waiting eagerly for her to come out. She runs out, banging the door enthusiastically and heads for her blue Ford Fiesta.

I start my engine up and creep slowly behind her. We head towards St Albans road and turn at Emerald Corner. This is actually the way to the college. Thank God, I was wrong. She is actually doing a course. Of course she is. But at the turning of the college car park, instead of pulling in she carries on straight. My stomach drops. I follow her, considering where else she could be going. She could be surprising Richard with a big present or something and she has to go miles away to get it. Yes, it's probably that. I follow her down quite a few muddy country roads and pass a sign stating Harpenden.

Within a few minutes we're on Harpenden high street. She pulls effortlessly into a parking space as I struggle to Parallel Park a little down the road. She puts on some fresh lipstick and jumps out, an excited smile on her face. She flicks her hair behind her shoulders and heads across the road into a bar.

I get out nervously, glad I came prepared. I pull out a red baseball hat, which perfectly matches my red t-shirt, and stick it on over my pony tail. I pull on a pair of sunglasses and grab my clipboard. I shuffle over to the other side of the road, making sure she's in clear sight of me. She'll never notice me. She'll just think I'm one of those annoying people asking you to sign petitions or asking you to complete a survey.

A few minutes later I watch as Cheryl's husband appears inside and they embrace each other tightly. Anyone that didn't know better might think that this was a good friend, but only I know their sordid little secret. They get some drinks and start talking intensely, leaning in closely. She looks worried and he holds her hand reassuringly.

What on earth could they be talking about?

'Excuse me miss.'

I'm thrown out of my concentration, turning around to see an elderly man with big milk bottle glasses smiling at me.

'I'd be willing to sign your petition, dear.'

'My petition?' I follow his eyes down to my clipboard. 'I mean, my petition! Yes, of course!'

I thrust the clipboard into his hands, realising that the piece of paper on it only contains my doodles of flowers and butterflies.

'And what is this petition for?' he asks narrowing his eyes at me.

Oh crap, I knew I should have given myself a back story, but it just took so long to get my pony tail in the right position so that I could wear the hat properly.

'Um...it's for....the tortoise hospital.'

Tortoise hospital? What the fuck is wrong with me? I feel myself redden and I quickly look away. Maybe I should just kick him and run as fast as I can. He looks like he'd go down pretty easy.

'Tortoise hospital?' he asks, smiling to himself, as if considering whether this is a joke.

Oh crap, this old man isn't as stupid as I first thought. I've got no choice, I have to just go with it.

'Oh yes.' I put on my most convincing tone. 'People forget about tortoises. It's all about cats and dogs, but tortoises need help too.' I smile as confidently as possible. Surely this is so ridiculous he has to believe it. Either that or he'll call the police.

'Oh right,' he says, staring at me strangely. 'And what's the name of this tortoise hospital?'

Seriously old man, don't you have anything else to do? Don't you have some Deal or No Deal to be catching up on? Some teenagers to tut at? Some slow walking to do?

'It's called....Tortoise Safety. Yes, Tortoise Safety. But like I've said, you probably haven't heard of it.'

'Oh, I think I have!' he smiles. 'Is Vanessa still working on reception? Good old Van.' He smiles affectionately.

'Um....I'm not sure.'

I glance over at the bar and to my horror they've gone. I look towards her car but it's still there. Where the hell have they gone?

'Well, when you see her, will you tell her that Betsy is terribly unwell,' he says, a sad expression on his face.

'Betsy?'

'My terrapin,' he nods.

What the hell is going on here?

'Yes, I'll tell her.' I grab the clipboard from him, eager to get away, but he clasps his hands round mine.

'You won't forget now will you dear?' His big green eyes stare up at me with serious hope.

'Of course not. Betsy, the terrapin, gotcha.'

I throw his hands off me and start running, but she's nowhere to be seen. I run further down the high street wondering if they've found a little hotel to have their rendezvous at. Maybe they meet up so regularly that they've gone as far as to rent a small studio and it's filled with paintings full of their naked bodies.

But then I see them. Kissing each other goodbye, as if it's the last time they're ever going to see each other. I feel a stab in my chest, my heart. How could she be doing this to Richard? He loves her so much, but she doesn't love him. It's pretty clear that she is madly, deeply and unconditionally in love with Cheryl's husband.

He walks away and blows her a kiss while I try to catch my breath. What a whore. She opens the glass door of the offices and goes in. I watch her with contempt. It's only after a few minutes that I realise she's just gone into a divorce lawyers.

*   *   *

When I get back to the flat it's 7.30pm and I'm starving.   I go into the sitting room to find all of my furniture re-arranged. The fact that it actually looks better is irrelevant. I still shoot Jazz an irritated look.

'Hey Chick, you OK?' she smiles, completely ignoring my annoyance.

'Yeah, but I'm starving,' I moan as I throw myself on the sofa.

'Me too! What are you gonna make us?'

'Why does it always have to be me?' I complain, but the truth is that I secretly love it.

I walk into the kitchen, Jazz following, and start inspecting the fridge contents. We've only got a few eggs and peppers.

'Omelette it is then,' I say under my breath. 'What time are we supposed to be going to Nobo? It's late now.'

God, I hope she changes her mind.

'Oh yeah, did you make a friend?'

'Sort of, but I doubt she'll be meeting us there.'

'Thank God!' she exclaims. 'I don't fancy it. This working full time shit is hard work.'

'Thank God. Anyway Jazz, I kind of need a favour,' I say carefully.

'Really? What?' she asks, her small grey eyes lighting up in excitement.

'It's kind of a long story but...can you pretend you want to buy a flat and put a fake offer in?'

She stares back at me completely puzzled. 'Why on earth would I do that?'

Because I want to make it so that Lilly can't buy the flat so she won't be in complete financial ruin.

'Like I said, I can't tell you. Can you do it?'

'Yeah, suppose,' she says, already losing interest in the conversation. That's my girl.

The front door slams, making us both jump. We freeze and stare at each other as men's footsteps come closer and closer.

'Hey Po Po,' Ollie sings, sticking his head round the door. 'Ooh, omelette. Go on then!'

I mutter under my breath, but crack another few eggs.

'How did you even get in? I thought I took your key away from you?'

'Yeah,' he smiles. 'I had another one cut.'

'Well that might have been OK when it was just me, but Jazz is here at the moment. You can't just walk in unannounced. She could be naked!'

They both go red and smile at each other.

'Yeah, that kind of happened the other day,' Ollie explains, smiling cheekily at Jazz.

'Oh my God, Ollie!' I shout, hitting him with my spatula. 'I'm so sorry Jazz.'

'Don't worry,' she smiles, putting her hand on her hip and sticking her chest out proudly. 'I've got nothing to be embarrassed about.'

'You're right there,' Ollie says, shamelessly checking her out.

'Ollie!' I shout, horrified.

What the hell is going on with them?

'Anyway,' Ollie says, turning to Jazz, 'I wondered if you wanted to come to Leicester with me.' He looks down a little sheepishly. 'You know, just so I don't have to go alone.'

'Oh,' Jazz says, seeming taken aback. 'Yeah....cool. When?'

'Wednesday. I'll text you about it.' He looks at me as if my being here is terribly inconvenient.

I grab the tweezers and start attacking him playfully with them.

'I know you just want her there so you can bang her!' I say as I attack him.

'Shut up,' he says, shoving me so hard I fall into the cupboard. Shit, my elbow!

What is going on with these two? Why has Jazz even agreed to go along? I thought she was happy with Jake. I really hope she doesn't ruin it because of Ollie. Of all people my dumbass brother Ollie.

'So anyway,' Jazz says, turning to me, her cheeks unusually flushed. 'How did the spying go?'

I dig her in the ribs, having not told Ollie about my little adventure. I was hoping I wouldn't have to. He looks back at me accusingly, instantly knowing that I'm keeping a secret.

'Ok!' I shout, throwing my hands up in defence. 'I've got something to tell you about Annabel, but you have to promise not to tell Richard....or anyone for that matter.'

'Yeah,' he smiles, leaning eagerly in like an old lady leaning over the fence for the morning gossip.

'She's....well, she's....' I lower my voice to a whisper. 'Having an affair.'

'Why the hell are you whispering?' Jazz shouts.

Ollie leans back against the worktop and purses his lips together.

'I thought as much,' he muses to himself.

'What? You thought as much? Why didn't you fucking say?'

'Dunno,' he shrugs. 'Just a few things Richard mentioned. Well, a few things he'd said to Henry. You know how those two are close.'

I nod knowingly. Those two have always been thick as thieves. It's like Richard almost resents me and Ollie for being the youngest. Feels we got more than he did, which is ridiculous. Ollie and I were in the smaller room in bunk beds until we were eleven and thirteen, when Dad built the loft extension.

'So what did he say?'

'Just a few things,' Ollie shrugs. 'That she's been really distant lately and that's why he suggested they try for a baby. He thinks she's just a bit bored and wants to feel more involved. That's why he's signing her onto the business too.'

'Business? What are you talking about?'

'Yeah, she's going to become a partner.'

190

He has to be joking. She's expecting to become a partner in my Dad's business, the business that he spent years building up.

My Dad owns a very small building company called Windsor & Sons which he started up when he was just twenty two and penniless. The story goes that he'd started labouring at sixteen and had worked for the same slave-driver of a boss for years. He was desperate to start out on his own and be his own boss, but never had the guts or the money behind him. When he married my Mum and she quickly became pregnant with Richard he realised money was going to be tight. He asked for time off to go with her to the first baby scan, and when his boss refused he says he saw red. He couldn't bear the thought of missing out on his first child's scan and told him where to stick his job. It was only when they were living off baked beans in their bedsit later that night that he realised what a giant mistake he'd made. He pleaded with the boss to take him back, but he refused.

He took a part time job in McDonalds and said he honestly didn't know how he was going to afford to raise a child. But one night he received a letter telling him that his father, who he'd never known, had died and could he call them to find out what he had inherited. He only expected to inherit debt, so delayed calling for a while. When he eventually got round to calling them they explained that he'd inherited two grand! Two grand to him might as well have been a million. He used the money to set himself up with tools and equipment and the rest is history. He now employs ten men, plus Richard. Ollie occasionally works for him, when he can be bothered to get off his back side.

And she's expecting to inherit all of that? Then the images of the divorce office flash in my head. Wait a minute. If she signs as joint partner with Richard and Dad, but then files for divorce she could demand a third of the business. They might have to pay her thousands of pounds to get out of it. My lovely Dad could lose everything he's ever worked for because of some silly little slut who can't keep her legs closed.

'She can't become partner! She's planning to divorce him!'

'Divorce?' he asks, horrified. 'Are you sure?'

'Yes! Look, we have to stop her! Talk some bloody sense into him.'

191

'OK, OK,' he says, his face looking hassled. 'Let's just go to a bar and talk through it, OK?'

*   *   *

An hour later we're in the local wine bar knocking back glasses as if our lives depend on it.

'So anyway, you're going on a road trip with my brother? Why?'

Jazz avoids my gaze, pretending to look around the bar.

'He just said that he doesn't want to drive up alone and I might as well.'

'He totally wants to shag you.' I sigh heavily at the mere thought of it.

'No he doesn't! We're just going as friends,' she says, trying to hide a smile.

'Why would you want to though? I thought you were happy with Jake?'

'I am! I'm just friends with Ollie. We're just going as friends, OK!' she suddenly explodes, throwing her hands up defensively.

'OK, calm down! Total over-reaction.' I sigh again. I don't think I could cope if those two got together. They both cause me so many problems separately, let alone if they joined forces. They'd probably be in jail within a week.

'I am calm. Anyway, where the hell is he?'

Hmm, she seems awful keen to change the subject. I must grill her about this later. I look around the bar for inspiration and spot Craig in the crowd. He's Ollie's friend that turned out to be gay after years of me fancying him and maybe sending him the occasional love poem. I wave over politely, expecting him just to wave back, but to my surprise he comes bounding over.

'Hey gorgeous, small world or what!' he smiles, squeezing my arm. It's such a shame he's gay. His arms really are beautiful. All tanned and hairy, just how I like them.

'Yeah I know. If you were straight I'd swear you were following me, ready to drop a date rape in my drink.'

'You should be so lucky,' he laughs, exposing his crooked teeth. He really should get them fixed. I'm surprised he hasn't been shunned in the gay community.

I tap Jazz on the shoulder, who seems to have been distracted by a good looking guy.

'Jazz, this is Craig.'

'Nice to meet you,' she purrs seductively. 'So how do you two know each other?'

Craig does a double take of Jazz's chosen outfit, which I have to say she has outdone herself with. Grey sequinned baggy shorts, a loose fitting 80's crop top that hangs over her bronzed tummy, legwarmers and Jimmy Choos. The most upsetting part of it all is that no matter how ridiculous she dresses, she always seems to pull it off.

'I was friends with her brother when I was younger,' he explains, winking at me.

'Oh my God!' She spits out her mojito. 'You're not Craig that Pops used to fancy when she was younger and you turned out to be gay?'

Oh. My. God. If I had a knife I would stab her.

'Um...maybe,' he says, smiling awkwardly at me. 'I am gay. Poppy? Did you...fancy me?'

'No! Of course not! Jazz is...obviously thinking of someone else,' I shout, my voice shrill. I shoot daggers at Jazz with my eyes.

'So, who you here with?' he asks looking round.

'Ollie actually. He's around here somewhere,' I say desperately scanning the crowd for him.

When we finally find him, Craig and his friend, who I assume is gay by his pink leather trousers, suggest going to a local gay bar.

'Gay bar? Sounds great!' Jazz beams, clapping excitedly, already half way outside.

I turn to follow them, Jazz already dancing off down the street, when I spot bakery goth girl running down the street towards me in a red fifties style dress. I almost don't recognise her.

'Hey!' I shout at her. 'Bakery girl!'

She turns to stare at me and then smiles, recognising me. She looks absolutely stunning, her big blue eyes lined with black kohl pencil.

'I didn't know you lived in St Albans,' she says, still unenthusiastically.

'Yeah, small world or what? I take it you stood me up at Nobo then?'

'Yeah,' she says, smiling sheepishly. 'I was out with a few old work friends but it's finished early.'

'Actually we're just going on to a gay bar with a few friends if you fancy it?'

She narrows her gaze suspiciously. 'Are you SURE you're not a lesbian?'

*   *   *

When I get home from work on Friday I dump my bag down in the hallway and throw myself into bed, kicking off my flat shoes. Even flat shoes hurt. Everything hurts.

'Pops?' Jazz pops her head round the door.

'Jazz?'

'Who else would it be?' She runs and jumps into bed with me, nestling herself in the duvet. 'God, you really have a way of making a bed cosy. I don't know how you do it.'

'What're you doing here?' I ask, sleepiness taking over my body as my eyelids start to close from the weight.

'The festival, remember!' She grabs my cheeks and squeezes them.

'Oh crap. I completely forgot.' I wonder if she'll let me cry out. I seriously cannot even contemplate going to a festival right now. In fact, just going to the fridge seems too far. And I'm desperate for a tea.

'You're not still tired from last night are you?'

'Yes actually, I am! I don't make a habit of dancing to Madonna in gay bars till two in the morning. Especially on a school night.'

'Well, you really should. I love Craig! He's fab! So funny.'

'Yeah, he's great, isn't he?' I sigh, remembering how devastated I was when I caught him snogging Peter Morris at Ollie's 18th birthday party.

'Totally! I can see why you fancied him.'

194

'Yeah, thanks for that by the way.'

'No probs,' she smiles. 'Even your friend Goth Girl loosened up after a few shots.'

We should really find out her name.

'She's actually quite a laugh if you just get her annihilated. I couldn't believe it when she flashed the barman,' she says, giggling at the memory.

I try to smile but I'm too tired to even try.

'Yeah, but you were hardly any better. Kissing that bouncer on his bald head and calling him your Buddha.'

'Ha ha, yeah I'd forgotten about that.' She laughs, seeming proud of herself. 'What about you! You kept asking everyone if you looked like a lesbian! What the hell was that all about?'

'Oh....I don't know,' I say, playing ignorant. 'God, I'm just so tired. Victor made me colour code all of his files and then he decided he didn't like the colours.'

'Well, don't worry,' she waves, completely dismissing how soul destroying that must have been. 'We've still got an hour before we leave. Oh and Izzy's convinced Grace and Ryan to come now.'

His name makes my body tense in response. It feels like I haven't seen him for days. Only the odd polite conversation in the morning. I still haven't brought myself to ask about Big Tits Tabitha.

'Really?' I ask a little too enthusiastically.

'Yep. Two of Jake's friends had some dodgy curry or something, and now it's coming out of both ends.'

Gross. I glance at my watch, suddenly aware of how quickly she got here.

'Did you finish work early?'

'Erm...' she looks around sheepishly. 'Yeah....I got a half day.'

'Jazz,' I say warningly. 'Tell me the truth.'

'I am telling you the truth!' she shouts defensively, sitting up, pouting her lips.

'Really? Pinky swear?' I hold up my pinky finger and watch her reaction. Jazz is the only adult I know that genuinely believes if you pinky swear something that isn't true you'll burn in hell, getting tortured by evil pixies.

She opens her mouth to say something and then decides against it. She slumps over and exhales heavily.

'OK!' She throws herself face down on the bed. 'They kind of fired me,' she muffles through the duvet.

'They what?' I ask, dragging her head up by her hair.

'Ouch! Don't touch the hair bitch.'

I let go and open my mouth to ask what happened, but the truth is that I'm too exhausted to ask.

'Let's just try and have fun,' she smiles. 'We'll talk about it properly on Monday. Come on.' She jumps out of bed and whips the duvet back, exposing me to the cold.

I look outside into the dreary summer evening, clouds looming above, threatening to rain. Hardly the type of weather needed to sleep in a field.

'Ok, what do I need?' I start searching around for my rucksack unenthusiastically. She's not going to give up.

'You just need something to wear now.' She opens her wardrobe.

'Plus a pair of fresh knickers, socks and a new top for tomorrow. Oh, and baby wipes and make up. That should cover it.'

She places a pair of miniature shorts, that look like they could fit a Barbie doll, on the bed with a pink top.

'Jazz,' I take her hand. 'If you're gonna force me to go, I'm going in my own clothes.'

*   *   *

'Jake's here!' Jazz calls from the front door.

I'm actually really looking forward to meeting him. Especially as Jazz seems so excited whenever she talks about him. I just hope my brother doesn't screw it all up for her.

I walk out into the hallway and find her snogging his face off. I cough slightly to show that I'm here and they look up, not nearly as embarrassed as they should be.

'Oh, Jake, this is Poppy,' she says, smiling as if she slept with a hanger in her mouth.

'Hi, nice to meet you.' I smile politely, looking at the child that stands in front of me.

Don't get me wrong, he's gorgeous – all short blonde hair and blue eyes set against bronzed skin, but my God – he's so young! He must only be about 19! Has he got his Mum's permission to come this weekend? They would have really gorgeous children though.

'You too,' Jake nods. 'Are you driving down with us?'

I look at Jazz, unsure. Is he even old enough to drive? 'I don't know. Who's driving?'

'I'm driving,' Ryan says, jogging down the stairs in jeans and a black t-shirt.

I feel a tingle of excitement go through my body and end up in my stomach, bouncing around the edges. He's so dreamy.

'Are you bringing Izzy and Grace?' I ask him, trying to sound casual and stop the smile spreading on my face. I hate how I act like a geeky teenager around him.

'Yeah. Girls! Are you ready yet?' he shouts up the stairs as if he's their Dad.

'Yes! We're just coming,' Izzy shouts. They both appear, lugging enormous suitcases.

'You do know we're only going for one night, right?' he asks, looking at their cases in concern.

'Yeah I know,' Grace says, as she drags her giant black and white case down the stairs. 'These are just my essentials.'

I smile at her joke, but then realise she's deadly serious. Ryan catches my gaze and we both burst out laughing. Grace shoots me a look which says 'watch out bitch'. It makes my stomach churn.

'Well, it looks like your car is full, once the luggage is added, so I'll just go with Jazz and Jake.'

Jazz and Jake. I didn't actually realise how alike their names were until I just said it now. It sounds kind of ridiculous really, like a children's TV programme. The adventures of Jazz and Jake.

'We'll meet you there then,' Ryan says. He smiles his delicious smile that never fails to make me weak at my knees.

I miss him already.

Izzy runs over and gives me a quick kiss, while Grace stares on, daggers in her eyes. I desperately want to jump into Ryan's arms and hug those tight arms round me. I mean, you never know when the last time you see someone will be, do you? You should make the most out of every day and all that. But instead I just smile and walk towards the car, trying not to look bothered and desperately trying not to look back at him.

Chapter 15

Two hours later and we're finally here. I've been introduced to Jake's friend Ringo, who I have a terrifying feeling that Jazz and Jake are trying to fix me up with. He's a bit short, still taller than me, obviously, but still short for a man and he's got dark hair which he's shaved close to his incredibly round head. It reminds me of a bowling ball.

We park up amongst what seems like hundreds of cars and begin to unpack the boot. The weather hasn't improved much since we left, and I wrap my cardigan round myself, wishing I hadn't worn flip flops.

'Right,' Jake says, getting out a map. 'If we walk this way then we'll get to our blue camp.'

Blue camp? How big is this place? I thought it was just a little festival, not something big enough to have colour coded camps.

'How big is this festival Jake?' I ask, after a few minutes of walking, glad the girls have to carry the tent.

'Well, there are five stages.'

'Ok...and how many people normally attend?' I ask, noticing that we've still not managed to even walk to the end of the car park.

'Eighty thousand,' he says casually.

'Eighty thousand people?'

Oh my God. I think I'm going to hyperventilate. There was me thinking that this would be just a little festival with a few hundred people and it turns out to be one of the biggest festivals in England. I mean, are there even that many people living in England? Of course, I suppose there must be.

'So, are you into rock then Pops?' Ringo asks me as we walk. Still in the car park, I might add.

I hate how he's already shortened my name to Pops. I've only known him two hours and he already thinks he's my new best friend. Maybe I'll call him Ring and see how he likes it. I hope Jazz hasn't given him false hope about hooking up with me.

199

'Sorry, did you say rock?' I ask, thinking I must have miss-heard.

'Yeah...you do know that this is a rock festival, right?'

'Oh...yeah, of course. Love all the rock. Even eat it sometimes!' I laugh nervously.

He narrows his eyes at me suspiciously as I get my phone out of my pocket, hoping that he'll stop talking to me. Jazz glances back and smiles nervously. I discreetly put my finger up to my neck and drag it to the other side, signalling that when we're on our own she is dead. I do think that the fact it's a rock festival should have been brought up in conversation when describing this. But of course, she knew I wouldn't have come. She grimaces slightly and turns back.

'Shall we ring the others and tell them where to go?' I ask, suddenly wishing that Ryan were here to reassure me.

'I've text them and said we'll meet them at camp,' Jazz answers coolly, swigging from a bottle of vodka.

'But...if there are eighty thousand people...' God, it panics me just even saying that number, 'then, how do you expect them to find us?'

'They won't be that far behind us.'

*   *   *

An hour later, I'm starting to panic. Its 9pm, getting dark and I'm sat round a fire that Ringo and Jake have made, wondering where the hell they are.

'So, are you girls ready to go and see a band?' Jake asks getting to his feet excitedly.

My body tenses. Please, please, please God, don't make me go.

'I'm just going to try their phones one more time.' I get out my phone and press re-dial, not holding out much hope.

'Hello?' I don't believe it! I've never been more pleased to hear Izzy's voice. 'Izzy! Thank God! Where are you?'

'We're in the blue camp, but I don't really know...Oh wait, Ryan wants to speak.'

'Hi, Poppy?' Ryan asks, sounding disgruntled. Just hearing his voice, no matter how pissed off, makes me feel calmer. Something about him makes me feel safer. Maybe it's because I'm currently with children, who I feel I should be being paid to look after.

'Hi,' I swoon, almost breathless.

'We're in blue camp, but what are you near?' he asks, sounding rattled.

'Um...' I look around desperately for some kind of sign or big feature that I can direct him to. 'I'm not actually sure. Jake, what are we near?'

'Tell him we're in section 205.'

'Did you hear that? Section 205.'

'Yeah ok, I heard him. We're in section 205 but I still can't see you. Jesus, I didn't realise that so many people were gonna be here.' He sounds thoroughly pissed off.

'I know! Me neither. Wait, there's a chair here I can jump on.' I jump up on a stranger's chair and try and ignore the looks I get from the strange bearded owners. I look around, still on my tip toes and start calling his name.

'Wait, I can hear you,' he says, a bit of relief showing in his voice.

'Of course you can hear me, I'm shouting in your ear!'

'I mean I can hear an echo, idiot,' he snaps.

'I'm waving like an idiot too,' I add, ignoring his impatience.

'Oh wait, I see you. Be there in a sec'. He hangs up.

I remain stood on the chair, just in case they can't see me, when eventually I see them weaving around someone's tent, lugging the giant suitcases and tent equipment.

'Thank God!' I squeal running towards them. I throw myself against Ryan and hug him tight without thinking. 'I never thought I'd be so glad to see you,' I say, before realising how clingy and mental I must look. I quickly pull back.

'Poppy! I'm trying to carry everything if, you hadn't noticed,' he snaps, his face flushed.

'Well, sorry for breathing,' I retort, hurt. I turn back to the others and try not to take it personally.

'Well now that everyone's here, why don't we go and see a band?' Jake asks, eager as ever.

'Actually, I'm pretty tired. I could do with just chilling here tonight,'
Grace says, lighting up a cigarette.

For once, I'm actually glad to hear her speak.

'I agree,' Izzy chimes in. 'Plus, I'm not really a mad rock girl.'

'Oh, well...ok,' Jake says, seeming deflated.

I start to settle back down onto the chair that doesn't belong to me.

'Come on then Pops,' Ringo says, holding out his hand.

'Huh?' I ask confused, looking at his hand in horror.

'You love rock, remember?' he reminds me, like I'm his best friend.

'Oh, *P-o-p-s*,' Ryan says, accentuating my name as if to show he finds
it hilarious that Ringo has shortened my name already. 'I didn't
realise you loved rock so much.'

I look back at his smug smiling face and shoot him the meanest look I
can muster. He's not going to help me get out of this. He's just going
to watch on in amusement.

'Well actually, I only started loving it after hearing so much about it
from *you*.' I smile devilishly. I turn back to Ringo and Jake. 'You
see, Ryan here is a *massive* rock fan.'

Damn it, if I'm going down then he's coming with me.

'Oh great!' Ringo says, enthused. 'Come on then guys – AC/DC are
headlining'.

Ryan glares at me, all previous amusement gone. Izzy and Grace look
on, smiling as they begin to set up their leopard print tent that Izzy
insisted on buying. At least it will be easy for me to remember which
tent I'm sleeping in.

'I have to set up my tent and stuff,' Ryan says, obviously playing for
time.

'We'll help,' Jake offers.

'Oh....OK, thanks,' Ryan says, glaring at me again.

Jake and Ringo help him set up his tent and when they're all up I'm
suddenly glad to be going for a walk. There's so many tents here its
making me feel claustrophobic. Miles and miles of tents as far as I can
see.

It's completely pitch black by the time we set out walking, the only
light coming from small fires and the dim temporary lights along the

main pathways. It reminds me of every scary movie I've seen, but I feel safer knowing that Ryan is with me. Unlike short arsed Ringo, he's strong enough to fight off a crazed killer. Ringo probably couldn't even fight off Justin Bieber.

It takes us a good half hour before we get to the stage and when we do, I can't believe the size of it. If I thought that the tents were making me feel closed in, then this was sure to make me lose my mind. There must be at least twenty thousand people dancing in front of this stage alone, and they all look completely off their faces on drugs; their pupils black and crazed.

'Come on,' Jake signals to us, weaving himself through the crowd to try and get a better spot.

Ryan follows him and I cling instinctively onto the side of his t-shirt, scared of getting parted from him. Everyone seems taller than me, and images of me being crushed underneath them flash through my mind. I probably wouldn't be found for days. But then it would probably be a cool way to go. Everyone would think I was a cool, mad rocker who parties all the time. They'll say 'she died doing what she loved best – partying hard'. Then they'll put on that song 'we like to party hard' and everyone will dance around my coffin.

Jake finally finds a spot he finds acceptable and starts dancing around like a crazy person. I say dancing, it's more jumping up and down and waving his hands in the air. Like Dad dancing, while having an electric shock. I look around, still at a loss. We're still miles away from the stage, the performers seeming like tiny ants, listening to shit music, being crushed by thousands of people and the beer stand is about, well about two thousand people away.

I seem to be getting pushed continuously, from either side, as women with rainbow coloured hair in dreadlocks, and body hair down to their knees dance around me. Each time I turn automatically to apologise, they ignore me, seeming on another planet; their blood shot eyes reminding me of an animal. It's far too un-nerving.

Ryan catches my eye and I know he's just as miserable as me.

'Do you wanna go?' he shouts in my ear, resting his hand on my lower back so I can hear him.

My skin burns at his touch and I shudder, wondering if he has any idea of the effect he has on me.

'Yeah, do you?' I shout back, loving how close I have to get to him so that he can hear me.

'Hell yeah,' he shouts, smiling widely. We both collapse laughing and I feel warm, loving how we have our own inside joke. I begin to imagine what it would be like to be with him, to own him. Images of us laughing on our wedding day flash through my mind. Then us laughing over our baby spitting out porridge at the breakfast table. I know I'm getting ridiculously ahead of myself, but I allow myself the indulgence for half a second.

'We're going,' I signal to the others, getting a hold of myself. There's no way they'll be able to hear me.

Ringo comes running over.

'I'll come with you guys,' he shouts, signalling at Jazz and Jake who're snogging each other's faces off again.

Oh great.

Ryan puts his arm around my waist and guides me out of the stage arena. I feel so safe and protected when he's around. When we get out of the stage arena and begin walking amongst hundreds of tents, his hand drops. The urge to grab hold of it, with it being so close to mine that I can feel the heat from it, is unbearable. Literally unbearable. Every now and again the back of his fingers will brush against mine and we'll awkwardly apologise to each other.

'You getting tired Pops?' Ringo asks me after about twenty minutes of walking, breaking me out of my concentration not to touch Ryan.

'No, I'm fine,' I lie, wishing he'd just leave me alone. He's really beginning to annoy me.

'Don't worry,' Ringo says, slipping his arm round my waist. 'You can always lean on me if you're tired.'

I look down, horrified, realising that he intends to leave his hand there. Oh God, this is terrible. His clammy hand is staying draped around me. I resist the urge to throw him off and punch him in the face, reasoning that it would probably be mean. Ryan looks over, a comical grin on his face. I try to show as much discomfort on my face as possible but he just seems to find it even funnier.

Luckily it's not long until we're back at camp. I spot the leopard print tent first and then Izzy and Grace who seem to have been getting to know the bearded guys in the tent next to us a lot better. They're sat on fold up chairs, flirting outrageously and smoking what I'm sure is weed.

'Hey guys.'

'Hey, you're back,' Izzy slurs. 'Have a beer. These are our new friends.'

She goes around the group and introduces them to us, but I forget their names as soon as she's told us, more interested in what their tattoos are of. So far I've spotted an eagle eating a chicken, a dog on a motorbike and a 'love you mum'.

I get a warm beer and sit around the fire, as far away from Ringo as I can. I down the first one, thirstier than I thought and then grab another. My body begins to de-clench and I relax, glad to no longer have Ringo touching me. I listen to the distant hum of the rock music and stare into orange and blue flames of the fire.

It's funny, but from here the band doesn't actually sound half bad. Plus, it seems that I judged the bearded guys we've adopted a bit too early. They're actually really nice, with Butch telling me about his mum and the history behind his tattoo. Something to do with an ex-girlfriend and fried chicken.

'You want some Poppy?' Butch asks, offering the joint.

'No thanks,' I refuse politely.

Ryan takes a quick puff and I stare at him disapprovingly.

'What?' he says, glaring back at me.

'Nothing,' I snap.

If Ryan gets stoned then I really will have no-one to look after me. Calm down Pops. You can look after yourself. You're a grown woman. Yet the nerves still seem to be getting to me. I need to get really, really drunk. A familiar nagging begins in my bladder.

'Izzy, where's the toilet?'

'I don't know. Somewhere over there,' she slurs, pointing vaguely into the distance. Her eyes are completely glazed over and I think that it's probably the first time I've seen her well and truly smashed.

'Ryan,' I ask, embarrassed that I have to show that I do in fact wee. 'Do you know where the toilet is?'

'Um...I think I saw a sign for them on the way back,' he says, sounding vague.

'Could you show me? Or better still...come with me?' I whisper, feeling pathetic.

He studies my face for a second, obviously wondering if I'm joking. 'Yeah, OK. But quickly, otherwise your boyfriend will want to come with us.' He smiles towards Ringo and I dig him in the ribs.

We begin to walk into the darkness again and the same urge to hold onto Ryan takes over me. It feels like every nerve ending I possess is on high alert. Get a hold of yourself Poppy.

'God, it's really dark isn't it?' I say, breaking the awkward silence. 'Duh.'

Well that was comforting. I grab on to the edge of his t-shirt and clutch on tighter as we get further and further away, my mouth becoming dry with panic. I should have told him to stick to the main paths instead of picturing him naked.

'Why are you so panicky?' he asks, his eyes wide with confusion.

'I'm not!' I protest a bit too quickly. 'I'm fine. Oh look, there it is!' I point to a sign that says toilets. Behind it is a row of porta-loos.

'I'll wait here,' he says, sticking his hands in his pockets.

I take another look at the line of porta-loos, immediately wishing I hadn't. They look so grubby. There's only one temporary light next to them which flickers every couple of seconds. It's like a horror movie set. When the lights aren't flickering it's completely pitch black. Basically, the place you pee if you want to get raped.

'Well?' he says, giving me a quizzical look. 'Are you gonna go or what?'

'I...I don't think I can,' I whimper, trying to ignore my bulging bladder.

'Are you fucking joking?' he roars, exhaling sharply with the strangest expression on his face. Anger flashes in his eyes, making him look hostile, even furious. 'Did you seriously make me walk all of this way just to change your mind?'

I'm slightly stung, despite myself. He looks so pissed off that I wonder if it would be safer to just chance it and wee in these toilets. And possibly get raped.

'I just...I'm kind of...scared,' I stammer, dropping my eyes to the floor in a flush of embarrassment.

'Scared? What the hell are you scared of?' he snaps, abruptly exasperated.

Right, that's it. How dare he make me feel this stupid. My temper starts to flare and I glare defiantly at him.

'The fucking lights broken and it looks like a scene from crime watch. Call me stupid, but I normally listen to that sixth sense which says DANGER. I'm not one of these little twits you're used to dealing with who you can scare into doing anything. I have my own mind thank you!'

Surprise flits across his face and I wait for him to say something, out of breath from my little rant.

'Woah! Over reaction or what?' he laughs.

Yet again he's made me feel pathetic. Why do I set myself up every time!? I don't even know why I like this guy, he's a complete knob.

'Do you want me to come in with you?' he asks, trying to catch my eye.

I turn to glare at him, but the minute he catches my eye I fight the urge to burst into tears. Why is it that whenever I get angry it ends up with me wanting to cry? My emotions always betray me.

'Ok,' I whisper, afraid that my normal voice would break.

'Come on then.' He guides me in, seeming a lot more patient. Probably terrified that I'll cry.

I look inside at the toilet seat, black from grime, vomit still in the bottom of the bowl.

He huffs as we both squeeze into the porta-loo. 'I never thought you'd be the scaredy little girl type,' he smiles.

'Just shut up,' I snap. He turns round to face the door and I lower my knickers. I hover over the toilet, suddenly feeling really shy. I really don't want him to hear me pee.

'Can you cover your ears or something?'

He snorts. 'Why, I've heard you get sick.'

'Just shut up and sing or something will you!'

He covers his ears and starts singing some rubbish pop song, really struggling to hit the high notes. I hope he's taking the piss and he doesn't honestly think he can sing.

'All done,' I say, pulling his hands away from his ears. I pull the flush with my elbows, desperate not to touch anything with my hands.

'What a shame, I was just getting to the chorus.'

'Oh, how will we live,' I say sarcastically.

When we walk out into the fresh air there's a midget dressed up in an orange felt suit with black stripes drawn on with felt tip pen. I think he's supposed to be a tiger. Could tonight get any more surreal?

'Go to the tiger show! Free entry! Free shots!' he bellows.

I smile widely but try not to laugh. I mean, that would be cruel.

Ryan politely takes a voucher from him.

'You fancy it?' he asks out of nowhere.

'Really?' I ask, taken aback by his sudden mood change. 'I mean, you don't want to trek back a hundred miles to sit around a field with a load of hairy bikers?' I ask sarcastically.

He laughs and grabs my hand. God, it's so warm. I shut my eyes and drink it in for a second. We follow the tiger's instructions to the show which seems to be held in a large green tent. We stick our head through the hole and are straight away ushered to our seats by a lady with purple hair.

'Quickly, the shows about to start,' she says, as she gives us a shot each.

'So, what do you think the show will be about?' he asks me before knocking back his shot.

'I don't know. Something to do with tigers I guess?'

He takes the shot instinctively off me and does that one too.

'Don't want you getting sick again, do we,' he chuckles.

I dig him in the ribs and settle back to watch a random show about tigers, just glad to still be with him, completely uninterrupted from Grace and her giant breasts.

The curtains open and a woman painted orange comes out onto the stage dressed in a strappy bikini and hooker heels, with random bits of fur stuck to her and whiskers drawn on. Rock music blares out of speakers, slowly at first, while she dances artistically around the stage. Maybe this is going to be one of those arty farty affairs where you realise how sad it is to be a tiger. This could be beautiful.

Just then a male tiger comes out, then three men dressed in black with balaclavas over their faces. The minute they arrive I know it's going another way. The music cranks up into a faster pace and two wooden crosses are wheeled onto the stage. I turn to look at Ryan, but his face is transfixed on the stage and I can't read his expression.

The balaclava guys start running after the tigers and captures them, tying them up to the crucifixes. Then they take out these weird looking steel instruments while the woman screams. I'm suddenly not sure whether this is really part of the show or if they've broken in here. 'Oh my God, should we help her?' I ask Ryan, clutching onto his t-shirt again.

'No, it's part of the show...I think,' he says, his forehead crinkled.

I turn back to the stage and before my eyes, the ninjas start piercing the tiger's body parts. First they pierce the man's nipples. I watch the rest through the tiny gaps in between my fingers, it's too intriguing to look away. The ninja's pierce the woman's nipples, her breasts completely on show now.

A sickening feeling creeps into my stomach and I get the overwhelming urge to run away. I probably would if I wasn't so frozen in my place. They cut off the man's boxer shorts, exposing his giant penis. My mouth falls open in shock, before they pierce that too. I lean into Ryan, burying my head into his chest and this time he comforts me, hugging me with his arms. I pray that I'll pass out from shock, but I can still hear the screams and rock music, even with my hands over my ears. It's like a nightmare.

After about five minutes the music stops abruptly and I look up to see all of them un-chained and bowing like it's a normal play. Like it's Shakespeare or something!

'OH MY GOD!' I shout at Ryan over the clapping. 'Why the hell is everyone clapping? That was horrific. It was like watching a horror movie live.'

'Yeah...well, that was...different,' he says, with a broad grin.

'Different? That was fucking awful! Come on, I need a drink.' I stand up and drag him out of there.

We stumble upon a cute little outside bar, which reminds me of a pool bar on holiday. It's made of cheap wood and looks like a firm shove would push it over, but it's kind of pretty. A few plastic flowers and twinkle lights tied around the roof make it look slightly magical.

We settle down at the bar and order a few shots. I know I don't normally do them, and Ryan does look a bit worried as I knock them back, but I honestly need them. Once I've done them I immediately feel the confident, blurry haze take over me, and I'm glad. I need to feel pissed for this evening to even start to feel normal again.

'Do you do cocktails?' I ask the barman, looking for a menu.

'Sorry darling. Only cocktails we do here are shandies and they're only for pussies who can't take the pace.'

'Well two beers then,' Ryan says chuckling. 'So,' he says, turning to me. 'Do you reckon she's single?'

'Who?' I ask confused, looking around.

'Miss Tiger,' he smiles playfully.

'I think she's out of your league. I mean, I think she's in a whole other league. Or planet, whichever you prefer.'

I burst out laughing, a mix of drunkenness taking over my body and the release of the stress I've been carrying in my stomach since the show started. He joins in and before I know it we're laughing so hard that I've snorted a few times and tears are falling out of his eyes.

I need to ask him about the Annabel situation before I forget my name.

'So Ryan,' I begin, mustering up all the strength I have. 'You work in family law. You must know about divorces, right?'

He looks back at me strangely.

210

'Why? You're not secretly married are you?' he smirks.

'Obviously not,' I snort. 'But if someone was planning on getting a divorce, but they signed on to the family business beforehand would they still be entitled to it?'

'Yeah of course. If it's signed in their name it would be theirs regardless.'

'So if my....I mean, if this someone's husband owned a third of the business they would have to buy out their half?'

'Yeah,' he says seriously. 'Actually in the divorce she'd probably also be able to claim half of his share in the company too.'

'You are joking?' I say to myself.

This evil witch is going to ruin my family.

'Why? Who's in trouble?' he asks.

'No-one!' I shout sharply. 'No-one at all!' I laugh unnaturally.

I get my phone out and frantically text Ollie to warn him.

DO NOT let her sign those papers. Under any circumstances!

'So how's Tabitha? Is it going well? I ask as casually as I can.

'Yeah fine thanks,' he says vaguely.

'And have you still managed to abstain from her?' I ask, a large grin on my face.

'Yep. No sex for me.'

'Well cheers to that,' I say, a warm glowing feeling going through my body. No sex means they're barely going out. They're basically cousins.

We carry on drinking and before I know it we're both so drunk that we've sung karaoke and danced on the bar to Bon Jovi. How it didn't collapse I don't know. I've won a competition for best air guitar, gaining us free drinks for the rest of the night. The next time I needed the toilet I've just gone to the nearest corner and held onto Ryan while I've squatted and peed, managing to wee on my own feet a little bit. But I don't even care! I'm having the most wonderful night. I really don't want it to end. Ryan has totally cut loose, showing me a side I never knew he had. He's so care free. And beautiful. So so beautiful.

'I'm afraid that we're closing up for the night guys,' the grey haired bar man says to us.

I look around and notice that we're the only ones left.

'How old are you?' I blurt out.

'Poppy!' Ryan slurs.

'Sorry, I'm just interested,' I slur back.

'I'm sixty-three, but I don't feel a day over twenty-one,' he says, smiling kindly.

'Well, you look g-g-great'.

'Maybe time to take her home, hmm?' he says to Ryan.

Why is he talking about me like I'm not here? Ryan is just as drunk as me, but he nods back, as if I'm some huge liability.

'Come on, miss aggressive drunk,' Ryan says, dragging me off my bar stool.

'I just want to finish my drink.' I clutch onto it for dear life.

'I think you've had enough,' he says, taking it out of my hand and placing it on the bar.

'Wait!'

'What?' he says, stopping in his tracks, seeming alarmed. Maybe I was a bit loud.

'I can't walk with these stupid things on.' I throw off my flip flops and place my bare feet on the warm grass. 'Aah, that's better'.

'You really are a bit of a hippy aren't you?' he says, with a wicked grin.

'Whatever,' I slur trailing on behind him, not caring that he's again decided to walk off the main path. It's more private this way.

We walk for another few hundred yards singing Bon Jovi and getting shouted at by people trying to sleep in their tents. Wimps.

'My feet hurt,' I wail.

'Don't be such a baby Pops. We're nearly there,' he says playfully.

I hate being called a baby. It instantly puts my back up. Unless someone's saying 'nobody puts baby in the corner'. That's *obviously* different. I'll show him. I'll prove to him that I can walk for miles.

'Do you want a lift?' he asks, humour curving his lips.

'No! I'm fine on my own thanks,' I say defiantly. 'I have two feet.'

God – I'm not even making sense.

'Come here,' he says, flinging me on his back into a piggy back, before I can protest. I wrap my hands round his neck and lean my face against his. It's so warm and soft.

'You know, sometimes you're so moody,' I say.

'Ri...ght?'

'But tonight you were so fun. I like fun. I like lollipops too.' I literally can't stop this shit coming out of my mouth. It's like my tongue doesn't belong to me anymore!

'Yeah, I like lollipops too. And, I'm not moody, I'm just misunderstood,' he says, his voice serious.

'That's something that moody people always say. You and Grace should get married. You could have beautiful moody children...and you could get a moody dog...and maybe even a moody parrot.'

He laughs. 'You think I'm beautiful, do you?' he asks, his voice husky.

'But moody. Let it be noted that I think you're moody.'

'Don't worry, I think I get the hint that I'm moody. But you're too nice.'

'Too nice?'

'Yep,' he nods. 'It's funny. You get yourself in loads of trouble from just being too nice.'

'Well, I'm *sorry* for being too nice,' I say like a moody child.

'Well maybe that's why we complement each other. I'm moody and you're too nice. Together we're probably a normal person.'

'Yeah, we'd have normal children. But Grace is very beautiful. I would love her,' I slur, wondering why I'm not walking. That's right, I'm on his back.

'Well, then you can marry her. I'm not interested.'

'Good. Beautiful people should not get together. It's too perfect.'

'Well I guess there's no hope for me and you then,' he chuckles.

'Huh? You think I'm beautiful?' I slur, surprised.

'You're alright I suppose,' he says, after a pause.

It's enough for me to start singing.

'You really love me, you want my babies, you want to marry me and kiss and squeeze me,' I sing to him.

'OK,' he says drily. 'We're back now anyway.'

He puts me down in front of my leopard print tent and I look inside to see Izzy and Grace passed out, still fully clothed.

'Well, goodnight,' he says, punching me on my shoulder.

'Ouch!' Night.'

I crawl into the tent, but something stirs in my stomach. I really don't want the night to end. I don't want to be away from him. I crawl out and go up to his tent.

'Ryan,' I whisper through the material. 'Ryan, are you awake?' I unzip the tent and he looks up just as he takes his top off, exposing his beautiful soft skin.

'Alright trouble. I thought you went to bed?' he whispers.

'Well, I don't want to. I want to cause more trouble,' I giggle. 'And your wife is snoring too loud.'

'I'm tired though,' he says, pushing his hair back with his hands.

'Me too. Can I sleep with you? I mean, you know...just to sleep.'

'OK, but I've only got the one sleeping bag.'

'That's OK,' I say already jumping into it. 'I can share.'

I snuggle into his pillow and feel him try and squeeze in next to me. I lay silent and melt when he wraps his arm around me, his hand resting in between my boobs. His legs go in between my legs. I breathe deeply as he pulls my hair away from my face and kisses me on the neck.

'Night Pops.'

'Mmm,' is all I can manage before I give up fighting the tiredness and drift off into my dream world.

Chapter 16

When I wake up I search for his hand before I open my eyes. All I feel is the cold sleeping bag. I open my eyes and look around the tent for him, but again nothing. Where the hell is he? My dream flashes up in my head and I remember vaguely that me and Ryan were lollipops that got married, and Grace was a mars bar that melted in the sun. How random.

'Ryan?' I call quietly, suddenly feeling vulnerable.

What time is it anyway? I glance at my watch and see that it's 9am. I unzip the tent door and find him sitting on a chair in front of the fire, his forehead wrinkled up in deep thought.

'You ok?' I ask quietly as I walk around the silent tents. It doesn't look like anyone else in the camp is awake yet.

'Yeah,' he says, looking up and smiling weakly. 'Just thinking.'

'Oh, ok. Anything...interesting?'

I feel so awkward. Last night all of the walls were down. Well, almost all of them. I don't know if we're being so candid today and it makes me feel tongue-tied.

'Nah,' he says, looking at me, his eyes enigmatic.

OK, what the hell do I say to that? I gaze at him expectantly, waiting for him to speak.

'I was just thinking that life is complicated,' he sighs.

'O...kay. What brought on this sudden bought of depression?'

'Nothing. It's just...I seem to always make things difficult for myself,' he says, seeming to be torn by some internal dilemma.

'How?' I ask, removing the sleep from my eyes.

'I just...I just think me and you are best as friends,' he blurts out quickly.

'Oh.' I'm still too asleep to be as truly upset as I know I will be later.

'Yeah, that's fine,' I shrug, trying not to look bothered and hoping my cheeks aren't blushing.

'I just think you'd be better off without me.' He looks into the fire, his expression blank.

215

Did I come on to him last night or something? I must seriously be giving off majorly desperate vibes for him to have to be clarifying it to me like this.

'Anyway, happy birthday. What do you want for breakfast?' He smiles, seeming to be pleased to have got that off his chest.

I'm so mortified. I shouldn't have to feel this humiliated on my birthday and it's only 9am.

'There's a choice?' I smile. I look around for this supposed food while I desperately try not to show my disappointment.

'Yep. There's beans or the burger van?' His dazzling face is friendly, a slight smile on his flawless lips, but his eyes are careful. Probably scared to lead me on in case I'm still planning our wedding.

'Shall I wake the others?' I ask, desperate to get myself out of this situation.

'Yeah, you better do. I'd hate to see Grace hungry. I reckon she'd murder someone,' he says, with a cheeky grin.

I laugh gratefully, pleased that he's lightened the mood. I love it when he laughs with that twinkle in his eye, like we're both in on some private joke. But we're just friends remember. Yeah, I remember, I think sadly.

I go into the leopard print tent.

'Guys, wake up. We're going to get breakfast.'

I hear Grace grunt from the black sleeping bag. Izzy stretches out, yawning so wide that I can see her tonsils.

'Morning Pops. Happy birthday,' Izzy claps. She immediately flinches and touches her temples. 'God, I can't believe how much we drank last night.'

'Yeah I know.' I'm only too aware of my own headache.

'God, if any of my clients could see me now they'd be horrified.'

I laugh because I feel I should, but my hearts not in it. What Ryan said is starting to sink in. I'm so pathetic. I feel just like I'm back at school and the popular boy's told me I don't stand a chance. I might as well have my braces back.

'So anyway, happy birthday to you,' she starts singing. 'Happy birthday to you. Happy birthday dear P – o – p – p – y.'

216

'Shut the fuck up!' Grace shouts from underneath her sleeping bag.
'Happy birthday to you,' she whispers, ending the song and sticking two fingers up at the sleeping bag.

'I'm going to wake Jazz'. I get out before Grace can rear her ugly head.

'Knock, knock,' I say outside Jake's tent. 'Jazz – can I come in?'

I *really* don't want to find them having sex. I slowly unzip the door of the tent, peering in to check the coast is clear. I'm relieved to see that they're both asleep.

I crawl in and lay down next to Jazz. She looks so cosy, even in last night's smudged eye liner. So cosy that I'm tempted to just forget breakfast and crash here for a while. That's exactly what I fancy doing - hiding away from Ryan. But then I remember the others.

'Jazz,' I whisper in her ear. 'Wake up.'

She stirs slightly and then slowly opens her eyes like an angel.

'Morning babe,' she croaks, stretching out.

'How you feeling?'

'I'm OK actually.' She clears her throat and grabs a cigarette out of her bag.

'How was the rest of the concert?' I ask, knowing that it would have been shit.

'Yeah it was good,' she says, unconvinced as she lights it and inhales deeply. I roll my eyes. 'Oh, what am I saying, it was shit and you know it was shit.'

I laugh, but quickly cover my mouth with my hand, trying to stop myself as I remember Jake still sleeping.

'Oh, don't worry about him. He'd sleep through a hurricane.'

'Really?' I examine his face closer.

'Totally! I saw a spider one morning and screamed for about ten minutes, and when I ran in to get him he was still asleep! I had to practically sit on him to wake him up. It's really weird! He blames it on living in a house full of noisy men. He's apparently learnt to just tune them out.'

'Weird. Have you been to his house?' I enquire, eager to learn how serious this relationship is.

'Yeah, although, it makes our place look like a palace,' she snorts.
I grimace. It must be a bloody squat.
'Ok Pops, no need to look *so* horrified.'
I quickly snap my face back to normal, feeling bad.
'Oh sorry, I didn't mean to. Anyway,' I lower my voice a whisper
again, 'how bloody old *is* he?'
'I was waiting for you to ask this.' She rolls her eyes. 'He's 21,
which isn't actually that much younger than us.'
'I know, but he looks twelve!'
'Shut up!' she giggles. 'For now, it's...fun.'
'And what about Ollie?'
'What *about* Ollie?' she asks avoiding my gaze. 'Anyway, where the
hell did you two sneak off to last night?'
'What do you mean?' I ask innocently, trying not to grimace as I think
of Ryan and how I must have behaved after the first drink. Why am I
such a drunken lush? 'We came back to the tent didn't we,' I say
vaguely. Hopefully by the time they got back Grace and Izzy were
asleep and would stack up with my story.
'Yeah,' she smiles knowingly. 'But then you went off, apparently to
the toilet, and never came back.'
'We did come back!' I retort quickly. Probably a bit too quickly in
hindsight.
'Well, eventually! What time did you make it back?' she asks sitting
up, her eyes wide with interest.
'Um...it was...about 3am, I think?'
A wide smile spreads across her face.
'Well that's a lie straight away. We went to sleep at 4.30am and there
was still no sign of you.'
'Oh....Ok, it was...a bit later than that then.'
She studies my face for a moment. 'You don't know what time you
got back, do you?' she smiles accusingly.
'Yes I do! It was....a bit after 5am...I think.'
'Ha ha! I knew it! You dirty scaly wag! You have no idea what time
you got back.' She lays back, laughing hard.

'Oh, whatever.' I fold my arms over my chest. 'Look, do you wanna come for breakfast or not?'

'Oooh! Tetchy about your night with Ryan are we? Why ever could that be?' she teases.

'I'm going. Be ready in five minutes or we're going without you.'

*   *   *

An hour later, and after trekking the distance to the nearest burger bar and queuing up for what seemed like forever, we all have bacon and sausage rolls with teas, lying on some nearby grass eating them. It's actually a nice day today, a clear blue sky with blinding sunshine. I'd appreciate it more if I didn't have Ringo squashed up against me like an eager little puppy.

'So, what did you guys get up to last night?' Izzy asks smiling towards me and Ryan.

I glance quickly at Ryan, wondering how much he remembers. Unfortunately for me, I can now remember everything. All of the little cringe worthy words I said – everything! No wonder he felt the need to tell me clearly this morning that we were just friends and nothing else. I behaved like a love sick puppy. How could I have been that drunk but then still remember it all? It seems really unfair.

Every time I look at him my mouth goes a bit numb at the memory of being curled up in his arms. Probably because I know I'll never be able to do that again. It's not something friends do often. Well, unless you're me and Jazz after a night dancing and a greasy kebab.

'Um...we just saw a show and had some drinks,' I answer as casually as I can. I just wish my voice wasn't quavering as much as it is. I stuff a big bite of my roll in my mouth so that I can't answer any more questions.

'Really? What show?' she asks, seeming genuinely interested.

I point to my mouth and smile. Ha ha – she can't make me swallow this.

'It was a...modern art show,' Ryan adds grinning at me.

219

'Yeah, that's right. And after that we went for some cocktails at a nice bar,' I add, playing along.

His grin breaks into a laugh and I join in against my better judgement. I just hope he doesn't take my un-lady like snorts for another sign that I'm in love with him. I look back at Izzy and suddenly notice everyone staring at both of us like we're mad.

'Sounds like a nice evening,' Izzy says, her mouth pouting in confusion.

'Anyway,' Grace interrupts, placing her untouched food onto the grass beside her. 'What time are we leaving?'

'I thought that maybe we'd catch another band before we go,' Jake smiles, as eager as ever.

I see Jazz grimace discreetly.

'Ok, sure. Whatever you want,' Jazz smiles un-convincingly.

'Can I catch a ride with you guys?' I ask Ryan. I don't really care anymore about hurting Jake's feelings. I just want to get out of here.

'Yeah course,' he smiles.

I look over to Jazz. She looks like she wants to kill herself rather than go to another gig.

'Ok, I'll see you later then,' I say to her.

'Yeah, I'll see you tonight.' She smiles and kisses me on the cheek.

'Why, what's happening tonight?' I ask, confused.

I was looking forward to an early night after the fiasco that was last night.

She stares wide eyed at Izzy and Grace. It suddenly dawns on me. Of course, they've planned something for my birthday! It's obvious. They've gone behind my back and organised a surprise birthday party for me. I'd actually almost forgotten it was today myself.

'Nothing! Nothing at all. I meant, you know...I might pop round,' she says, in her high pitched Oxford voice. Her face looks unnaturally flustered.

Well two can play that game.

'OK, because, it is my birthday today,' I say innocently. 'You do remember, right? You haven't even wished me happy birthday yet.'

'Your birthday?' she says, in mock surprise. 'Oh, of course! It's your
birthday! I'd completely forgot!'
She really is the worst actress in the world. They're definitely
planning a party.
'Oh. Well, maybe I'll see you later then,' I say, playing my part,
smiling on the inside.
'OK. I'll call you or something.'
They really are the worst liars in the world. I know I said I didn't want
to do anything but it's nice that they've gone out of their way to
organise something. I suppose I should be grateful. And truth be told,
I am actually pretty excited. I need some cheering up.
'Pops, let me get your number first,' Ringo says, jumping up.
Damn it.

*   *   *

The drive home always seems longer than the drive to get somewhere.
It doesn't help when you're crushed between Izzy and Grace's
enormous suitcase. Happy birthday me.
'I'm just gonna get a drink. You guys want anything?' Ryan asks as
we pull into a petrol station.
'Nah, I'm cool,' Izzy says.
'Me too,' Grace says.
'Ok, back in a minute.'
As soon as the door is shut, Grace swings her head back to us, an
excited grin on her face. I don't actually think I've ever seen her face
be anything but mean. It looks strangely unnatural.
'So guess what?' she says, giddy with excitement.
'What?' Izzy says, excitedly clapping her hands.
'I think tonight's going to be the night with Ryan,' she announces,
twirling her honey highlights with her fingers.
My mouth drops open. Did I just hear her right?
'Do you think?' Izzy asks, almost jumping up and down in her seat.
'Completely,' she smiles smugly. 'He's been giving me the eye all
day.'

'Sorry? Did I just hear you right? You and Ryan are going to....' I swallow the lump in my throat. 'You're going to...sleep together tonight?'

Her expression instantly changes to a nasty disgusted look, as if she's just smelt bad fish.

'Sorry, but who invited you into the conversation?' she sneers.

'Err, it's a bit hard to ignore when I'm in the same car as you,' I retort defensively.

'Well maybe you should mind your own business,' she snaps.

'Then maybe you shouldn't talk about it in front of people!' I say, my voice erupting in an angry growl. I should be angry, but instead I feel I could burst into tears.

'Gracie, she was just asking,' Izzy protests. I smile gratefully at her.

'For your information, me and Ryan used to have a thing,' Grace says, pulling out a mirror and inspecting her reflection.

'Yeah I know that.'

'Well, then you'll know that things have been hotting up recently.' Her voice is rising in conviction. 'I keep catching him looking at me and I just know he's picturing me naked.'

Oh my God. Have I really been that much of a fool to think that he'd been staring at me? He's obviously into Grace. I mean, who wouldn't be? She's like a beautiful movie star. I've even imagined her naked a few times – in a very heterosexual way of course. Just purely from envy. That's why Ryan let me down gently this morning.

'What about Tabitha?'

'Please,' she smiles, 'as if she's any competition for me. They haven't even slept together.'

'Well, good luck,' I say under my breath.

'I don't need luck honey,' she smiles smugly. 'Look at me.'

She's probably right. She might just snap her fingers and he'll run into her bedroom and strip naked. Then I remember his cruel words about her last night. Surely he can't be into her if he's talking like that? For some unknown reason I suddenly feel sorry for her. She can't help it that she's obsessed with him. Hell, if I can't help it how could she? I should open a support group. Call it ROL – Ryan's obsessive losers.

'OK. I just don't want you getting hurt.'

Her eyes bulge open and her throat physically retracts, as if she was taking a large intake of breath.

'Me get hurt? Oh, don't worry honey. I know Ryan, unlike you. If anyone's going to get hurt it's you.'

'Me? What have I got to do with it?' I ask in a flush of embarrassment.

'Oh, don't pretend I don't catch you looking at him, all pathetic and puppy eyed,' she says, in mollifying tones. 'It's quite amusing actually. Me and Ryan laugh about it sometimes.'

'What?' I ask, swallowing the second lump in my throat. 'First of all I don't know what the hell you're talking about and second, you and Ryan are laughing at me behind my back?'

'Let's just say we find you very amusing,' she smirks.

Oh my God. Paranoia sweeps over me. I've been so naive. Such an idiot.

'Gracie! Don't be such a bitch,' Izzy says shortly.

'Well, I'm sorry if the truth hurts,' Grace snaps. She turns back to the front just as Ryan opens the door. He smiles at me, but I turn my head.

'Pops, I know you said you didn't want anything, but seen as you are the birthday girl, I got you a little present.' I turn my head in intrigue to see him holding out a pack of jelly babies.

I still feel sick from his betrayal. I can barely look at him. I turn to stare out of the window; ignoring him completely as a feeling of complete empty sadness takes over my body.

'O...kay. I take it you don't like jelly babies then,' I hear him say under his breath as he starts the engine.

When I get home I run to my bedroom and spend a good couple of hours crying alone in my bedroom. Happy fucking birthday. Why is it every year I get a terrible day? Normally I just injure myself, but this year it's far worse. To have my feelings hurt this badly. I mean, I thought I knew Ryan. Little did I know he just finds me amusing to have around. Like a stupid little jester or something.

I stare at my phone, declaring myself pathetic that no-one has text me to wish me happy birthday. Not even my parents. Does no-one in the entire world love me? I scroll down to Jazz and press dial. She's bound to have planned something for my birthday.

'Hello?' she shouts, loud rock music playing in the background.

'Hey Jazz, it's me. Listen, I know I said I didn't want to do anything for my birthday, but I've changed my mind. Do you want to go out?'

'Huh? Sorry Pops, I can barely hear you! I'm still stuck at this stupid festival. To be honest, I don't actually think I'll be able to make it back tonight. Jake's talking about staying for another night.'

I know her game. She's planned a surprise birthday party for me, I know it. As if she would stay at a festival just for Jake. Surely I'm way more important?

'Oh yeah, is this your fake ruse?' I say smiling to myself. 'It's ok Jazz, I want to celebrate my birthday now. You can tell me all about the surprise party. I promise I won't get mad. I'm kind of looking forward to it actually.'

'What party? Chick, you told us not to do anything for you. There's no party. I'm really sorry babe, but why don't we go out for lunch tomorrow to make it up to you?'

My stomach drops and the same depression begins to creep over me again. No-one cares about me.

'Oh...OK. Yeah I suppose that's great.' I try not to sound ungrateful. She doesn't even have her usual high pitched Oxford acting voice on to make me doubt her. She must be telling the truth.

'Great. Can I call you tomorrow then?'

'Yeah, fine.' I just want to get off the phone so I can cry.

'OK, love you babes. Happy birthday.'

'Thanks,' but she's already hung up.

I bury my head under the duvet and let out some loud sobs, hoping no-one can hear me through the wall.

My phone rings again and I pick it up before checking who it is.

'Happy birthday darling!' my mum's shrill voice sings down the phone, before I've even had a chance to say hello.

'Hi Mum,' I say, my voice flat and boring.

'Hi darling. Well...are you running late or what?'

What is she talking about?

'Huh?'

'Your birthday lunch round Auntie Beryl's. We've all been here for about half an hour and I just wondered where on earth you are?'

'Lunch? I don't remember any mention of lunch?'

'Darling I sent you an e-mail,' she sighs heavily, as if I'm a massive inconvenience to her.

'E-mail? I never got an e-mail?'

'Really? I'm sure I pressed send?' She doesn't sound too convinced herself.

'Well you obviously didn't Mum. Did you not get Ollie to help you?'

'Excuse me Poppy, but I am more than capable of sending an e-mail. Since the college course, I'm what they call a whizz kid at computers.' Meaning she can just about turn it on.

'OK, whatever. Look, I didn't get it so I'm not sure if I can make it.'

'Don't be so ridiculous! I've baked a cake! Well, I've bought one. I'll tell them you'll be here in half an hour.'

'But the train will take me at least forty-five minutes!'

'See you soon darling!' she sings, ignoring me. 'Oh and do me a favour and be careful will you? We don't want any more accidents on your birthday.'

'Bye mum.'

Chapter 17

When the taxi pulls up at the familiar white terrace house my stomach starts getting butterflies. Why on earth are we having a birthday lunch round here anyway? Probably Mum not wanting a mess at her house.

'Thanks again Tony,' I say to my regular taxi driver as I get out.

'No probs love. But remember, be careful today. I don't want to be picking you up tonight and taking you to hospital like last year.'

'I'll try my best.' I slam the door a little too hard and run up to the familiar yellow front door.

Auntie Beryl swings the door open. She's wearing a floral pink and yellow dress which is far too short for her age group, and holding what looks like a flower vase full of wine.

'Darling! What took you so long?'

'Sorry Auntie Beryl.' I hug her tightly, suffocated by her strong floral perfume. 'But Mum forgot to tell me about it.'

'Why am I not surprised?' she smiles at me before throwing her head back laughing.

I follow her through the house and breathe in the stir fry smell which always seems to linger in the kitchen, even though I've never actually seen her cook. Her cookery books are dusty and yellowed at the edges from the sunlight, never seeming to have been touched.

Despite this, I love her house. Even though the yellow wallpaper is peeling at the edges, with patches of damp, and the ceiling is just as yellow from the years of smoking, it reminds me of being younger. It was modern then, everything brand new. She used to get these massive sheets of paper, almost as tall as me and I'd spend entire afternoons drawing wedding dresses while her and Mum smoked and drank coffee.

'See! She's not a total tom-boy,' she'd whisper to my mum.

'Yes. I suppose there's still hope for her,' Mum would say, sighing heavily.

The same pink happy birthday banner that they use every year hangs above the sofa.

'They're all in the garden' Auntie Beryl says, gesturing towards the French doors. 'Drink?'

'I'd love a beer,' I sigh.

'You know I can't get you a beer in front of your mum. I'll get you a gin and tonic.'

She walks off towards the drinks cabinet and I walk through the French doors into the garden. My three brothers and Dad are there grimacing, probably already sick of Mum's constant moaning. Some friggin' party.

'Happy birthday love,' my Dad says, hitting me on the shoulder.

I put my hand up to my shoulder, it already throbbing, and smile. I must get my awkward body language from him.

'Yeah, happy birthday Po Po,' Ollie waves as he puffs on his cigarette. God, it's at events like this I wished I still smoked. We used to always sneak off at family dos and have a cheeky fag. My Dad would always come looking for us and end up having one himself while we all basically hid from my mother.

'Here's your drink darling,' Auntie Beryl says, handing over my gin and tonic.

'Darling! Beryl just told me you asked for a beer?'

I turn to face my mum carrying out a Marks and Spencer's birthday cake, dressed in linen trousers and a smock top exposing far too much cleavage.

'You know you shouldn't be drinking anymore,' she says, shaking her head disapprovingly.

'Why not?'

'You're in your late twenties now darling. You need to be drinking water. It fights wrinkles apparently. Oh and what are you wearing?' She looks me up and down.

'Well I didn't have much time.' I cross my arms defensively, suddenly feeling like a boy.

'Well you could have still made an effort. And no make-up? Where's my make-up bag? I'll put some on you myself.'

She goes fussing around for it as I watch her and Auntie Beryl. They couldn't be more different, yet so similar at the same time. Even though they have the ridiculous matching names of Beryl and Meryl (I'll never understand my Grandma's logic), they look so different. Unlike Mum, Auntie Beryl has short dark hair, which she always wears down, straightened to within an inch of it's life. Her big brown eyes are always painted in far too much eye shadow, and her cheeks, once as sculpted as Mum's, have now gone a bit chubby. Yet they both have the same attitude to life. It's their way or the highway. Their opinions are the right ones and everyone else is insane.

'Here's your present anyway,' Richard says, handing over a purple shiny bag. 'Annabel picked it.'

Right on queue Annabel walks into the garden wearing a pale green short summer dress which shows off her olive skin perfectly. Hussy.

'Happy birthday,' she smiles innocently, wrapping her arm round Richard's waist.

'Abbey sends her apologies,' Henry smiles shyly.

'Cool. Are you excited about the wedding?' I ask, trying to make small talk. At least she's not another Annabel.

'Yeah, not long now,' he says politely, as if I'm a work colleague rather than sister.

I've never been close with Richard and Henry. They've always resented how much attention I got for being the much wanted girl, even though it turns out that I was a massive disappointment, refusing to wear a dress as soon as I could talk.

The household seemed to be split into two camps almost as soon as I was born. Mum's camp consisted of Henry, Richard and obviously Auntie Beryl. They were the over achievers. Always striving for better – a better house, better car, and better appearance.

Then there was my camp. Me, Ollie and Dad, who are quite happy to get pissed and watch Eastenders. Striving for better always sounded like far too much hard work. Although it does stand to reason that Ollie still lives at home at the age of twenty-eight and I'm living alone, soon to be eaten by cats.

'I still can't believe we're going to have a ginger in the family,' Mum says, as she paints blusher onto my cheeks.

'Mum!' I shout, shoving her slightly and nodding towards Henry.

'What?' she says, confused, as if she's done nothing wrong.

'Actually she's strawberry blonde,' Henry says, defensively, his arms tensely at his side.

'OK darling,' she smiles. 'I just hope that your genes take over and we don't have a ginger grandchild on our hands. That would really be something!'

'Mum! You can't say these things,' I almost shout, grabbing hold of her arms.

'Why not?'

'Strawberry blonde,' Auntie Beryl mutters under her breath with a muffled snort. 'How ridiculous.'

I smile an apology over to Henry, feeling in some way responsible for our insane Mother.

'Anyway Poppy,' Auntie Beryl suddenly shouts in excitement. 'What do you think of my new addition to the garden?'

Oliver and Dad roll their eyes as I search the garden desperately. How the hell would I know what was new? Every spare space in this garden is filled with something. There are hanging wooden wind chimes, hanging baskets, decorative pots, butterflies, cat ornaments. The concrete bench is filled with hundreds of multi-coloured scatter cushions with tiny mirrors and beads hanging from them. Auntie Beryl's still smiling wildly in anticipation.

'Um...I'm not sure,' I admit.

'Honestly Poppy! It's the new lemon candles.' She gestures to the centre of the table.

'Oh...lovely!' I say, with as much enthusiasm as I can muster.

'Yes, anything to warn off those bastard mosquitos that keep getting me.' She narrows her eyes as she looks around the garden.

I'd forgot about the mosquitos which she's sure stalk the garden, even though no one's ever been bitten.

'Anyway, let me give you my present.' She hands over a blue card.

I barely open the envelope before she shouts out 'It's pottery classes!'

'Pottery classes? Since when did she retire?' Ollie snorts.

'Oh do shut up Oliver!' she snarls at him before turning back to me. 'I thought that you might meet someone there. You know, like in Ghost.

It could be very romantic.' She stares off in the distance, a whimsical look on her face.

It's this very ridiculous romantic attitude that means she's alone living with three cats.

'Oh, thanks,' I say, trying desperately to sound enthusiastic.

'But she already has a man!' Mum corrects her.

'Oh yes, but I got it before the announcement,' Auntie Beryl says, topping up both of their wine glasses.

'What announcement?' I ask, puzzled.

'Oh...nothing,' Auntie Beryl says avoiding my gaze.

'I got you a manicure and pedicure,' Mum says proudly. 'You need to start looking more groomed now you're twenty-six. It might have been fine to look scruffy at twenty-five but now that you're on the wrong side you need to start looking after yourself.'

'Thanks,' I drool sarcastically.

'That's why I told the boys to get you anti-ageing cream.'

'Oh thanks for ruining the surprise!' Richard huffs.

'Anyway! Let's cut the cake!' she says, ignoring him. 'But none for you darling. Too many calories.'

'Oh, before the cake, why don't we get the business out of the way?' Dad says, turning to Annabel. 'Sign those documents?'

'Yes, great,' she smiles.

Shit. I feel my insides clenching. They're going to sign them now?

'Let's go into the study,' Dad says smiling eagerly, ushering Annabel out of the room.

'Doing business on Poppy's birthday. Ridiculous,' Mum mutters under her breath.

Richard, Annabel and Dad start walking out of the room. A new swoop of fear goes over me. I stare at Ollie and he looks back just as panicked.

'We'll be witnesses!' I exclaim before I think if this can even be done. Dad stares at me strangely before nodding. We follow him in, Ollie's eyes are nearly bulging out of his sockets. He's really not good in an emergency.

'So here's the contract,' Dad says, putting on his reading glasses and handing over a thick wad of paper. 'It's just what we discussed.'

There's a fountain pen next to it on the table. Ollie and I spot it at the same time. He looks at me and raises his eyebrows. I give him a nod. His hand covers the pen as he discreetly slides it off the table and puts it in his pocket.

'I'm sure it's fine,' Annabel smiles.

'Great. Where's that pen?' Dad asks, scanning the table.

'Beryl?' Dad calls. 'Do you have a pen we could borrow?'

'Don't worry,' Annabel smiles. She gets a pen out of her pocket and places it on the table. 'I have one.'

Crap. I feel my jaw tighten. My pulse quickens, my breaths become shallow.

'Could I see it?' I ask, sweat trickling down my neck.

I pick it up before I've had a response and pretend to scan over it seriously. I inhale a deep breath and muster up the loudest, wettest fake sneeze I can, covering the contract in my germs.

Dad and Annabel look back at me horrified.

'Whoops!' I laugh. Even my laugh sounds strained. 'Sorry. I think I ruined it.'

Dad snatches the contract back, his chubby cheeks red with frustration. He wipes it with his sleeve.

'No, I'd say it's still fine,' he smiles, handing it back over to Annabel.

I'm suddenly ill with panic. This can't happen, it just can't. My stomach curdles at the thought of Annabel taking away my Dad's business.

'I don't think you should do it!' I shout, a little too loudly. Everyone looks bad at me alarmed. 'I mean,' I swallow, trying to calm myself.

'I've got a really bad feeling about this. Almost like a...psychic feeling. It's like....some greater force is telling me it shouldn't be done today.'

Dad and Annabel look back at me confused. Ollie walks to the other side of the room with his head in his hands.

'You have a....a psychic feeling?' Annabel asks in disbelief.

It's funny, but now she's saying it back to me, I suppose it does sound kind of ridiculous.

'Yeah,' I nod, looking down, hoping they won't see me as I swallow hard, trying to compose myself. 'And....well, I think its bad luck for business to be done on my birthday.'

'But Poppy,' Dad tries to reason, 'this will take five minutes at the very most.' He smiles warningly at me.

'Don't worry,' Annabel smiles to Dad. 'Luckily I don't believe in superstitions.' She picks up the pen, flicking to the back page.

'Has it been done yet?' Mum asks, walking into the room holding a glass of wine.

'Almost,' Annabel smiles, trying to find the right page.

My insides are starting to turn to liquid. I can't breathe. The witch is going to ruin everything.

'But....but,' I say, struggling for anything, absolutely anything that could help.

I look at Ollie, desperate for him to come up with something.

Annabel's pen is almost touching the paper as little beads of sweat gather on my forehead. He opens his mouth, but then shuts it again.

'I've got a girl pregnant,' Ollie blurts out.

Everything happens quickly. Annabel drops her pen on the table, Mum drops her glass of wine on the floor and Dad falls back into the wall. I stare at him, dumbfounded.

Mum holds onto the table, her face as white as a ghost.

'You've....' she swallows, as if she is holding back the vomit. 'You've got a girl....pregnant?' she asks in disbelief.

'Yes,' he nods, meeting my eye for long enough to let me know this is a rouse. With him I wouldn't be shocked if it was true. Which is why this is such a brilliant excuse; it's so believable.

Dad steadies himself against the wall, his face red and blotchy.

'How could you have done this?' Dad asks him. 'I thought I always taught you boys to use a condom.' His voice is low and beaten.

'Don't say condom,' Mum cries, tears streaming down her face.

'Well maybe if we'd said condom a little more often when they were growing up he'd have learnt how to put one on!' Dad shouts.

'Maybe now isn't the best time,' Annabel says, getting up and backing out of the room.

'I can't believe this,' Mum cries, sinking dramatically to the floor. 'You've ruined your life! Got some little slut pregnant.'

'Whoops,' Ollie shrugs.

*   *   *

By the time I've made it to the front door, full fatigue has set in. Two hours of arguing really does take it out of you. Luckily Ollie remained vague and refused to tell the family who the girl that he'd got pregnant was.

I put the key in the door and am about to let myself in, when I remember my surprise party. I've been thinking about it on the train and I reckon Jazz is double bluffing me. Of course there's going to be a party. She and Izzy would have planned something for sure. Jazz must have just taken some acting classes. They might still be making arrangements now.

I knock on the door, just to let them know I'm coming in. There's no answer so I slowly walk into the hallway. I walk in the kitchen sure to find them frantically putting away banners and balloons, but everyone seems to be acting so ordinary. Izzy's doing squats, Grace is lying on the sofa in her knickers and a crop top watching A Place in the Sun and Ryan's making tea. Surely they wouldn't genuinely be ignoring the fact it's my birthday unless they're getting ready to take me out? So I perk myself up, have a shower and steal some of Grace's expensive body wash. I blow dry and straighten my hair and moisturise my skin with some of Jazz's coconut oil. By 8pm I'm getting a bit concerned that no-one's tried to get me out of the house. I mean, surely the guests should be starting to arrive by now?

I walk into the sitting room and find the three of them squashed on the sofa watching TV. Grace is still in her knickers and crop top, Izzy's in her stripy pink pyjamas and Ryan's in tracksuit bottoms and a tomato ketchup stained t-shirt. These really don't look like the kind of people that are about to host a surprise party for me.

'Hey Pops, you want some cheese on toast?' Izzy asks holding out a piece to me.

'No, I'm fine thanks,' I say pushing it out of my face. 'Actually I was wondering if anyone wanted to go out. You know, to celebrate my birthday?' I ask hopefully.

'Oh, sorry hun,' Izzy says, grimacing. 'I thought you said you didn't want me to do anything? The truth is I'm pretty knackered from last night and could do with just chilling.'

'Yeah me too,' Grace and Ryan chime in.

It seems that they're more in tune than I thought. Images of them together flash through my mind and I force them out again. I doubt they'd eat lasagne off of each other's naked bodies anyway.

'Oh, OK,' I say, deflated. 'Maybe I'll just watch some TV with you then.' I settle down on the floor and wrap my arms around my legs. This is some good quality acting these guys are doing. I mean, any minute now they're going to tell me we have to go out. Any minute now. Yet the clock keeps ticking and they only seem to be getting sleepier and sleepier.

When the clock strikes 9pm it dawns on me that there was no acting today. There really is no party. And I shouldn't be upset, I mean, I told them not to organise anything. But now I'm desperate to do something. I mean, you only turn twenty-six once, don't you?

'Izzy, are you sure you don't wanna pop out for a few drinks? We could go somewhere quiet?' I plead pathetically.

'Well...oh, OK,' she smiles sympathetically. 'Go get ready and I'll throw on some clothes.'

'Great.'

I run into my room and throw on one of Jazz's tight dresses. I don't care if it's a pity outing. I just want to get out of this house. A hum of conversation vibrates quietly through the wall and I press my ear to it to eavesdrop.

'Yeah, but I feel bad. I mean, no-one's bothered to celebrate her birthday with her.'

'But she said she didn't want anything,' I hear Ryan protest.

'But still. I can't be horrible,' I hear Izzy say before she runs up stairs.

234

Well this birthday is awful. It's like the universe is setting out to let me know that nobody cares about me. I mean, am I that awful that people just either find me totally hilarious or a giant pain in the arse? I fight back my pride and the tears pricking at my eyes and leave with Izzy, plastering on a fake smile.

'The local pub OK?' she asks.

'Um...yeah, of course.'

I'm a tad over dressed for The Old Swan, but right now I just want to go out for a few drinks and then crawl back into bed where I can cry myself to sleep.

Izzy makes the best of it, chatting pointlessly about fitness, or running, or something like that. But I'm not interested. I can't help but think about Grace and Ryan at home alone together. I mean, what if they're having sex right now? Going 'how ridiculous was Poppy earlier' and throwing their heads back laughing before continuing to lick each other.

'Poppy, I know I'm awful, but I'm really kind of exhausted. Do you mind if we call it a night?' Izzy asks apologetically.

I glance at the clock on the wall. 10pm. I've stayed out on my birthday until 10pm?

'Yeah, of course.'

We walk down the couple of streets back to the house as I feel the emotion brewing in my body. Nobody wants to spend my birthday with me. Not my best friend, barely my family and now not even Izzy. What is wrong with me?

I take my shoes off, giving in to the crushing, and walk barefoot in the street for what seems like forever until we reach the shiny red door. I'm going to just run in and sob heavily into my pillow. I'm going to wallow in my own self-pity and never resurface. I honestly can't wait. Izzy unlocks the door and we stumble into the dark house. Ryan and Grace must be in bed. Maybe even together in bed. God, the thought of it makes my heart ache. Them lying in bed laughing about me.

'Night,' I whimper. I run into my bedroom closing the door firmly behind me.

Sleep. That'll make it better, it always does. Whenever life gets hard, have a nap. I lie flat on the bed and let the full embarrassment flood over my body. What a loser. I brace myself, clutching my pillow, ready to release my body into full on sobs.

'Poppy! Did you leave the oven on? Something's burnt in here!'

Oh for fucks sake! Is it not enough that everyone hates me, now I'm going to get blamed for burning something? You burn one piece of garlic bread and nearly set the house on fire once and they hold it against you forever. I stomp out of the room and head for the kitchen.

'No! It must be Grace and Ryan!' I shout moodily into the dark.

The lights flick on, blinding me momentarily.

'SURPRISE!'

I open my eyes to see a room crammed with people. Everyone's wearing stupid birthday hats and letting off party poppers and there are happy birthday banners hung on the walls.

It's too much.

Without any self-control I burst into tears, and not just tears, heavy sobs. I turn and run out of the room, throwing myself face down on the bed. I hear some muffled voices next door and then music is turned on loud.

'Poppy! Are you ok?' Jazz asks, hovering over me.

'No!' I cry into my pillow. 'How the fuck could you do this to me?'

I look up, furious, to see Jazz looking back puzzled.

'Wait, I'm confused. We've had this party planned for well over a week and we're worried you'll go mad and say that you don't want a party. Then today you ring me up and say you do want a party and we think, great – she won't be cross. But now you're crying. What the fuck?'

'It's just...it's just....Well, I honestly thought that no-one gave a shit about me.'

'Oh babe!' She throws herself on top of me, crushing me into the mattress. 'You're such an idiot.'

'Oh thanks.' I push her off me. 'But....you were all such good actors. I just...didn't think you had it in you.'

236

'I know, right!' she beams proudly. 'I was so good when you rang me earlier. I was at home ringing round making sure everyone was still coming, and Jake was just playing rock music on the CD player. Apparently he said that normally when I'm acting I put on some weird posh voice, so I tried really hard to sound normal.'

'Really? A weird posh voice? I've never noticed.' I desperately try not to smile.

'I know! I said he was a weirdo. So anyway, have you gotten over your little melodrama, nobody loves me saga? You coming back out?'

'I suppose. I'm just...God, I'm just so embarrassed in front of everyone now.'

God, they're all gonna think I'm a nutcase running away like that.

'Don't worry, we'll just tell them you're on the blob,' she shrugs.

'Jazz! Don't tell anyone that!'

'Ok chill out,' she laughs, flicking her curls back and already re-applying red lipstick.

'Ok, how do I look?'

She studies me for a while, seeming to be wondering whether to tell me the truth or not.

'A bit like my Mum after her face lift; red and puffy.' She pulls a face. 'But you'll do, come on.' She drags me out into the kitchen before I have time to fix it.

*   *   *

Two hours later and the party is in full swing. Everyone I love is here and they're all in the party spirit. Jazz seems to be going between snogging Jake on the sofa and smoking with Ollie in the garden. I'm not sure I like this new relationship they've developed.

Lilly's here with her long suffering boyfriend Alex who she's spent the entire night either arguing with or slagging him off to me in the toilets. Cheryl from work is here, engrossed in what looks like a deep conversation with some girls from work, who Lilly must have talked into coming. Craig is dancing to Vogue with Bakery Girl. My brothers Henry and Richard are here too. Henry's brought Abbey, who keeps looking round at the place as if she might catch a disease, while Richard stands by awkwardly. Thankfully no Annabel tonight. After that, I don't really recognise the rest of them. Jazz must have just invited everyone she knows. But who am I to complain. If it were just my friends we could have held the party in the bathroom.

'So, we really fooled you?' Ryan asks in my ear, his silky irresistible voice making my pulse jump.

I swivel round to face him, suddenly feeling flustered.

'Oh...yeah. You were all so horrible, I totally believed it.'

'Good,' he says, with a smile. 'So it seems you've had your first birthday without bad luck.'

I force myself to look away from the intensity of his stare, his gaze making me lose my breath. Grace's words still flash through my mind, stabbing me like a dagger.

'Yeah, don't jinx me yet,' I snort, trying to keep it light. Very attractive.

'I say we make our own luck,' he says, his voice smouldering and his eyes gloriously intense.

'Yeah, well...anyway,' I say flushing. 'I should probably...you know...' I slowly back away.

I glance over at Ollie shamelessly flirting with Jazz. Ryan and my brother are actually more alike than I thought. To think, I used to pity those ridiculous girls who fell for Ollie's charms and followed him around like a lost puppy. Now I'm one of those pathetic morons.

'Happy birthday Poppy!' a recognisable high pitched voice comes from behind me.

I turn round to face Annabel. What the hell is she doing here?

She grabs me, kissing me on both cheeks.

'Sorry I'm late, but I had to get some work stuff finished.'

A stone drops through my stomach as I look into Annabel's excited eyes and then over my shoulder at poor Cheryl.

Chapter 18

Oh my God. Cheryl is only a couple of metres behind me. If she sees Annabel she's going to kill her.

'Annabel! You shouldn't be here!' I whisper quickly, my voice wobbly.

'What are you talking about?' she asks, as if I'm mad. 'I see Richard! See you later.'

She runs off towards him and I watch as she kisses him on the cheek. God, they make such a convincingly happy couple. It scares me to think how many other couples might be like that.

Cheryl is so close to her. She could easily recognise her any minute. I dread to think what she might do. But then, would she really recognise her? I mean, we were far away and she might not have got a good enough look of her.

I go to the fridge to get myself another glass of wine to steady my nerves.

'Pops?'

I turn to face Jazz whose usual relaxed pretty face is re-arranged into a serious, concerned expression. Serious and smashed.

'Ollie just told me you're pregnant?' she slurs.

'WHAT?' I shout, dribbling out my wine.

'Thank God it's not true!' She throws her arms around me and squeezes while I try to remember how to breathe. 'I just reacted totally the same. He told me your Mum had told them all, but said you were in denial and not to mention it to you.'

'For fuck's sake! I told her she had it wrong.'

'Yeah, but you know your mum.' She pulls a face. 'But listen Pops, I just want you to be happy,' she slurs, wrapping her arm around me. 'I may have a few drinks inside me, but...I love you babe.' She hiccups.

'Well, I'm still quite sober. I just think you're nice,' I joke, squeezing her affectionally on the shoulder.

She stares at me blankly for a second and then giggles huskily when she eventually gets it.

'I'll go tell...you know, what's his name, that you're not preggers.'

'You mean Ollie?' I ask, surprised how incredibly drunk she is.

'Yes!' she says, throwing her hands in the air. 'Ollie!'

I watch her stumble off in Ollie's direction, Jake watching her closely. He must be wondering what she's doing talking to him all night. In fact, I'm starting to think the same thing.

Henry starts walking towards me, a stern expression on his face. What's his problem?

'Poppy, I need to speak to you,' he says seriously.

'Ok?'

He looks back at Jazz who's still talking to Ollie and laughing animatedly. Jake's no longer there, probably sick of watching them.

'Is Jazz the girl Ollie got in trouble?'

I stare at him trying to comprehend what's happening. In trouble? Uh-oh.

'In trouble? Do you mean...'

'Yes,' he interrupts. 'I mean pregnant. Is Jazz the girl Ollie has got pregnant?'

'What?' a man's voice says from behind me.

I turn round to see Jake staring at me horrified.

'Jazz is what?' he asks, his face filling with fury.

'No! Jake – ' I try, but he's already flying off towards Jazz and Ollie. I watch on, desperately thinking what to do. I want to run over and protect her, but my feet seem to be glued to the spot. I've never seen anyone so angry before. He's really scary.

'You fucking bastard!' Jake screams before powering a punch in Ollie's face.

Ollie stumbles back in confusion and drops his Becks bottle. Jazz jumps in front of him protectively.

'Whas? Whas your problem?' she slurs.

'You're sleeping with him! You two are welcome to each other,' he screams before fleeing from the room, slamming the front door behind him.

For a second I copy everyone else; just staring at them, complete shock and confusion on my face. I eventually get my feet to move and rush over. Jazz and I help him up while everyone looks on.

'Sorry Pops,' he says, grabbing a tea towel and holding it to his nose. 'I'm out of here.'

'No, don't go,' Jazz pleads, tugging on his arm like a toddler.

'I am,' he says to her. He takes hold of her cheek. 'I'll see you soon, OK?' He smiles and leaves, with Jazz still seeming to be hanging on his every word.

'Whatever,' Jazz says, before stomping off to dance.

Jesus, the drama! Are they sleeping together? I didn't hear either of them denying it, and touching her cheek; surely that's not normal friendly behaviour?

I'm suddenly aware of Grace behind me from the strong vixen perfume she insists on wearing.

'So, wish me luck tonight,' she whispers seductively in my ear.

'Sorry, are you talking to me?' I ask, swivelling round to face her. She's wearing a short red dress with huge gold hoop earrings. She actually looks a bit like J-Lo tonight.

'Yes, of course I'm talking to you,' she hisses, jutting her jaw out in temper.

'Oh, well...yeah, good luck,' I say as evenly as I can, willing my voice not to break.

'I know you like him, you know,' she says, her voice accusing.

I turn away from her, burnt by her words, trying to think of a reply; some kind of put-down, a witty remark. But my thoughts are too jumbled. Instead I spot Cheryl dangerously close to Annabel. Cheryl is talking to some girls from work, seeming to be telling a story, probably about her child. Annabel is laughing at a joke Richard's told. Cheryl looks up at the crowd as they laugh at her story. She looks straight at Annabel.

I hold my breath.

A quick flash of recollection goes through her face. Every muscle in my body tightens. Now she's looking down at her glass of wine, as if to think of where she knows her from. Please don't remember. Please don't remember.

I make a silent prayer in my head. Dear God, please don't let this happen. I'll go back to church, I promise. And I'll volunteer somewhere. Anything, please!

'Are you listening to me?' Grace says scathingly.

'Oh...yes,' I mumble, remembering she's there.

I turn quickly back to Cheryl's reaction. She knows, I just know she knows. She's glaring towards Annabel and I think her hands are shaking. Please Cheryl, don't cause a scene.

'I wasn't born yesterday,' Grace snarls to my left. 'I just want to warn you – you don't stand a chance.'

'Oh,' I say, not really listening. 'Well, you've got it all wrong anyway.'

Cheryl walks over to Annabel, her hands now definitely shaking, and taps her on the shoulder.

I stare at them helplessly, feeling sick with fright, not daring to move a muscle. Cheryl, if you can hear me and have become telepathic, please understand there is no need to cause a scene.

'What the fuck are you doing here?' she slurs at her. I didn't realise she was drunk too.

'Excuse me?' Annabel asks, leaning back from her. 'Do I know you?'

Richard looks at Cheryl bemused, sure she must be a lunatic. Probably just assuming if she's my friend she must be insane.

'Just watch your back,' Grace whispers in my ear, sending a chill down my spine.

'You don't know me. But you know my husband,' Cheryl slurs.

'Really?' Annabel laughs, seeming completely oblivious.

'You should do. You've been screwing him!' Cheryl explodes.

'Are you fucking listening?' Grace snarls, shoving me on the shoulder.

'Grace, I've got to go.'

I don't have time for her shit right now. I turn and start to walk across the room, my stomach flipping from nerves, towards the unfolding drama that everyone's turned to watch.

As I put my right leg in front of the other I feel something in its way. I try to miss it, but can't and the tightness of my dress means I can't steady myself. There's nothing I can do. I'm going down. I'm going down and it's going to hurt.

Slam! I hit the floor, face down. An overpowering black, heavy pain takes over my forehead, spreading across my entire head. I press myself up slightly and open my eyes, but the rooms spinning as if I've drunk tequila. A sharp hot sting starts on my face, just above my eyebrow. Why won't the room stop spinning?

'Shit, Poppy! Are you ok?' I hear Izzy shout.

'I...I...'

I try to look up at her, but moving my head even an inch starts a throbbing so strong I clench my eyes shut. Someone grabs me under the shoulders, swooping me up to standing in one swift movement. My head almost explodes from the fastness. I open my eyes and realise that I'm on Ryan's lap and he's inspecting my face.

'I don't know what you're talking about,' I hear Annabel shout. 'Who *is* this crazy woman?'

'Che....Cheryl,' I stammer, trying to point towards them but instead only managing to point at a wall.

'My name is Cheryl. Cheryl Foster!'

I look up again and this time I manage to focus in on Annabel's face, through the purple spots. Sudden recognition is written all over it and Richard seems to notice.

'Let me see your head,' Ryan demands.

I look up to him, my head still blurry. He looks kind of worried. A fresh sharp sting takes my attention back to my eyebrow. I put my hand up to it and feel something warm. I look at my hand to see dark red blood in between my fingers. I swallow convulsively, my stomach heaving.

'Oh my God, oh my God, oh my God,' I say over and over to myself, suddenly shaking hysterically.

'Is she bleeding?' Jazz asks from the other side, struggling to stand still.

I swing my head round to her but only manage to let the vice tighten around my skull. I close my eyes, trying to hear through the ringing in my ears.

'It's pretty deep,' Ryan clarifies. 'Plus I think there's still a bit of glass in there.'

'I honestly don't know who this woman is!' Annabel shouts. I open my eyes to see the entire party now watching closely to see how this plays out.

'I know it's you! Me and Poppy saw you with our own eyes!' Cheryl screams.

Annabel freezes rigid and Richard reacts as if he's been slapped in the face. He looks over to me, devastation in his eyes.

'Poppy,' Ryan says, clicking his fingers in front of me. 'Do you think you could stay still while I try and pick it out?'

'Can't you see a drama is unfolding?' I attempt to shout, but instead my voice is weak and shaky.

'Poppy?' Richard walks towards me, his face furious. 'Is this right? Did you see Annabel and her husband?'

I slowly raise my head, afraid to see his face.

'Um...I...I may have,' I admit. I'm still so dizzy.

'WHAT?' He stares at me, completely horrified and disgusted. 'You knew she was having an affair? And you never fucking told me!?'

'I'm...I'm sorry.' I can feel my lip trembling.

'I can't fucking believe this!' he shouts, the vein in his forehead bulging out.

I close my eyes again and try to fight the nausea with all of my strength, clamping my lips together.

'Mate, I think you need to get out of her face. Can't you see she's got a head injury?' Ryan says, putting his hands up and trying to push Richard away.

'Who the fuck are you?' Richard asks, his face hostile.

'I'm Poppy's housemate and right now you just need to get out of her face so we can take her to hospital.'

'Richard, let's go,' Annabel pleads reaching for his arm with tears in her eyes.

'Get off me, you fucking whore!' he snaps, throwing her off.

This is really not going well.

Richard storms out, Annabel running after him, while the whole party watches in shock.

'Jesus,' Ryan sighs once they're gone. 'Drama follows you around, doesn't it? Anyway, do you think you could stay still while I try and pick it out?'

I nod and swallow, my stomach heaving from the thought of the blood. Izzy holds my head still and Jazz holds my hand while he pokes around in my wound.

'Aaaah!' I cry, trying to wrench my head away from him.

'I'm just trying to get the glass out of it!' he shouts back frustrated.

'Why is there glass in it anyway?' I ask, still disorientated.

'You fell on some broken glass,' Izzy explains, squeezing my hand. 'I think it was your brother's Becks bottle.'

'Only you could get these bizarre injuries,' Jazz snorts, still hiccupping.

'She needs to go to hospital and get it sorted out,' Ryan tells Izzy.

'Ok. Jazz, will you come with us?' Izzy asks her.

'I'm coming too,' Ryan says, lifting me off him and standing up.

'No. It's fine,' I protest, tears pricking at my eyes as the sting turns into an itch.

'I want to come,' he says, still supporting me with his arm around my waist.

'Well I don't want you to,' I snap, getting up and walking towards the door before I burst into angry violent tears.

*　　　　　*　　　　　*

'I'm afraid that you'll need stitches,' the greying lady doctor says to me, as she pulls the last shred of glass out of my wound and places it in a grey paper dish.

'Stitches? Are you sure?' I ask, my voice unnaturally shrill. 'Can't we just put a large plaster over it or something?'

245

'I'm afraid not.' She smiles politely, but isn't able to fully conceal her smirk. Probably thinking how ridiculous I am. 'But, seen as it's your birthday, you can bring your friends in with you.'

'Oh great,' I scoff.

'Where have they got to?' she asks, pulling back the blue curtain. Just at that moment Izzy and Jazz spin round the corner in wheelchairs, pushing themselves along frantically. They giggle hysterically, trying to push the other into hospital beds and staff, desperate to win the race to some imaginary finish line.

The doctor looks at me accusingly. I grimace apologetically. It's not my fault my friends are drunk and insane.

'Hey Pops,' Izzy says, as she parks up, out of breath. 'How's the patient?' she directs to the doctor.

'She'll need stitches. You know you really shouldn't be playing with those,' she snaps.

Izzy immediately looks regretful and shuffles back and forth on her feet.

'Sorry.'

Jazz gets off her wheelchair, still two beds away from us, and stumbles over, seeming to be having problems putting one foot in front of the other. Her face is pale and her forehead shiny.

'You OK Jazz?' I ask, praying she won't cause a scene.

'Of c-c-course,' she slurs. She opens her mouth into a wide smile and then projectile vomits all over the floor. She pulls her head up, wipes the remains of her vomit with the back of her arm. 'Maybe I'm b-b-bit ill.' She looks at me with big scared eyes and then passes out.

*　　　　　*　　　　　*

When we eventually arrive home, it's 5am and the birds are out to greet us. We almost fall into the hallway, all exhausted from the drama of tonight. That and having to fight a transvestite for our cab. Ryan comes running to the door as soon as it opens.

'Poppy, how are you?' he asks, helping me in as if I'm a cripple.

'I'm fine,' I snap, my eyes so heavy I can barely keep them open.

I wish he'd stop fussing and leave me alone. I wonder if he's just stopped having sex with Grace.

'I'm gonna crash in Izzy's room,' Jazz says, sipping her bottled water. 'Will you be OK on your own?'

'Yes! For fuck sakes, I've had stitches, I'm not disabled!'

'Alright moody,' Ryan says, smiling at Izzy and Jazz.

'Night, love you,' Jazz and Izzy sing in sleepy voices, kissing me on the cheek. Jazz still smells of vomit. I turn and head towards my room without bothering to say goodbye to Ryan.

'Can I see it?' Ryan asks, following me into my room.

I flick on a lamp and sigh heavily. I turn my head so that he can have a good look, while still maintaining a healthy distance. I don't want him touching it or anything.

'Do you trust me?' he asks, coming closer and hovering his hand over the wound.

Do I? Do I trust him? I honestly don't know.

He places his hands gently on either side of my face and carefully traces the line of the stitches, making me tingle.

'Shit. That's gonna be a fucker of a scar.'

'Yeah, well you can thank your girlfriend,' I snap, my voice full of disdain, as I pull away from him.

'Huh?' he asks bewildered.

'Grace. She's the one who tripped me.'

'No, she wouldn't do that.' He shakes his head. 'And she's not my girlfriend.'

'Well, that's not what she told me. Was going to jump your bones tonight. Thought I'd leave you to it. Was it fun?' I ask sarcastically, my face like thunder.

'You know what,' he sighs heavily. 'I was going to give you your present, but if you're gonna talk crap I'll just leave.'

Present?

'No! I mean...you got me a present?' I ask, embarrassed by how spoilt I sound.

'Yep.'

247

He walks towards my wardrobe. He reaches behind it and pulls out a large shape wrapped in brown paper. He places it down in front of me and I look up to him confused.

'Well, open it then,' he smiles encouragingly.

I tear at the paper, my hands tired but excited. I stand back to see that it's a large black photo frame. I turn it round to face me and inside it's an old Singing in the Rain poster. I'm stunned. He remembered it's my favourite film. He bothered getting a poster and putting it in a frame.

'You like it then?' he asks, his face suddenly serious.

'I...I love it,' is all I can mumble out.

'Good,' he says, seeming chuffed. He leans closer into my face, his features serious again. 'And remember...don't believe all the crap that comes out of Grace's mouth.'

He stares at me for a second, his eyes so intense that I'm sure he's going to lean in and kiss me. Instead he turns and leaves the room. Forget what Grace said. Game on bitch.

Chapter 19

I'm woken up by a strange sound in the hallway. Like someone is bouncing off the walls, the door frames shaking. Oh my God. What if it's an earthquake? I mean, you hear about these things happening all of the time. You think you live in a quiet country with no natural disasters and then – BAM! You're in the middle of one. A tsunami. How far away are we from the Thames?

'Come here! Come here!' I hear Ryan shouting.

Is he calling me? I jump out of bed and throw on Jazz's dressing gown and slippers. I don't want to be found amongst the rubble in just my tatty pyjamas. I put them on, careful not to catch my face against any of the fabric. The wound is already stinging badly enough. I open the door and peer out.

A furry brown creature turns and locks their brown eyes with mine. Terror creeps into my stomach. This is far worse than an earthquake. A dog. And I've made eye contact with it. They say never to look them in the eye otherwise they'll attack. It's mouth opens exposing sharp white teeth, slobber falling onto the carpet.

It widens its paws on the floor and leans back slightly before sprinting full speed towards me. It happens so quickly I don't have time to think. I dive instinctively out of the way just in time for it to miss me and go bounding into my room. It quickly turns back at me, jumping up so high it's almost touching my face. It's going to bite my face!

'Aaah! Get it off me, get it off me!' I shout running through the hallway, desperate for an escape.

I jump on the kitchen table, losing a slipper in the process. The vicious dog continues to jump, trying to reach the top of it. Where the hell did this dog come from?

'Oh my God,' Ryan says, walking in almost doubled over laughing. 'That was the funniest thing I've ever seen.'

'Is it your dog?' I ask, my heart still beating too fast in my chest. It's still jumping.

'She's my Grandma's. She's got friends over all day today so I said I'd have her.' He's still trying to compose himself.

'Her? I thought all dogs were boys?' I ask looking for a dog penis. His eyes crease and he doubles over again into loud hysterics.

'Stop, you're killing me,' he says, breathless, his face slightly red.

'Oh shut up will you,' I snap, still trying to balance on the rickety table. Please God, don't let it collapse from under me. I feel dizzy enough as it is.

'Sorry,' he says, looking at me confused. 'Are you seriously still on that table?'

I glare in response.

'Oh, come on,' he scoffs. 'You can't really be scared of this little dog can you?'

I look down at the cream and brown haired creature and I know that a normal person would probably think it was cute. Yet all I can seem to notice is its big teeth and extremely large paws. That and how it can seem to jump six foot. It's going to get me any minute now, I can feel it. I'm going to die. It's going to bite me on my neck and I'll bleed out in a second.

'Yes, OK!' I shout abruptly. 'I happen to have a serious phobia of dogs. Can't you just tell her to leave me a-alone?' I stammer, sweat dripping from my forehead.

'Sorry? You want me to reason with an excitable dog, to leave you alone?' he asks, enunciating every syllable, as if he were talking to someone mentally handicapped.

'Yes. Is that really *too* much to ask?'

'God, you're hard work,' he sighs. He scoops her up in one arm. 'Come here and I'll hold her.'

Next to him she does look kind of small and pathetic, but that doesn't stop my body shaking.

'You're sure you've got her?' I ask my mouth dry with anxiety.

'Yes.' He sighs, seeming frustrated.

I tentatively put one foot down onto the floor, but flinch when I see her try to wriggle from his arms.

'Come on, I've got her,' he says, his voice suppressing laughter.

I take a deep breath and then quickly jump off before I can talk myself out of it. I open my eyes to see that I've made it. Both feet are on the floor and I'm still alive. I take another deep breath and slowly walk over to the sofa to sit down, Ryan sitting down next to me. I sit as far away from him as I can, all too aware of the dog's teeth and it's massive blood red gums.

'Poppy, this is Toffee.' He extends his arms out to me so that she's nearly in my face.

'Please,' I beg, my voice breaking as I put up a shaking hand in defence. 'This isn't funny. Dogs creep me out. She's gonna claw me, I know it.'

'Don't be stupid,' he says, muffling a snicker. 'Let me just put her down next to you.'

He places her slowly down onto the sofa and I clench my body, ready to bolt out the door if she makes any sudden movements. Yet to my surprise she manages to sit calmly, her big brown eyes staring at me as if I'm the freak. I try to avoid looking at her straight on, sure it'll aggravate her. I suppose she is kind of cute. Her ears are far too big for her head and they flop over her eyes, almost like a pretty girl with unruly hair. Maybe there is an exception to the rule.

'There you are,' Ryan smiles looking back and forth between me and her. 'She's fine.'

He looks at me, unleashing the full devastating power of his eyes, as if trying to hypnotise me into calming down. It only seems to make my heart beat faster.

The sound of someone walking down the stairs startles me away from his beautiful face as the dog jumps off the sofa, circling in a mad frenzy.

'Aaah!' I scream. 'I'm going to die!' I wail.

I jump onto the back of the sofa, a sudden urge to get as high as possible, while the dog runs from the room. I crouch down, taking deep breaths, trying to bring myself back from the hysterical panic.

'Calm down,' Ryan says soothingly, but his eyes are mocking.

'Hey Toffee baby,' I hear Izzy say from the hallway.

251

Izzy walks in with Jazz and Grace, cradling Toffee in her arms like a baby.

'Hey Pops. Are you OK?' Izzy asks, widening her eyes in suspicion.

'She's scared of dogs,' Ryan explains, rolling his eyes, a tight smile on his lips.

'You're joking?' Izzy asks, a wide smile creeping up on her face.

'How can you be scared of little Toffee?'

Toffee licks her face in response. Ugh - gross.

'Hello? Don't you remember one of my stories from last night about her being bitten?' Jazz reminds her, smiling at me sympathetically.

Jazz had decided, once gaining consciousness, to tell loads of stories about the bad luck I'd suffered on my many birthdays.

'Oh yeah,' Izzy says apologetically.

'Why am I not surprised?' Ryan says, shaking his head as if I'm a major liability.

'Yes. You're very accident prone aren't you,' Grace smirks. 'How *is* your head?'

What a two faced bitch. Acting all nice in front of Ryan. She makes me physically sick. Just looking at her face makes me want to take up boxing.

'It's...OK,' I shrug. I don't want her to know how uncomfortable my face feels.

Ryan's phone rings and he leaves the room to take it. The minute he's gone I decide to confront her.

'Look Grace, I know it was you that tripped me. What the *fuck* is your problem?'

'What?' she asks, fake innocence all over her face. 'I don't know what you're talking about.' She smiles discreetly, as if to let me know she realises exactly what I'm talking about.

'Poppy!' Jazz shouts, completely shocked.

'No Jazz, she fucking tripped me and I know it. I'm not scared of you Grace.'

Maybe I am a little, but I'm not gonna let this bitch know that.

'I honestly don't know what you're talking about,' Grace says, her bottom lip trembling.

Wow – this bitch is good. If I didn't know better I'd believe her.

'Poppy, you can't just assume it was Grace,' Izzy protests. 'Look how upset she is'. She walks over to Grace, putting her arm around her shoulder.

Ryan walks back in the room and looks confused by the sudden tense atmosphere. He looks from face to face.

'What's going on?' he asks eventually.

Grace runs over to him, pushing her face into his chest.

'Poppy accused me of tripping her.'

Ryan looks at her and then back to me, shaking his head in disbelief. 'No, you must be wrong.' He looks at me for reassurance. 'She's wrong, right Poppy?'

Izzy and Jazz look away, the tense atmosphere growing by the second. Oh God, well now I look like an awful witch. I'm turning red.

'Um...no. Actually I did accuse her...but only because I know she did it.' I'd attempted to make my voice sound strong and confident, but I've ended up sounding like a squeaky mouse.

'Poppy, you can't just go around accusing people!' he shouts, his voice making my skin retract in fear.

Why do I suddenly feel like I'm being told off by the headmaster? It's the same humiliating feeling, the feeling that I've been caught doing something wrong. I've done nothing wrong. Grace smiles at me from Ryan's chest, showing off her victory. What a sly, sly bitch.

I've got to have a really good come back for this. A really good answer, an explanation, showing Grace to be the true back stabbing bitch she is.

'Whatever,' is the best I can come up with. Pathetic.

'I think you should apologise to her,' he suggests.

I let out a short laugh.

'You think I'm going to apologise to her. I don't think so.'

Grace lets out a pathetic little cry.

'Don't worry Gracie,' Ryan says, squeezing her tighter. 'I know Poppy doesn't mean it.'

'Don't speak on behalf of me! I do mean it, she's a sly bitch!' I shout, my voice erupting in an angry growl.

'Poppy that's enough!' he shouts, silencing me.

How dare he speak to me like this? How dare he take her side over mine? I feel more betrayal than I know I should, but I can't help it. I thought he'd be on my side. How can he not see through her? Oh, I remember, because her massive tits are in the way.

Silence fills the room and I look around to see that Izzy and Jazz have begun backing out of the room.

'Well, I think it's clear that we're not going to make up today. Maybe just keep out of each other's way for now?' Ryan suggests.

I fold my arms across my chest as I begin a staring contest with Grace.

'Anyway,' Ryan says, his voice softer now, 'I'm really sorry guys, but I need to go and sort something out. Would you be able to keep an eye on Toffee for a little while?' He looks at Izzy and Jazz, with an expression that also says 'and try to keep these two from killing each other'.

'Yeah of course,' Izzy says, putting Toffee down on the floor.

'Poppy, you're OK with that?' he asks smirking.

'I'll be fine,' I growl.

*   *   *

Two hours later I'm in the park with Izzy and Toffee. Grace and Jazz wisely ran for the hills soon after Ryan left. Yet Izzy somehow managed to talk me into yet another walk, giving me a lecture on how it will not only calm Toffee, but how it's good for health, cellulite, and mood. So here I am, walking through a field full of cow shit with a mental little dog, who I'm sure is waiting for me to relax before going for my jugular.

'How's your face?' Izzy asks warmly.

'It stings, but I'll live I suppose.'

Her phone starts to ring with the latest pop tune and her face lights up. 'Hey Maria! Long time. I know, it's been ages!' She mouths 'sorry' to me. She places her hand over the receiver. 'Pops, I'm just gonna take this, it's a bit private.' She thrusts the lead into my hand and jogs off.

I look down at the lead to the dog attached to it. She's left me with Toffee. I'm alone with the dog. OK, don't panic. Just breathe. Toffee looks back at me and I flinch. But then it's like she's actually smiling to reassure me. What am I actually worried about? I mean, she's a cute little dog. She's almost like a really hairy toddler. I shouldn't be intimidated by her. I can do this. How hard can it be? I breathe in the fresh air and start to relax, looking up at the sky.

A dirty dark cloud creeps over my head, bringing with it a chill in the air. Toffee looks back and smiles again, but this time my stomach doesn't settle. I don't have a coat with me. Please don't rain, please don't rain. I slow down my pace, scared of losing Izzy. The sky darkens completely, as if it's ten o'clock at night. Images of every horror film flash through my head.

Boom!

I jump from the loud sound of distant thunder. Rain begins pouring, slowly at first, but big fat drops soon start coming down heavily. Within seconds I'm soaked straight through my clothes. Toffee runs to my side, seeming scared. She makes a weird whimpering noise, kind of like she's crying.

'Don't worry Toffee. It's only a bit of rain. Come here.' I try to muster up the courage to pick her up and reassure her. I don't even know how I'd go about doing it. Would I go under her shoulders or her stomach? Maybe I can just pat her on her head instead?

Crackle!

Close thunder breaks through the sky and I jump so hard I almost swallow my tongue. Toffee barks so loudly my eardrums wince in disbelief. She bolts. I try to hold onto the lead but she's so strong that I feel the fabric whip my skin with a friction burn. I look down in disbelief at my empty hands. Toffee is running through the open field as fast as a whippet.

'Toffee! Come back,' I yell running after her.

But it's no use. She's so fast and it seems she's been well and truly spooked. I stop running for a second, watching her run to a distant field and crawl under a fence into what looks like someone's garden.

The sky around me has become crowded with dirty black clouds, thick persistent rain drops falling from them. The mix of the darkness and rain means it's a struggle for me to see in front of me, let alone into the next field.

I run as fast as my legs can take me towards the field, the grass gets muddier each time I make contact with it. I slip over a few times, but the panic tightening my throat is spurring me on. I cannot lose this dog. They'll all say I did it deliberately because I don't like dogs. They'll probably start a hate campaign against me in the local paper and people will spit on me in the street.

When I make it to the wooden fence I realise just how high it is. I can't find the hole she went through but I'm sure it was this garden. I can hear her whimpering on the other side.

I glance up at the tree next to me. I haven't climbed a tree since I was a teenager and Sean King convinced me there was a butterfly nest worth seeing. What a gullible idiot; the only thing he showed me up there was something far less pretty and definitely not worth seeing.

I wrap my arms around it and straddle it with my legs, but I struggle, feeling splinters digging into my fingers. I hoist myself up as far as I can, with my legs wrapped tightly around the bark, and then I see her over the fence. The poor thing looks at me, confused and scared, drenched from the rain.

'Don't worry Toffee. I'm going to get you,' I shout, desperately trying to find a way though to her.

I can see the tiny hole that she went through now, but there's no way I'd get through that. Getting stuck trying won't help anything. I climb carefully back down and walk over to the tiny gap, sticking my head through, trying to coax her.

'Come on Toffee. I've got a treat for you.' I fumble in my pocket for something, anything, but of course it's empty.

The rain is coming down so thick and loud that I'm not sure if she can even hear me. I look around for someone to help me, but the place is deserted. Where are all the joggers that were here a few minutes ago? And where the *hell* is Izzy?

'Izzy! Izzy! I shout, but the pathetic sound that escapes my throat sounds more like a sob. I'm just so tired. Tired of things like this happening to me.

I get my phone out of my pocket, but of course the battery is dead. My throat starts contracting, the lump in it getting bigger by the second. Try not to cry.

Why did this have to happen!? What am I going to do? I can't leave her here to get help; what if when we get back she's gone? I give in to the tears, letting them fall down my face as I think about how I'd break it to Ryan that I'd lost his Grandma's dog. In fact, I don't think I'll ever be able to go back. I'll have to run away too.

No – think calmly! There must be *something* I can do. I look around, desperate to come up with a solution. The only thing that seems to be offering any kind of solution is the tree. I suppose I could try and lower myself into the garden from it. Maybe hold onto the washing line or something.

I suck at my bleeding friction burn on my hand and then grip the tree, hauling myself up it. I straddle it with my legs and try to ignore every pain I'm feeling in my hands. They're just superficial pains. The pain I'll feel if I lose this dog will be far worse.

I climb until I'm by a branch over hanging the garden and I can see a washing line filled with old bras and knickers. They mustn't be in; if they were, surely they would have run out to save their washing. I shimmy along the thick branch and try not to look directly down or think about how it wobbles every time I move. All the while I try to keep my eyes locked on Toffee, whose tail is wagging as if she's amused by this show I'm putting on for her.

I accidentally glance down and feel dizzy from how high I am. I try to focus myself and breathe deeply. My hands are shaking as I grip onto the branch and try to lower myself down, using every muscle in my body. Why couldn't I be stronger? Note to self: book in a body pump class.

'Poppy!'

My head automatically swivels round to see Izzy running towards me. My hand slips and I lose my grip, feeling myself falling. The helpless feeling of not having some part of me on the ground is enough for me to close my eyes, knowing that this is going to hurt.

When I open my eyes I can hear Izzy frantically shouting my name. I must try to regain my senses. I'm wet, cold and lying in mud. Was I knocked unconscious? I sit up and sudden sharp pain shoots through my ankle, making my head spin. Toffee jumps on my lap and for once I'm glad to see her. I grab hold of her in my arms, trying not to think about how sharp her claws are.

'Poppy! Are you OK?' Izzy shouts from over the fence, her voice seeming to break from stress.

'Yeah, I'm fine.' I close my eyes and try to hear through the ringing in my ears. 'I just need to figure out a way out of here,' I shout over the thudding rain.

'Pass me Toffee through the hole,' she orders.

I try to get up again but the pain shoots through my ankle as if I'm being stabbed by a thousand knives. What the hell have I done to myself? I crawl over to the hole, careful not to put any pressure on my ankle and pass Toffee out to her.

'How the hell am I going to get out?' I shout, wincing from the pain of my own voice.

'You're going to have to climb back over,' she says, looking doubtful.

'I can't! My ankle's agony.'

'I'll have to call someone to help us.' She gets her phone out of her pocket.

But I can't wait. I'm too wet and cold to be waiting for someone to save me. Before I can think what I'm doing, I punch the fence with my bare hands, ripping at it with all of my force. The weak rickety wood rocks unsteadily and I manage to get enough shards off it so that I might just get through. I lie on my stomach and begin to crawl through, trying to block out the idea of the mud and possible insects deciding to move into my pants. I'm almost half way out when I seem to run out of floor.

'Help, I'm stuck,' I shout, not quite believing how ridiculous my life is.

'You're joking?' she asks, a smile threatening to break on her face.

258

'I swear to God. If you laugh I'll kill you,' but the giggles rise in me too.

Izzy drops to her knees in hysterics.

'Come on Toffee, let's dig her out,' she says, hoping that this will be the day she learns how to speak human. 'Come on; stop being so well trained for once.'

'Izzy, she's not holding back. She just doesn't know what the fuck you're on about.'

'Well I'm sorry for trying to help,' she snaps.

'HEY YOU!' an angry voice shouts from behind us. 'Get out of my fucking garden!'

'Oh my God,' I whisper, too scared to move.

Izzy jumps up and down trying to see across the fence.

'Shit. It's a woman and she seems really pissed off. Quickly, get out of there!'

'I can't!'

'I'm calling the police! Do you hear me? THE POLICE!'

I've only one option. I'm going to have to dig myself out. I brace myself for the mess, take a deep breath and plunge my hands into the wet slippery mud, dragging it from side to side.

'You could help you know,' I shout at her.

'I would,' she says, holding up her French tips. 'But I've just had a manicure.'

Chapter 20

A warm hand on my face wakes me up.

'Poppy, wake up.'

I open my eyes to see Ryan hovering over me, confusion and amusement all over his face.

'Hi,' I croak, shivering from the cold.

'So....do you wanna explain or...do I have to guess?' A smile is threatening to show on the corner of his mouth.

I sit up and look around. Toffee is curled up on my stomach, her cream and brown coat still covered in mud. The carpet is covered in muddy foot prints from both me and Toffee. I'm still in my wet clothes, my hair stuck together with clumps of dried mud.

'Ah. It's a bit of a long story,' I say, my voice a squeak.

'Well, at least you don't seem scared of Toffee anymore.' He strokes her head affectionately.

'It turns out I'm the biggest danger to myself.' I stand up and immediately wince from the pain in my ankle. 'Fuck.' I hold if off the floor to take the pressure off the pain.

'What's wrong with your foot?' he asks, his forehead creasing in concern.

'Part of the long story,' I say, barely having the energy to roll my eyes. 'I'm fine though.'

I try to walk again, but when I put it back on the floor the pain is unbearable, freezing me to the spot and bringing water to my eyes.

'Sit down,' he orders, pushing me roughly back onto the coach. He takes hold of my ankle and pulls off my muddy trainer.

'Ouch!' I say ungratefully, almost kicking him in the face.

He pulls off my sock and I nearly pass out from the size of it. It's swollen to nearly twice the size and is a deep purple colour.

'Fuck,' I blurt out, surprised.

'Yeah, fuck indeed. Maybe you should see a doctor.'

'Nah, I'm fine. I'll just have a shower and put some ice on it.'

I take my foot away from him and stand up, trying unsuccessfully to hobble out of the room. One step is all it takes for me to realise that this is impossible, the pain almost blinding me. I stand there, silent but too embarrassed to look back and ask for help. Maybe I could discreetly crawl out of the room and he wouldn't notice.

'You really are stubborn.' He exhales sharply and walks round to the front of me. 'Come on.'

He bends down and throws me over his shoulder into a fire man's lift, dangling me upside down.

'Put me down! I hate being upside down – please! I'm gonna be sick!' I yell desperately.

'Be sick then,' he says, chuckling to himself.

He walks up the stairs and ignores my squirming and weak punches. I eventually give up and let him carry me the last few steps to the bathroom in silence as all of the blood rushes to my head.

'There you go,' he says, plonking me down on the toilet seat.

'Thanks,' I say through gritted teeth.

'You need help getting undressed?' he asks, his eyes wickedly amused.

'No, I think I'll manage thanks.' I cross my arms and roll my eyes.

He laughs and turns the shower on, flicking some water into my face.

'All yours princess. Oh and one last thing,' he says, his expression turning serious.

'What?'

He leans over me, resting his hands either side of me. His face is so close that I can feel his cool breath against my chin. I can't remember how to breathe. A chill that has nothing to do with my wet clothes makes me shiver.

'Try not to drown.'

When I get out of the shower I feel one hundred times better. I didn't realise how much mud I had on me until I tried to wash it away. It really was everywhere. I wonder how much mud has wrecked downstairs. How am I going to fix that? Plus where the hell did Izzy go? The last thing I remember was her helping me in and saying she was getting in the shower. I must have closed my eyes for a second and instead passed out.

I hobble down the stairs, struggling to take my weight on my swollen ankle, holding my towel around me. My ankle is a bit better from the heat of the shower, but it still throbs like hell. I pop my head round the kitchen door to survey the damage. Oh dear. Ryan's on the floor scrubbing at one of the many footprints and Toffee's lying down on the floor next to him, soaking wet.

'God, sorry about the mess,' I grimace.

'That's OK. It's my own fault for leaving you with her,' he shoots back, his face tense.

I flinch from the resentment in his voice.

'Well, I'm sorry I'm so incapable,' I say hurt by his sudden change of mood.

He ignores me and carries on scrubbing. Not even an insult, this must be bad.

'How did you wash Toffee if I was in the shower?' I enquire, attempting more conversation.

'I got her with the hose.' He looks at her fondly as she lets out a yawn.

'The hose! Poor thing, she must have been frozen.'

'Oh, look who suddenly cares. This morning you just wanted her the hell out of here and this afternoon you're best friends,' he growls back. What the hell is his problem? We scowl at each other in silence for what seems like an eternity. I decide to speak first, trying to keep myself focused. I'm in danger of being distracted by his livid, glorious face. The way his forehead wrinkles and his jawline tightens. Even when he's pissed off he's hot. Maybe hotter.

'It's strange actually, they normally say dogs are like their owners, but she doesn't seem to have erratic mood swings,' I say icily.

He just glares in response and continues to scrub the floor.

I go back into my room and get changed into baggy jeans and a vest top, too knackered to even attempt to wear anything pretty. I place my slippers carefully on my feet, mindful not to aggravate my ankle. I'm

halfway through towelling my hair when I hear the front door slam.
Did he just leave? Then I hear Grace start to shriek.

'Oh my God! What the fuck happened here!'

'Oh calm down Grace,' Ryan snaps at her.

Oh God – Grace is going to *literally* kill me.

'I will not calm down! What the fuck has that dog done! And what
are these foot prints? Was this Izzy?'

'No...It was....Look, it doesn't matter who it was.'

'I know who the fuck it was!' She bursts my door open and barges in.
Thank God I'm dressed.

'Poppy, what the fuck do you think you're doing bringing all this mud
into the house?' she screams, her face red and blotchy from anger, her
eyes scrunching up in frustration. This is the first time I've seen her
truly ugly.

I stare at her dumbfounded, frozen in fear.

'Well? What's your answer? What's your excuse for wrecking my
house?'

'I....I....'

I start to feel tears pricking at my eyes. Do NOT cry Poppy. Don't be
a baby.

'Leave her alone Grace!' Ryan jumps in front of me.

'No, why the fuck should I? She swans in here like she owns the
place, accuses me of pushing her over and then wrecks the house. I
know it was never the best house, but it was ours and you've just
wrecked it like you don't give a shit.'

God, she's right. If someone did that to me I'd probably be just as
mad. I mean, look how upset I get when a pillow gets ruined.

'I'm sorry. I'm really so sorry,' I say, trying to look at her over
Ryan's protective shoulder.

'No, don't apologise to her Poppy', Ryan interrupts. 'She's well out of
order, storming into your room like this.' Ryan to my rescue. Swoon.

'ME OUT OF ORDER!?' she screams, her eyes bulging out.

'Yes, you! Look, Toffee is my dog and if you want to take it out on
anyone take it out on me.'

'But it's HER fault!' she shrieks. A vein in her neck is bulging now. Wow, she really hates me.

'I don't care,' he says coolly, still standing protectively in front of me.

'I'll pay for it to get fixed,' I say impishly over his shoulder.

'Pay for it to get fixed! You think you can just throw your money at it do you!?' she screams, her eyes mad and bulging with anger.

It's like she's possessed. Maybe at first I could sympathise with her, but now she's just acting un-hinged, her face getting redder by the second. God, she's ugly when she's mad.

'Come on Poppy,' Ryan says, putting his arm around me and guiding me past her. 'We're going out.'

'But...I don't have...'

It's too late. He practically drags me out of the house and into his car before I realise what's happening. He leans over me to strap my seat belt on, giving me the opportunity to smell his hair. It annoys me that he treats me like I'm incapable of doing it myself, but having him so close to me still makes my heart splutter hyperactively.

He disappears into the house, only to appear a second later with Toffee in his arms. He opens my door and places her on my lap. The smell of wet dog is so powerful, but I just pull myself together, scared of making more of a fuss. You've wrecked his house. Don't moan. He gets in the car and takes a big deep breath.

'The fucking cheek of her,' he huffs, starting the engine.

'Yeah, but I did kind of wreck the house. I'd have probably gone mad too.'

'That's not the point,' he says, a new blast of anger broad siding him as he pulls out of the space and onto the road. 'She just thinks she owns the place and to hell with everyone else.'

'I suppose,' I say, stroking Toffee's head.

They say the closest thing to hate is love. Him getting this angry just makes me realise that Grace is right. There really must be something between them.

'Anyway, it was nice for you to pull me out of there, but there's really no need for you to just drive around aimlessly. We can go back now. I'm big enough to fight my own battles.'

I just want to go home and have a little cry.

'Hmm, yeah looks like it. How's the ankle?' he snickers.

'Its fine,' I lie through my teeth. 'Seriously, we can go back now.'

'We're not going back,' he says, a smile breaking across his face as he stares ahead at the road.

'Then…where the hell are we going?' I ask, suddenly panicked.

'We're going to drop Toffee back.'

'Oh.' Then it hits me where Toffee lives. 'We're going to your Grandma's house?'

'Yep,' he says, a soft enchanting laugh escaping.

Oh my God. I'm going to visit his Grandma dressed like a tramp, with wet hair and no makeup.

'I can't! I haven't got any make up on! And my hairs wet. And I'm in SLIPPERS! Please, can you at least go back and get my make up? Or a jacket? I haven't even got a bra on!'

'Oh I know, I noticed,' he says, eyeing my boobs and smiling playfully.

I immediately cross my arms over them and start to panic. Ok, calm down. I pull down the mirror and look at myself. My hair doesn't look that bad. It's drying into its usual un-tamed waves, but it's not horrendous. At least there's no more mud in it. My skin is clear, but without make up I look so pale I could pass as a vampire, small purple bags under my eyes.

I pinch my cheeks and start looking around his car. He must have something here that an old girlfriend left behind. I go through the glove box and throw out the contents.

'Hey, are you trying to wreck everywhere today?' he asks with a flash of irritation.

'Ha ha,' I shoot back, still rifling through.

I feel some kind of fabric and pull it out, hoping it might be a small jacket, but all that comes out is a tiny pink diamante thong.

'Get many visitors in your car, do you?' I ask holding it up with one finger.

'Shit, how did that get in there?' he laughs, but not before I see a flush of embarrassment.

I throw it on the floor and carry on looking through, but I can't find anything! Why couldn't there be a mascara in here!?

'What's wrong?' he asks, amusement still clearly in his eyes.

'I can't find any make up! I seriously cannot meet your Grandma like this. I'll have to wait in the car.'

'You look fine. And anyway, I didn't think you were one to be bothered about make up.'

'That's when I had the chance to wear it! Your Grandma's gonna think I'm a gremlin.'

'She'll love you. Plus, anyone that saves her dog is going to be top in her book.'

'Save her dog? Who told you that?' I look at him bewildered. I never told him.

'I called Izzy when you were in the shower and she filled me in. Said she didn't have the heart to wake you up once she was out of the shower.'

'How embarrassing.' I drop my eyes to the floor as I feel my cheeks get hot.

'Well anyway,' he says, suddenly grabbing my hand. It stings as if an electric current has passed through us. I turn to look at him. 'Thank you.' He squeezes my hand.

I might actually pass out from excitement.

'Are you OK?' he enquires, his eyes narrowing. 'Did I hurt your hand?'

Oh God, I must look pained. Not exactly the look I was going for.

'Um...yeah. It's a bit sore.' I pull my hand closer to me. It does actually look pretty rough, tiny scratches all over it from climbing the tree.

'Hurt from climbing trees is it?' he asks, smiling warmly as he locks his eyes with mine.

'Y...yeah,' I slur, drunk from his eyes.

I'm going to kill Izzy. How many embarrassing details did she tell him?

'Well, here we are.'

He pulls up outside a small, but perfect bungalow painted a welcoming yellow. It's got hanging baskets full of bright flowers everywhere and has such a perfect front lawn that I wonder if she cuts it herself with nail scissors. This is clearly a woman that likes perfection. Not someone to welcome a gremlin in pink fluffy slippers.

He rushes around to open my door for me and I step out, my stomach contracting with nerves. Suddenly my ankle is not the only thing I'm worried about.

'Don't worry, you'll be fine,' he says, smiling at me, his eyes warm. He puts Toffee onto the ground and offers me his hand. 'Come on.'

I give in and take it, trying desperately not to react this time. I let him drag me, limping, towards the house, the warmth from his hand making me feel woozy. I'm already dreading when he's going to let go.

We walk to the old fashioned front door, with frosted glass and an old knocker with a lion's head. He knocks just as I notice some balloons tied to a hanging basket.

'Is it somebody's birthday?' I enquire.

At his comical expression I feel the blood draining from my face.

'Yep – she's eighty today.'

'What?'

But it's too late. The door swings open and an old man smiles at us.

'Hey Teddy,' Ryan smiles.

'Hello Ryan, I haven't seen you in a while! Come through, the party's still going. Oh and is this your girlfriend?' he asks smiling warmly at me.

'No, just a friend,' he says, smiling arrogantly.

I smile politely but remove it when I see Teddy notice my erect nipples. Why couldn't I at least have a bra on? Ryan turns to laugh silently at me the minute Teddy's back is turned, enjoying my misery. We follow him into the back of the house where there is an open plan kitchen leading onto a conservatory. It's filled with old people drinking sherry as Billy Holiday plays on the stereo.

I don't need to be introduced to Ryan's Grandma to know which one she is. I can tell straight away. Through the crowds I notice a chubby round faced lady with the same brown curly hair and big brown eyes that he has. She's quite beautiful for eighty, with only a few laughter lines on her face. She also looks like the kind of person who doesn't suffer fools gladly. And today I am a fool. Ryan has clearly brought me for the entertainment.

'Ryan, sweetheart!' She rushes over, embracing him in a tight hung.

'Ok Grams, I only saw you this morning,' he laughs pulling himself away like a moody teenager.

'Oh, I know, but I'm always happy to see my favourite Grandson. And is this Poppy?' she asks, smiling warmly at me.

Has he talked about me before now?

'Hi.' I lift my hand and awkwardly wave to her. It feels too formal to shake her hand, but now I just feel foolish.

She grabs both my hands, her palms like silk, and steps back to have a good look at me. Paranoia sweeps over me as I notice her perfectly set hair and gold bracelets. I turn to stare at Ryan, a little discomfited at being on display and he looks away, his cheeks seeming a bit flushed too. I don't think I've ever seen him embarrassed.

'Happy birthday,' I blurt out. 'And sorry for the way I look. I didn't know I was coming here,' I add, disgraced by my outfit.

'You look lovely dear. Nothing worse than when a girl slaps too much paint on her face. You have natural beauty.'

I blush and instantly warm to her.

'And I hear you saved my dog today? Come on, I'll get you a sherry. Oh and I love your slippers.'

*   *   *

Two hours later and I've been introduced to all of her friends, each asking if I'm Ryan's girlfriend. We've talked old films, music, everything! Plus she's made me a cup of tea in a perfect china tea cup with roses down the side of it. I honestly feel closer to this woman in the last two hours than I do to my own mother. She's the down to earth mum I always wanted, not the judgemental, trophy mother that I got. She's even insisted on wrapping my swollen foot up in a bandage and making me several cups of tea, worried I'll get a cold from being out in the rain.

'Oh Ryan, I love this song. Dance with Poppy, will you?' she says, swaying along to the tune.

'Grams, she might not want to dance,' he grimaces.

'Well, you'll never know until you ask her,' she smiles encouragingly. He sighs and rolls his eyes. He turns to me, raising his eyebrows.

'May I have the pleasure of this dance?' he asks, bowing in front of me playfully.

I smile at him, then at his Grandma (who insists I also call her Grams). I take his hand to be led onto the dance floor, where a few other old couples have started dancing too.

He takes my right hand into a formal dance pose and puts his other hand round my waist. He's even taller when we're this close and my palms tingle from his touch.

'You know I can't dance properly to music like this. Especially with my foot.'

'Don't worry, we can just sway,' he says reassuringly.

He takes my hands and wraps them round his neck, my shaking hands trying to stay still. He starts swaying, his hands generating heat on my waist. It sends tingles of pleasure down my spine and I just want to kidnap him, tie him up and force him to marry me.

'Your Grandma's lovely,' I say smiling over at her as she stares at us.

'Yeah, and she loves you.' He looks down at me from under his lashes, his face close. The desperate urge for me to close the little distance between us is overpowering. To grab him and burrow my head deep in his chest.

'I'm sure she's like that with everyone you bring here.' I have to remind myself that I'm not special. That we're just friends.

'Yeah,' he sighs. 'She probably likes you a bit more than the elephant trainer but a bit less than the brain surgeon. She *really* thought she was special.'

'That's good to know,' I joke back.

The song finishes and he stops dancing, pulling back from me. The loneliness from the distance over shadows me immediately. As if he knows, he continues to hold my hand, leading me back to sit with his Grandma. Once we're seated, it eventually breaks off.

'Well, we'd better be going Grams.'

She grabs him and pulls him into a tight embrace. 'Love you sweetheart.'

'Love you too.'

He goes off to say goodbye to everyone else and his Grandma turns back to me.

'Thanks so much for having me,' I say politely.

'Thank you for coming dear. It's so nice to see Ryan with someone whose company he enjoys.'

'Well, yeah...he's a good friend.'

That's all he'll ever be.

'Yes, for now.' She grins mischievously at me.

'Sorry, but do you know something I don't?' I ask, praying desperately that I don't snort with laughter.

'All I know is that I know my Grandson. Better than he knows himself and he's happy. You're the first girl he's brought back here since...her. Don't go breaking his heart, mmm?'

She grabs me into a tight hug, almost choking the air out of me, before I can respond. Her? Who is 'her'?

'Aah, there you are,' says Teddy, walking towards me. 'I want to get your phone number. My Grandson would love you.'

'Oh...well...I'm really not looking to get into anything right now,' I stall.

'Nonsense. You never know when you're going to be swept of your feet my dear.'

'Leave the poor girl alone Teddy,' Grams complains to him.

'I will, when I get her number,' he says, insistent.

I begrudgingly type my number into his phone hoping that I'll never get a call.

When we finally get out of the door it's 10.30pm, but it feels more like midnight, the cold dark sky above us.

'Here,' he says, taking off his hooded cardigan and handing it to me. 'You look like you could do with this.'

I think about what a romantic gesture this is, until he smiles and I realise he's staring at my erect nipples.

'Cheeky bastard!' I shove him before throwing it on and zipping it up. 'If you were a real gentlemen you would have offered this to me when we were arriving.'

'Yeah, but where would the fun in that be?' he smiles.

I hit him on the arm in response, lingering to feel the dark thick hair on them. When I get in the car I snuggle up against the chair and let the hum of the engine drift me off to sleep.

*   *   *

'Poppy.'

I wake up in the car to see Ryan in my face, rubbing my cheek softly with the back of his fingers.

'We're home,' he says, his soft voice overwhelming.

I stretch my arms out in front of me and let him help me out of the car and up to the door. I'm so sleepy that I almost fall asleep against the wall as he fumbles with the key in the door. Once it's open I head straight for my bedroom.

'Poppy?' he whispers in the dark so as not to wake anyone.

'Yeah,' I whisper back, my eyelids heavy.

'Thanks for coming today. She loved you.' His voice is alluring, whether he's aiming for that or not.

'I didn't have much choice,' I whisper, smiling coyly even though he probably can't see me.

The darkness just seems to add to the electric atmosphere. Only the glare of the streetlight shining through the top window of the door highlights his eyes.

He edges closer and my heart stalls, any chance of breathing gone. He stretches out his hand and places it on my cheek looking deep into my eyes.

'Well, goodnight,' he says.

271

He pecks a kiss on my lips before pulling them away from mine. For two agonising heart beats he doesn't move. I stare at him, trying to not let him see me shiver from the electric current that just passed through us.

'Goodnight,' I whisper, looking into those amazing brown eyes glittering in the darkness, as need, desire and flat out frustration push me over the edge.

Before I have time to reason with myself I close the tiny space between us and peck another quick kiss on his warm, delicious lips. As I step back and look at his confused expression I wonder whether I've done the wrong thing kissing him back. I've done it. I've completely misread the signals. He's just being a nice guy. I'm mortified.

'Well, I'll see you in the morning,' he says.

He strokes my cheek and leans in for another kiss, this time lingering his lips on mine for a second too long. He pulls back leaving me cold and alone from his withdrawal and backs away. He continues to stare as he walks up the stairs, both confusion and amusement showing on his face.

I lean against the wall, struggling to take in breaths, more confused than ever.

Chapter 21

Why would he kiss me? I thought he was still going out with Tabitha? Plus, I really don't know if I can trust that he has no feelings for Grace. I'm so confused. Maybe it was just a friendship kiss and I'm just reading too much into it. That bitch would probably be very upset if she knew. I know it's wrong but whenever I picture her crying about it, a smile creeps over my face. Someone needs to bring that bitch down a peg or two anyway. She's probably still horrified how any man can reject her.

I know her sort; always getting what she wants, whether it be a man or a new car from Daddy. The popular girl from school who always dated the cool guy that everyone wanted and made sure everyone knew about how happy they were, flaunting it in everyone's faces. She makes me feel like the same gangly teenager that I was then, all braces and frizzy hair. Where she would have big hair and boobs, I'd have a big spot and bruise from where I'd fallen down the stairs. Again. God I hated school.

I'm still not so delusional to think that Ryan would choose me over her or Tabitha. I mean really, he did just kiss me goodnight. A normal reaction for a friend. I kiss Jazz goodbye all the time and don't bat an eyelid over it. Why was he any different? But I know why. Because he's a Greek God of a man. All jawline and cheek bones, his scruffy hair falling round his eyes. Oh God, just thinking about him gets me aroused.

It was a bit awkward this morning at breakfast but luckily Grace and Izzy were there too so I was able to just stare at him awkwardly over my Weetabix.

'Hey Pops, how are you?' Lilly asks as soon as I get to my desk.

'OK,' I say feeling exhausted.

'God, that really is going to be a big scar,' she says, grabbing my face for a closer look.

'Thanks for the support,' I say sarcastically.

'You know I love you Pops,' she smiles.

'Poppy!' Victor shouts at the top of his lungs.

Lilly looks horrified and runs off as I scramble for a pen and paper.

'Poppy!' he shouts again, frustrated. Shit, he sounds pissed. My stomach starts churning.

'Hi, sorry I just had to get a pen,' I say flustered at her door.

'Why did you book these?' he asks, hitting a piece of paper in his hand.

'Your flights? I...thought you told me to?' I'm trying desperately to un-jumble my thoughts.

'No I never! Why would I say that!?' His face is reddening and his stare is turning dangerous.

'Sorry. I thought you told me to book them,' I whisper pathetically.

I bloody know he told me to book them, but there's no point in arguing with him. It won't get me anywhere.

'Well I didn't!' he shouts furiously. He puts the paper down and places his hands on his temples. 'Poppy shut the door,' he whispers. Shit. Whispering is never a good sign. I turn round to shut the door and feel the nerves taking over my body.

'Poppy,' he says, his voice a malicious whisper.

I hate this voice. It's actually more intimidating than his shouting.

'When I tell you to book something, I'd like you to book it. But in this occasion, I did not tell you to book it. Do you understand?' He looks at me as if I'm mentally retarded.

'Yes, sorry,' I say swallowing my pride. 'I just thought you had. My mistake.'

'Are you calling me a liar?' he asks aggressively, the vein in his forehead throbbing.

'No!' I shout back, too startled to be diplomatic.

'Good,' although it sounds anything but OK. 'You'll have to just get it sorted.' He throws the piece of paper in the bin and turns to the window.

'Sorry...get it sorted?' I ask, barely looking up.

'Yes! Ring the airline and get it sorted. This is the last thing I want to hear about it.' He waves his hands at me. I suppose that means I'm dismissed.

I turn to walk out, feeling completely deflated.

'Oh, Poppy?'

'Yes?'

'Terrible injury on your face there.'

'Oh yes.' I pull my hand up to my face instinctively. 'Just had a small fall.'

'Well perhaps you should drink less. It looks very bad on the company, me employing someone who could be an extra on Shameless.'

Dick.

'Goodbye.'

*   *   *

Two hours later and I've rung everyone trying to get it sorted. The travel agent, the airline, even my friend that works for the airline, in a desperate last bid attempt that she could somehow hijack the system. But nothing can be done. The only thing left is to just burst into tears and threaten to kill myself.

'Damn it! I fucking hate this place,' I say to myself, a little too loudly.

'Mind your language please, Poppy,' Cheryl says, over her computer.

'Oh fuck off,' I snap, shaking from the sudden adrenalin running through my veins.

'Well! There's no need for that!' She huffs loudly, turning round offended.

'Sorry! I didn't mean it. I'm just...having a breakdown.'

'Oh...right,' she says, perplexed, but not caring enough to ask. 'Well your phone went off with a text.'

I reach for my phone and find a text from Jazz.

'Hey sex pot, Mission for today is to say yes to everything.
EVERYTHING! See what new doors it opens for you. Have fun
chicken xxx'

For goodness sakes! Why couldn't her life be a little more stressful? Just a little bit more – I'm sure it would make me feel better about myself. Even when she's five grand in debt she doesn't seem to have a care in the world.

'Hi Poppy,' Neville says, making me jump. 'Having a bad day?'

Bless Neville. He's hardly the best looking or funniest guy in the world but he's probably the nicest.

'Yeah, a bit of an understatement actually,' I cringe.

'Well...I was kind of wondering...if you're not too busy.' His face starts turning a shade of purple and sweat has suddenly appeared on his upper lip.

Oh my God. He's going to ask me out. Damn it. Why the fuck didn't I listen to Lilly? She always says you can't be nice to boys without them assuming you fancy them.

'What?' I ask quietly, hoping I'm wrong.

He takes a deep breath, seemingly for courage.

'Would you like to accompany me to lunch today?'

Oh. Lunch. That's not so bad. I have lunch with Lilly every day, no big deal. And I've got to say yes to everything anyway.

'Yes.'

His face lights up as if he's won the lottery.

'Great, see you then.'

* * *

'No, no! I insist on picking this up,' Neville says, as the waitress places the bill on the table.

'Are you sure?' I ask, hoping he won't argue.

'Of course,' he smiles. 'I've had a great time.'

'Me too,' I smile back.

And the truth is that I have had a great time. So what if Neville isn't Brad Pitt? So what if I don't fancy him one little bit? I still had a great time. He's really funny when he's relaxed. We spent half the lunch taking the piss out of everyone else in the restaurant. To be honest, I feel like I needed someone to adore me for an hour. It seems so long since anyone really gave a shit. I just hope he realises we're better off as friends.

The waitress walks over to get the cheque and fiddles around with the card machine when he asks the question I've been dreading.

'So...do you fancy doing this again?'

Oh dear. How do I tackle this one? Carefully I think. Very carefully. The waitress says something under her breath in a foreign language and laughs to herself. God knows what it was, but Neville's back immediately goes up.

'How dare you!' Neville shouts.

'Oh, I'm sorry,' the waitress says, taken aback. 'I didn't realise you spoke Portuguese.'

'Yes, well that's very clear,' Neville says, still furious. 'Perhaps next time you should think before you speak.'

'I'm...I'm really sorry,' she stammers. 'It's just that...well, I just don't see it with you two.'

She looks at me and then at Neville and laughs again to herself. How dare this woman judge us!? And poor Neville looks so embarrassed, his cheeks practically puce.

'Well, maybe you should look a bit closer,' I say getting up abruptly. I drag Nevile up and tuck his arm into mine. 'Come on Neville.'

He smiles at me in wonder and amazement, before smiling triumphantly at the waitress.

'Well, good day to you,' he says.

He leads me towards the door but stops midway. I look at him confused.

'I forgot to leave a tip,' he says apologetically.

'Tip? Are you crazy? Come on, you're ruining our great walk out.' I drag him towards the door before he can change his mind.

The minute we're on the pavement we both collapse in helpless laughter.

'That was the best lunch I've had in ages,' he says, smiling warmly.

'Um...thanks.'

*   *   *

That night as I walk towards Mum and Dad's house I pull out my phone and take another deep breath. This is no big deal. I'm sure it's not proper fraud and you're doing this for a friend. She'll thank you eventually.

I dial the number and wait for someone to pick it up.

'Hello, Grenada Estate Agents, how can I help you?'

'Hi,' I say in the most official PA voice I can muster. 'This is Miss Windsor here, PA to Miss Jasmine Green. I'd like to make an appointment to see a flat.'

'Oh marvellous,' the woman says, clearly smelling a sale. 'Can I ask the flat in question?'

'Yes, it's property number 652, a flat on Brenville Road.'

'OK, let me have a look.' I listen to her tapping on her computer and brace myself for her answer, my stomach a bag of nerves. 'Oh dear. I'm afraid that we've had an accepted offer on that flat and it's been taken off the market.'

'Well, Miss Green is willing to pay over the odds.'

'I'm afraid there's nothing I can do,' she says apologetically.

'You do realise that I'm talking about Miss Jasmine Green? Daughter to the porn tycoon Reginald Green?'

'Oh....wow. No, I didn't'. I can hear her thinking. 'When you say willing to pay over the odds....how...how much more are we talking?'

'Let's just say that Miss Green knows what she wants and money is no object to her.'

'Crumbs!' She laughs nervously.

'Look, it's up to you. If you'd rather miss out on the commission...'

'Oh no! No, no, we'd love to help! Let me speak to the seller and get back to you. If I could just take a number.'

I smile to myself and give her my number. Thank God, for once things are going my way.

I let myself in and stop for a minute to breathe in the overly perfumed house. It normally over powers me, but today I find it soothing. This afternoon with Victor was torturous. I had to explain that we couldn't change the flights and if we booked something else we'd have to lose the money. To say he wasn't pleased is an understatement. He actually threw a stapler.

'Hi, Mum, are you in?'

'Hey Po Po,' Ollie says, walking out of the kitchen eating toast. His eye is completely black now from Jake's punch. Far worse than I thought it would be.

'Hey bro. Where's Mum?'

'She's in the sitting room arguing with Dad in front of Abbey.' He rolls his eyes.

'Oh great,' I sigh. 'How did she react to the black eye?'

'I don't want to talk about it,' he says dismissively. 'Let's just say not well. It's this fucking wedding stressing her out. It's all she's been talking about for the last year. It's driving me crazy.'

Thank God I have one normal brother.

'Tell me about it. Apparently I'm here for a fitting for a dress she's picked out for me.'

'Ha ha! Good luck. Oh and wait till you see the new sitting room,' he smirks. He turns and stomps upstairs like a moody teenager.

I take a deep breath to brace myself and enter the room.

'All I'm saying is that Abbey might not want you wearing a white dress,' Dad says, as diplomatically as he can.

'And why the hell shouldn't I? Your mother took over my wedding and completely ruined it, and by the looks of it I'm not going to have the pleasure of giving Poppy away, so this may be the only wedding I get.'

'Only wedding you get? My God, Richard only got married last year and you nearly drove Annabel mad with your ridiculous planning. And you're doing the same again.'

'Oh, hi darling,' Mum says, when she sees me. 'Come and give Mummy a hug.' She puts down her glass of wine and opens her arms wide.

'Hi Pops,' Dad says, seeming exhausted by Mum's usual antics.

But I can't respond yet. Oh my God. The room. It's Moroccan themed. It's bloody ridiculous! She's laid new red patterned carpet and there are low slung red sofas covered in hundreds of cushions,

each a different luxurious fabric – silk, velvet, woollen – every one of
them embroidered in over the top patterns.

There are tiny tables placed around the room with floor cushions
around them. Even the walls are draped in fabric – red, purple,
yellow. I look up and the chandelier is now surrounded by billowing
fabric. God knows how it's even staying up there. How much did this
cost?

'Darling? Are you OK?' Mum asks concerned.

'No...It's just the room,' I say gesturing around.

'I know! It's fabulous isn't it? I'm so glad you like it.'

'Hi Abbey,' I nod, noticing her on the edge of the sofa.

'Hi,' she says, looking glum as she downs her wine.

'You must be getting really excited about the wedding now then?
Only a week to go,' I say, faking excitement as I try to find somewhere
to sit down amongst the thousands of cushions.

'Mmm, I would be if it wasn't so stressful.' She looks over at my
Mum as she says it.

'Yeah, did I hear right Mum? Did I hear you say you're wearing a
white dress?'

'Yes you did actually! And I'm well within my rights to wear it!' she
shouts defiantly.

'For goodness sakes Meryl! When will you just grow up and realise
everything isn't about you!?' Dad shouts.

'Mum! You cannot wear a white dress. And anyway, I don't think
white suits you very well. Abbey, what colour did you say the
bridesmaids were in?'

'They're in brown,' she says, uninterested.

Brown? What the hell? Why would you choose the colour of poo for
your wedding day?

'Aah, brown! Well Mum, I've always loved you in brown. It really
suits your skin, you know, all bronzed and stuff.'

'Mmm, I suppose I could look nice and tanned,' she says, mulling it
over.

'Oh completely. I think you'd look fab. You should really do it.' I
hope I'm winning her over.

'Oh, you're right. What the hell, I'll wear brown. I'll get a fabulous brown dress made for me. 'Carol,' she calls, turning to the family seamstress. 'I know Poppy was booked in for her dress fitting, but do you think you'd have time to do me first?'

'I...' Carol starts.

'Of course you do, fabulous! I'll just go and get my strapless bra on.' She turns and runs out of the room.

'Poppy, thank you so much!' Abbey says, running over and hugging me. 'You've literally saved my life. My Mum said she'd punch her in the face if she turned up in white. I've been having sleepless nights about it.'

'Don't worry about it. We know what she can be like.' I smile knowingly at Dad.

'You're a lifesaver. Listen...I know you were booked in to just get a normal dress fitted that your Mum bought for you, but I was thinking...do you want to be one of my bridesmaids?' she asks jumping up and down in excitement.

'Bridesmaid?'

I see Dad's face break into a smile and I'm so tempted to hit him.

'Yeah, what do you say?'

'Um...I'd love to?'

'Yay!' She hugs me while jumping round in a circle. 'Henry will be so pleased!'

Really, as he's always kind of hated me, I want to say, but instead I smile sweetly.

'I'm back!' Mum says, jumping into the room dressed in only her bra and knickers.

'Jesus Meryl! Put some clothes on,' Dad shouts.

'Oh, stop being a prude Douglas!' she shoots back. 'What were you girls talking about then?' she asks as she positions herself next to Carol.

'Poppy's just agreed to be my bridesmaid,' Abbey says proudly.

'Oh marvellous! Make the most of it Poppy. It may be the only time you'll carry a bouquet in a church.'

'Thanks Mum,' I say rolling my eyes.

'And your eyes will really pop next to the brown,' Abbey says, her eyes lit up.

Brown. I shudder involuntarily every time I hear it.

'Oh yes,' Mum sniggers. 'My little green eyed monster.'

I sigh in response. I hate when she calls me that.

'Yeah, Poppy. I have always wondered. Where did you get your green eyes from?' She looks between Mum and Dad's blue eyes. 'Is there an Aunt or something that you take after?'

'We don't know,' I say, sick of the same question I've had to answer my whole life.

'I think Meryl had her way with the gardener!' Dad teases.

'That joke never gets old, does it Dad,' I say drily.

'It is strange.' She looks at me closely, as if I were an alien. It reminds me of the times when Mum would pick us up from school and the girls would say I was adopted.

'So Poppy, is there anything new with you?' Dad asks, thankfully changing the subject.

'Um...not really. You know I'm living at Jazz's at the moment don't you?'

'In trouble again is she? When will that girl grow up and settle down?' Mum tutts.

'She's fine actually. I'm just glad to have the company to be honest.'

'Are you seeing anyone?' Dad enquires, trying to be casual.

'No,' I say sadly.

'Well I was wondering darling,' Mum interrupts, 'Why don't you ask Stuart to the wedding?'

'Stuart? Are you fucking insane?' I shout, instantly losing my temper.

'Just a suggestion sweetheart! No need to have a heart attack.'

'Anyway, has anyone heard anything from Richard?' I enquire, trying to sound casual. Or more specifically has anyone heard about his whore of a wife.

'Richard?' Mum says, alarmed. 'Why? What's wrong with Richard?'

'No! Nothing's wrong! I was just...making conversation.'

'Oh. Well I haven't spoken to him in a few days.'

Great. So they're keeping it a secret. Abbey looks at me as if to communicate that she knows more but can't say.

'Anyway darling,' Mum says, taking me over to a quiet corner. 'Have you thought anymore about your *situation*?'

'I haven't got a situation. How many fucking more times do I have to tell you! I'm not pregnant!'

'That's what I keep telling her,' Dad shouts.

'Darling, there's no need to lie to me. A mother just knows.'

'Well it seems I'll just have to wait nine months to prove you wrong.' I get up and storm out of the house.

Chapter 22

'And this is Matilda at the park...oh and look at her on the swing,' Cheryl croons across the table with her camera.

'Ah, cute.' I smile politely as I try to ignore Lilly pretending to stab herself behind her.

'Anyway, I must go. Gotta go ring the Nanny and check my baby's ok,' she smiles before she leaves.

'I swear that woman used to be fun before she ruined her vagina forever,' Lilly snorts.

'She's not that bad,' I protest, feeling bad to slag her off. Her whole world is crumbling around her.

'Oh, come on! All the woman talks about is that baby. If I ever get like that just shoot me, OK.'

'Don't worry, the very minute.' I make a finger gun and stick it to her head.

'That's sweet. Anyway, have you seen any of Neville today?' she teases.

I had of course filled her in on everything the minute I got back from lunch yesterday.

'I've been avoiding him like the plague, poor thing.'

'You do know that this is your own fault,' she says, with no sympathy.

'Yes. You did remind me a few times. I just can't be horrible to him. He's so lovely.'

'You really do have a problem. It's almost a disability.'

'Whatever. You're just mean.'

'Ah thanks,' she gushes, taking it as a compliment instead of an insult.

'Anyway, I haven't told you about Alex and the washing machine incident.'

'No, what happened?' I ask, bracing myself for the latest rant from their stormy relationship. Well, I say stormy, more like Lilly shouts and he just tries to calm her down.

'Well, so I'm in the kitchen, loading the washing in the machine and he comes in. Then he starts – '

My phone ringing stops her in her tracks. I glance at the phone, sure that it'll be Jazz, but it's an unknown number. I'm always a bit nervous about picking these up, but I'm too curious to ignore it.

'Hello?' I say carefully down the phone.

'Hi, is that Poppy?' says an unfamiliar male voice.

'Um...yes, but who's this?' I ask afraid that it's my bank.

'Um...this is Lewis. I'm Teddy's Grandson.'

Oh my God. I'm going to pass out. I've been set up with a stranger.

'It's a bit awkward, but I was wondering if you wanted to go out for a drink sometime?'

'Um...well....I'm not sure.' I don't know how to let him down gently. Lilly starts waving her hands in the air and mouthing 'who is it?' over and over again.

'Look, I know I'm a total stranger calling you up, but the truth is that my Granddad won't stop pestering me to call you and take you out and he won't stop until I do. I just really need to get him off my back.'

'Oh, so you don't really want to go out with me at all?' I say with humour in my voice.

Lilly looks like she might pass out from anticipation and starts shoving me on the shoulder, still mouthing 'who?'

'Well, I don't know. I haven't seen you yet,' he laughs.

'But I'm sure you agree it's what's inside that counts, right?' I ask, shocked that I'm flirting.

'Oh of course,' he says playfully. 'Unless you're a dragon. So what do you say?'

I think for a moment. What have I got to lose? Ryan's hardly talked to me since Sunday, probably scared to lead me on in case I'd pounce on him again. Plus, if it goes well I could get a date for the wedding and get my Mum off my back.

'Ok, I'll go out with you. Tomorrow night, 8pm at Whispers bar in Shepherds Bush.'

'Ok great, see you then,' he says, hanging up.

'What the fuck!?' Lilly exclaims, throwing her hands in the air dramatically.

'My thoughts exactly.'

My phone rings again and me and Lilly stare at it in shock.

'It can't be him again can it?' she asks. 'Or have you been giving your number out to more random strangers?'

I glare at her and answer it. 'Hello?'

'Hello, is that Miss Windsor?' a posh voice bellows down the phone.

'Yes,' I say cautiously.

'This is Caroline from Grenada Estate Agents. You wanted a viewing for Belvedere Road?'

'Um...yes, that's right,' I say, pulling away even more from Lilly. If she hears this I'm dead.

'Well the seller is willing to have Miss Green view the property. How's tonight for you?'

*   *   *

'I can't believe you're making me do this,' Jazz moans as we walk towards the flat. It's an old Victorian terraced house which has been split into two maisonettes. 'And you're still not gonna let me know why I'm doing it?' She stares with wide suspicious eyes.

'Um...let's just say it's to help a friend,' I say vaguely.

'How is putting in a higher offer helping a friend?'

'It's a long story, OK. So just shut up and act rich and obnoxious.'

'Fine,' she snaps.

The door of the flat swings open and a beaming estate agent smiles wildly at us. She's about forty-five, got pink lipstick on her teeth, and has greying wiry hair.

'Miss Green!' she bellows, as if she's know Jazz forever. She turns to look at me. 'And you must be her PA! Please come in!'

We follow her into the pale green hallway and then into the sitting room. It's got three long sash windows and a massive original fireplace. It's painted a pale pink and the floors are a cheap laminate which is bowed slightly underneath our feet.

'This is the sitting room. As you can see it still maintains many of the original features.'

We nod appreciatively. Then we're led into the kitchen. It looks like it's had five different kitchens fitted over the years and each cupboard door is different to the other one. It has a tiny window leading onto the garden. Suddenly I feel bad. I can see Lilly living here. I can see why she loves it, it's totally her in a flat. Not perfect, but perfect for her. Who the hell am I getting in the way of their happiness? Maybe they'd be able to afford this flat once she gets made redundant anyway. Maybe she'll get a job straight away. Or maybe she'll be out of work for two years. Oh God, I just don't know.

'It's only minutes away from The Broadway with many shops, bars and restaurants,' the estate agent continues. 'The closest station is Cricklewood National Rail.'

'Yes thank you,' I cut her off. 'I'd like to talk over an offer with Miss Green.'

'Of course,' the estate agents bows, as if to a queen, slowly backing out of the sitting room.

'So, you want me to put a fake offer in?' Jazz asks, her bottom lip sulking from boredom.

'Yes.'

'Oh, fine.' She falls back onto the sofa with her arms out dramatically. I see something colourful flash through the corner of my eyes and then an almighty crashing noise. Jazz and I stare at each other, our eyes wide, neither of us knowing what just happened.

'Please don't tell me you just broke something,' I say, my voice strained.

'OK.' She looks onto the floor. 'Then I definitely won't tell you I just smashed a vase in half.'

I look down and sure enough there is a red and black vase in two on the floor.

'Shit.'

'Don't worry!' she shouts. 'I have some nail glue in my bag.' She runs over to her silver and gold bag and pulls out a little tube.

'Are you OK in there ladies?' Julie the estate agent's voice says through the door.

Shit.

'Stop her!' I hiss at Jazz. Jazz runs to the door.

'We'd just like a few more minutes,' she shouts, holding onto the door knob.

I quickly pull the glue out and dab it along the edges. Thank God it's a clean break. I fuse the edges together and push tightly together. I blow my hair out of my face, my forehead sticky.

'Miss Green,' Julie shouts. 'The owners are here now and they're keen to talk to you.'

Jazz looks back at me in panic. 'Is it dry yet?' she whispers.

'I don't know,' I say, my throat tight.

Jazz suddenly falls back, Julie barging through the door, her face red and flustered.

'It seems we were having a bit of trouble with the door there,' Julie says, looking at us suspiciously. 'Not that there's any problem with the door of course,' she corrects herself.

A couple in their sixties walk in. The woman is tall, slim and has long blonde hair. Her face is full of Botox and her teeth are clearly veneers, but you can still see her true age. She's dressed in a flowery maxi dress with sparkly flip flops. The man has grey hair and a massive nose. He's short and a bit rough around the edges.

'This is Mr and Mrs Clennel,' Julie presents proudly.

They smile politely, their gaze eventually dropping to my hands, still holding the vase. Jazz turns to look at me and looks at me as if to say 'put the vase down'.

I smile nervously. 'Beautiful vase you have here. I was just examining it.' I walk over to the table and place it down, feeling everyone's eyes on me. They obviously think I'm a freak or something. I try to leave it there, but it keeps getting attached to me. I shake my hands a bit more violently but the vase is still attached to me. Have I really managed to glue myself to it? *Of course* I have.

I pick it up again and stand tall. 'Actually it's so beautiful I'd like to take a closer look.' I pull it closer to my face while everyone looks on in horror.

'I'd like to make an offer,' Jazz says loudly, seeming to be trying to be taking attention away from me.

'Excellent!' Julie beams.

'Yes,' Jazz agrees. She keeps looking at me in confusion, her eyes shooting daggers. 'Put down the vase,' she's desperately trying to communicate.

'How much would you like to offer?' Mr Clennel asks, clearing his throat.

What the hell am I going to do? How am I going to get this vase off my hands? I start discreetly shaking my hands, then trying to pull them with all of my force off them. How the hell can nail glue be so strong?

'Um...' Jazz says. 'I'd like to offer a million.'

Three stunned faces look back at her.

'You...you want to offer a million?' Julie asks, her face pale. She looks like she's about to pass out. 'You do realise that the current offer is only at £200,000?'

For God's sake Jazz.

'Oh, really?' Jazz shrieks. 'Did I say a million? I meant....half a million....well, actually half of half a million,' she smiles nervously, glancing from me back to Julie. 'I meant £250,000. Yes, that's right. £250,000.'

Mr Clennel eyes her suspiciously. 'And this is a genuine offer?'

'Of course!' I shout before I can stop myself.

He narrows his eyes on me. 'Can I have my vase back please?'

'No!'

'No?' he asks, his voice as deep as a headmasters.

'I mean....I love it so much....um, I'd like to buy it! Yes, Jazz would like to buy it from you.'

'Yes!' Jazz shouts, shuffling in her bag. She pulls out a cheque book and a pen. 'How much? Name your price.'

'Oh, I'm afraid it's not for sale,' Mrs Clennel says with a girlish laugh. Mr and Mrs Clennel and exchange smiles. 'You see, that vase was given to us on our wedding day from my Mother, God rest her soul.' What? Is she for real? We've broken a priceless vase.

'A million!' Jazz shouts. 'A million for the vase! Surely you can't say no to a million?' Her forehead is sticky and she's biting her nails.

Mr Clennel scratches his head, clearly wondering if this is a dream. He glances at Mrs Clennel and she shakes her head.

'No, I'm afraid it's not for sale,' he says sternly, while his eyes seem to be wondering what he'd do with a million.

Jazz looks at me in horror. What the hell am I going to do? Jazz raises her eyebrows as if a sudden genius idea has come to her.

'Run!' she screams, running into the hallway.

I stand there frozen, them all looking at me in disbelief. Oh sod it. I run out into the hallway, pushing Mr Clennel out of the way. Jazz is at the front door struggling with the lock.

'They must have locked us in!' she shouts. 'Help me!'

'I've kind of got my hands full at the moment!'

Three sets of footsteps slowly follow us out into the hallway, their bewildered faces staring. They stare at us, still unable to speak as I feel my cheeks getting redder and redder. I actually want to die. This is the worst thing that's ever happened to me. Much worse than that time I pissed myself laughing in secondary school. That seems tame compared to this, and that's saying something. I was called Poppy Pissy Pants until I left.

'Tah dah!' Jazz exclaims, shoving jazz hands in the air.

'Sorry?' Mr Clennel says. Julie's face is getting redder by the second.

'That was a little performance we've been working on,' Jazz explains. 'We're playing at the local theatre next Saturday and you've been lucky enough to witness a scene from it.'

'Really?' Julie asks carefully. 'What's it called?'

I look at Jazz hoping she can pull this off.

'Oh, it's...the best title ever. It's called 'The Stolen Vase of Dreams.' They stare back at us and this time I think they're considering calling the police.

'My hands are glued to the vase,' I say, admitting defeat.

Jazz looks at me hysterically. 'Ha ha! How funny! Another part of the play. Ok, now cut Poppy. We don't want to give the whole play away!'

'No Jazz, I mean it. We're not getting out of this. I'm so sorry, but I broke your vase.'

*   *   *

I really do think calling the police was a tad dramatic. I mean, it was clearly an accident. Although, it didn't look too good when the policeman said we'd just received a caution a couple of weeks ago. Mr and Mrs Clennel thought we were some kind of criminals that stole vases from unsuspecting couples. Even when I explained that it had been a fire, not a robbery, they didn't seem to relent. God I hate the middle class. Although I suppose in hindsight, Jazz shouting 'I'm not going back to that place!' hysterically didn't look good. Anyway, thankfully the policeman saw that it was all a bit of an embarrassing situation and let us go. Well, after we'd soaked my hands in hot water with fairy liquid for half an hour. I think I even saw him giggle. It'll probably be a great story at the station by tonight.

As I put the key in the lock I'm pleased to hear no noise. Thank God, they must all be out. I walk towards the kitchen and dump my bag down, flipping the kettle to boil.

'Hey Pops. I'll have a tea thanks,' Ryan shouts from the sofa. Shit.

'OK,' I say in a strangled voice.

I make the tea, finding a china cup with a scary looking clown on the side for myself, my hands now shaking and carry them in towards him. My hands are shaking so much I struggle not to spill it on the carpet. Get a hold of yourself, Poppy. It's only Ryan. Delicious Ryan. I hope Izzy and Grace are in there with him but have decided to take a pledge of silence. The awkwardness is killing me. When I turn the corner, I nearly drop it. He's just so pretty. He literally takes my breath away

291

every single time I see him. It's like I've been deprived of him and that first glimpse is how I imagine a heroin addict is when they get their next hit.

He smiles his devastating smile, his lips twisting to one side and sits up from lying on the sofa.

'So how was your day?' I ask, trying to sound like a normal friendly housemate. I congratulated myself for managing to talk without my voice cracking or trembling.

'Yeah really good actually.'

I hate how he never elaborates.

'OK....anything else you want to say on the subject?' I say, my mouth twisting with an urge to giggle.

'No. That's about it,' he smiles with a glint in his eye.

I take a sip of my tea and think desperately for something to say. But the atmosphere. My God – it's so electric! I can barely sit still.

'Are Izzy and Grace out?'

'Yeah I think so,' he says, his eyes glued to the TV.

'So...you don't actually know.'

'Nope,' he says, his voice flat and uninterested. 'Anyway, you look tense. What's wrong?'

'Do I?' I shriek a little too loudly. 'Oh, no, I'm fine. Absolutely fine. Totally fine.'

Perhaps too many fines in that answer. I almost put my hand to my mouth to shut myself up.

'So wait,' he says, turning seriously to me. 'Are you...fine?' he asks, a mocking smile on his face.

'Shut up!' I hit him on the arm playfully.

'Aah! Aaah!' he cries as his tea spills all over his arm.

'Shit sorry!' I jump up. 'Quick, give me the mug and I'll help you clean up.' I clasp at the mug.

'No, its OK,' he says, flicking his hand around to get the tea off.

'No really, just give it to me,' I say grabbing his mug a bit more forcibly.

'No. Poppy, stop!'

But it's too late. The cup flies back at him and the remaining tea slops out onto his crotch. His fucking crotch!

'Fuck! For fucks sake!' he screams as he jumps up, his tracksuit bottoms soaked through.

'Sorry! Shit, I'm so sorry!'

I want to kill myself.

'Don't worry,' he says, his lips pressed into a hard line, all signs of humour gone. 'Just get me something will you?'

'A biscuit?' I blurt out.

He glares at me. 'No, of course not. A tea towel,' he says frostily.

'Oh yeah. Obviously.'

I should physically kick myself. What an idiot.

'You know what, don't worry. I'll go get changed.' He walks out of the kitchen.

'OK. Sorry...again.'

I hear him walk up the stairs and I hit myself several times on the head. I try to clean up, dabbing the stains on the sofa with a tea towel. Luckily this sofa wouldn't have won any beauty contests before anyway.

The front door slams and Izzy's giggles echo through the hallway.

'Come on through,' she shrieks, sounding half cut. 'Hey Pops,' she sings, skipping into the kitchen with a short dark haired guy on her arm. 'This is Greg.'

'Hey,' he nods.

Grace is the next to come in with another short guy, but this one has golden hair and is much better looking. She obviously called dibs. They all look thoroughly pissed, Izzy smiling from ear to ear, her forehead shiny. Grace still looks like she could have just walked off the catwalk, although her actual walk is a bit wobbly.

'Good night then?' I ask, feeling rather nervous at how drunk they are. I mean, it's only 8.30pm. How could they already be this drunk?

'Oh Pops, we had an awesome night, you should have come,' Izzy says, sitting on the floor cross legged.

You'd had to have invited me.

'Wine?' Grace says, giving each of them a glass out of the cupboard and pouring it to the top. 'Oops, we've done the bottle.' She lets out a little seductive giggle.

The man with the golden hair seems captivated by her. I don't blame him. Even I find myself not being able to look away from her in her skin tight red dress.

'Hey girls,' Ryan says, walking in with new tracksuit bottoms on.

'Hey Ry Ry,' Grace purrs pouting her lips towards him.

Ry Ry? What the hell? He gives her a strange look and catches me looking at them. I quickly look away and try to look uninterested. Grace holds the empty bottle above her head and for a second I think she's actually going to drop it on the floor.

'I know. Who fancies a game of spin the bottle?' she smirks.

It's my worst nightmare. I'm a gangly thirteen year old with braces again. I thought I was safe from this game now I was an adult.

'Yay!' Izzy shouts, spilling some of her wine on the carpet.

'What do you think?' Ryan says to me, a mischievous smile on his face.

'I don't know,' I say hoping someone will come up with an idea to play twister instead.

'Oh come on Pops, it'll be fun,' Izzy wails.

'Yeah, come on Poppy. Don't be such a spoil sport,' Grace says, her words cutting me like glass as she holds my stare.

'O...kay,' I finally spit out.

We all instinctively sit on the floor, my palms already sweaty from the panic. I sit in between Izzy and the golden haired man, who still hasn't been introduced to me. I hope my breath is fresh. I probably still smell of tea. I hope I don't get picked. Is it too late to back out of this?

Grace spins the bottle and I wipe my sweaty forehead, trying not to look as nervous as I feel.

'Greg!' they all sing.

Greg picks the bottle up, smiling at Izzy, who it's obvious he wants it to land on. He spins the bottle again and it begins to slow down, painfully slow. I hold my breath, begging it to keep going. It finally stops, pointing at me. Of course. I shift slightly in my seat, hoping that someone will agree it's Izzy, not me.

'Poppy!' Izzy sings. 'Poppy and Greg!'

I look up at him and my stomach does a nervous flip. I can't be rude and refuse the kiss, but I really don't want to kiss this guy. As I look at him closer I realise his lips are chapped. Ugh! I don't want those lips cutting mine to shreds.

I glance round at everyone else wondering if they'll agree that was just a practise run. Ryan is looking at Greg a bit strangely. Could it be jealousy? No, it can't be, it's probably just sympathy. Pity that the poor guy has to kiss me. I really don't want to kiss him, but what can I say? Sorry everyone, but I'm secretly in love with Ryan. I don't think so.

I take a deep breath and slowly lean forward into the circle, almost crawling like a dog towards him. He leans in eagerly and I try not to grimace as I catch a whiff of his breath, a mix of beer and wine. I decide to just take the initiative and get it over and done with. I quickly peck him on the lips and then sit back, smoothing my hair back self-consciously.

'What?' Grace says shortly. 'That's not a kiss. I want a real kiss, tongues and all.' Her expression is stern.

'Yeah, come on, a proper kiss!' Izzy wails clapping her hands.

I look back at him and he looks embarrassed too. At least it's not just me living this nightmare. I lean into him again, but this time I catch Ryan staring at me, which makes me all the more nervous. He looks away quickly when he sees me notice him. This time I decide to just place my face in front of him and close my eyes.

His lips plunge onto me, forcing my lips open so that he can caress my tongue, it rolling sloppily around my mouth. There's so much tongue in my mouth I struggle to breathe. How long is this tongue? I know they said they wanted a proper kiss, but this is a bit ridiculous. I lean back, trying to retract myself, but he leans back with me. I lean back even further, to the point where I'm almost lying down on my back, but he's still raping my mouth. I put my hands up to his chest to try and push him softly off me but he seems to think I'm trying to encourage him and kisses harder, darting his tongue like an angry pecking bird.

He finally sets me free and when I open my eyes, to remove the remaining slobber I seem to have on my chin, I notice that Ryan's hand is on Greg's shoulder pulling him back.

'That's enough,' Ryan says protectively.

Thank God someone saved me.

'Sorry dude. I didn't realise you two were dating,' Greg says.

I look at Ryan, my cheeks beginning to burn, but he looks away and goes back to his seat.

'We're not,' Ryan says flatly, staring at the floor.

'Oh,' Greg says, darting his eyes between us both confused.

Everyone seems to have gone silent as they watch this scene play out. God, the awkwardness is too awful. Someone say something – PLEASE!

'God, awkward turtle,' I say, doing my turtle tongue.

Five horrified faces stare back at me as if I've just told them I shag sheep.

'What?' I ask, my cheeks going even redder.

'Awkward turtle?' Ryan says, biting his lip to stop a smile which is quickly spreading on his face.

'Yeah. Have you never heard of that expression?'

I can't believe they haven't heard it. They're the mental ones.

'I can honestly say I have never heard anyone say "awkward turtle",' Grace says, looking smug and superior.

'Oh...well, maybe it's just something my family say then,' I say attempting a laugh.

'Who're your family? The Hillbillies?' Grace snorts.

'No!' I say, my voice barely audible. I feel so hurt and humiliated that tears are threatening to break from behind my eyes.

Do not cry. Do not cry.

'Right, whose go is it now?' I ask desperate to break the silence.

I grab the bottle and spin it quickly, ignoring the stares. It lands on Grace first and then Izzy. I think they're going to decline but then they start making out in front of us all, their hands exploring each other's bodies. It's almost like soft porn. I'm so astonished, there are no words. The guy's mouths are all open as they watch with curiosity, probably nursing hard ons that could cut ice.

'Wow, I didn't think you were gonna do it,' I say, still startled when they come up for air.

'That's spin the bottle, baby. You get who you get. And besides, Gracie's always been a good kisser,' Izzy says, winking at her.

Who'd have known it? I'm living with a pair of lesbians.

Izzy spins the bottle and this time it lands on Ryan. He rolls his eyes, as if he's far too cool for any of this. Grace suddenly sits up and takes notice, pursing her lips together. She must be desperate for it to stop on her. Probably creaming her knickers already.

I however, would rather it didn't land on me. I'm still confused by the other nights kiss, let alone anything else. I think anything else would just push me over the edge and I'd explode.

'Poppy!' Izzy claps excitedly as it stops on me. Oh crap.

I look up at Ryan and feel breathless, my heart pumping hard in my chest. How the hell am I going to do this? Is my breath OK? My head starts thumping as a million questions go racing through my mind. Grace looks disgusted and gets up to walk into the kitchen.

He leans back behind Izzy and I go behind her too, glad of the privacy her small body will provide.

For a second I forget about everyone else in the room. It's just me and him looking at each other, as nervous as could be. His burning eyes lock with mine, releasing their full power on me, turning my legs to jelly. When that mesmerising gaze drops to my lips I lose my balance, falling slightly to the right. He flashes his gleaming smile, dazing me momentarily before I lean in a bit further, taking an unsteady breath. He leans his head in until he's close enough for me to smell his sweet breath. My own breathing is erratic, short spurts of breath making me almost choke. My mouth is almost turning numb from the nerves and my stomach's full of flutters. He takes my face in his hands and draws my mouth up to his. I close my eyes, melting into it.

His plump lips meet mine, so soft and yet firm. His silky palms against my cheeks make me want to feel those strong hands moving all over my body, one slow inch at a time. I hear both of us take a sharp intake of breath through our noses and then he ever so slowly parts his lips, poking his tongue onto mine for just a second, then taking it back out. He continues to tease me with the pleasure he's withholding. I tremble. He kisses me harder. He pushes his hands into my hair, my whole body shivering from the pleasure. His hands move down to my neck, his thumbs circling small patterns. I let myself get lost in it. The kiss goes on until I feel I'm going to melt with the heat roaring through my body, and we're both gasping for breath. He slowly pulls away and when I open my eyes I'm still in a daze, everything around me seeming fuzzy.

'Wow,' I whisper before I can help it.

He smiles at me, his lips red. I try to pull myself together but I just can't stop staring at him.

'Wow. That was hot!' Izzy chuckles.

Ryan gets up and walks into the kitchen. I sit still, trying to regain consciousness.

'OK, we'll leave Poppy out for now,' Izzy says, laughing at me as I sit there still in a dream world.

I get up, my legs still like jelly and decide I'll get a beer from the kitchen. And if Ryan just so happens to be there, so be it. I walk through the doorway and stop in my tracks as I see him cornered by Grace, her hands on his face. Kissing him.

Oh my God. Oh my fucking God. OK, try not to react. Just quickly get the hell out of here and pretend you haven't seen it. Go somewhere where you can cry over your broken heart. I turn hastily and in the process knock over a glass on the worktop, it smashing into a million pieces on the floor. Damn it! Why am I such a klutz!

Ryan pulls away and turns to look at me, his eyes wide with horror.

'Oops.' I look anywhere but at him.

I bend over to pick up the pieces, covering my face with my hair so that I can't see them anymore. Ryan bends down and tries to help me, collecting the remaining glass into his hand as Grace stares on from behind him, her arms crossed.

Why can't he just leave me alone? Why does he keep doing this to me? Grace was right all along. He's been leading me on just for a bit of entertainment. He thinks I'm a joke. He's been laughing with Grace about me behind my back. The two of them, rolling back and forth in bed naked, their bodies crushed against each other as they relay the latest ridiculous thing I've done.

'OK...well, sorry for interrupting,' I mumble before turning sharply and running out of the room into my bedroom, just as the tears begin to fall.

Chapter 23

The next morning I'm still recovering from my loss. For I have lost my lovely dream world where I fantasised that Ryan was secretly in love with me. He's not in love with me. Of course he's not. He's barely friends with me, and what did I expect? Honestly, did I expect him to just ignore the charms of Gorgeous Grace and settle on little old boring me? I feel so foolish for even wishing that were true.

He thinks I'm a joke. Well I'll show him what a joke I am. I'll show him how fabulous I can be. No more pushover Poppy. At least today I'm having my stitches taken out. I am so ready to have these out! I can't begin to tell you how they've interfered with my cleansing routine. They itch so badly and seem to gloat up at me every time I look at them, reminding me that Gorgeous Grace always wins.

I'm nearly fully dressed when Jazz flashes up on my mobile.

'Hey hun.'

'Pops, I'm so sorry, but I'm not gonna be able to go to the doctors with you today.'

'What? You were supposed to be my moral support so I didn't act like a complete baby!' I shriek, panicking.

'I know! I know! I'm so sorry, but I've got a last minute interview.'

'Interview? What for?'

'It's just...for something else. I can't really say much about it. Anyway, are you sure you'll be OK without me?'

'Yeah, that's OK. Don't worry about it,' I lie.

I mean, why couldn't she have told me this last night? She's known since Monday about this appointment and she only knows to tell me this at 8am in the morning? And why the mystery about the interview? She's not normally so secretive.

'Are you sure babe?'

'Yeah, honestly it's fine. I've gotta go, love you.'

'Love you too. Call me later.'

Great – now I have to go by myself. Why the hell couldn't she be more responsible – just for once!?

I wander into the kitchen and hover over the cereals, not really feeling brave enough to eat. The truth is that I'm terrified to have them out. I mean, even thinking about it gives me the creeps. I don't even know how they're gonna do it. I tried to Google it but I couldn't bear to watch any of the videos that flashed up.

'Hey Pops,' Ryan says, walking in with a devastatingly handsome suit on, his hair still wet from the shower.

How can he act normal? Like nothing's happened. And calling me Pops. How dare he shorten my name!

'Hi,' I say trying to act natural and not like the spoilt brat I want to be. What I really want to do is run over and punch him hysterically and scream 'why don't you love me!?' But I have a feeling that would be slightly pathetic and needy.

'So...today's the day then' he says with a warm smile.

How can he act so normal? He's a heartless arsehole.

'Yep. After today I'll be normal again.'

'Well...I wouldn't go that far,' he says, with a wicked grin.

'Gee, thanks.'

'So, what time you meeting Jazz?' he asks, pouring himself out some cereal.

It really does escape me how someone can manage to eat coco pops as much as he does and still manage to keep a fit physique. Not that I'm looking at his body. Not anymore.

'Oh...I'm just on my way to meet her now,' I lie.

I don't want his pity. I'm starting my new fabulous me today. No more Poppy the joke.

'Morning Pops,' Izzy says, bounding into the room, a ball of her usual energy. 'Jazz just called me and explained. I'd totes go with you, but I'm already running late for a client.'

I stare at her, trying to explain with my eyes that she's totally blown my cover.

'What?' she asks innocently as she peels a banana. 'Anyway, good luck.'

She runs out of the house and I turn begrudgingly to face Ryan and his accusing gaze.

'You better get going. You don't want to miss Jazz,' he says sarcastically.

'Ok, OK, I lied! I just didn't want you feeling sorry for me. I'm totally fine to go by myself.'

'You are funny,' he says, amusement all over his face. 'But it's your lucky day. I've got a late meeting this morning and I've got my blackberry with me, so I can go with you.'

'Really? I mean...no, I'll be fine. I'm fine, but thanks.'

'Pops, stop being stubborn and pretending to be brave. I can tell you're shitting it. It's all over your face. You're even paler than usual.'

'Oh thanks,' I say rolling my eyes.

'Just shut up and let me come with you, OK.'

I stare at him for a moment, trying to work out his hidden agenda, but the truth is that I could really do with someone being there while I wee my pants.

'OK,' I say reluctantly, feeling like a pathetic baby. If my brothers could only see me now, they'd laugh their arses off.

*   *   *

'So...once I get them taken out I can just act like normal again?' I ask the extremely hairy male doctor.

'Yes, although do still try and take it easy. The last thing you want is for the skin to come apart again,' he says, smiling warmly.

How can I trust this man? I mean, first of all he looks like a werewolf, with the most body hair I've ever seen on anyone. His thick black hair is escaping from the sleeves of his shirt, running down to his fingernails which are too long. Plus he's got a worryingly thick gold chain round his neck with a gold hoop earring in one ear. I mean, are you allowed to be a doctor and have an earring? Isn't it one of those unspoken rules? And which ear is it that tells people you're gay?

'Oh, OK,' I say as I begin to feel myself tremble. Don't panic Pops. This is going to be over so quickly. It's not going to hurt at all.

'Right, let's get on with it then,' he says, taking my face with his weird werewolf fingers.

I try not to show how visibly repulsed I am. He picks up some weird looking scissors and starts coming towards me with them.

'And, will I have to put any special cream on?' I ask, pulling myself away from him.

'No, back to normal,' he says, with a flash of irritation. He leans in again.

'And! How long have you been a doctor?' I ask, my voice a squeak.

I mean, maybe he's just a crazy person that's broken in off the streets and put on a doctors jacket. Yes! That's it, that's why he's got an earring. He's not a doctor at all, he's a con artist. A gay con artist!

He looks back up rubbing his face wearily and sighs.

'Pops, maybe you should just let him get it over and done with, hmm?' Ryan says, taking hold of my hand, his warm touch making me quiver. 'I'm sure it's pain free...right doctor?'

'Oh yes. You'll barely feel a thing.'

'Barely? So I *will* feel something?'

Oh my God. It's going to kill. What if I pass out from the pain?

'Barely anything at all,' he reassures.

Ryan looks at me, raising his eyebrows as if to communicate that I'm being ridiculous. I cannot be ridiculous. I'm fabulous Poppy now. Fabulous Poppy is brave like Tarzan. She rips the stitches out with her teeth! But obviously I wouldn't do that. Oh God, I shudder just from the image.

'OK,' I say reluctantly as my breathing grows erratic. 'OK, you can do it.'

'Maybe don't look at it while I'm doing it,' Doctor Werewolf says, as he takes my head again and I begin to hyperventilate.

I stare at him, feeling completely overwhelmed. At least when I had the stitches I was a bit pissed. This is full on sober and the thought of what's about to happen is making my skin crawl. The urge to just run straight out of this office and never come back is overwhelming. But then what would that achieve? I can't have these stitches in my face forever. Can I?

I just hope he isn't pissed. You hear about drunk doctors all the time. And I mean, what if he takes them out wrong and my face is scarred horrifically forever? I'll be in one of those weekly magazines with a headline like 'Doctor butchered my face, now I can't find anyone to love me'. God I can see it. I'll be surrounded by all of the cats I've had to buy. And they'll be weird looking cats, with one eye, and three legs and hacked off tails, because I'll have related to their odd looks. I'll have understood what they were going through.

'Just look at me Pops,' Ryan says, swivelling my head to face him.

I look up at his big brown eyes and feel myself calm as I look into the deepness of them. I've never realised before, but up close the colour around his pupil is lighter, almost a whisky colour. They're so beautiful, especially surrounded by his long eyelashes and bushy eyebrows. I try to concentrate on just this while I feel some pulling on my face. Just imagine it's an eyebrow wax. Don't think about it. Don't think about the gay werewolf doctor pulling stitches out of your face.

'There we go; good as new,' Doctor Werewolf says, breaking me from Ryan's stare.

'What?' I say feeling my face. 'It's done?'

I thought it would take at least half an hour.

'Yes, as easy as that,' Doctor Werewolf smiles.

'Well thank God that's over,' Ryan says, sighing with relief. 'I thought it was going to be awful.'

'What? You weren't saying that a minute ago!'

'Well, *obviously*. Would you have gone through with it otherwise?'

'Well...I suppose not.'

'Exactly.'

'I just don't like being lied to, that's all,' I say defensively, crossing my arms across my chest.

'Oh really? It's a good thing I'm not so sensitive isn't it?'

The doctor stares at us both confused.

'You can go now Poppy. Just make sure to keep it clean and come back if you get any severe itchiness or swelling.'

'OK thanks,' I say as we get up to leave.

The minute we're out of the door I turn to Ryan again, still confused by what he said.

'What did you mean? When have I lied to you?'

He's got a cheek. The way he's been confusing me lately.

'Oh please! Let's make a list shall we? You lied about being Jazz's cousin from Spain, then about Jazz coming with you this morning. It begs the question what else you've lied about?'

'Well...'

'Exactly!' he says, muffling a snicker.

'I thought I was a good actress,' I say, a little laugh escaping.

'I may be pretty, but I'm not dumb,' he says, cocking his eyebrows at me.

'I wouldn't even say pretty,' I say before he digs me playfully in the ribs.

'So, are you going back to work?' he asks.

'Yep. Victor won't be able to drink coffee without me. It's a very important role I have you know.'

'I can see that,' he says, playing along. 'I could always...'

'What? You could always what?' I ask, a little too desperately.

'Well, it's a nice day. I could always walk you to work. Your office is only a few tube stops from mine.'

He wants to spend time with me?!

'Yeah OK,' I say as casually as I can, but in my panic to try and act like a normal human being, I end up dropping my handbag, all of the contents spilling out onto the pavement.

'Shit.' I crouch down to pick them up.

He crouches down too and starts picking things up for me. God I've got a lot of crap in this bag, I really must clear it out when I get home. Oh my God. I notice my thrush cream on the floor next to him. Ok, don't panic. Just quickly lean forward and pick it up and he won't even notice.

I take a quick deep breath and reach my hand out to the cream. I'm nearly there and he hasn't even noticed yet. Thank God, this is going to be fine. He's still picking up random bits of eye make-up.

'Oh, let me get that,' he says, reaching for the cream.

Oh my God. If he picks it up, if he even removes my hand from above it, he'll see the words. He'll think I've got thrush. And he's a man – he probably doesn't even really know what thrush is – he'll just assume that it's a terrible sexually transmitted disease. He'll just assume that I'm a horrible nasty slut and if there was ever the smallest possibility of him fancying me, it will be ruined forever. Forever when he thinks of me images of a spotty vagina will flash into his mind and he'll vomit.

'Noooooooo!' I shout, leaping for it.

I dive for it, but in my panic fall and manage to take him down with me. I look up to see that I'm basically straddling him on the pavement. Oh God, people are starring and he's looking at me like I'm insane. But the main thing is that I have the thrush cream. It's in my hand.

'Whoops,' I grimace.

'Poppy, what the hell?' He pushes me back.

'Sorry. I....I lost my balance.'

'Really?' he asks raising his eyebrow. 'Why did you shout "no" then?'

'Um...just because...I knew I was falling.'

I crawl away from him pushing the rest of my things into my handbag, not feeling brave enough to look at him yet.

'O...kay.' He looks completely unconvinced as he begins to pick up my loose change.

'No, leave the penny,' I say taking the rest of the change from him.

'Huh?' he asks looking at me as if I've finally lost the plot.

'You should leave it there.' I stand up and try to get over the feelings of embarrassment.

'What for?' he asks studying me with curious eyes.

'You know...so someone else can find it and have good luck.'

He stares at me for a moment.

'Are you for real?' he asks, a smile breaking out on his face.

'Yes. Wouldn't you want someone to see it and pick it up, feeling that they're going to have good luck?'

'Well, to tell you the truth I've never really thought of it,' he says, his voice sounding like he's suppressing a laugh.

'Well maybe you should,' I snap.

How dare he make me feel stupid. He's the idiot that doesn't know about the penny rule. I stomp off towards the tube station, not caring whether he's following me or not. I HATE how he makes me feel stupid.

'You are funny,' he says, catching up with me in one stride of his long legs.

Great, probably funny like a clown. No-one fancies a comedian do they. Of course they don't. You don't ever see clown porn do you? Oh my God, why the hell am I thinking about clown porn? Images of creepy men dressed as clowns with their dicks out are flashing through my mind.

We jump on the tube and travel for a while in silence.

'You fancy getting a coffee before you go in?' he asks casually.

'Yeah, whatever,' I say still feeling moody.

When we get off at my stop I'm in a better mood, even though the weathers taken a turn for the worst. I must be the only person in the world that prefers a good thunder storm to tropical sunshine.

'Look at those clouds,' Ryan says, glancing towards a couple of big dirty grey clouds looming over us.

'Yeah. They look like shapes of things.'

'Really?' he asks, looking up at them again confused.

'Yeah, look.' I point upwards at them. 'There's a banana, that's the Eifel Tower and that's a clown.'

God, why can't I stop thinking about clowns!?

'You really are a fruit cake,' he laughs, shaking his head while he reads his blackberry.

'No I'm afraid that you are just a bore.'

'Thanks,' he says, rolling his eyes. 'In here OK?' he asks gesturing towards a Cafe Nero.

'Actually...could we go in there?' I point towards my normal bakery.

'Yeah, whatever.'

As we walk towards it the rain starts and we hurry our pace to miss it. The smell of fresh bread hits me the minute we walk through the door and it instantly calms me, like it always does. I look around at all of the beautiful, mis-matched, hand painted china tea cups. I'm home. Ryan shakes his wet hair like a dog and gestures towards a small table with two chairs.

'This is a nice place. You been here before?'

'A few times.'

'Hey Poppy,' Glenda says, walking past and blowing my cover. 'Shall I get you the usual?'

Damn it.

Ryan turns to smirk at me, my cover completely blown.

'Um...OK then. Ryan, what do you want?'

He stares at me for a moment, amusement in his eyes.

'I think I'll have the usual too,' he says, smiling at Glenda.

'Are you sure?' I check. 'You don't even know what I'm having.'

'I know. But I'm a risk taker. I'm crazy like that.'

Glenda rolls her eyes, winks at me and then walks away.

'So, you never come in here then?' he asks, cocking his eyebrow up.

'I may be a bit of a regular,' I smile.

'How come? Don't you have a Starbucks closer to your office?'

'Yeah, but it's not the same. There's nothing like a good bakery. The smell of fresh bread, iced cupcakes. It's all so lovely,' I gush, inhaling heavily.

'Wow. You really like bakeries,' he laughs.

'Well, my Grandma used to own one when I was little.'

'Really? That's pretty cool.'

'Yeah it was. I used to pop in every day after school and she'd make me a hot chocolate and give me the cupcake of the day. And she'd always have rock and roll playing on the radio and flour all over her clothes.'

God, just remembering her makes me miss her all the more. How can someone be gone for so long and the pain still feel so fresh?

'So, you two were close?'

'Yeah, really close. She totally got me, unlike my Mum,' I say rolling my eyes.

'Two usual's,' Glenda says, placing down two teas and two big pink cupcakes.

'Nothing much has changed then,' he says, humour curving his lips.

'So, did she sell it?'

'No. She died.'

'Oh.' Ryan's face drops as he tries to smile sympathetically.

'It's OK. It was a sudden heart attack when I was fifteen. My Mum and Auntie inherited the bakery.'

'And sold it?' he guesses.

'Yep. I'll never forgive them for selling it. Especially to those people that turned it into a porn shop.'

Ryan spits out tea as he suddenly laughs.

'Shit, sorry,' he says, rubbing a napkin over his mouth. 'I just...wasn't expecting you to say that.'

'I know. Anyway, now whenever I'm feeling a bit crap I come here or to another bakery. The smells remind me of her. It kind of comforts me, you know.'

'Yeah, I get it.'

He leans forward and places his hand over mine. I quickly move it away and stuff a bit of the cupcake in my mouth.

'So. I've been asked out by Teddy's Grandson.'

'What?' he says, suddenly alert, his jaw wide.

'Yeah,' I say coolly. 'Called me yesterday and asked me out tonight.'

'And you said yes?'

'Yeah. That's normally how these things work,' I say sarcastically, glaring up at him from over my hot tea. All I see when I look at him now is him kissing Grace.

'Oh right. I just didn't think you'd be interested,' he says, his tone cutting.

'Well, tell me. Is there any reason why I shouldn't go out with him?'

I wish he'd tell me not to go. To stay home with him.

He stares at me intently as if he's trying to figure out what to do. For a brief second his stunning face is unexpectedly vulnerable.

'No. I suppose I can't,' he says indifferently.

'Well, then I'm going,' I say defiantly.

'Have fun,' he snorts.

How fucking dare he. Snort about my date. Like it's some big joke. Well, I'll show him. I'll show him just how gorgeous and attractive to another man I can be.

'I will.'

'I was actually going to invite you to a work do in a few weeks, but now I'm not sure if your new boyfriend will get upset.'

'What work thing?' I ask eagerly.

'It's this charity event they do every year. Probably really lame, but I can't really be arsed to get a proper date.'

'Oh thanks!' I exclaim, sounding more peeved than a normal friend should. 'Why don't you just ask Grace?'

'Why would I do that?' he asks innocently.

Because you were kissing her in the kitchen last night.

'Well...I think you two make a good couple.'

'Well, I don't think we do,' he says, as he breaks his cupcake apart with his hands.

'Really? You looked pretty cosy last night,' I say, not being able to resist.

'That wasn't what it looked like. She kissed me. I'm not interested.'

'OK, I believe you,' I mock.

'Look, do you want to come or not?' he asks, pissed off.

I pause, pretending to mull it over.

'Yeah OK. I suppose I've got nothing better to do.'

'Well I'm very honoured that you'll grace me with your presence,' he says sarcastically.

'Pops!' someone calls.

I turn round to see Lilly and Neville walking in. What the hell are they doing here?

'Hey Lilly, Neville. Have you met Ryan?'

'Yes, I met him at the party. Alright?' she smiles. Ryan smiles back politely.

'I haven't met him,' Neville says, looking a bit peeved at me having coffee with another man.

'Oh, of course. Neville, this is Ryan. My housemate.'

Neville looks him up and down as Ryan brushes the crumbs from his cupcake off his hands and extends it to him.

'Hi, I'm Neville,' he says, taking his hand. 'I'm Poppy's boyfriend.'

I choke on my tea and start spitting it out. Did he just say boyfriend?

I look up to see Lilly completely lost for words. A complete rarity.

Ryan's looking at Neville as if he's mental and Neville looks like he might punch Ryan any moment.

Boyfriend? Where the hell did he get that from?

'Um...come on Neville,' Lilly says, dragging him towards the counter. 'Let's get a coffee.'

She looks back at me and mouths 'what the fuck?'

I turn back to face Ryan and he's smiling smugly.

'Boyfriend? You're honestly going out with him?'

'No, of course not! I don't understand how he's come to that conclusion, trust me.'

'Then, why don't you just tell him?'

'I can't be that mean to him!'

'Oh and it's not mean to keep leading him along like this?'

'I...' Shit, I don't have an answer for this. 'It's...complicated.'

'Hey!' I hear Lilly shout. 'Get to the back of the queue.'

I turn round to see a rough looking guy staring angrily back at Lilly. He's in dirty jeans and a ripped duffel jacket. I'm guessing that he's homeless.

'I was here first,' he snarls.

Oh God, I really don't like the look of him. He looks like a heroin addict.

'No you weren't!' she screams, never one to miss out on the dramatics.

'I'm afraid that we were before you,' Neville says, nervously, straightening up his glasses.

'And who the fuck is this cunt?' he says, squaring up to him.

Oh my God. Hearing that word before lunch time is really shocking.

Everyone in the bakery turns to stare at the drama unfolding. I glance back at Ryan and he's already getting up. He stands protectively in front of me.

'Um...my name is Neville.'

Oh God, he's a walking bloody victim. He's going to get himself killed.

'Don't you call him that word!' Lilly says aggressively, like a little Rottweiler.

'You can shut the fuck up as well.'

I feel the anger rising in my body. How dare he speak to Lilly that way? How dare he come into my lovely bakery and scare everyone? I have to say something. I jump up and walk around Ryan up to him.

'You know, you really should pick on someone your own size,' I say before I realise what a mistake I've made.

'You fucking what?' he says, glaring at me with his blood shot eyes.

'You...you heard what I said,' I stammer, trying to stand my ground while Ryan grabs onto my waist, pulling me away.

'Sorry about her. Come on Poppy, let's go,' Ryan says, as he tries to drag me away.

'No! Don't apologise for me,' I say to him, furious.

'Come on Pops,' Lilly says. 'Scum like that's not worth it.'

'Yeah, go on, go,' he spits. 'You should keep your dog on a tighter lead mate.'

Oh my God. What a nasty bastard. I look up, humiliated. Ryan's face has changed in an instant. His jaw is locked tensely, his body stiffened.

'Ryan, don't worry, come on,' I say, attempting to pull him away, but it's no use. He's so strong there's no stopping him.

'What did you say?' Ryan growls, going right up to the man's face.

'You heard what I said,' he sneers.

My stomach contracts with nerves as I realise a fight's about to erupt. Why, oh why did I have to open my big mouth?

Ryan pushes him, the man pushing him back. The guy laughs and for a second I think he's going to walk away, but he turns and smacks Ryan in the face. Ryan loses his footing for a second, stumbling back onto the tiles.

312

'Oh my God, Ryan!'

I run over to him and touch his eye which is already bright red. He doesn't even look at me, but flings me off in one swift movement. He plunges towards the guy and decks him in the face. The guy falls straight back onto the floor, and Ryan climbs on top of him, continuing to punch him repeatedly in the face.

'Ryan! Stop! Please, just stop!' I yell, pulling at him, not wanting to look at the man whose nose is now bleeding.

It's like he's possessed!

'Shit, Pops! Stop him,' Lilly screams.

'I'm calling the police!' Glenda screams.

'Let's all just calm down, shall we?' I hear Neville say. He's so British. He'll be telling us to have a cup of tea next.

I jump in front of Ryan, above the man's battered face, holding my hands up to him in defence. I'm not sure if he'll even notice and end up knocking me out too. When I open my eyes he's stopped and is getting up.

'I'm sorry,' he says, looking around embarrassed.

He turns and storms out of the bakery.

'Glenda, I'm so sorry.'

There's blood all over her floor.

'Don't worry darling. You go after your man,' she smiles.

'Actually, I'm her boyfriend,' Neville says.

'Shut up Neville,' Lilly snaps. 'Pops, I'll see you back at work.'

I nod and run after him, but I can barely keep up, still out of breath from the drama. When I catch up with him we walk for a few minutes in complete silence.

'Well, that was scary,' I eventually spit out, sick of the silence.

He ignores me and carries on walking, his face hostile.

'How's your eye?' I ask, trying to touch it with my hand. He knocks my hand away angrily.

'I don't know why you're being so mean to me! I wasn't the one you were having a fight with!' I shout feeling hurt.

'No. You were the one that got me into the fight in the first place,' he says, hostility still in his eyes. 'You and your stupid friends.'

'Hey! They're not stupid! I'm...sorry. But I mean...you didn't have to fight him,' I try to reason.

'Didn't I Poppy? That's the difference with men and women. Women can go around starting fights with men but they'll never get punched. But the minute a guy is around they'll always get into a fight.'

'Well, that's wrong straight away. Jazz got punched in the face by some guy in a Uni bar. Look, that's not the point. I said I'm sorry, but I don't know why you fought him anyway. You could have just left it.'

'What? And let him insult you?' he spits, his face still tense.

'Yeah. I don't care!'

'Well maybe you should.'

'What do you mean?' I ask, confused.

'Nothing. I'm just pissed off. Now I have to go to a meeting with a black eye,' he says, staring at himself in a shop window. 'How the hell am I going to explain this?'

'Err...you could say that you stopped an old lady getting mugged?' I offer.

'Well thanks for everything,' he fumes sarcastically. 'I'll see you later.'

Oh my God. Have I really just ruined everything?

I think it's safe to say that I'm not fabulous Poppy today. I wouldn't even say I'm the joke Poppy. I'd say I've been promoted to disaster zone Poppy.

Chapter 24

'I have to leave! Bye!' Victor shouts, running out of the office.

I breathe a sigh of relief, pleased that this afternoon will be a bit more chilled out without him. Hang on a minute. He's gone and his Chinese visa hasn't arrived yet. He's flying tomorrow afternoon. Shit. OK, don't panic. I'll just call the visa people and check that it's on its way.

'Hello, Visa Application. How may I help you?'

'Hi. I'm expecting my boss's Chinese visa back today and I still haven't received it. He's flying tomorrow lunchtime and I'm getting a bit nervous. His name is Victor Darlington, order number 073843.'

'OK. Let me just check for you.'

I drum my fingers impatiently on the table. God, I need a manicure.

'It says here that it's due to be delivered to you around 6.30pm. Will that be OK?'

'Not really. We'll have closed by then. Can we change delivery address?'

'Yes, that shouldn't be a problem.'

Great. I'll just get it couriered back to the house. That way I'll have it in my hands and won't be panicking all night. I give her my address and let her assure me for the third time that it'll be OK. I'm sure it will be. Of course.

*   *   *

Well, I obviously didn't bank on there being train delays, did I?

'Please, if you could go as fast as you can,' I say to the taxi driver as he turns the corner into our road.

I've already rung the courier company three times to explain that if I'm not in they could leave it with a neighbour or post it through the door, but you can't trust these courier people can you? A load of jobs worth's.

As we turn the corner I see him. Red and yellow uniform heading
back towards his car.

'WAIT!' I scream out of the window.

I throw the money at the taxi driver and run towards him.

'WAIT!'

He hasn't heard me. He's closing the door. Why is he doing this to
me? Why is he out to ruin my life?

I run faster.

'WAIT! WAIT!'

I can hear the engine starting. Please God no. Please fucking God,
don't do this to me.

I run to his window, music blaring from it and practically throw
myself against it.

'WAIT!' I wail.

The poor man jumps out of his skin, probably thinking I've just been
murdered and rolls down his window slowly.

'You alright love?'

'Yes!' I say, panting. 'I just want my package.'

'I posted it through the door darlin' no probs.'

Oh thank you God. Someone in the universe is rooting for me.

'Brilliant! Thanks so much.'

'No probs. That's what we at E & L do best. Get packages to people.'

'OK great.'

What a weirdo. He drives off and I take a deep breath, smiling to
myself. See Poppy, when things are stressful, there's no need to fret.
Things always work out in the end.

I open the door and what I find sends a chill down my spine.

Toffee is here. She has the package in her mouth. Her drool is
dangling down it. Dear God, if that drool leaks through and runs the
ink of his passport. No wait, if she rips it apart with her bare teeth. If
she poos on it. For the love of Lassie, there are so many terrifying
possibilities.

'Toffee,' I say carefully, edging slowly towards her.

No quick movements. I don't want to scare her off.

'Why don't you give me the package? Hmm?' I smile sweetly.

Dogs can see when you smile, right? I know they can't see black and white, or was it colours? Anyway, I'm sure they can see smiling, or just catch the general vibe.

She looks up at me and smiles. Maybe she remembers that I rescued her that day.

'There we go.'

I reach for the envelope in front of her, now released from her jaws, edging my fingers slowly closer to it. It's nearly within my grasp, when she jumps and picks it up again.

Shit.

I knew dogs were evil. Especially this one, she's got that crazed look in her eye.

I grab hold of the envelope and try and pull it from her. She pulls back just as hard. Jesus, if she pulls too hard it will just be ripped apart.

'Give it to me,' I almost sing, hoping to lull her into a false sense of security.

But this bitch isn't going to give up. She yanks it away, harder this time.

'I said give it to me!' I shout, scaring myself a little bit.

She hardly flinches. I try to touch her mouth to de-clench her teeth from it, but they're too gross. We go back and forth, while I begin to sweat profusely.

'Poppy? What are you doing?' Ryan asks, popping his head around the corner, his eye now completely back.

Well, I must look ridiculous.

'I need my package! Please, just tell her to give it to me, will you?'

He raises his eyebrow and smirks.

'Toffee. Treat time,' he calls, pulling a treat from his jeans pocket.

Just like that Toffee drops the envelope and runs towards him. Thank Jesus.

I grab the package and run into the kitchen, trying to remove the slobber from it. It is pretty crumpled and she's even ripped a corner, but I'm still holding out hope that it's not ruined. I carefully remove the documents, my heart racing.

If his passport is ripped I'll literally kill myself. Izzy will find me hanging in the bathroom. Mind you, I'd hate for Izzy to have to find me. She might be completely traumatised and need counselling for years. Maybe I'll jump off a bridge. But then what if I cause a massive traffic hold up with that? Hmm, I'll have to think about it. I remove the papers and it's a miracle! They're not ripped! They're totally intact! I'm so elated I actually do a little spin round. I better just check that everything is ok. I fumble inside the envelope to find his passport. Where is it? Where's his passport?

I scan the first page of the document. KIP Solicitors? This isn't visa documents.

'Dear Miss Windsor,
It has been brought to my attention that my client, Mr Ryan Smith, has received several letters and presents from you and your Mother, Meryl Windsor. My client denies having a relationship with you and questions your mental health. It is therefore with regret that I have to tell you to stop harassing Mr Smith or we will have to get an injunction against you'
Oh. My. God.

What the hell has Mum done?

And more importantly, where the hell is the visa?

'Everything alright?' Ryan asks.

I'd completely forgotten anyone else was here. This is a disaster. A total fucking disaster.

I take out my phone and ring E & L, but it says that their offices are now closed. I dial the visa centre, but their offices are closed too.

Why!? Dear God, why!?

'Where's our sharpest knife?'

'Err, why?' he asks, bemused.

'I just need to stab myself with it. Or even better, you could stab me.'

I look up at him, hopeful, but he just seems scared.

'You want me…to stab you?'

'Yes. Just a little bit. Just enough so that I'll be in hospital for a few days and I can escape this nightmare.'

'I'm not going to stab you,' he says, eyeing me suspiciously.

318

'Well, you don't have to actually do it. You could just hold the knife and then I could run into – '

'Poppy! Stop this. It's not funny. What the hell is wrong?'

God, he's a drama queen. One little stab, is that really too much to ask?

'Oh God, it's just work. It's just Venomous Victor ruining my life again. And your little dog didn't help.'

'Hey! Leave off Toffee.'

'Sorry.'

I sigh heavily and try to compose myself. This is not the end of the world, remember that.

'Wine?'

'Love one! But I can't get too pissed. I've got that date with Teddy's Grandson.'

He ignores me and starts filling up my glass.

Three glasses later and I'm feeling quite pissed and generally better about the whole thing. I've sent Victor an e-mail explaining that I'll get it sorted out tomorrow. Ryan's told me how he did lie to his work and claimed to have saved an old lady from a mugging.

My phone rings, making me jump. Maybe I'm not as relaxed as I thought I was.

'Hello?'

'Poppy, it's Victor,' he says, his voice tired sounding.

'Hi.'

'Well it never rains, it pours doesn't it!' he shrieks.

'Yep, pretty much,' I slur.

Compose yourself Poppy. You cannot be drunk while speaking to your boss.

'I need you to sort out these flights as well. I need them changed. I have my hair booked in at 2pm so I can only make after around 5pm.'

'Oh. Well, couldn't you move your appointment?'

You're feeling brave Pops.

'Move my appointment? Are you insane? I've been waiting months for this appointment at Red and Go. Sting goes there!'

'Oh, well OK. I suppose that's worth it.'

'Exactly! Anyway, just *fix it*, will you.'

'Ok, I'll e-mail you tomorrow.'

'Yes, look Poppy, I have to go.'

The line goes dead.

How can he do that? Ring me at 7.30pm and then make out that I'm the pain in the arse. That I called him or something?

'Problems?' Ryan asks.

'Nothing I can't fix with a bit of this.'

I reach for the bottle and pour it into the glass, to the very top. I take a slurp, the cool bubbles fizzing down my throat. See, this is why I work. So that I can afford wine.

'Why do you let everyone boss you around so much?' he asks.

'I don't,' I say, offended. 'The person you're talking about is actually my boss. He's meant to boss people around.'

'Yeah, but to the point of you worrying about it every night? Is it really worth it?'

'Well...yes. It's a job, isn't it?'

'Really? Are you on great money then?'

Well, no actually. I'm on shit money, far too little for a PA in the City. I found out what a few friends are on and I'm way below the average, but I'm not going to tell Mr Swarmy pants that, am I.

'I do....OK.'

He raises his eyebrows in surprise. 'Really? I didn't realise you were so comfortable.'

Oh God, now he thinks I'm a frigging millionaire.

'I'm OK. I wouldn't say I was comfortable.'

'And do you love it? Do you love what you do?'

'Well, nobody loves their job, do they?'

'I love my job,' he says seriously.

I think about it for a second. Do I? Do I love it? The crazy thing is that I do quite like my job. I love the buzz and the fast paced days, but I just hate Victor. He makes my life hell.

'I do like my job. Just not Victor. But sometimes I think maybe its better the devil you know and all that.'

'That's why you're staying in your job? Because you think you might find a worse job?'

'Well...yeah, kind of. And I love Lilly.'

'Yeah, but what if Lilly left for bigger and better things? What would you do then?'

Oh my God, what would I do then? She's my lifeline. Without her I'd probably be found in a corner rocking back and forth whilst foaming from the mouth.

'I don't know. Look, just stop bothering me, OK?'

'Why? Because you don't want to face up to reality? When are you going to stop being such a doormat?'

He's really starting to bug me now. Why can't he just leave me alone? It's none of his business anyway.

'Well?'

'Oh just fuck off Ryan. It's none of your business.'

He stares back at me, seeming angry and hurt. Maybe I was a bit mean.

'You're right. It's none of my business. Get walked all over as much as you like. You'll be late for your date.' He turns on his heel and leaves, leaving me feeling like a giant bitch.

*   *   *

When I arrive at the bar I catch myself in a mirror and almost purr back at myself. I look amazing if I do say so myself. I've done my eyeliner to look like a cat, with lashings of mascara and I'm wearing a strapless top, which shows of my shoulders amazingly, with jeans and high heels. It might help that I am slightly tipsy, but still.

I've just ordered myself a vodka when a man with spiky brown hair and trendy glasses taps me on the shoulder.

'Are you Poppy?' he asks smiling, exposing perfect teeth.

'Yeah, how did you know?' I ask taken aback.

'Granddad said you had a cut on your face and I can see your scar.'

Oh, well that's embarrassing.

'I love your top – it really suits you.'

'Thanks. Well...I know nothing about you, so why don't you tell me a bit about yourself?'

God, I sound like Cilla Black on blind date.

He goes on to tell me that he's twenty-nine, works as a marketing manager and has recently got out of a long term relationship. This guy really is lovely and he's quite sexy, but all I can think about is Ryan. And I can't help fighting the feeling that in some way I'm cheating on him by being here tonight, which I know is ridiculous.

'So, I had a great time tonight,' he says, as he pays the bar bill.

'Yeah me too.'

Oh God, I can feel it coming. He's going to ask me out again.

'Um...well, if we're going to see each other again I need to tell you something,' he says, suddenly shy.

'Oh, OK. What is it?' I ask, hoping it will be something that I can use as an excuse not to see him again.

'Well, my Granddad likes to think he knows me well, and I mean to some extent he does. But, well, the thing is...I'm actually gay.'

'What?' I almost shout. A few people at the bar turn round to stare at me and I laugh nervously.

'I know. I'm so sorry for wasting your time Poppy. But my Granddad was adamant I had to take you out and I just wanted to please him, you know?'

'Actually, I know exactly how you feel,' I say imagining my Mother.

'So, your long term relationship, that was with a guy?' I ask intrigued.

'Yep. Paul. We were at the stage where we were either going to move in with each other or break up and...Well, it just seemed he was scared of commitment.'

'Oh, I'm sorry. And I've kind of been there myself anyway,' I smile.

'Well, you actually seemed kind of relieved when I told you. Was I that much of an awful straight man?' he asks smirking.

'No! It's just that...'

'There's someone else isn't there? You've got that puppy love look in your eyes,' he laughs.

'No! Not like that anyway. But...well, I like someone.'

'Oooh, really? Do tell!' he says, suddenly very camp.

'Well...oh, why not! It's my housemate, Ryan. He's actually your Granddad's friends Grandson. If that makes sense,' I say realising how confusing this must be to him.

'Ryan Davis? You've got a crush on Ryan Davis?' he asks, his eyes widening.

'Oh my God, do you know him?' Shit, I should have kept my big mouth shut.

'Yes, of course. We practically grew up together. He was actually a great help at school. Thugs used to pick on me for being...well, shall we say flamboyant?' We both mutually laugh. 'He used to stick up for me and saved me getting my arse kicked a few times.'

'Oh God, he's so great.' I physically swoon at the thought of him.

'I know. I actually had a crush on him myself at one stage.'

'Really?'

'Oh yeah, but can you blame me? That jawline, with those abs – wow! But...'

'But what?' I ask, intrigued by his sudden change of facial expression.

'He had a rough time about a year ago.'

'Really? Before he went travelling?'

'Yeah. That's actually the reason. He had a long term girlfriend, was mad about her. Anyway, she suddenly ran off and got married to his best friend.'

'Oh my God, that's terrible.'

'And then his friends that he'd spent years building up, they were all suddenly gone, not caring if he were dead or alive.'

'Oh my God.'

I really can't believe this.

'Yeah, my heart broke for the poor guy. But he was back to his old self when he got back from travelling. The guy I used to know before he got swallowed up in all of that corporate bullshit. He'd gotten so serious and stuffy.'

'I think he's pretty serious now,' I laugh.

'Yeah, he comes across as that. But that's only because he's a massive thinker.'

'Oh. I don't know why I'm bothering anyway. I haven't got a chance.'

'It's not something you can control. He just has something about him.'

'I know,' I swoon, despite myself.

'Well, anyway, I have to scoot. But it was so lovely meeting you. We should go shopping or something soon.'

'Yeah I'd love that,' I say as he kisses me on the cheek.

'Oh and good luck with Ryan. Maybe get a push up bra?'

*   *   *

When I get home I throw my shoes off at the door and stumble into the kitchen to make myself some toast. I flick the kettle on and jump when I see Ryan still up at the kitchen table.

'Fuck! You scared me!'

'You're so jumpy,' he says, rolling his eyes as if I'm a massive inconvenience.

I sigh and put some toast on, trying not to stare at his massive black eye.

'So...how was your date?' he asks raising his eyebrows in interest.

'Yeah, good thanks,' I say not feeling generous enough to elaborate.

I get some hot chocolate powder from the cupboard and start mixing it with water. I need the sugar.

'What are you doing?' he asks.

'Making a hot chocolate. You want one?'

'No thanks, I'm thirty-two,' he says, sniggering to himself. I turn back, choosing to ignore him.

'Which grandson was it anyway? Lewis or Graham?'

'It was Lewis,' I say, busying myself by buttering my toast.

'Oh' he laughs. 'So...do you think you'll see him again?'

I wait, pretending I haven't heard him for a second while I butter my toast.

'Well?'

'Look, you obviously know he's gay, so just stop winding me up OK!'

'Lewis, *gay*? I don't believe it! Tell me it's not true!' he says, being sarcastic and mocking.

The front door slams and Izzy comes skipping in.

'Hey,' she sings, smiling at both of us. 'Oh God, Ryan! What happened to your eye?' She rushes over and fusses, while he attempts to push her away.

'Why don't you ask Poppy,' Grace says, as she walks into the kitchen in just her bra and knickers. Is it really that hard for her to put clothes on?

Izzy turns to stare at me with a quizzical expression as I attempt to back out of the door. How could he tell her!?

'You...you punched Ryan?' Izzy asks, her mouth twitching into a smile.

'No! Of course not.'

'Thank God for that. I thought you'd lost the plot' she says, relaxing.

'What happened then?' She looks between me, Grace and Ryan.

'I'm knackered. I'm going to bed,' I sigh, not feeling up to him telling them all it was my fault.

I'm barely in my room when there's a knock on my bedroom door.

'Hello?'

'Hey,' Ryan says, walking in.

'Look, if you've just come in here to have a go at me, don't bother. I've been punished enough tonight,' I say as I crawl into bed.

'Your date was that good then?' he asks, amusement showing in his voice.

'What did you tell them?' I ask from underneath the duvet.

'Who? The girls or work?'

'Fine! Rub it in even more.' I push the covers back. 'You hate me, I get it!'

'God, only you could turn this round so it's me feeling sorry for you.'

'I don't want your pity,' I practically spit to him before turning to face the wall.

'Well, I told Grace the truth.'

'You total fucking traitor! Of all people, Grace!'

'Alright, calm down drama queen.'

'Like she doesn't hate me enough as it is. Now I've gone and broken her boyfriend's beautiful face!'

'How many fucking times!? I'm not her boyfriend.'

'Whatever. Didn't you spend the night with her?' I ask before I can stop myself.

'Spend the night? What the hell do you mean by that?' He looks offended.

'You know exactly what I mean.' I sit up in bed to glare at him.

'No,' he insists, moody.

'What, have a headache did she?' I say like a bitch.

'Oh shut up. Surely you could see that *she* was kissing *me* last night. She cornered me.'

'Well, I didn't see you beating her off,' I say, pretending to inspect my nails. 'Or was it another girl tonight? I can't keep up with your conveyor belt of women.'

'Well I would have stopped her if you wouldn't have come in and smashed glass all over the floor like a clumsy idiot.'

'I'm very sorry for being such a massive inconvenience,' I snap. We both glare at each other in silence for a minute.

'So, were work really mad?' I hadn't had a chance to go into it properly earlier.

'Work?'

'Yes! About your eye,' I say, annoyed that he can't seem to keep up.

'My boss was actually really impressed that I'd stopped an old lady getting mugged.'

'Oh, well, you see! You might end up getting a promotion over it.' I smile, glad that something has worked out.

'That's what I thought. I was going to thank you actually.'

'Great! See! Some things happen for a reason,' I say smugly.

'That was until he was so impressed he organised for the local paper to come round and do a story on it.'

'You are joking?' My face drops.

'I wish I was,' he says, smiling weakly. 'He thinks it'll be good for the company. Lawyers You Can Trust.'

326

'I'm so sorry.' I sigh heavily. 'It just seems that everything I touch lately turns to shit.'

'Pretty much,' he says, smiling and walking out of the room.

What a charmer. No wonder I fell for that one.

Chapter 25

The next morning at work I'm ringing the airlines desperately trying to change Victor's flights to later in the day so he can go to his stupid hair appointment. I've finally managed to do it, but I still need to go to the E & L depot to collect Victor's visa. Stupid courier people still sent it to the work address so I have to treck all the way down there. I just hope I have enough time.

I grab my bag and am nearly away from my desk when Tiffany, a young temp with glossy red hair and too much blue eye shadow, comes by my desk.

'Hi Poppy. I just heard something hilarious,' she says, smiling widely.

'Really?' I enquire, intrigued despite myself.

'Yeah. Neville said he's going out with you,' she snorts, holding onto her sides, while she's overtaken by uncontrollable laughter.

Oh, for goodness sakes. I'd almost forgotten about that drama.

'Oh. That.'

'That?' she asks confused. 'You're not actually going out with Neville are you?' she laughs.

'No, of course not.'

'I was gonna say. I mean, what a freak he is! I totally laughed in his face when he told me. As if he could get anyone!'

What an evil bitch. Who the hell does she think she is? She's hardly Elle MacPherson herself. He may have gotten it all deluded in his head, but Neville is a good person. He doesn't deserve little bitches going around laughing at him.

'It's just too funny,' she says, continuing to laugh as if it's the funniest thing she's ever heard.

'Actually it's not that funny,' I snap, feeling embarrassed on behalf of Neville. 'We may not be going out, but...but we're having sex.'

'What?'

Yeah, what?

'Yes! We're having hot, passionate sex. And let me tell you, don't let that sweet innocent look fool you. Behind closed doors he's an absolute animal!'

Tiffany stares back at me completely stunned. I should stop. Stop there. Just let her imagine the rest. But I can't.

'Oh yeah, it's true. And he's hung like a donkey. I thought I'd had orgasms before him, but my God I had no idea. The doors he's opened to me. I'm so thankful to him,' I gloat, flicking my hair around as I imagine a sexual goddess does.

'Are you...are you serious?' she asks, looking as if her head might explode any moment.

'Oh yeah. He's such a generous lover. I mean, I *wish* he'd go out with me! I begged him, I really did! But he told me he didn't want to be tied down. He said he'd play along at work if I told people. That's probably why he told you.'

She nods, her eyes darting helplessly from side to side, trying to make sense of it all.

'To be honest, I don't know if I'll be able to move on from him. I mean, I think he may have ruined me for any other man. They'll never be able to satisfy me like him.'

'Wow,' she gasps. 'I had no idea.'

'Yep. They always say it's the quiet ones.'

She nods, completely in awe.

'Anyway, I have to go. Promise me you won't tell a soul?' I ask, fully aware that it will be around the entire office within the hour.

'Of course. I won't breathe a word,' she promises, her mouth still gaping open.

'Bye!'

I run out of the room, round the corner and almost straight into Neville.

'Neville! Come with me!' I shout grabbing him and dragging him into the lift.

I close the doors and push the emergency button, suspending the lift in the air, as Lilly and I have done many times in an emergency.

'Poppy, are you OK?' he asks, seemingly concerned that I've lost my mind. Maybe I have.

'Listen, I'm too rushed to be sensitive, OK?' I say, conscious of the time.

'OK,' he nods.

'Neville, we're not going out. I love you as a friend, but I don't see you romantically like that.'

'Oh.' His face drops.

'But I've lied to people and told them we're sleeping together.'

'What?' he asks in surprise.

'I'm gonna help you out. If anyone asks you any questions you are only to say "a gentleman never tells". Do you understand?'

'A gentleman never tells,' he repeats slowly. 'OK, got it.'

'Nothing else, promise?'

'Promise,' he smiles.

'Cool. I'm taking you shopping tomorrow lunch and giving you a makeover.'

'Really? Do I need one?' he asks looking over his tartan shirt and green dickie bow.

'Yes,' I say bluntly. I don't have time to beat around the bush. 'Will you meet me?'

'Yes. I'll be there!' he says with fresh enthusiasm.

'Great.'

'But Poppy, why are you doing this for me?' he asks, as I press the emergency button again making us move.

'Because you're a good guy Neville and a lot of the little bitches here need a lesson teaching to them. It's just all about good PR.'

The door pings open and I quickly wrap my arms round Neville's neck and plant a quick kiss on his lips. I turn round and as I predicted, Tiffany is already at reception telling the receptionist Suzanne my gossip. They both turn to stare at us, their mouths gawking open.

I pretend to straighten my hair, wink at Neville and then run out, hearing Tiffany say 'I told you!'

*   *   *

330

I arrive at the passport place at 11am. I'll make it. I just need to make sure I don't get delayed. The lady on the phone said I just need to quote the order number and they'll give it to me. As long as I'm in and out I should get to the airport in time.

'Next!' a lady behind a glass counter yells.

It's a bit like a normal post office really. Hopefully they'll be as efficient as Harry from ours. And not make so many racist jokes.

'Hi. I'm here to pick up a package for Victor Darlington. It had attempted delivery last night. It's order number 2398JLK.'

I smile up at the moody woman. She's about forty with blonde frizzy hair and crooked teeth.

'I'm afraid only Mr Darlington can collect it,' she drawls, yawning.

'Sorry? You must be mistaken. I called up three times. They said I could just quote the number.'

Please God, let her be mistaken.

'Sorry, but the computer says no.'

Did she seriously just say "computer says no?" Am I on a hidden camera show? Is this a massive joke?

'You can't be serious.'

'Afraid so. Sorry.' She looks anything but sorry.

'Can I speak to your supervisor please?'

'She's on a break.'

'I'm willing to wait,' I say, standing my ground.

'Fine,' she snarls through gritted teeth. We glare back at each other until I finally lose my nerve and look away.

'Please stand out of the way madam. Next!'

'I don't think so! I'm waiting here until I can speak to your supervisor.'

'Excuse me,' a young girl with plaited brown hair says, trying to barge me out of the way.

'No, sorry! I'm not moving until I get my package.'

'Why don't you just go,' plaited girl says to me giving me a little shove.

Did she seriously just shove me?

'I'm not going anywhere,' I say, shoving her back a little harder.

'I think you need to wait your turn!' she growls, pushing me away hard.

How can she have so much attitude for a nineteen year old? Who does she think she is? Probably here to collect a Polly Pocket toy from her pen pal in Austria.

'Why don't you just back the fuck up,' I shout, channelling my inner ghetto princess.

I shove her as hard as I can. She flies back, falls over and hits her head on the top of the desk. Maybe a little too hard in hind sight.

'Oh my God, are you OK?' I ask, rushing over, a sickening feeling creeping into my stomach.

I didn't mean to kill the bitch.

'What on earth is going on?' a deep authoritative voice says.

I look up, panicked. Please don't say it's a police man.

I look through the glass window at a bulky mixed race woman with long black curly hair. I recognise that face. I swear I do. Her stern face breaks in recognition too.

'Poppy? Is that you?'

Shit. What's her name? I went to school with her. I sat next to her in French. She went out with Barry Reynolds and lost it to him in a ditch in the countryside on our sponsored walk. But what the hell is her name?

'Oh my goodness. Is that...you?' I ask.

'Yes, it's me! How strange, I was just talking about you the other day,' she squeals, full of excitement.

Crap. Did I do anything horrible to her? Trace back your mind.

'Oh really?'

'Hello! Has everybody forgotten about me?' plaited girl shouts, still leaning her head dramatically against the counter.

'Oh pipe down,' I hiss.

'Yes.' She lowers her voice to a whisper. 'I heard through the grapevine that you're knocked up.'

Oh dear. What has my mother done? No, what have I done? One little teeny weeny lie and it's multiplied and spread round London like the plague. I still need to speak to her about stalking poor unsuspecting Ryan Smith.

'Err...' I don't know what to say. I'm literally lost for words.

'You're preggers?' plaited girl says, horrified. 'Pregnant women shouldn't be going round starting fights. Especially when they can't end them.'

'Well, maybe you shouldn't go around pushing pregnant women,' my long lost friend says.

'But...I...,' plaited girl protests, stamping her foot.

'No buts. I think you should go to the next desk before I call the police and tell them you've been hitting pregnant women.'

She huffs and puffs, before stomping off, flicking her plaits in my face.

'Thanks,' I say, picking plaited girls hair out of my lipstick.

'You poor thing. Heard he'd left you as well.' She leans her head sympathetically to the left.

Now I remember. Felicity Dunbar. She was always a smug bitch.

'You're trying to pick up someone's package?'

I nod, still unable to speak.

'Well we don't normally do that,' she says, clicking her tongue.

'But I rang, three times! Is there nothing you can do? For an old friend?'

'Well, I'm not sure. It is procedure.' She studies her nails, clearly enjoying the power trip.

'Come on Felicity. For old times? Remember French class? Please! Or should I say s'il vous plait?'

'I'm really not sure. I could be fired if anyone found out.'

'Well I'm not going to tell anyone. It can be our little secret,' I whisper, smiling as nicely as I can muster.

She still looks slightly unconvinced.

'It's just, I'm so stressed at the moment. Being knocked up and everything.' I quiver my chin and discreetly poke myself in the eye, trying my best to look like I'm on the verge of tears.

She looks at me, as if she's trying to work out a calculation in her head.

'Well...OK? Here it is. Good luck with the baby.'

I grab it greedily and run out of there.

'Thanks!' I shout back.

So what if I maybe confirmed I was pregnant? So what if she used to be the biggest gossip in school? That doesn't necessarily mean that she'll tell *everyone* I went to school with. Maybe a few of them will be on holiday.

*   *   *

I arrive at the airport at 2pm, slightly flustered. How did I know the bus would break down? I'd planned to get here earlier and be totally calm and composed. I'd be sitting in Starbucks with a tea, reading the paper when Victor would come in all panicky. I'd smile, hand over his documents and tell him I need a raise. Well, that's clearly out of the window.

I get myself a tea and struggle to get a seat, weaving through everyone's suitcases. A man gets up, answering the phone and bumps into me, spilling my tea down my shirt. Damn it.

Where is Victor? He was supposed to meet me here. By 14.05 I'm starting to get anxious. By 14.18 I'm panicking. By 14.30 and four voicemails on Victor's phone later, I'm having a meltdown. Where the fuck is he? He can't board the plane without me. Has he had an accident?

My phone rings and I pull it out frantically. 'Hello?'

'Poppy, I'm zzzzz late zzzzz flight zzzzzz do?'

'Victor? I can't hear you. It's a really bad line.'

I get up and weave through the people, trying to get a better reception.

'I said zzzzzzzzzz flight zzzzzzzzzzzzzzz visa.'

God, this reception is awful. I can't make out a single thing he's saying. I leave the Starbucks area and go into the middle of the airport.

'Victor, I really can't hear you.'

'Can you hear me now?' he asks.

'Yes! I can hear you now.'

'Thank God. My driver's car has broken down. Tell them to hold the flight. I'll be there soon.'

'But – '

The phone's already gone dead.

OK, don't panic. I'm sure they'll hold a flight for a totally deranged mad man. It's only 2.30pm, there's hours yet. My phone rings again, flashing up with 'Jazz'.

'Hello?'

'Hey Pops. So your brother's a total dick. I hate him! You'll never guess what happened last night.'

'Last night?'

'Yeah, we went to Leicester, remember?'

'No, not really? Look, Jazz this really isn't a good time. Can I call you later?'

'I suppose,' she sighs. 'OK, love you.'

'Love you too.'

I hang up and turn round, walking towards the Starbucks area, eager to get another tea. Swarms of people are walking out of it very quickly with slightly alarmed expressions on their faces.

'What's going on?' I ask, grabbing a ladies arm as she walks past me.

'There's a bomb scare,' she says, looking down at her arm which I'm still gripping tightly onto.

'You're joking?'

'No. Apparently there's an abandoned bag. Airport security are checking it out now.'

'God, that's horrible.'

'I know. They're evacuating the airport.' She throws off my hand and walks briskly off in the other direction.

A loud female voice comes from the tannoy.

'Evacuation. If everyone could please evacuate the airport immediately. Please remain calm.'

People start running and screaming, dragging their children along with them. This is awful. I wonder if I'll be on the news. I take a deep breath, ignoring my sudden need to have a wee, and make my way towards my nearest exit, elbowing people out of the way. As I pass the Starbucks area I take a deep breath. It's probably nothing. Just get out of here as quickly as possible. I can't help myself sneaking a glance towards the drama.

Policemen in black uniforms are stood back, speaking into their radios. A man in a big kind of space suit is walking slowly towards a handbag on the table. That's funny, because it kind of looks like...

Oh my God. My body goes numb, but I try and regain feeling of my shoulders. Is there a handbag on them? I lift my hand up to my shoulders and as suspected there's no handbag hanging on them.

That's my handbag. I've caused a terror alert.

Shit shit shit.

I walk over to the nearest policeman, wondering what on earth I'm going to say.

'You can't go in there miss. If you could please evacuate.'

'No, but I just need to get - '

'I'm afraid you'll have to get your coffee from somewhere else, now if you could please just leave the building.'

Maybe I should just go and leave it here. It'd be a hell of a lot easier. But what about Victor? He'll be here any moment and his passport is in that bag. And so is my purse with my driving licence.

Just take a deep breath.

'It's my bag,' I say quietly, not even wanting to admit it aloud.

'Sorry?' he asks seriously. 'I didn't hear you miss. Do you have some information on this terrorist attack?'

I wish he'd stop calling it a terrorist attack. It clearly isn't.

'Yes, it's my handbag, OK! I left it there by accident.'

'What?' He looks at me completely perplexed. 'That is your handbag?'

'Yes!' I shout, tears threatening to break behind my eyes.

'Boys!' the policemen yells. 'We've got another one. Dozy mare left her handbag. There's nothing in it.'

They all release their tense stances and the guy in the space suit grabs my bag, emptying the contents on the table.

'Yep,' he shouts over, removing his helmet. 'Just a loud of make-up and shit. And apparently she's got thrush.'

What a bastard! I should really remove that cream from my bag.

'You know I could arrest you for wasting police time,' the policeman says to me.

'What? I only left it for a second. Please, be reasonable!' I plead, sweat trickling down my forehead.

'I dunno. What you think boys?' he asks, smiling wickedly at them.

'If anything at least now you know how you'd handle something like this. And I must say, you guys have done a great job.' I smile sweetly.

'Well, thanks,' he gushes. 'I suppose, we can let you off.'

Thank God.

*   *   *

When I get home I'm so hot and flustered I don't know what to do first; have a drink, strip off or just pass out. I can't believe the unpredictable weather. It's sooo hot this afternoon. Sweat drips from my upper lip, my cleavage and the hair at the back of my neck. Gross. My hands are swollen, the veins in them raised to resemble a tube map.

I run to my bedroom and peel off my shoes and then my clothes, stuck to me as the strangers on the tube had been. I throw myself on the bed in just my bra and knickers, too tired to think clearly. Water. That's what I need – lots and lots of water.

'Pops?' Izzy calls, sounding like her usual ball of energy.

I take a deep breath and drag myself up, stumbling into the kitchen, not bothering to put anything over my bra and knickers. I'm frankly too hot to care. Jazz, Izzy and Grace are buzzing around in nothing but their bikinis. Jazz has on a yellow string bikini with pink polka dots and wears a matching giant yellow flower in her hair. Izzy has a pink stripy sporty one with matching flip flops. Grace has a red and gold bikini which squeezes her breasts tightly together and it matches her lipstick.

'Hey Pops,' Jazz says, 'strawberry margarita?'

337

She shoves a load of ingredients in the blender with a bagful of ice and starts blending. I steal a cube from the bag and put it against my wrists, then the back of my hair. Oh yeah, that's good.

'What you doing here?' I ask, too hot to be diplomatic.

'Nice to see you too!' she scoffs.

'Well?'

'Isn't it obvious?' She looks at me as if I'm mad. She looks to Izzy and they both smile knowingly.

'Margarita party!' they both chime.

Are they serious? Margarita party? Do they think this is a sorority house like in one of those American universities? They have clearly been watching too much TV.

'I'm not sure if I could drink it. It's too bloody hot,' I complain.

I'm so hot, it's hard to even talk to her, or stay conscious, let alone get smashed.

'Stop being a pussy,' she snaps. 'I've bought your bikini.' She goes to a carrier bag and presents a jewelled green bikini that I've never seen before.

'That's mine?'

'Well, it is now,' she says, her eyes lighting up, as they always do, when shopping is involved.

'You went shopping!' I say accusingly.

I can't believe her! How can she be so irresponsible? Five grand in debt and she's acting like she owes me a fiver.

'Chill! It's only Primark.' She hands it over to me and I inspect it. It is beautiful and the padding around the bust is amazing. I'm talking proper hard-core padding.

'Jazz! It says La Senza!'

Jazz and Izzy giggle at each other.

'I told you we should have cut the label out,' Izzy giggles.

'Well I just thought you'd appreciate the padding,' Jazz says, pointing towards my chest.

Grace flicks her hair around to glance at my boobs, and sniggers cruelly.

'Look. Just try it on,' Jazz demands. 'If you like it keep it. OK?'

'OK. I suppose trying it on can't hurt.'

My God! I can't believe how a bikini can transform your figure so much. My small boobs are now bulging bouncy bosoms and the bottoms are cut such a way that my legs look a lot longer and more slender than they are.

I walk into the garden feeling strong and confident. Jazz and Izzy turn around, dipping their sunglasses and wolf whistling. I know it's silly and childish but I do a little bow and spin, pleased by the attention. I join them on one of the towels they've laid out on a tiny bit of concrete.

They really need to clear this garden up. It's a mess. Completely overgrown grass up to my knees, with ferns and weeds running amok. The four of us are squeezed on to the tiny bit of concrete. It's pathetic. If I had a garden like this I'd really turn it around.

'Have you ever considered cleaning up this garden?'

Grace ignores me as usual, but Izzy looks up, a demented excited smile on her face.

'Oh God!' Jazz sighs, dipping her sunglasses so she can roll her eyes. 'Don't get Izzy started.'

I stare at Izzy confused.

'I've been wanting to get it cleaned up for ages but these guys won't help me!' she explains.

'Lazy cow!' I hit Jazz playfully on the shoulder. 'Why don't we do it this weekend?'

'Sweet!' Izzy squeals. 'It's a date.'

'And Jazz, you're helping.'

'Ugh! Fine!' She rolls over to her front and I just about make out her saying 'Hitler's taken over' under her breath.

'Where's Ryan anyway?' I ask.

Grace looks up at the mention of his name.

'He's shopping,' she says, smirking at the thought of knowing more than me about him.

'Yep. He hates the heat,' Izzy adds as she leans back, basking in the sun.

'I know how he feels.' I down my strawberry margarita and apply more factor thirty.

The faint sound of the door knocking stops me from applying another layer. Everyone pretends like they haven't heard it so I jump up to get it. It's only when I open the door and see Big Tits Tabitha on the doorstep that I remember I'm only in a bikini. Something about having a massive pair of fake tits thrust in your face makes you remember that yours are the size of an average twelve year olds.

'Tabitha! Hi, come in' I say, my voice squeaky and fake.

She's dressed in a pink and white summer dress, her breasts heaving over it. She must be boiling.

'Hi! Poppy, isn't it?'

'Yep, that's me.' Just Ryan's housemate Poppy.

'Is he in?' she ask, barging past me into the kitchen, pouting her lips all the way. I wonder if she's had those lip injection things. They look huge. They look like blow job lips. Slag.

'He's out at the moment, but he'll be back soon.' I smile and sit at the kitchen table. I grab a newspaper, hoping she won't engage me in conversation.

'Can you show me where his bedroom is?'

His bedroom? I look up at her in disbelief.

'Sorry...what?'

'Well, he's been holding out on me in the bedroom department, probably too much of a gentlemen. So I thought that I should show him how much I want him, if you know what I mean.' She reaches beneath her dress and exposes her neon pink bra at me.

Oh I think I know what you mean, you slag.

'So, could you tell me where his bedroom is?' She gets her bag and walks towards the door.

Oh my God. This tramp is trying to bed him. I spent all my energy telling him to wait, but never did I think that she'd force herself on him. And he's a red blooded male. Of course he's going to say yes. They're going to have sex upstairs...while I'm in the house! I'll be able to hear the springs creaking and the headboard knocking. And then it will really be game over.

'No!' I protest, my voice a squeak.

She stops and turns towards me. I think she's trying to crease her forehead, but she's had so much Botox I can't make out any lines of real expression.

'Sorry? No?' She narrows her eyes at me. She's clearly not used to being told what to do.

'I mean…not *no*…but...you just can't.' Every muscle in my body is tightening. Please don't sleep with him I want to plead.

'Sorry, but why can't I?' Her tone has quickly changed to one that someone doesn't argue with.

'Because...because...' I can feel the sweat on my upper lip as my mind races. Why can't she? Think Poppy, think!

'Because what?' She puts her hand on her hip and leans in, as if to challenge me.

'Because...he's...gay!'

Oh dear, what the hell have I done.

'He's...gay? He's *gay*? What are you talking about?' she demands, her face getting red with distress.

Gay must just be on my mind from my date with Lewis.

'Well, he's very...confused at the moment. He knows he should like women, but...whenever he looks at my poster of Jared Leto he just...melts.'

Oh God, I can't stop this crap from spilling out of my mouth.

'Is that why he wouldn't sleep with me?' she asks, her eyes darting from side to side as if she's doing a long multiplication in her head.

'Yes, that's why! Very confused, as I said. He keeps forcing me to watch Singing in the Rain. One of his favourite films apparently.'

'Oh my God. That's what you were watching the other day!' she says, her eyes still not meeting mine. 'He really is gay. I can't believe I haven't seen it until now.' She stares at me completely dazed.

'Yeah. I'm really sorry to break it to you like this. Please don't tell anyone.'

'No, of course. But thank you.' She smiles gratefully and backs out of the room, still clearly in shock, banging the door shut.

As soon as it slams shut I cradle my head in my hands. What the hell have I done? What is wrong with me? I walk into my room and look into the mirror. A scared vulnerable little girl in a posh bikini stares back at me. Since when did I turn into such a compulsive liar? My mum raised me better than this. Well, my Grandma did. She used to say 'Never tell a lie. You'll never escape from a lie without being made to cry.' I hope just for once Grandma would be wrong about these few recent ones.

I wander back into the garden wondering how I came to be such a loser.

'I still need to tell you what a dickhead your brother was,' Jazz says, rolling back over to face me.

'Oh yeah, I completely forgot. What happened?'

I'm glad for the distraction.

'Well, he asked me to Leicester didn't he and I go all the way there with him and he ends up going off and shagging some random girl in the club.'

Typical Oliver.

'And? You guys aren't dating or anything are you?'

'Well...no, but...'

'But what?'

Izzy and Jazz exchange glances and I'm aware I'm missing something.

'What?' I demand, sighing heavily. Why do I always feel like a parent?

'Well...we've kind of been sleeping together,' Jazz announces, avoiding my gaze.

'WHAT?' I exclaim, spitting on her in shock.

'See! This is why we decided to keep it a secret! Because you always make a big deal out of things!'

'Oh really,' I mock. 'What would I have said? That someone always gets hurt? That's just happened!'

342

'No it hasn't! I'm not in love with him or anything. I just...well, I didn't know it bothered me until I saw him with someone else,' she says, a little sadly.

'Aren't you supposed to be dating Jake anyway?'

'We're not exclusive!' she shouts rolling her eyes.

'Jazz! How many times!? This exclusive excuse is totally American. We're British and once you sleep with a guy more than once it's just an unwritten rule that you're kind of going out and won't sleep with anyone else.'

'Sorry Jazz, but I agree with Poppy,' Izzy says, looking slightly afraid of Jazz's reaction.

'But he hasn't asked me to be his girlfriend!' Jazz protests.

'Well then it's fine,' Grace says, stretching out like a cat. 'I'm with Jazz. If it's not exclusive she can sleep with whoever she likes.'

Tramp.

'Anyway,' Jazz says, demanding our attention back to the problem. 'I'm furious with him. He made me go all the way to Leicester just so I could watch him go off and fuck some slag.'

'This is what I was worried would happen! You two will hate each other and won't be able to be around each other anymore and I'll be like a child whose parents are divorced and have shared custody.'

'Don't be silly Pops. It'll be fine,' she smiles reassuringly.

'Promise me?'

'Of course,' she smiles, before I notice her grimace at Grace when she thinks I'm not looking. 'So anyway, how was your day at work?'

I give her a run-down of the nightmare with the visa, but manage to keep out the terror alert I caused.

'What a nightmare,' she sympathises.

'Yeah. Oh and then I helped Neville, this guy from work, out. Some bitches were being mean to him so I ended up sort of lying and telling them I'm sleeping with him.'

'That is so cruel! *Why?*' she says, outraged.

'I know,' I nod.

'Why would a parent name their child *Neville*?' She shakes her head, still seemingly horrified and doesn't seem to notice the look I give her.

'Anyway...now I'm meeting him tomorrow for a bit of a makeover.'

'Let me come!' Jazz says, sitting up and clapping her hands together.

'I love a makeover!'

I think about quiet little Neville getting bossed around by Jazz and decide I'd probably scare the crap out of him.

'He says he just wants to go by himself,' I lie.

'That's a shame,' Jazz pouts.

Yeah, real shame, not.

God, it's just too damn hot! I'm practically cooked like a chicken.

'I'm going to cool down,' I announce, springing to my feet and rushing to get inside.

'Wimp!' Jazz calls after me.

I ignore her and open the fridge. Oh, it's so nice and cool in here. Ah! I pick up a bottle of water and then a packet of cheese. I put one to my head and the other on my lower back. Aah! Finally cool.

'You alright there?'

I spin around in shock from Ryan's voice, dropping the cheese and then the bottled water on my foot.

'Shit.'

Why do I always have to act like such a dick around him? I bend down to pick them up, desperately trying to ignore his smirk as he watches me.

'Don't help or anything,' I snap.

'Ooh, moody are we?' he teases.

'I'm just so bloody hot,' I moan like a bratty child.

'Yeah, I know. It's unbearable,' he says, as he starts unloading some shopping into the fridge.

'Well...I'm going back out there.' Why do I feel the need to tell him that?

'Ryan's back,' I say to the others as I sit back on my towel.

Grace perks up and starts reapplying her lipstick.

'I hope he got more ice,' Izzy says, draining most of her glass.

He appears at the back door, lifting the bottom of his t-shirt to wipe some sweat from his forehead. His stomach is so brown and toned that I can't help but stare, mesmerised by him.

'Margarita party is it ladies?'

'Woo!' they all sing, raising their glasses.

I'm guessing this is a regular occurrence.

'Apparently it's supposed to be this hot for the next week,' he says, seeming horrified by the thought of it.

I watch him from the corner of my eye as he discreetly glances at Jazz's boobs, then Izzy's, then Grace's. What a pig. Wait a minute. He just checked out mine! My boobs are worthy of being checked out!

He catches me watching him and quickly looks away. He lifts his t-shirt over his head, fully exposing his abs and his low slung jeans. Wow. They're too low slung really. You can almost see...well, you can almost see. He picks up the hose and turns it on over his head soaking his brown curls. Is it me or did he just turn into slow motion? He turns around and his back muscles flex as he moves the hose around.

He looks up, this time catching me being a pervert and I quickly avert my gaze. Damn. Why did he have to catch me? He smiles to himself and squirts the hose briefly over all of us.

'Ryan!' Jazz shouts. 'I just covered myself with cream!'

'Sorry,' he laughs, jumping down onto the end of my towel and shaking himself like a wet dog.

'Thanks,' I say drily, secretly loving the feel of his droplets.

'The weirdest thing just happened,' he announces.

'Really?' I say, trying to sound relaxed and uninterested.

'Yeah, what Ry Ry?' Grace purrs.

'I just bumped into Tabitha and she broke up with me. She just said that she couldn't go out with me. I'm not her type anymore apparently. What the hell is that all about?'

'How bizarre!' I shriek, far too suspiciously.

'You need some cream on,' Grace says, crawling suggestively over to him, her boobs spilling out. 'Poor baby.'

She goes behind him and starts spreading cream over his back, making sure to press her boobs up against him at any opportunity.

'I'm really not going to be out here long enough anyway,' he tries to protest.

She ignores him and keeps touching him even when there's no cream left. She's practically dry humping him. I feel myself cringing for her.

'Oh, Ryan!' Jazz says, sitting up. 'I forgot! I had a dream about you last night.'

'Oh really?' he enquires. 'Doing anything interesting was I?'

'Yeah, it was a sex dream actually,' she says, throwing her head back cackling.

'Why....why....why would you dream that?' I ask, sounding slightly more desperate for the information than intended.

'More importantly, was I any good?' Ryan asks raising his eyebrows mischievously.

'You were pretty damn good,' Jazz says, fanning herself. 'Woke up sweating and stuff, really weird.'

'Interesting,' he smiles. 'Because in my dreams I'm surprisingly inadequate.'

'Well, let's just say last night you definitely knew your way around, if you know what I mean,' she says, cackling some more.

'I love it when we share,' I say under my breath. 'I think I'm going to go in.'

No point torturing myself. Between Jazz's dreams and Grace's groping I'm about to explode with jealousy.

'No Pops! We're going to get a take away later,' Izzy says, looking surprisingly hurt.

'It's too hot to eat. I think I'm just gonna shower and go to bed.'

No point staying here and making myself miserable.

Chapter 26

When I wake up the next morning I see it on the kitchen table. The picture of Ryan with his black eye and the dramatic headline shouting out at me from the front page.

LOCAL HERO SAVES OLD LADY GETTING MUGGED

Oh crap. I grab it, reading it quickly.

Ryan Davis, 32, from Shepherds Bush, bravely saved an old lady from getting mugged on Wednesday 19th. Ryan had been enjoying the sunshine, while on his way to a meeting, when he noticed an elderly lady getting harassed by some teenage thugs. He bravely decided to interject and although he suffered a black eye, he managed to save the elderly lady from any harm and give her handbag back to her. The lady is thought to have gone home flustered. Ryan says 'Anyone would have done the same thing. It's just instinct'.

If you saw this incident or know the thugs, thought to be between 15 to 28, of medium build with black hooded cardigans, please contact crime stoppers.

Oh dear. When I put it down I notice a post-it stuck to it that I hadn't seen before with Ryan's handwriting.

This is your fault!

So I think we're safe to say that he's slightly pissed off with me. Then I notice another little story with the headline 'Crime Duo Targeting Couples'. I scan over it, praying that it's not about us.

'Mr and Mrs Clennel were horrified to find them trying to steal their vase, a wedding present given to them by Mrs Clennel's deceased mother. 'They're just animals!' she says of the incident. 'Anyone that can do that to someone, it's just horrific!' The police were called to the incident but they were let go with a warning.'

Let go with a warning? Tried to steal the vase? There's nothing in there about it being an accident! About my hands being glued to it. What a bunch of lying bastards.

'The first woman is described as tall, thin with blonde curly hair and small grey eyes. She is thought to be impersonating a rich child. The

second woman is described as quite short, chubby with black hair, green eyes and freckles'

Chubby? Fucking *chubby*? When have I ever been described as chubby? So I may not be as thin as Jazz, but I mean who the hell is? She makes Kate Moss look like a fat bitch. I mean, *chubby? Really?* I try to push it to the back of my mind as I walk hurriedly along Oxford Street during my lunch hour. Neville's waiting for me outside Topshop as agreed, dressed in a dark green pinstriped suit and tartan shirt.

'Hi Poppy,' he says awkwardly.

'Hey Neville. Right, no time to waste. I hope you've got your credit card.'

I link arms with him and drag him into Topman, picking up clothes as we go through.

'Go to the changing rooms and strip naked. I'll be over in a minute.'

'Oh. OK,' he says, seeming unsure, shuffling from one foot to another.

'Don't worry Neville. I'm not going to steal your clothes. I'll be there in a minute.'

By the time I get to the changing rooms I've got two baskets full of clothes. I knock gently on the door and he peers around, his face bright red with embarrassment.

'Can I come in?'

'Really?' he asks, going redder.

'I promise I won't look. It'll just be easier.'

'Oh...OK.'

He pushes the door back to reveal a pale white body in grey stripy boxer shorts. Who'd have known it, but Neville actually has quite a nice body. Yes, it's pale but it's not weird and skinny. And from the bulge in the boxers I'd say I wasn't lying too much about how he's hung.

'So did anyone ask you about us yesterday?' I ask as I throw clothes on over his head.

'Only everyone!' he chuckles, pushing his glasses up his nose. 'But I kept saying a gentleman never tells, like you said.'

'Brilliant. And did anything happen?'

'Yes! All the girls were swarming around me asking questions and...Well, I think a few of them might have even been flirting with me.'

'Really? See!'

'Poppy, these clothes are great,' he says, smiling at himself in the mirror. 'I think I'm going to take all of them.'

I've managed to pull together a great geek-chic look for him. Anything else would have been going against what he is. Instead his new wardrobe consists of skinny jeans, layered cardigans, t-shirts, smart blazers, and fitted shirts. I've even included a few bow ties, but instructed him as to what he can wear them with. He looks amazing. Next I drag him to the opticians where I force him to buy new black oversized frames, and then to the barbers. The barber cuts his curly light brown hair tighter to his head and shows him how to apply wax to it to keep it looking fresh.

I stand back to survey him and can't believe the transformation. He's like a shiny new penny. If I didn't know him and saw him on the street I'd do a double take. He looks gorgeous.

'Poppy, I really don't know how to thank you. I love it.'

'You're welcome,' I say, sneaking another look at him. I'm so proud. 'I can't wait to show it off back at work.'

'I know! Me too! Now, if anyone at work asks you out all you can say is "Maybe. If you play your cards right". You need to treat them mean to keep them keen.'

'That really works?' he asks, pushing his new glasses up his nose.

'Definitely.'

'Great. Thanks so much,' he beams, hugging me tightly before bustling up towards our office; a new spring in his step.

*   *   *

When I get in that night I'm tired. The weather's remained hot and clammy, and all I want to do is jump in the shower and then get an early night. My phone rings, flashing up 'Jazz'.

349

'Hey hun.'

'Oh my God babe, have you seen the paper? Ryan's on the front page?' she shouts excitedly.

'Yeah I know. It's all my fault,' I say sighing.

'Why? It's a good thing isn't it?'

'Not really,' I say quietly.

'Oh babe, what have you done?'

'It's...a bit of a long story.' I hope she won't have time to listen to me.

'Great. I'm coming to pick you up now. We're going to Emily's birthday.'

'Emily?'

'Yeah, you know – from Uni. She's hired a bar in Harrow. It should be a laugh.'

'Oh...I don't know...I'm really knackered.'

'Too late, I'm already in a cab. Be at yours in ten.' She hangs up immediately before I can protest.

*   *   *

'So Poppy, have you managed to bag yourself a fella yet?' Chris asks me, his onion breath on the back of my neck.

'Not yet,' I smile politely. 'I've just got to find Jazz to sort out a taxi. Excuse me.'

Well this night's been a disaster. Damn Jazz. Forcing me here tonight and then leaving me to endure everyone from Uni questioning me about my life. It's more like a reunion than a birthday party. And what have I got to say about myself? Nothing. Nothing is going well in my life. Everyone I speak to is either engaged, or married, or with kids. Hell, even the single people have amazing careers, or they've travelled the world. How do you make staying in watching telly and drinking tea sound fun?

I search around the bar for her, but all I find is more excitable people, trying to engage me in conversation. Where is she? Typical. She always goes off to places without telling me.

'Has anyone seen Jazz?' I ask random people as they pass me.

'Hey Poppy,' Tom, another guy I vaguely remember from Uni says. 'She's gone on to the after party.'

'You're joking! Do you know where it is?' I ask, hating being left this vulnerable. I swear to God, when I find her I'm gonna ring her neck.

'We're just going there now. Come with us.' He guides me outside and points towards a taxi.

I glance in the taxi and see a few girls in there. He holds the door open for me.

'OK thanks.'

As I step into the taxi the women get out of the other side and I'm left with just Tom and his friend with buck teeth that I haven't met before. A sinking feeling in my stomach tells me this doesn't feel right. I ring Jazz.

'Hey, this is Jazz...'

Straight to voicemail for the fiftieth time tonight.

'Hey Jazz, it's me. I've gone on to the after party with Tom. See you soon.'

'So, do you have a boyfriend these days then?' Tom enquires, grinning widely.

'No, unfortunately not,' I smile. 'What about you?'

'No-one special,' he winks.

I look away quickly, hoping I haven't led him on. I should have just told him I was a lesbian or training to be a nun.

'Here we are,' Tom says to the taxi driver a few minutes later.

We pull up outside a white semi-detached house in a residential street.

'Are you sure this is it?' I ask as I get out, aware that there's no noise or lights on.

'Yeah course I am,' he says, putting his hand on my waist and ushering me in.

A sickening feeling creeps into the pit of my stomach as I reluctantly get pushed into the house. The stench of stale beer and sweat welcoming me once inside makes me gag. By the time I've got into the sitting room I realise there's no party here tonight. It's only us three.

'W...where's the others?' I ask, trying to remain calm.

'What others?' he asks locking the front door with a key and putting it in his pocket.

'You know...the others. For the party,' I smile, kicking myself for being so stupid.

'They're probably on their way.'

I look over to his friend, sat on the sofa lining up some coke and feel myself start to sweat. This is a disaster. I'm going to get raped.

'I'm just gonna call Jazz,' I say, my voice breaking as I get out my phone.

'Hey, this is Jazz...'

Again with the voicemail! What the fuck!? OK, don't panic. I'm sure Izzy will be available. Izzy goes straight to voicemail too. I try Jazz one more time in desperation.

'Just me again! *Please* call me as soon as you get this, OK?'

The trick is not to panic. It's going to be fine. You've just gone back to a friend's house. You knew Tom in Uni. Well, sort of. Enough to trust him, right? Enough to be sure he wouldn't force you to do something you don't want to do.

'Sit down darling,' Tom says, pushing me towards the sofa. I fall back on it and quickly sit up straight, crossing my legs tightly together.

'You want a line?'

'No, I'm...I'm fine thanks,' I say, my voice barely audible.

'Really? Might loosen you up a bit.' He smirks before snorting one himself.

Loosen me up for what? Oh God. They're going to attack me. I can just feel it. My hands start shaking and my upper lip starts sweating. I sit on my hands to stop them from noticing

He moves closer to me on the sofa as he rubs some remaining coke into his gums, his eyes suddenly crazed. Unease creeps over me. His shoulders are pretty massive and I suddenly remember he used to play rugby at Uni. He leans closer again, his huge physical presence threatening. Would I be able to fight him off? Would he let me?

'This is a lovely road. What's the name of it?' I ask, standing up and carefully edging closer to the door.

'Don't worry about that sweetheart. Come and sit on my knee.'

352

'Actually I think I should go.' I walk slowly towards the door, still facing him.

With one fast move he blocks me.

'Where you going?' he asks, his eyes wide, staring at my breasts.

'I...I told you. I've got to get home,' I say, a tear escaping from my eye despite trying to remain strong.

'You can stay here tonight,' he says, a lewd whisper.

'Just tell me what area this is and unlock the door,' I say, trying to sound strong and determined, but it instead coming out as a weak pathetic whisper.

'Come on sweetheart. Don't be shy.' He moves closer and wraps his arm round my waist.

'Please. Just let me go,' I say, thick tears starting to fall.

I look into his wide unhinged eyes and see that he has no intention of letting me go. Not until he's got what he wants. Oh my God. This is happening. I'll be able to fight him off, right? But what if he gets a knife and threatens to kill me? Would I rather get raped and live, or die? OK, think straight. There must be a bathroom here someone, it must have a lock. Just get there and ring someone.

'I'm...I'm just going to go to the toilet.' I attempt a natural smile.

I turn and bolt for it, running to the top of the stairs as quickly as my legs will carry me. I dive into the bathroom, turning round to shut the door. I've almost closed it when something wedges in its way. His foot. How did he get up here so fast? I look at him, pleading with my eyes for him not to touch me.

'You freshen yourself up sweetheart. You're gonna fucking love this,' he snarls, smirking as he reaches out and strokes my breast and begins to remove his belt.

'O..OK, I will,' I stammer, throwing his hand off and slamming the door shut, locking it as fast as I can.

I sit on the toilet seat and sob, my whole body trembling. How could I have been so stupid? I'm one of those stupid cows you see on Crime Watch that walk down dark alleyways alone at night. I've brought this all on myself. I get my phone out and call Jazz again.

'Hey, this is Jazz...'

Fucking voicemail! OK, think, think! I call Izzy again, but no answer. I would call Oliver, but I know he's on a stag weekend in Bournemouth. I can't call Richard or Henry. I just can't. They think I'm an idiot as it is. They'd probably just shout at me. There's only one person I can call and I really, really don't want to call him.

I type in his name and he picks up after two rings.

'Hello?'

'R...Ryan,' I stammer down the phone in between sobs. 'I'm...I'm in trouble.'

'What's wrong? Where are you?' he says, his voice full of concern.

'I don't know where I am! I'm at this guy Tom's house and he just...well...I just get the feeling that he won't let me go.'

I can't seem to say what I suspect might happen if I unlock this door. That would make it too real.

'Poppy, what are you talking about? Just walk out the door.'

'He's locked the door. You don't understand. He's being really forceful.'

'Poppy, you need to call the police. They'll be able to trace your call.'

'No! I don't want the police. What could I say? I think someone might try it on with me, but I'm not sure. They'll just laugh at me. Can't you just pick me up?'

'But if I don't know where you are?'

'Please,' I beg, the sobs thick and heavy on my chest.

'OK, calm down. Look out of the window and describe to me what you can see.'

I pull back the blind and open the top window so that I can see out. The fresh air on my face reminds me again that this isn't a horrible nightmare.

'I'm somewhere near Harrow. We were in the car for about five minutes. Um...I can see a church tower and there's a train station next to it, but I can't see what the name of the station is.'

'Did you pass Homebase?'

'Yes! Yes, I remember a Homebase.'

'I think I know where you are. Stay there. I'll be there soon.'

He hang ups and I press my ear to the door, trying to sense whether he's still lurking outside. I think he's gone. Not that it means that I'm leaving this toilet. No way.

About ten minutes later Tom knocks on the door.

'What's the hold-up sweetheart?' He sounds even more wasted.

'Um....I'm just getting ready. Be out soon.'

Please God, Ryan, find me and be quick. Another ten minutes later I hear a knock at the door. That can't be Ryan. Can it? How would he know what house I was in?

I hear a few loud shouts and my stomach flips even more nervously. What if he's called some friends? What if they all think they're going to have a party with me? I lean over the sink and pull my hair back as I heave violently. Footsteps creep up the stairs. Someone's coming up the stairs. They're coming to get me. That pathetic lock won't hold it. They're going to get me.

I frantically open the bathroom cabinet trying to find some sort of weapon. My shaking hands throw the contents into the sink. I sift through it all until I find some small nail scissors. They'll do. I clasp it in my hand, ready to stab them in the eyeball. I'm ready. I'm tough and I'm ready. Someone bangs loudly on the door and I instantly cower away from it, no longer feeling brave.

'Go away!' I shout as aggressively as I can.

'Pops, it's me,' Ryan calls.

'Ryan?'

I open the door to find him flustered, his curls in every different position. I throw myself into his arms, not caring how desperately pathetic I look. He pulls me close into his chest as I break into angry urgent sobs. I'm finally safe. His strong arms will protect me.

'Are you OK?' he asks, stroking my hair.

I nod unconvincingly, not even breaking away from his chest to look at him.

'How did you know which house it was?' I ask, breaking myself away from him for an instant, before throwing myself back into his arms.

'Jazz phoned home saying her battery had died and had we heard from you. I asked if she knew this Tom and she gave me his address.'

'Oh.'

He pulls back and points to my clenched hand. 'What's with the scissors?' he asks raising an eyebrow, smiling.

'It's a weapon, obviously,' I say wiping my nose.

'What were you planning on doing? Manicuring him to death? Come on, let's go down.'

'I don't know,' I hesitate. 'Are you sure we're safe now?'

'Pops, it's over. Come on.'

I walk very slowly behind him down the stairs, straining my head to hear anything, but all I get back is an eerie silence. I peer around the corner and see Tom and his friend on the floor, cradling their heads. Blood is coming out of Tom's mouth and his eyes are red and puffy, as if he's been crying.

Ryan walks over and takes Tom by his neck, dragging him towards me. I flinch back.

'Tom's got something to say to you,' Ryan snarls.

'I'm sorry Poppy. I didn't mean to,' Tom cries. His shirt is ripped and he looks pathetic. But that doesn't stop me wanting to run away from him.

'Can we just go?' I ask Ryan, wanting to leave this nightmare behind.

'Course. Come on.' He guides me out to the car, wiping tears from my face. 'You're safe now.'

*   *   *

'Can we get a McDonalds?' I ask, my stomach growling as we queue up in the petrol station.

'In a minute,' he snaps. 'God, you're like a child sometimes.' He smiles.

'Well I'm very sorry! But I'm starving.'

He rolls his eyes.

'Jazz is probably eating by now,' I say under my breath, my stomach growling.

'Have some crisps then.' He grabs some off the shelf and hands them over to me.

'Oh yeah, thanks.'

I rip the bag open and stuff some in my mouth, letting the strong flavour of salt and vinegar take over. My God, it's like I haven't eaten in years. Let alone something this delicious!

'Mmmmm,' I moan before I can stop myself.

'You OK there?' he says, looking at me, his mouth twitching in amusement.

'U-huh,' I say, my mouth full.

'I can't believe this queue.'

'EVERYBODY GET FUCKIING DOWN!' a gruffly voice shouts from nowhere/

'What the?'

But I'm already being pulled to the floor by Ryan. I look around and everyone's on the floor, the whole queue. A man behind me is praying, his eyes closed, rosary beads in his hands. Who the hell carries rosary beads around with them? The woman behind him is crying.

Whereas I still don't know what the hell is going on! I try to look towards the front but I can't see anything, shelves of car oil blocking my view.

'What's going on?' I whisper to Ryan who's got his arms protectively around me.

'Some kids are robbing the place,' he says, not looking at me.

Oh my God. I'm one of those people you see on the news. I've been a victim of crime. I thought there was more chance of you getting hit on the head with a coconut or something like that? I was sure I'd heard it on the news? Or maybe it was something Jazz had read in one of her stupid magazines. It probably wasn't a fact at all.

A woman in-front with frizzy hair turns to face us, tears streaming down her face, her whole body shaking so uncontrollably that her teeth chatter.

'Don't worry,' I whisper holding onto her hand. 'It'll be over soon.'

Since when did I get so calm in an emergency? But then I suppose, I have already had a pretty traumatic night. Maybe I'll never be scared again.

But then I think of Jazz. What if she comes looking for us? What if she gets involved in it all and ends up getting shot? Or kidnapped or something? Oh my God! Now my teeth are chattering.

'Hey,' she says, suddenly seeming a little calmer. 'Aren't you the guy from the paper?'

I follow her gaze and realise she's staring at Ryan.

'Yes! You're the man who saved the granny from those muggers!' she says, getting all excited.

His expression changes quickly as we both realise what she's talking about.

'No! No, he's not,' I shout. 'He gets that all the time, don't you Ryan!' I laugh nervously.

'Yes, it is you! Ryan David or something like that?'

Why did I say his name! What an idiot.

'What are you waiting for? Go up there and help out,' she says eagerly.

'What?' he says, staring back at her as if she's mad.

'Everyone,' she whispers to the others around us. 'This guy has dealt with this kind of thing before. He's going to help us.'

'Oh thank Jesus in heaven,' the man with the rosary beads says.

'No! No he's not! He's staying here.' I desperately look from face to face as I hear the men's raised voices get louder.

'Poppy. It's fine,' he says, his face seeming afraid but determined.

'No it's not! Don't you fucking DARE!' I cling onto his arm like a child.

He's trying to get up! He's actually trying to stand up! He's fucking insane.

'Just promise me you'll stay here,' he says, looking at me seriously.

'No!' I whisper loudly, holding onto his arm so strongly I'm sure I'm cutting off his circulation. 'No!'

'Just stay here!' he barks, throwing me off him. He walks away, past the shelves, until I can't see him anymore.

'Stay here. Do what he says,' the frizzy woman says to me.

'Are you fucking crazy!? This is your fault! I'm going after him.' I get up, zoning in my hearing to him attempting to reason with them.

He hasn't got a chance. People that rob shops aren't normal people you can have a conversation with. You can't just get them a tea and tell them to calm down dear.

'No! He said to stay here.' She clutches onto both of my arms, restraining me. 'He knows what he's doing.' She smiles reassuringly. She's crazy!

'No he doesn't! This is all my fault you stupid bitch! He doesn't have a –'

But I stop mid-sentence. I stop because I hear a gun shot.

Chapter 27

For a second I'm frozen. My body trembles, my stomach dropping.
My throat contracts, my tongue going numb. I look from face to face.
First at the frizzy woman, who's frozen still, then at the man praying.
Please no. Please no!

Before I can think I jump on top of the woman, shaking her with all of
my force.

'WHAT THE FUCK HAVE YOU DONE!?' I scream, shaking her
violently. 'WHAT THE FUCK HAVE YOU DONE!?'

I get up slowly, my legs complete jelly, and try with all of my force to
walk towards the front of the shop. The thugs have gone, but in their
place is a small crowd of people that a second ago were queuing with
me, waiting to pay for petrol.

I try to run over to them, but my body's not working. My eyes begin
to sting with tears and I put my hands out in front of me, as if to try
and help myself forward, but they're shaking so violently.

'R-r-r-yan,' I stammer.

As soon as I've said his name something jolts inside my body. Ryan!
I run over to him, pushing the people roughly to one side and find him
on the floor, sitting up.

'Ryan!' I cry, crouching down to him.

He's holding onto his shoulder and there's red blood dripping down
from it, through his t-shirt.

'Oh my God. Oh my God. Someone call a fucking ambulance!' I
shout, my voice not coming out as loud as I want.

'Ryan, are you OK? OK, stupid question. Are you...are you alive?'

'Of course I'm alive,' he says, rolling his eyes. 'I've just been shot.'

'*Just* been shot? You've been fucking SHOT Ryan!'

'I'm fine,' he smiles. The blood is draining from his face, telling me
he's anything but ok.

Oh my God. He's bleeding to death right in front of me.

'I can't hear anyone calling that fucking ambulance!' I shriek at
everyone. They just seem to be staring.

'Someone's called it. They're on their way,' a man with an afro shouts.

'Great. Don't worry Ryan. I'm here.' I take off my jacket and put it to his wound. 'Lie down will you.'

I practically push him down flat on the floor and press the wound with all of my might, desperately trying to stop the bleeding. Just like they do on Casualty.

'Here, let me take over,' the afro man says.

I let him, as he's clearly stronger than me. I lie down on the floor next to Ryan and grab hold of his face.

'Hold on Ryan. They'll be here in a minute.' I wipe a tear off my face. 'Just hold on.'

'God!' he says, rolling his eyes. 'You sound like an actress from one of those action films.'

'What? Trust you to be an arsehole even when you've been shot. I don't know how to act! Normally people don't get shot around me.'

'I'm surprised,' he says, smiling weakly, but then seeming to suck in the air from pain.

'Oh my God,' I sob. 'Please just hold my hand.'

I clasp my fingers through his and gaze into his big brown eyes. They seem to be getting weaker, the life being sucked out of them. He's trying desperately to be strong, but I can tell he's hurting. He squeezes my hand tighter and starts breathing deeper and slower.

'Don't worry. They're almost here,' I whisper.

'OK. It...It kind of hurts,' he says weakly.

'Of course it hurts, you idiot. You've been shot.' I smile and rub his cheeks with my other free hand.

He doesn't say anything back. His face is almost pure white.

'Excuse me miss,' someone says to me, budging me out of the way.

I turn and see that it's two paramedics. I didn't even hear them pulling up. Was their siren even going?

'What's your name son?' the grey haired one asks.

'It's Ryan. His name is Ryan.'

'Yes thank you miss,' he says, annoyed. 'But I need to talk to him. We need to find out how coherent he is.'

'Oh...sorry.'

'Ryan. How are you feeling?'

'It hurts,' he says weakly. Shit, it must be bad. He's not even being sarcastic or giving a witty response.

'Don't worry mate. We'll have you at the hospital in no time.'

'Why can't we go now!?' I scream. 'Why the fuck are we waiting so long?'

'Please miss, calm down.'

'Sorry. Just hurry!' I cry desperately.

They load him in the ambulance and I automatically jump in with him.

'Would you like your girlfriend to go with you?' he asks Ryan.

'She's not my girlfriend,' he croaks.

Oh. So he can get shot and be on his death bed, but still he manages to let people know I'm not his girlfriend.

'You want me to come with you, right?' I ask, already making myself comfortable on the end of his bed.

'No. You should drive my car home.'

'Oh...right. OK.'

I slowly jump out, in total shock, as one of the men slams the door and it drives off, sirens blaring.

I can't believe this. Ryan's been shot and he wants me to drive his car. What kind of mental person gets shot and is still rational enough to ask someone to drive their car home? Who cares about the car!? If I'd been shot I'd be asking for people to call my love ones and a priest, dramatically confessing all of my sins and telling people I love them. But I mean...a car?

I get in the car and start the engine, but then I realise. I don't know which hospital they'll have taken him to? I take my phone out and ring home hoping Jazz will be back by now.

'Hello?' Jazz answers.

'Hi,' I stammer.

'Hey babe, where are you?'

'Um...Jazz, I...'

'What? Where abouts are you?'

'Something's....something's happened,' I finally manage.

'What? Are you OK?' she says sounding panicked. 'What's happened?' Izzy says in the background.

'OK, I don't want you to panic. Promise?'

'Yeah, of course babe. What's happened?'

'Ryan's...he's been shot.'

'WHAT?'

'He's been – '

'I fucking heard you the first time! He's been shot! Where the fuck is he?'

'He's just gone in an ambulance to the hospital.'

'Oh my God, which one? And why aren't you with him?'

'That's why I was ringing you. He's gone in an ambulance but I don't know which one.'

'Oh, OK. Don't panic. They've probably taken him to Hammersmith. We'll meet you there.'

*   *   *

'Hi. Ryan Davis. Where is he? He was brought in with a gunshot,' I say to the sulky looking receptionist.

'Was he in an ambulance?' she says through chewing gum.

'Yes of course he's in an ambulance!'

'Please don't use that tone with me madam. What relation do you have to him?' She eyes me suspiciously.

'I'm...I'm his fiancée.'

'Oh, OK then,' she says, suddenly friendly. Thank god I lied.

'According to this he's up on the Elizabeth ward. It's floor 4.'

But I've stopped listening to her. I'm already running towards the lifts.

'Ryan Davis? He came in here with a gunshot wound?'

The nurse looks back at me blankly. 'I'll try and find out' she says, disappearing.

I grab another nurse as she walks past.

'Please! I'm trying to find Ryan Davis. He's been admitted for a gunshot wound?'

'I'll try and find out for you,' she says, also disappearing.

You know what, fuck this. I'll find him myself! I wander around the rooms, sticking my head round the curtains. I manage to find everything but him - a fat naked man, a nurse and patient making out, but not Ryan. Where the hell is he?

I go into another room with two empty beds and sit down on one. This is useless. I'll never find him. I throw myself back on the bed, tears escaping thick and fast and cradle a blanket or something to my face. Actually, it smells. I sit up and hold it away from me to see what it is. Damn NHS. It's probably a blood stained cloth that they've left here. But it's not. It's Ryan's bloody t-shirt. Well, a bit of it anyway. It's been cut in half.

But where is he? The bed's empty. A sickening feeling creeps over my entire body. It's like it knows something bad is coming. Oh God. I want so desperately to know if I'm right. Because the pain of not knowing is killing me. Nerves appear in my stomach, intuitions way of telling me I'm right. It's true.

A nurse walks round the corner and I grab her.

'Tell me it's not true,' I beg. 'Tell me!'

She looks awkward and apologetic. She stands back.

'I'm so sorry,' she says, dropping her head to the floor.

'Sorry? Sorry for what?' I want to hear her say the words. 'Is he...dead?'

'I'm so sorry for your loss.'

OH. MY. GOD. He's dead.

The shock blinds me for a moment and I pray I've misunderstood. It must be wrong. She must be wrong. But I know. I know it's true. It's happened and there's nothing I can do about it. My throat starts to close and my chest tightens. A dull aching thud appears on my chest, suffocating me. My throat is being strangled. Strangled by grief. Breathe, Poppy. Breathe. But all that comes out is a noise. A weak little noise, almost a silent sob. The tears start falling down my face and my whole body begins to tremble. My lips are wobbling and my whole body starts to convulse as the sobs come thick and fast. I'm sobbing so hard and so fast I can't breathe. But I don't want to breathe. I want to die.

'No!' I scream hysterical as I fall to the floor.

I sob so hard that I heave. I'm going to vomit. Grief is taking over me. Intense grief, taking over my entire body, making me heave. I want to be sick. I want to feel the pain I'm feeling. I want to wallow in my own sadness. I want to die.

'Rachel? Is everything OK?'

I look up and see the red head Irish nurse from earlier.

'She's just upset, Ann. Let her be,' she says, ushering her out of the room.

'Let her be? Why?'

'She's just lost her husband.'

'No she hasn't' she says, shaking her head at her.

'Yes she has'. She turns to me on the floor. 'You're Mrs Walsh aren't you?'

'Mrs Walsh? No. I'm here for Ryan Davis,' I say in between sobs.

'Oops! Wrong room! So sorry.' She turns and runs from the room.

'Wrong room?' I say at the Irish nurse. 'You mean...he's not dead?'

'No dear. He's in the next room. Come on.' She lifts me up from the floor, my legs like jelly. 'I'll take you to him.'

When I walk in the room he's sitting up in bed in a horrible hospital gown with Jazz next to him.

'Ryan!' I run over to him, practically throwing myself on the bed.

'What took you so long?' Jazz says, looking at me wildly.

'They...they told me you were dead!' I shout, snot still running down my face.

'You're joking!' she says. 'You should sue!'

But I'm not listening.

'Ryan, are you OK?' He still has a face as white as a sheet.

'I'm fine,' he says, looking away annoyed.

'What happened? Have they operated on you?' I look around for a nurse.

'Excuse me, nurse! When the hell is he going to be operated on?' I shout frantically.

'Poppy, I'm fine. I don't need an operation. It just grazed the top of my shoulder. The bleedings stopped and they've just put a bandage over it.'

'A bandage? But...you've been shot.'

'Poppy, I'm fine.'

'I'm going to speak to a doctor.' I leave the room and grab a nurse.

'Excuse me, but I want to speak to you about Ryan Davis's injury.'

'I'll send a doctor out to you.'

I wait around tapping my foot. I mean, what the hell do I pay my taxes for if a doctor can't even see me and tell me what's going on with him?

'Ah, are you Ryan's fiancée?' an Indian doctor says to me.

'Yes,' I say trying to act smug. That's how engaged people act isn't it?

'Well, Ryan's been very lucky. The bullet just grazed the top of his shoulder. We don't need surgery and we've managed to stop the bleeding. He can go home in the morning.'

'Oh thank God.' A big sigh of relief escapes my lips.

'No problem,' he smiles.

'Is there anything else I can help you with?'

I consider telling him about his thick nurse that told me Ryan was dead, but then I decide to leave it. Karma and all that. It's probably good karma that he didn't die if you think of it!

*   *   *

'Well, I've spoken to Grams and she's going to get here as soon as she can,' I say when I go back into the room.

'What?' he says, looking up disgusted.

'What?'

'You called my Grandma?'

'Yeah,' I say in a quiet voice. 'Was I...not supposed to?'

'No, no. You go ahead and call my eighty year old grandmother and give her a heart attack. I'm sure she'll be fine.'

'Oh. I hadn't thought of that.'

'That's your problem Poppy. You don't think.' He glares at me thoroughly pissed off.

'What?' I'm suddenly very aware of Jazz being here.

'Yeah, it was you that got me in this whole fucking mess. If you wouldn't have started the fight with the drunk, I wouldn't have had to lie, I wouldn't have been in the paper and I wouldn't have been shot.'

'I'm...I'm sorry.'

'Ryan that is some kind of twisted logic. I mean, Poppy didn't know this was gonna happen.'

I look at Jazz and smile. Thank God someone is sticking up for me.

'Oh whatever,' he says, looking away. 'I'd like to be left alone now. It's late.'

'OK. Well, we'll see you soon then,' Jazz says.

He ignores us. We walk awkwardly out into the hall by the lift.

'Come on, let's go,' Jazz says, taking my arm. 'You've had a pretty rough night.'

'No. I have to wait for his Grandma.'

'Are you sure? You don't have to feel responsible for this you know?'

'I know. But I do.'

She kisses me goodbye and I wander back towards his bed and sit down next to him. His eyes are closed and his head is rolled to the side but I'm sure he's faking.

'Are you asleep?' I whisper, just in case I'm wrong.

'Yes.'

'OK.'

'Don't speak to me,' he growls, still with his eyes closed.

*   *   *

A hand on my shoulder wakes me up.

'Poppy, dear.'

367

I look up to see his Grandma and realise that I've fallen asleep leant over his bed. Ah, my back aches. I look at Ryan and he's still sleeping peacefully. I glance at my clock and realise its 6am.

I put my finger up to my lips to signal to be quiet around him.

'Let's talk outside,' she whispers.

I follow her out, feeling a slight sting on my leg as I walk around the bed.

'Don't worry. He's totally fine. The bullet just grazed him.'

'I know dear. I spoke to one of the nurses. What I'm more interested in is that she says you're his fiancée?'

'Oh, shit. Oh, sorry, I didn't mean to say shit. Oh god, I just said it again!'

'Calm yourself darling.'

I take a deep breath and try to chill out. 'I'm not his fiancée. But I just had to see him and...It's all my fault anyway...and...'

'And your leg's bleeding,' she says, looking down.

'What?'

I look down and sure enough dark red blood is dripping down my leg. 'How the hell?'

I follow the small trickle of blood back to the bed and find that I've caught it on a bit of rusty bed.

'Nurse!' Grams says, grabbing the Irish one. 'She just caught her leg.'

'Not another one,' she sighs. 'Sorry love, but you'll need a tetanus.'

I break into pathetic heavy sobs.

'Come on love. I'll come with you. We'll get a tea and you can tell me all about it.'

Chapter 28

The next morning it's full action stations. We've decided to surprise Ryan with a made over garden. It's the bloody least I could do after nearly getting him killed.

A knock at the door startles me. I swing it open to see Lilly with red puffy eyes and a mini red suitcase.

'Lilly? What's wrong?'

'Oh, fucking everything!' she says, bursting into tears. I hug her tightly and pull her off the street, dragging her suitcase with me. 'Can I stay here tonight?'

'Yeah of course. Why, what's wrong? Is it Alex?' I pull her into the sitting room and settle us both on the sofa.

'We got into this massive fight about the flat,' she sniffs, blowing her nose in an already crumpled tissue.

'What about the flat?' I ask. My voice is high and unnatural, I notice.

'The sellers have taken it off the market!'

'What?'

'They said something had happened to them recently which made them realise what was important in life and that they didn't need to upgrade anymore. Someone about a vase or something. I think they're just kooks.'

Oh my Jesus. I only wanted to put an offer in to delay it. I had no idea they'd lose out on their dream flat for definite.

'Oh my God, I'm so sorry.'

'It's OK,' she says, pushing me away. 'But he started saying that maybe it wasn't meant to be. Can you believe that!? And I was like, well maybe you just don't want to buy with me. Maybe you're having second thoughts about the whole thing! And he was like you're always so paranoid and I was like paranoid? Your mother's paranoid.'

'You...' I take a deep breath. 'You mentioned his mother?'

She looks down at her tissue. 'Well I mean....maybe I did slightly over react, but then he said I spent too long blow drying my hair in the morning and I told him I hated how he never washed out the bath and before I knew it I was packing a bag and telling him I needed space.'

'Oh hun.' I pull her close into my chest, albeit awkwardly.

'I don't need space! I hate space. I just want him and I've messed it all up.'

'Lill, you haven't messed it all up.'

Jazz and I have done that for you.

'Come on. We're clearing up the garden, why don't you help?'

She looks at me in horror. 'You think manual labour is going to help me?'

'Well...maybe not. But surely bossing people around will help?'

'I don't know what you mean,' she smiles. 'Where are they all?'

Before I've even had a chance to open my mouth she's jumped off the sofa and is outside. I look out of the window and see her charging in, briefly introducing herself and ordering people to do things.

Everyone's looking a bit confused and put out, but wisely they've decided to just do it.

*　　　　　　*　　　　　　*

As I walk down the long hospital corridor that afternoon, I start to rehearse the speech in my head. Ryan, I'm really sorry for all of the pain I've caused you but I think we should both move on and you should forgive me. I imagine he'll smile, shrug and tell me to forget about it. Then he might drop to his knees and tell me his near death experience has made him realise he wants to marry me. And have five kids. Well, *maybe* I went a bit too far with that bit, but you never know.

I take one last deep breath before I turn the corner and see him sat on the bed in his horrible green hospital gown.

'Hi.' I attempt a smile as I look into his gorgeous face.

'Have you got my clothes?' he asks, avoiding eye contact.

'Yeah.' I hand over the bag containing some tracksuit bottoms and a t-shirt. 'How are you feeling?'

'I've been better,' he snorts. He turns to face me, holding his tracksuit bottoms. 'Can you turn round?'

'Huh?' I look at him bewildered. 'Oh, you mean so you can get dressed?'

'Yes,' he says, slowly as if I'm special.

I turn round, trying desperately to remember my speech. What was it? Something about forgiving me. I knew I should have written it down. 'I'm ready.'

I turn round to face him, but he's already half way down the corridor. I run after him to the car and we spend the entire journey in awkward silence.

I pull into our road and attempt to park, ending up with one half on the curb, almost touching the lamppost and the back end sticking out into the road. Not that I'm going to admit it's an awful park. I turn the engine off and open the door.

Ryan pulls my arm. 'You're not seriously leaving it like this?'

'What?' I say, playing innocent and hoping he doesn't notice the sweat on my forehead at the thought of having to try and correct it.

'The car. You have passed your test, right?'

'Yes! I have, thank you very much. I passed with flying colours. And first time!'

'Really,' he laughs. 'Were you by any chance wearing a short skirt at the time?'

'What? How dare you! You think I just passed my test because I'm a little slut. You're way out of line.'

The fact that I've still got my lucky denim mini skirt hanging proudly in my wardrobe is not something I feel I should share.

'Sorry,' he scoffs, sounding anything but. He sighs heavily. 'Just give me the keys. I'll fix this.'

I throw the keys into his lap and slam the door behind me, but not before I hear him mutter 'like I always do.'

I slam the front door behind me, shaking with rage. He's such an arrogant prick! How can someone be shot and still make you want to kill them?

Izzy comes running into the hallway. 'Where's Ryan?' she asks, her face beaming with excitement.

'He's in the car,' I growl, reminding myself that I shouldn't take it out on Izzy.

'Why? Are you OK? You look kinda red?'

'I'm fine,' I snap.

The door swings open and Ryan walks in, throwing his bag angrily on the floor like a moody teenager.

'Ryan!' Izzy sings, throwing her arms round his neck and straining on her tippy toes for a hug. 'How are you?'

'I'm fine,' he shrugs.

'Well...' she says, smiling mischievously at me. 'We've got a surprise for you.'

'Really?' he asks, scrunching his face up. 'What is it?'

'It wouldn't be a surprise if I told you,' she giggles, hitting him playfully on the chest. 'Come on.'

She places her hands over his eyes and he instinctively crouches down, so as to make her job easier. Bless her, she's short.

A strange feeling of jealousy overwhelms me, as I wish it was me with my hands round Ryan's face. *Totally* irrational. I don't even like him.

'Keep your eyes closed,' she sings, as she ushers Ryan through the house.

'I am, but I can't see where the hell I'm going,' he says, as he stumbles around.

'That's the whole point,' she says, giggling. God, he really doesn't get this. 'Poppy, help me will you?'

I take his arm, pleased to have some excuse to touch him.

'Ow!' he shouts as he stubs his toe on the banister. 'Poppy! For fucks sake.'

Why does he instantly blame me? What about Izzy?

'Just a little longer now,' Izzy says, leading him outside into the garden. She smiles at me. 'OK. Open your eyes.'

'Surprise!' Me, Izzy, Lilly, Jazz and Grace shout, before he's even opened them.

His eyes flick open and widen as he takes in the transformation.

'Wow,' he breathes, looking from one side to the other.

I smile as I look around. It does look incredible, if I do say so myself. No longer do we have to look at the over grown grass and rusted rotting furniture. On the freshly jet hosed patio there's a new bamboo table which I found at the dump. In perfect condition! Well, I mean, the top was kind of scratched and there were a few fag burns, but you don't notice it. I've covered it with a multi coloured bed sheet, which I think passes as a table cloth, and placed different coloured tea light holders on it.

My Mum's old gazebo has been given to us and is erected at the end of the garden with a couple of brightly coloured duvets and cushions inside it. Around the garden walls are brightly coloured pots bursting with geraniums and Busy Lizzie's. Lanterns are placed on the floor next to bean bags from the local charity shop. Auntie Beryl even gave me a wooden wind chime.

'You like it then?' Izzy asks excitedly.

His jaw is still open. He runs his hand through his hair, clearly trying to compose himself.

'I...I just never knew the garden was even this big,' he says, letting out a nervous laugh.

'I know! Me neither!' Jazz exclaims, jumping on the grass and putting her arms wide. 'It was Poppy that told us it was wasted.'

I smile modestly, trying to make out this is no big deal. But really I want ALL of the credit.

'She wanted to do something special for you after....well, the incident,' Izzy adds looking sheepish.

'She means after Poppy got you shot,' Grace adds, quickly at his side.

I glare at her quickly, wishing for once, just once, she'd know when to keep her mouth shut.

'How are you feeling Ryan?' Grace asks, practically purring.

'Fine. It was just a graze,' he shrugs, avoiding her gaze.

'You're so strong,' she says, flicking her hair back. 'Has Poppy even apologised yet?' She turns to shoot me an evil look.

'I think this is her apology,' he says, smiling knowingly at me.

'Excuse me! We did all help,' Jazz shouts. 'We've spent all day at it.'
She suddenly drops onto her knees and strokes the grass. 'Look at this grass – I mowed it!'

'Yes Jazz,' he nods, bemused. 'Very impressive.'

'And I jet hosed the patio,' Izzy says proudly.

'Great. And what did you do Gracie?' he asks turning to her.
Why does he have to involve her? She's just stood there looking like she's sucking a wasp.

'Um...I...I supervised,' she says finally.

'Well done,' he nods before stealing a quick grin at me.

'Ha! Supervised,' Lilly complains under her breath. 'Hi Ryan, I'm Lilly,' she says shyly.

'Yeah, we've met, right?'

'Yeah we have,' she beams, winking at me.

'Is this the old table?' he asks inspecting the bamboo table.

'No, it's new,' Jazz beams.

'Well, second hand...but new to us,' I add.

'It's cool,' he says finally, still seeming to be taking it all in.

'Great. You want a beer? Jazz is doing a barbeque.'
He immediately pulls a face the minute I mention Jazz cooking and I try to hide my smile. My phone starts flashing 'Oliver'.

'Hello?'

'Didn't you get my messages?' he asks, his voice frantic.

'Yeah, but I've been kind of busy,' I say backing away from the rest of them as they fuss over Ryan.

'Oh. Well, have you heard from Jazz?'

'Of course I have. Why?'

'Why? Because I've tried to ring her like a hundred times since Leicester and she's just ignoring me,' he says, irritated.

'OK and think about it. Is there any reason why she'd be pissed off with you?'
God, he's slow sometimes.

'I don't think so. I thought we were having a good time, but the drive home she was really off with me.'

I walk into the house so Jazz can't hear me. I lower my voice to a whisper.

'You don't think it's got anything to do with you sleeping with someone, when you invited her all the way to Leicester?'

'What do you mean?' he says, after a long pause. 'We're just friends.'

'Friends with benefits!' I spit out, still pissed off they've put me in this situation.

'W..what?' he asks, trying to sound innocent.

'Look, Jazz told me you've been sleeping together.'

'Yeah, as friends!' he laughs.

'Oh, for goodness sake! This is why that never works.'

'Anyway, she's still dating Jake....isn't she?'

'I think so.'

'I Just...' he tails off, sounding embarrassed.

'You just what?'

'I don't know. I just...kind of miss her I guess.'

'Really?' I ask a bit too enthusiastically.

I immediately start fantasising about them falling in love and getting married. Jazz would be my official sister and we could have babies at the same time. And we could buy houses next door to each other and build a gate into the fence so we could wander into each other's houses all the time.

'I guess,' he sighs.

Well, that's hardly a love confession, but its close. Jazz had said she'd been bothered about seeing him with someone else. Maybe they're both secretly in love with each other and they just need a little push.

I glance out into the garden and jump guiltily when I see Jazz looking around for me. I creep into the kitchen cupboard where she can't find me.

'Look Ollie, you could turn up later for the barbeque, but you'd have to accidentally turn up.'

'Accidentally? But you just invited me.'

'Jesus, are you that dense? Jazz won't want me inviting you. Just turn up and say you popped in to see me and then maybe Jazz will talk to you.'

'Ok, got it. Thanks Sis, I owe you.'

'Understatement of the year.'

I hang up and imagine him thanking me in the wedding speech. 'And of course we wouldn't have gotten here today if I wasn't for my fabulous sister and her amazing meddling.'

The cupboard door swings open and I scream, jumping out of my skin.

'Pops?' Jazz says, a confused expression on her face. 'What the hell are you doing in the cupboard?'

'Oh...I just thought it was...a bit cosy in there.' I smile brightly, hoping she'll buy it.

'Riiiiight,' she smirks.

'Did I tell you I spoke to Ollie earlier?'

'Oh really,' she says, pursing her lips together. 'Telling you about that slut he got with, was he?'

'No. He was just chatting. He said how much he missed you actually.'

'Well obviously he misses me. I'm fabulous. It's just a shame it's taken so long for him to realise that.'

'Better late than never though right?' I ask desperately.

'Nope. That ships sailed. Any chance he had with me has gone. I'm not interested anymore.'

Then why is it she's biting her hair? She always does that when she's confused or nervous.

'OK, whatever you say.'

Maybe in hindsight I shouldn't have invited Ollie.

* * *

'This really is a delicious pizza. Jazz, where did you get the recipe?' I ask in mocking tones.

'Ha ha! It's not my fault I burnt everything.'

'Really? Because I thought you cooked it?' Ryan adds, grinning.

'Yes, but....Well, I'm not used to cooking meat am I? Everyone always forgets that I'm a veggie. It's too inconvenient for them.'

Oh, here we go. Jazz is going to play the 'I'm a veggie and no-one understands me,' card.

'And the jacket potato?' Ryan asks, trying to hide a giant smile breaking out on his face.

'Just shut up!' She flicks her hair, looking the other way.

'Anyway, this pizza really is lovely. I'm kind of glad you burnt it,' Izzy says, smiling kindly at Jazz, as she moves the take-away box.

'Well thank you Izzy'. She turns to glare back at both of us. 'Nice to know *someone* cares about my feelings.'

'I'm just glad they've started doing salads at Pizzamia,' Grace says, as she tucks into her Caesar salad with no dressing.

I mean, who orders a salad from a pizza place? A mental case, that's who.

A knock on the door startles me. Shit, I'd completely forgotten about Ollie. Whoops. Please don't hate me Jazz.

'I'll get it,' Jazz says, bouncing into the house.

I lean back and try to quickly make a nice memory of tonight, before Jazz throws a hissy fit and falls out with me forever. Whenever I'm having a great time I try to sit back and remember everything. Like the smell of baked dough pizza and garlic bread. The sound of Jazz's Mariah Carey album that she's insisted on playing, wine being poured and Izzy's giggles. If Grace weren't here it really would be the perfect evening.

'Look who it is,' Jazz says sarcastically, as Ollie follows her out into the garden. She glares at me, seeing through me immediately, completely aware of my plan. I stare back at her as innocently as I can manage.

'Hi Ollie! I didn't know you were coming round!' I say, a little too dramatically.

'Yeah, just one of those spur of the moment things,' he grins.

'This is my brother Oliver everyone. Izzy, Grace, Ryan,' I point round, 'and of course you know Jazz.'

'Hi,' he smiles charismatically around at everyone. 'Pops, I thought you said you were having a barbeque?' he asks.

Damn it Ollie! Way to blow my cover. He's not supposed to know it was a barbeque!

'It was,' Ryan says, 'but Jazz burnt it, so we had to order a take-away.' Oliver chuckles. 'Let me guess, she used the "I'm a veggie" excuse?' 'So you know her well then,' Ryan says, laughing freely at her. Jazz goes and sits back in her chair. She decides to glare at Ollie, while seeming to still act like she doesn't really care. Which I know she does.

After another hour or so, the drink is flowing and everyone is getting on well. Ryan and Ollie seem to be hitting it off, talking about the latest BMW on the market. Grace sits next to him, her claws possessively on his thigh. Jazz has somehow moved to sit next to Ollie and is wrapped up in his oversized grey cardigan. She's clearly trying to pretend that she's not interested anymore, but the chemistry between them is undeniable.

Izzy has persuaded our neighbours Ralf and Karen to join us. They're both in their forties, with no children or pets. Which I myself find a little strange. I mean, fair enough – maybe they could never have children. But wouldn't you want an animal? A few cats or maybe even a bird or some goldfish? They keep commenting on how we should make the most of our young lives while we can. They look so prim and proper I can never imagine them being young and reckless.

'Well enjoy it while you can,' Ralf says, glugging his red wine, 'because believe me, once you're married it's over.'

'It's over? That's a bit of a pessimistic way to look at it, isn't it Ralf?' Karen asks him, laughing nervously.

'Is it Karen? Because since we got married I've had to give up all of my hobbies.'

'All of your hobbies? Do you mean sitting in your pants and scratching your balls while watching Deal or No Deal?' Karen retorts. Mortification floods over his face and his bottom lip starts to wobble. Awkward silence fills the table and everyone looks away, as if to pretend we didn't just witness it.

A knock on the door makes us all look up.

'I'll get it!' Lilly shouts, running as fast as she can inside before someone else can beat her to it.

'Well maybe that was the one thing I had left to look forward to in my life. I mean, it's not like we even have sex anymore!'

Wow. One point to Ralf. Jazz stares at me, willing me to say something. I instead decide to run for it.

'I'm gonna go lie down for a while.' I head for the gazebo, ignoring Jazz's look which pleads with me not to leave her.

I throw off my flip flops and lay under it, staring up at the twinkle lights that I've set into it. It really does look fantastic. Maybe I should be an interior designer. But I'm not sure if I could do all of the fake 'hi darling, mwah, mwah' crap. Thank God it's quieter down here. Karen and Ralf's argument seems like only a buzz of light conversation from here.

'You did a great job,' Ryan says, suddenly appearing.

I jump and try to regain my composure as he lies down next to me.

'Oh thanks.' I turn to face him, feeling the same electric atmosphere which is always charging between us.

'I mean, I suppose you felt guilty for getting me shot,' he smirks.

What an ungrateful little shit head. I'm here landscaping his garden like some kind of pathetic wife, while Grace swans around pressing her boobs against him and I'm just supposed to let him treat me like shit? Is he for real!? Anger bubbles up inside me. How dare he treat me like this and think he can get away with it. Who does he think he is?

'You know what? I've had enough of you being rude to me. So what, I might have somehow...in a roundabout way, got you shot. But I mean, I didn't pull the bloody trigger! I didn't force you to intervene! In fact, I think I was the one trying to stop you. But, oh no! You had to act like a stupid hero and nearly get yourself killed. Well, did you think about me? Did you think about your Grandma? Of course not! You were thinking of yourself!' I almost scream.

I sit back, shocked by my own outburst, still panting from the rant. I suddenly feel very self-conscious as he stares at me, a blank look on his face.

'I was going to say that you didn't need to though. I already forgave you,' he smirks.

'You're....so full of yourself,' I exclaim, exhaling sharply. 'Could this not just be me wanting to give you all a nice garden?'

He looks at me for a moment, trying to figure me out. I start to feel sick. He's just so close.

'No. I'm pretty sure it was because you felt guilty,' he grins.

'Ok, OK. Maybe it was a little bit.' I laugh and tickle him lightly on his stomach.

God, its firm.

'You know I'm not ticklish,' he says, looking at me disapprovingly.

'Really? I thought everyone was?'

'No. Not me,' he says, shaking his head, as if it be ridiculous to think someone as strong as him could have any weakness.

'Wait. Does that mean you are?' A mischievous smile spreads over his face.

'Er...no,' I say, my body tensing.

'Really? Maybe I should check.' He leans in, his hand reaching towards me.

'No!' I scream, tensing my body and attempting to make a run for it. But it's too late. He throws me back on the duvet and his fingers caress the skin on the side of my stomach, having the same effect as a feather duster. Oh my God, I've forgotten the pain of being tickled. It's unbearable.

'Stop! Please stop!' I shout between giggles.

Why do I always giggle when I'm being tickled? It's not even funny – it's agony!

'What do you say?' he says, climbing over me, his legs straddling me. If we were in a normal situation then I'd be having heart failure at him on top of me, but the tickling is too much. I'm using all of my mental energy not to pee my pants. Please don't pee your pants!

'What? What!?' I shout as I writhe in torment underneath him, hitting him in the chest and trying to grab his hands away from me.

'You say,' he pins my arms over my head, 'Ryan, you are amazing. You are the king of the castle.'

'Don't be ridiculous,' I laugh.

I kick my legs, in a desperate hope to hurt him or get him off me, but he's just so strong. I'm helpless against him.

'Well then,' he says, tickling me with his left hand, while still managing to pin me down with the other. 'Shall we see if you're ticklish under your arms?'

He brushes his hands against my arm pit and my skin tingles so much I'm sure it's going to burst.

'Seriously! I'm going to pee myself! Please!' I plead.

'Just a few little words,' he whispers in my face, so close I can feel his breath on mine.

'Never!' I shout, playing along, suddenly aware that I don't really want him off me.

I mean, sure I might be in agony. But Ryan is on top of me, not letting me go and touching me all over. It could definitely be worse.

'Fine. Then you'll eat some grass too.' He rips some out of the ground and starts trying to stuff it in my mouth. I wriggle my head around and lock my mouth shut. He won't be able to get it in. Not if I can help it.

'Open wide,' he says, plugging my nose shut with his hand.

I hold my breath for as long as I can, my own stubbornness willing me on, but even I can't hold it forever. I eventually breathe out and as I quickly inhale again he stuffs grass in my mouth. I spit it out, the taste of mud making me heave. Before I can take another breath his hands are tickling me again, leaving me laughing hysterically.

'OK, stop! Ryan's the king! You're the king!' I almost scream.

'The king of what?' he says, leaning in, clearly enjoying my pain.

'The king of the castle!' I say still writhing.

'There we go. That wasn't so hard was it?' he whispers into my ear. He's so close it makes me shiver. He leans back laughing, his eyes warm.

'Can you let me go now?' I ask. I try to act genuinely annoyed, but the truth is that I could stay here forever.

'Of course Princess.' He releases my hands but stays on top of me, grinning mischievously.

'Oh I'll move, shall I?' I say sarcastically while I slide underneath his crotch. I try to stand up but fall back, realising my hairs caught on something.

'Ah!' I whine as I try and tug it.

'What?' he says, moving away, not getting it. I move with him.

'My hair. It's attached to you or something,' I say, my head still down against the duvet.

'Oh my God,' he says, laughing wildly.

'What? What am I attached to?'

'You're...' he breaks into a heavy chuckle. 'You're attached to my zipper.'

'What?'

'Come on, stand up,' he says, trying to compose himself. He stands up and I try to, but I can only stay on my knees.

'Hey guys, are you...oh, sorry,' Izzy says, walking up to us. 'I didn't realise I was interrupting something.' She turns to leave.

'You're not, you idiot! Help me,' I shriek. It's like I can feel each individual hair being broken.

'Help you?'

Ryan's laughing so hard now I think he might wet himself. I might have to punch him in the face.

'My hair's caught in his zipper!'

'Oh,' she says, giggling nervously. I feel her tiny hands try to unpick it from the zipper.

'Any luck?'

'No. I can't get it out,' she says tutting, frustrated.

'Don't worry. I've got some scissors in my bedroom,' Ryan says, taking my hands and trying to help me stand up. I still have to crouch over, my head in his crotch.

'Scissors! You are not cutting my hair!' I wail, panicked. He ignores me, already walking towards the house. I trail after him.

'Wow. You guys don't waste any time, do you,' I hear Ralf say as we pass him.

'What can I say? They flock to me,' Ryan says arrogantly.

God I want to smash him in the face.

'I wish I had that luck,' Ralf scoffs.

'Maybe he takes the upper hand in the bedroom. Nice to see how a real man operates,' Karen snaps.

'Nearly there,' Ryan says, as we awkwardly go up the stairs, one step at a time.

'You are not cutting my hair. Do you understand? Not cutting it,' I shriek.

'OK princess. Chill,' he says patronisingly.

Oh God. Images of me walking around with a small bald patch flash through my head. And I really don't suit hats.

He opens his bedroom door and the scene in front of me is so terrifying I can't even put it into words properly. Let's just say that it must have been Alex at the door. And Lilly and Alex have been, hmmm, making up. Making up hard. On Ryan's bed.

'Aaaahhh!' I scream in horror.

Ryan swivels round to me, his face as horrified as mine, but in the panic, falls over onto the floor. I go with him, my hair being ripped out in lumps.

'Shit!' Lilly screams, wrapping the duvet around her. Alex falls out of the bed, his naked body far too close to me to mention.

Ryan quickly pulls me up as Alex jumps up again to cover himself with the duvet.

'Lilly! What the fuck!'

'Hi Poppy,' Alex smiles awkwardly, his face like beetroot.

'Sorry,' she giggles.

'It's not funny! This is Ryan's bed!'

'Well I'm very sorry. I didn't realise you were needing it tonight,' she says scornfully. 'And for goodness sakes Poppy, I get that you wanna give him a blowie, but stand up. At least wait until we've left.'

'What?' I exclaim, horrified. One blush blends into another. 'My hair is fucking caught! Now get out and go down to the barbeque and try to act like grown-ups.'

'Coming from the girl with her hair stuck in a boy's zipper.'

'You're hardly in a position to judge me right now,' I snap.

'I'm really sorry guys,' Alex says, grabbing his jeans and putting them on. 'Can we just pretend this never happened?'

'Trust me,' Ryan says, his face pained 'it's already forgotten.'

They trudge out, still half-dressed and Ryan sits on the bed, me crouching underneath him. Before I can come up with a solution he pulls off his jeans and hands them to me. I take them, struggling not to look at his half naked body in front of me. Do not look at his package. I put all my attention to the jeans. My hair has curled around the zip and formed a knot. I struggle around with it and after what seems like an eternity I manage to undo myself from it.

'Ah. Finally free,' I say relieved, sitting back on the floor exhausted.

'Can I have my jeans back now?' he asks, the hint of a smirk on his face.

'Oh yeah. Of course, sorry.' I pass them back to him, blushing. What a fool I am. 'Hey, you've got really hairy legs,' I say before I can stop myself.

'Looking at my masculine legs then, huh? God, you just can't stop yourself can you?' His eyes dance, he's enjoying the idea more than he should.

'Yeah, I guess you're just too much of a hunk for me to ignore,' I say drily, standing up to leave.

'So....You really are ticklish aren't you?' he says, standing up.

Am I imagining it or is he trying to make me stay here a bit longer with him?

'Oh, a little bit,' I say trying not to smile.

'Oh my God,' he says, looking beyond me. 'Did you do this?'

I follow his gaze to the photo collage I did for him, using all his Australia photos I found on his desk while snooping earlier. I just wanted to find a picture of his ex-girlfriend. That's not weird, right?

'Yeah,' I say, suddenly aware that I must look like a bunny boiler. 'It just seemed such a shame, you having all those great photos and them not being on display.'

'You're right. It looks great, thanks.'

'Sorry,' I say suddenly all too aware that this was too much. He hates how I've tried to take over. I'm suffocating him. 'Sorry. I didn't mean to go through your stuff.' I turn and quickly make a dash for the door.

'No,' he says, grabbing my arm and making me turn to him. 'I love it. Thank you.'

He locks his eyes with mine and every muscle in my body reacts. He walks forward and gently throws me playfully against the wall. My breathing starts to quicken as ripples of pleasure go along my body. He leans into me, but I look down at the floor. I'm too used to jumping to conclusions with him. I will not assume ever again that he is interested in me. The rejection is too painful.

He presses his forehead against mine and I look up at him. Now that we're so close I notice that he's panting too.

'Look,' I begin. 'I can't do this.'

'Do what?' he says, tracing his fingers up my arm, a look in his eyes which says he knows exactly what I'm talking about.

'You know...that. I can't do that,' I stammer, trying not to swallow my own tongue.

'Really? Why not?' he asks, still tracing his fingers, seeming as cool as a cucumber. But then he's probably used to seducing women, I remind myself.

'Because...' God. Why can't I? I really can't remember. It's like his fingers are erasing all sensible thoughts in my head. My hormones are just taking over.

'Because?' he grins, his soft voice overwhelming.

'Because I don't want to be another...thing on your bedpost.'

'Thing?' He looks amused, still not moving his forehead from mine. 'Do you mean notch?'

'Yes! Notch. That's what I meant. We should...just be friends.' Why couldn't I think of the word!? Now I look like a right idiot.

He runs both his hands up my arms, barely touching me but making me quiver. His wicked fingers run up to my shoulders, then my neck. His eyes are gloriously intense. I break away from the intensity of his stare, it too much to bear. Maybe I should just sleep with him. Get rid of this tension. Then I can go about my normal life.

His hands creep up from my neck to my face, making every hair on my body stand on end. He turns my head back to face him and I try to avert my eyes, not wanting to be entranced by his. But I can't help it. I look into them and see a night long of passion and ecstasy.

'Because you think I'm just going to hit it and quit it with you?'

I can't speak. I literally cannot make a sound. I'm just dumbfounded by him. I manage to nod.

'Well actually, no.' A wicked grin lights up his face. 'But then...maybe you're right. We should just be friends.' He smiles, kisses me on the cheek slowly and leaves me panting in the room. What? I mean seriously, what the fuck? Where was my expected speech about how much he adores me? Where he confesses to being secretly in love with me and how of course I'd never be a notch – a notch you idiot – on his bed post. How he'd want to wake up to me every morning. But no. It seems my first opinion about him was right. He's really just a man whore who enjoys playing with my emotions. I'm a little toy for him to play with when he's bored.

When I walk back down the stairs to join them he's already back sitting under the gazebo with Grace. He watches me, amusement all over his face, as I sit down with the rest of them at the table. How embarrassing – he's laughing at me. Well he can go jump off a cliff for all I care. Grace is lying down next to him, seeming to be chatting away, but he's just ignoring her and won't stop staring at me.

I try to act like normal and get involved in the others' conversation about the local rubbish man but I keep looking up to see if he's still staring. And each time he is. Grace starts trying to tickle him, clearly trying to relive our play, but he ignores her.

Maybe. Just maybe. I might be wrong.

Chapter 29

'OK, you can have a little rest now,' Izzy says to me as we walk into the kitchen after another power walk.

'O..kay,' I say between pants.

'But after that I'm gonna make us some eggs and then run you a hot bath.'

Why is she treating me like a baby? I know she thinks I'm some sort of project for her, but when is she going to realise it doesn't matter how many times she makes me do star jumps around the park – I will never be a size zero.

'You need to look your best for tonight.'

My body tenses at the mention of it. Tonight is Ryan's work charity do. He made a point of reminding me about it during the week and pointing out that I didn't need to worry. It was just as friends. He seriously enjoys taking the piss out of me. I'm so scared of having to dress up and try to be graceful. I don't get why he didn't just ask some bimbo instead. Some bimbo who knows how to act at these events. But still, it doesn't stop me nearly have a heart attack at the thought of spending an evening with him.

I have an hour's nap and then wake up to Izzy's boiled eggs with wholemeal toast.

'I've drawn you a bath too. It's ready when you are,' she says, with half a piece of toast still in her mouth.

'OK thanks.'

When I go up, the smell of bubble bath is already coming down the stairs. When I open the door the bath is full of bubbles and I sink in, my aching muscles sighing in relief.

As I walk down the stairs feeling as fresh as a daisy, I think I can hear familiar voices.

'Jazz? Are you here?'

'Ta-daaaaa!' she shouts, jumping out into the hallway.

'Are we greeting each other this way now?' I ask, smiling. 'Because I like that.'

'Come on,' she says, grabbing my hand, her eyes bulging out in excitement. 'I've got a surprise for you.'

'Really? What?'

I walk into the room looking quizzically at her and Izzy sat on the bed with the same wide eyed smiles. She opens the wardrobe and pulls out a hanger.

'Tah Dah!' she says, exposing a dress from underneath dry cleaners wrappers.

'Oh, wow,' is all I can mutter, mesmerised by its beauty.

Staring back at me is a long deep green strapless gown. It's ruched at the boob with a line of crystals and emeralds underneath it and the satin material is covered with an organza kind of material, hanging freely to the floor. It's probably the most beautiful dress I've ever seen.

'You like it?' Jazz says, apprehensively.

I can't even speak, I'm too shocked.

'She loves it!' she screams to Izzy.

'Yay!' Izzy claps jumping up and down on the bed like a six year old.

'Is...Is it for me?' I ask, hoping I haven't got the wrong end of the stick.

'No, it's for me. I'm going to wear it on the tube home. Come on dickhead, of course it's for you!' she shouts dramatically.

'But, where did you get it from?' I edge closer, feeling the material between my fingers.

'Well...you kind of...bought it yourself,' Jazz says, tracing her foot along the floor.

'What do you mean, I bought it myself?' I ask, baffled.

'Well...the bad news is that I hacked into your eBay account.'

'You hacked into my eBay account? What the fuck Jazz?'

'Ok, OK, don't get mad. Me and Izzy just couldn't let you go in that boring black dress of yours.'

'What's wrong with it?' I say defensively.

'It's just a bit...' Izzy tries to explain.

'It's a bit fucking boring and old fashioned, is what she's trying to say,' Jazz butts in.

'Don't be horrible. It's lovely – look.' I take it out of the wardrobe. Now that I put it up against the beautiful dress it does look kind of boring and fuddy duddy. I mean, it's hardly a wow dress, but still. It would work and the whole point was that I couldn't afford a new dress.

'OK, it's boring!' I sigh. 'I admit it!'

'Thank God – she's seen the light! Hallelujah!' Jazz shouts.

'Tad dramatic,' I say under my breath. 'How much was it then?' I ask, not really wanting to know the answer.

'It was *very* expensive,' Jazz says, winking at Izzy.

'Very expensive,' Izzy echoes with a massive grin on her face.

'How much?' I almost shout at them.

'The grand total of £7.50,' she says proudly.

'What? Are you sure they didn't make a mistake?'

Surely something this beautiful couldn't be that cheap.

'Nah – it was just a mum in Devon who wanted to get rid of her daughter's prom dress.'

'Daughter? Am I wearing a child's prom dress?'

'Why do you always have to see the down side of things? The main thing is that once you're done you're gonna look hot.' Her eyes start growing wide again.

'OK, well you start moisturising and then we'll help you with your hair,' Izzy says, clapping her hands in delight.

A knock at the door startles me.

'Is Ryan back already?'

'Nah, he's gone to his Grandma's for the day. Won't be back for hours. It's probably Lilly,' Izzy says, walking to the door.

'Lilly?' I say turning to Jazz puzzled.

'Yeah, Lilly,' she says, as if I'm mad.

I hear air kisses from the front door. Since when have they been best friends?

'Hey Pops,' she says, bounding into the room with two bags.

'Hey Lil. What're you doing here?'

'Helping you silly. Jazz e-mailed me and explained that she needed help getting you to look fabulous. The three of us had lunch, and now we're here,' she says, laughing excitedly.

'Sorry? So you three have been plotting behind my back on how to dress me up? I'm not a Barbie doll you know. And did you ever think that maybe I don't actually need your help?' I fold my arms defensively across my chest.

As if on cue the three of them double over in hysterical laughter.

'I'm sorry,' Jazz says, the first one to lift her head up 'it's just so funny.'

'What is? I can dress myself you know.'

She rolls over again as they get a fresh dose of hysteria.

'Stop, you're killing me,' Lilly says, wiping tears out of her eyes.

'Is she this funny at work?' Izzy asks her in between breaths.

'Oh yeah, she cracks me up,' Lilly says giggling.

'Please stop before I get offended. You guys are seriously mean!' I sit on the end of the bed, beginning to sulk.

'Sorry Pops,' Jazz says, sitting down next to me. 'It's just that we want you to look amazing and glamorous and...Well, like a girl! And we just know how to do that a bit better than you.'

'Yeah, I mean, if we left it down to you we couldn't trust that you wouldn't end up going in a trouser suit,' Lilly snorts.

The thought had actually crossed my mind.

'OK! Just do whatever you want. I'm in your hands,' I say giving in easily.

'Yay!' Izzy shouts.

'Let's get to work ladies,' Jazz instructs. 'We have very raw material and only a matter of hours.'

I roll my eyes in response.

'Please don't tell me that was the dress she was going to wear?' I hear Lilly whisper to Izzy.

Three hours later and I'm ready. My body has been squeezed into the teenager from Devon's prom dress, which does seem to accentuate my eyes, and I have the furry black wrap that Lilly brought for me.

I've got on some vintage emerald stud earrings with a matching hair broach that Izzy bought me. She said they were vintage but I have a feeling that means she found them in a charity shop.

My hair has been blow dried, then scooped up and teased into an up do, with loose curls falling delicately around my face. My make-up is done so well I feel like I've been to a professional make-artist. It's quite simple, but my eyes have been done up with green eye shadow, black kohl eyeliner around them. They smoulder at me in the mirror and even I have to admit it – I look amazing, if I do say so myself. It's just a shame that it takes a team of three people to get this effect.

The door bangs and it sends me into a panic. Ryan's here. No more fun girly sleepover. It's nearly time. Calm down! You're just friends, you idiot.

'Hey Pops. I'm running late – I'll just have a quick shower and be ready in ten,' he shouts as he bounds up the stairs.

'Well, it's nice to know he's putting the same amount of effort in,' Lilly says, making us all giggle.

'And I bet he'll still manage to look amazing,' I sigh pathetically.

They all smile at me and I quickly realise how that must have sounded.

'I mean, I'm sure he'll look fine,' I say, feeling my cheeks burning.

They all smile knowingly at each other and I feel like I've been left out of a secret.

'What? What is it?' I ask. 'What are you laughing at?'

'Just that you're totally in love with Ryan,' Jazz snorts.

'What! No I'm not!' I protest, a little too loudly.

'The lady doth protest too much,' Lilly says, chuckling.

'Shut up! I'm serious. And shut up saying that. I don't want Ryan hearing and getting the wrong end of the stick.'

'Oh come on Pops! You're all over each other!' Jazz teases.

'No we're not.'

I feel a thrill go through me as she says 'we' and I hate it. Why can't I control myself?

'Izzy – you must agree with me?' I plead.

'I'm sorry Pops, but it is pretty obvious. Especially since you've been doing your Mother Teresa act while he's been recovering. I mean, you don't see us running around after him making him tea every five minutes, do you?'

Maybe I have been fussing over him slightly since he got shot, but I mean – he got shot! It's a serious injury.

'Yeah, I don't even know the dude but I can tell you like him. Whenever his names mentioned you go all gooey looking in the face,' Lilly says, looking at me in pity.

'Shut up! And anyway Jazz, you're a fine one to talk! What the hell is going on with Ollie?'

'Oh, I don't know,' she says, exhaling heavily. 'I do kind of like him.'

'Which means you're mad about him,' I nod, understanding her language.

'But it's over. I'm with Jake now. I can't be with someone who just goes off and sleeps with other girls. Anyway, we're talking about you right now.'

I hear him moving around up on the landing and panic takes over. He cannot hear this.

'Listen here bitches. Don't say anything like this in front of Ryan. You're all totally wrong and I don't want it getting awkward between us, understand?'

'OK, OK, calm down drama queen,' Jazz says, putting her hands up in defeat. 'But it doesn't stop us saying good luck. You never know – looking like that – you may actually have a chance with him.'

'Oh thanks for the confidence,' I shoot back. 'But seriously, thank you for helping today.'

They really didn't need to, but they bothered to take time out to help me.

'To be honest, we kind of wanted to apologise to you as well,' Izzy says, grimacing.

'Why? What have you done?' I ask, alarmed.

'Nothing!' Jazz says, a little too quickly. 'All we did was go out with Grace the other night and she kind of got really drunk and admitted to tripping you and hating you.'

'I knew it!'

'This is the stunning bitch, right?' Lilly asks, confused.

'Yep. We're sorry we didn't believe you Pops,' Jazz says.

'Don't worry about it. She was pretty convincing.'

'Anyway, we've told her not to bother speaking to us until she confesses everything to Ryan and apologises to you.'

'So you'll be waiting forever then,' I laugh. 'Anyway, let's just forget about her.'

I look at myself in the mirror and take one last deep breaths as I hear Ryan running down the stairs.

'You ready Pops?' he asks knocking and sticking his head through the door.

'Oh...sorry! I didn't realise you had friends in here.' He backs slowly out of the door.

'No, it's fine. Come in.' I stand to face him and almost faint when I see how stunning he looks in his tux.

'Wow,' he mumbles staring at me. 'You look...nice.' He looks gobsmacked.

'Nice? She looks bloody amazing,' Lilly says, a tad aggressively.

'Oh, yeah...she does,' he says, staring at her as if she's mental.

'Ryan, you remember Lilly,' I say rolling my eyes as Lilly waves at him.

'So, you guys been having fun getting Poppy ready?'

'Fun? More like a mission! She takes a lot of work,' Jazz snorts.

'Don't be mean Jazz. You know it's been fun,' Izzy says, applying some more gloss on my lips.

'Anyway, it was nice to see you again Lilly, but we should get going Pops.' He looks anxiously at his watch.

'Yeah cool.' I edge out of the bedroom, trying to ignore Lilly mouthing 'he's so hot' to me.

When I glance back into the room to say bye, the three of them are dry humping each other, whipping their hair back and forth, tongues out, giggling silently. My God, they're immature.

I'm almost at the door when I remember I've forgotten my bag.

'Oh, I've forgotten my handbag,' I say turning round.

'Don't worry, I'll grab it,' he says, as he edges back into the room.

'No! I'll get it!' I say as I run after him.

As he enters Izzy, Lilly and Jazz are still pretending to dry hump and immediately jump out of position, pretending instead that they were touching their hair, or looking at the ceiling.

'Got it, let's go,' I say grabbing my purse off the side.

'Your friends are weird,' he laughs as we leave.

'You don't know the half of it.'

*   *   *

'It's the highest gynaecological killer of women in the UK and the fourth most common cause of death from cancer in women. Around two thirds of those diagnosed will die from it.'

'Oh yes, it's terrible,' I say to the bald man lecturing me on the facts of ovarian cancer.

'It's thanks to firms like these that support us and bring our cause more awareness.'

'Oh, yeah. My house mate has just joined the firm and he says they're all really nice,' I say desperately trying to change the subject.

'They are indeed. But we need more firms like these and more donations. Tell me dear, have you ever considered doing a fun run? We organise one every year and I'd love to put your name down on the list.'

'I....I'm not sure.'

'Why? Why wouldn't you want to run for a good cause?' he asks his eyes narrowing.

'I...well; it's not that....it's just...'

Oh God, I'm running out of excuses now. Maybe it would be easier to just agree with it and then break my ankle a week before.

'Poppy, I see you've met Harold,' Ryan says, swooping in with two glasses of champagne.

'Yes. This charming young lady was just volunteering to do a fun run for us.'

'Really?' He smiles at me questionably, as if he sees through my act.

'Um...'

'Yes – a very charitable girlfriend you have here,' Harold says, smiling approvingly.

'Oh, I'm not – '

'Oh, she's not – '

We both speak at the same time and look at each other embarrassed.

'We're not together,' Ryan says, smiling at him. 'Ooh, I love this song.'

He quickly puts our champagne down and pulls me onto the dance floor. I let him lead me away from Harold, breathing a sigh of relief. The band is playing some old rock and roll number I don't recognise. He pulls me into the centre of dancing couples, twirling me all the way. He begins to dance and I'm shocked with how easily he moves. Especially when he's supposed to still be taking it easy. He pulls me into him, twirling me round and out every so often. I laugh hysterically the whole way through, totally exhilarated by the evening. I want to scream from the tension between us.

The song ends and they slow it down, singing 'the way you look tonight'. He reaches his hands out to me.

'Shall we?'

'We shall,' I say putting my hand into his frame. I melt as he puts his other arm round my waist to my lower back.

The melodic piano plays softly in the background and seems to make everything around me seem so romantic. The lights seem dimmer, the people more in love. The whole scene makes me feel like I'm in a romantic fifties movie.

'You know, Harold must be the fifth person to think you were my girlfriend tonight,' he whispers in my ear.

I try not to convulse from his breath on my ear.

'Really?' I mumble back, him taking my breath away from his touch.

'Yeah, and it's funny because they all seem really shocked.'
'Shocked?'
Why would they be shocked? Shocked that he'd date someone as
average as me?
Oh my God. It dawns on me why. They must all still think he's gay.
'Yeah, but it's probably "the way you look tonight",' he laughs,
quoting the song playing.
I blush, even though he's only taking the piss out of the song.
'Because....you look beautiful tonight. They're probably shocked I
could get someone as good as you.'
I laugh awkwardly. 'You're crazy.'
'Am I?' he whispers back into my ear, sending shivers down my spine.
I ignore the question and instead bury my head into his chest, hoping
that I'll never have to leave it to face reality. This song is really how
I'm feeling. Tony Bennett is right, I'll always feel a glow just thinking
of Ryan and tonight. I didn't realise I could feel so happy and so sad
at the same time. Happy that this feels exactly how I want it to be; me
and Ryan dancing together happily, our bodies pressed together. Sad
because I know this isn't going to last, this isn't real. It's only for
tonight. When midnight strikes, like Cinderella I'll be back to my
dowdy life.
When the song ends I pull back to look at him and for a second it's as
if we're the only people in the room, his eyes enveloping me. I look
away, intimidated by his stare, not wanting to set myself up for
disappointment again.
'Another drink?' he asks, smiling awkwardly.
'Yeah, cool,' I mumble.
He goes to the bar and I move over to the side of the room. I spot
Harold edging towards me and so I weave through the crowd, hiding
behind a group of three women.
'Well, he brought that woman, but he's definitely still gay.'
'Oh yeah, it's so bloody obvious.'
'Yeah, she's probably just his fag hag.'
'Such a shame – Ryan's so lovely.'

'Excuse me,' I say tapping them on the shoulder 'but were you just talking about Ryan Davis?'

They all turn and I'm horrified to see that one of the girls is Tabitha.

'Oh hi again. I've forgotten your name – Polly or something isn't it?'

'It's Poppy actually. Anyway, look, Ryan's not gay, OK? You need to tell everyone that he's not gay.'

'But you told me he was?' She looks at me as if I'm insane.

'I know I did but I was wrong, OK? He's definitely straight,' I protest, sweat starting to form on my forehead.

'She's obviously just saying this to save his feelings,' her blonde friend says, looking at me sympathetically.

'No I mean it. He's not gay!'

'Yeah right,' she scoffs.

'Listen to me! HE IS NOT GAY!' I shout, just as the music comes to a standstill.

Silence, apart from a few muttered giggles fills the room and Ryan is suddenly at my side with two more glasses of champagne.

'Who's not gay?' he asks quizzically.

I feel myself sink into the floor as I wait desperately for the band to start playing music again. After about thirty seconds, but what feels like a lifetime, they start playing again.

'Poppy?' he says, looking from face to face, 'who's not gay?'

'Um...' I'm starting to sweat profusely.

'She was talking about you,' Tabitha says, amused.

'Me? Well, of course I'm not gay. Why on earth would you think that?' he says, both amusement and embarrassment on his face.

Without realising I've started to back away slowly, a sickening feeling creeping into my stomach. Intuition's way of letting me know something bad is coming.

'Because she told me you were.' She sticks her long bronzed finger out to point at me.

Ryan follows her finger and turns to me, disorientated.

'Poppy, what the hell is she talking about?'

I'm blinded for a moment, numb and dizzy from the consequences of my own actions.

'Um....it's a bit of a long story...'

'Excuse us a minute, will you ladies.' He smiles at them as he grabs hold of my arm and begins to drag me.

'Ow! Ryan, you're hurting me' I try to protest. He continues to drag me out of the banquet hall, ignoring my pleas. He opens the doors to the hallway and throws me angrily against the wall.

'What the FUCK do you think you're doing spreading lies about me?' he shouts outraged, pure hostile anger in his eyes.

I've never been so scared in all of my life. My whole body starts trembling and goes cold, apart from the throbbing of my arm.

'It's not what it looks like. It's - '

'Really? Because it looks like you're trying to make me look like a dick,' he spits.

'No! I never meant it to end like that. I just didn't want you with that bitch Tabitha and so – '

'And so you made up a lie,' he growls.

I flinch back from the disgust in his voice.

'Yes. Look, obviously now I know it was stupid, but I wasn't thinking. I'm sorry.' My voice is merely a squeak.

'Sorry! Sorry for what exactly? For ruining things with Tabitha? Or for spreading lies around the new company I'm working for? Or for making me look like a complete dick in front of all of those people?' His tone cuts through me, raising a lump in my throat.

'Um...all of it! I'm sorry, ok!' I cry back.

'You know what,' he says, his lip curling up in disgust, 'I'm sorry. I'm sorry I ever thought you were different to all the other bitches out there. You're just as bad as my ex-girlfriend, although at least she was more honest and upfront with it. What you've done is so sneaky and premeditated...it actually makes me sick.'

I'm stunned into silence. My throat starts to close and my chest is tightening.

'But, I didn't mean to – '

'I'm not fucking interested Poppy! Our friendship, or...whatever the fuck we were pretending to do – it's over,' his low voice cold.

He punches the door open and goes back into the reception.

I collapse onto the floor, the dull aching thud on my chest almost suffocating me. Tears start falling thick and fast as my throat starts to close up, it overwhelming me. I run to the toilets just in time to throw up.

Chapter 30

There's really nothing like crying on the tube wearing a ball gown.
'Hey lady. You get stood up? I could take you out,' a teenage boy
and his friends bellow from across the carriage, smirking. Judging me.
'Oh just fuck off!' I scream.
Not my finest hour.
I run home from the station, too upset and impatient to wait for a cab,
still crying and throw as many clothes as I can into a bag.
'Poppy? What's wrong?' Izzy says, coming into the bedroom. 'Why
are you back so early?'
'Because I fucked up!' I shout through the snot and tears.
'Why? What happened?' she asks, alarmed.
'I can't talk about it,' I say as I push past her.

                    *   *   *

When I finally get to the flat I knock on the door lightly, my body
feeling weak from emotion.
Jazz opens the door wearing my Minnie Mouse pyjamas, clearly not
expecting company.
'Hey Pops. What you doing here?' Her eyes wrinkle in confusion.
I want to answer, to tell her everything, but the only sound I can make
is one of a kicked kitten.
'Oh Pops! What's wrong? Come in.'
She guides me into the sitting room and I sit down on the sofa, the
chiffon material of the dress making a funny noise. It's the only sound
in the awkward silence.
'Tea?' she asks smiling sympathetically.
I just nod. I feel so numb, so...nothing.
She returns a few minutes later with two cups of tea and a tray of kit
kats and hob nobs.
'Here – drink it,' she says, offering it to me.

I take three large mouthfuls of tea and then stuff half a kit kat in my mouth.

'Better?'

'Mmm,' is all I can manage.

'So...are you gonna tell me what happened?' She tilts her head to one side, her eyes curious.

'I fucked up,' I say in a strangled voice, exhaling a big breath.

'Babe, I'm gonna need a little more description than that. You just turned up at half ten in a ball gown.'

'I'm too exhausted to even tell you.'

I realise that the tears are no longer running down my face. I'm numb.

'Please?' she begs.

'I...oh God, I can't even bring myself to say it.' I take a deep breath and try again. 'I did something really stupid and now Ryan hates me.'

'Well...what did you do?'

'I kind of....I sort of...told everyone he was gay,' I admit reluctantly.

'WHAT?'

I look up at her, ready for a lecture but she's already broken into a laugh.

'It's not funny!' I protest, suddenly feeling that I may also break into fits of hysteria.

'Sorry, but it kind of is! You told everyone he was gay and they believed you! So funny,' she says, doubling over again.

'I hate myself,' I say, suddenly too embarrassed to look at her.

'So...why did you tell them that anyway?'

'Well, he was going out with that Tabitha girl and she was horrible. And she was about to seduce him and then it just kind of came out.'

'Oh, I see!' She bites her lip to try and hide her smile. 'You didn't want this Tabitha girl around and that's why you lied.'

'Well, she was just so horrible and I couldn't bear for him to go out with her.' I put my head in my hands.

'Because you're so in love with him,' she states as if it's fact.

'No I'm not!'

'Oh really? So it had absolutely nothing to do with him?'

'Well…I just didn't want him to go out with a bitch, which she so obviously was.'

'OK Pops. You can lie to me if it makes you feel better.'

'Oh God! Then tonight he found out and went mental and told me whatever was going on between us is over.'

'Yeah, but he'll calm down eventually,' she says, taking a sip of her tea, as if it's no big deal.

'No, he really won't, Jazz. You didn't see him. I've never seen him like that before. He actually scared me.' I shiver at the memory.

'Oh.'

'And the worst thing is that it's all my fault. And the way he said "whatever it is we had going on" it just sort of proved that I wasn't imagining something. There was something between us.'

'Yeah, no shit Sherlock.'

'And it's all ruined because of me. Everyone at his work thinks he's gay, it's awful.'

The tears start falling down my face again and my body begins to tremble.

'Oh babe, don't get yourself upset.'

My lips wobble as I try and speak. I can't breathe again. The grief is coming over me again and this time I'm letting it. I actually want to be miserable. I want it to engulf me. I lay down on the sofa and close my eyes.

'And now I've ruined your life,' I continue. 'You won't be able to pay off your debt now.'

'Babe, don't worry about it,' she sighs, sympathetically.

'How can I not? I'm ruining everyone's lives.'

'Well…' she pouts, as if considering whether to tell me. 'The truth is that my debt is paid off. My mum caved and bailed me out.'

'What?'

I don't understand. Why on earth would she still be living here if she didn't have to?

'I didn't want to tell you because you were almost fully back to your old self again.'

I break down into more tears. Even my best friend thinks I'm pathetic.

'It's funny,' Jazz says, as she wraps me with a blanket and begins stroking my hair 'who would have thought a month ago that I'd be the sensitive shoulder to cry on and you'd be the lunatic.'

*   *   *

'Did he call?' I say as soon as I get in a few nights later.

'No...Sorry chick,' she says, her head tilted to one side in sympathy as she brings over a cup of tea.

This has been our new set routine since me moving back in. I rush home desperate to find out if he's called, only to be told he hasn't, and then Jazz makes me tea and biscuits. I have a little cry and then go to bed.

'But someone else called for you,' she says, not meeting my eye.

'Really, who?' I ask uninterested.

Probably just my mum reminding me about the wedding for the hundredth time.

'I'm not sure if I should tell you,' she says, dunking a hob nob into her tea, avoiding my gaze.

'Why? Jazz, who called?'

'OK, but promise not to get mad.'

Who the hell could it be?

She takes a big deep breath. 'It was Stuart.'

'Stuart?'

'Yep,' she nods.

'Why the fuck did he call me?' I say, anger bubbling up inside me. What the hell does that twat want?

'He says he desperately wants to speak to you and for you to call him back.'

'But what for?'

'I don't know, but he sounded pretty desperate.'

'Great. I'm desperate for Ryan to call and instead I get that twat hounding me. I wonder what he wants.'

'Dunno. Maybe you should call him and find out.'

'Ha! I don't think so. I'm depressed enough, let alone having him put me down.'

'OK?, don't bite my head off!'

'Sorry! I know I'm being a bitch. I just....oh God, I just wish life were more simple, you know.'

'Trust me I know.'

'It's like, when you're growing up you dream of marrying a prince and being a stupid nurse or whatever but no-one ever stops you and tells you not to dream so big. That you might not be a nurse because there are too many qualifications and you can't be bothered. Or that you might not find a prince. Or you might find him and you might tell his whole office he's gay. Do you know what I mean?'

'Err, sort of.'

'Oh, maybe me and you should just elope to Vegas and be massive lesbians.'

Her eyes light up animatedly.

'I thought you'd never ask!' she shouts dramatically before grabbing my face and kissing me on the lips, dragging me off the sofa.

God, she can be hilarious sometimes.

'OK!' I shout, throwing her off, laughing. 'So after we've become lesbians, what would we do?'

'Duh!' she says, as if I'm stupid. 'We'd buy a big butch van, get a goat and adopt a couple of albino children. That's the dream, right?'

'That's the dream,' I repeat through hysterical giggles.

'Anyway, do you think you'll be able to eat a dinner tonight?'

'I don't know. I just can't be bothered to eat.'

'Babe, the last couple of days all you've eaten is cereal.'

God – even cereal reminds me of him.

'OK, I'll try.'

And that was the first night I was able to eat a dinner and keep it down.

*　　　　　*　　　　　*

'Hey Pops, how are you?' Lilly says, as soon as I get to my desk.

'OK,' I say smiling weakly.

'It just wasn't meant to be, you know.'

'Thanks for the support,' I say sarcastically.

The last thing I want to hear is how it wasn't meant to be. It was meant to be, but I fucked it up. It's my fault and people should admit it to me.

'You know I love you Pops. I just think you need to move on.'

'Yeah, I know.' my voice threatening to break.

'Anyway, have you heard the latest with Neville?'

'No, what?'

'The two temps are fighting over him! He keeps telling them maybe he'll go out with them and it's driving them crazy.'

Shit. I should really speak to him and give him something else to say. I pick up my ringing phone, seeing that it's Suzanne on reception.

'Hey Suzanne.'

'Hi Poppy. Victor's visitor is here, but there's also some animal protestors outside. They've got banners and everything!'

'What? Why the hell are they here?'

'Apparently they say some of our products have been tested on animals. Do you think they are?'

'Oh fuck, I dread to think. This is a big meeting for Victor – he'll go mental. OK, don't worry – I'll be down to sort it out. Maybe call the police in the meantime?'

'Yeah OK.'

'Lilly, there are animal protestors downstairs! Will you help me get rid of them?'

'Normally I'd love to, but I've got a meeting with Hugh.' She smiles apologetically.

Hugh? Shit, is she going to be made redundant now? Today? I brace myself before going in to Victor's office.

'Victor, your visitor is here.'

'Put them in the boardroom.'

'But...there's also a problem. There's some animal rights – '

'Poppy, I don't have time for problems. Today is a big day. It's D day for redundancies. Just sort it out.' He dismisses me with his hands as he plays with his iPhone.

Fuck. Today *is* redundancy day. I was right. Oh my God, I didn't have time to prepare myself for this. I was too busy worrying about myself.

When I get to reception the scene is far worse than I'd first suspected. There must be two hundred people outside, all in brightly coloured clothes holding up banners with slogans like 'There is no excuse for animal abuse' and 'Being cruel isn't cool'.

I welcome Brady Thomson and usher him quickly into the meeting room. When I walk back out a few of them have actually come into reception and are bothering Suzanne, who looks terrified.

'Hey! What the hell are you doing in here?' I shout in my best intimidating voice.

The tallest guy steps forward, his blonde dreadlocks down to his bum. 'We're here to stop animals being tested on! You've got blood on your hands!'

'Hey, look – I don't even think we do test on animals.'

'Yes you do!' a purple haired girl protests.

'Look at this,' the dreadlock guy says, handing me over a piece of paper. It's an article in the newspaper saying that one of our companies we buy products from tests on animals. It's there in black and white.

'This can't be right,' I protest.

'It is! And until you stop doing it you're a murderer! We want to speak to your CEO.'

Oh my God. Victor is going to be coming down any minute and if he finds this he's going to kill me.

'Well you can't. The police are on their way and if you don't leave reception I'm going to have to call security.'

I don't dare tell him that we don't actually have security.

Dreadlocked guy stares at me silently for a minute. He signals to the others and they leave. Thank God!

'Poppy.'

I turn around to my name to see Lilly by my side, her eyes red from crying. Shit.

'Lilly, are you OK?'

'Did you know?' she asks, her voice shaky.

'What? Did I...did I know what?' I stammer, my stomach doing summersaults.

'You fucking did know!' she screams, finding her voice. 'You knew I was being made redundant and you didn't fucking tell me!'

'I...I couldn't...I mean, they'd have fired me.'

'So you chose your fucking job over me? Your fucking job that you hate, over your best friend? How long have you known?'

'Um? A....few weeks.'

'A few weeks! I assumed you'd only been told this week!'

Well if I'd have known that I wouldn't have admitted it.

'So what, I'm only your friend if I work here? The minute I'm leaving I can go fuck myself? I'm dead to you?' She's shouting, but tears are falling fast out of her eyes and her words are choking.

'Lilly, please! I never meant to hurt you.'

'I can't fucking believe this! How did you think I'd react?'

'Um...' I can't even respond. I can never win this.

She closes her eyes and pinches her nose with her finger. 'Please, please don't tell me it was you and Jazz that made us lose the flat too?'

'What?' I say, alarmed. How the hell does she know that?

'It was you! Alex read out the description in the paper, but I told him no way would you do that. Why the hell would you do that? Are you sick in the head or something?'

'No! Lilly, you don't understand,' I start.

Suddenly all two hundred or so protesters start barging into reception. Oh my God – they're going to kill us.

'You know what,' she says, her angry vein popping out of the side of her head. 'I should have known it was you. The minute they said she was chubby!'

I take it like a bullet to the heart. I can't even speak.

'MURDERER'S!' the protestors scream.

'Poppy! Help!' Suzanne calls. I look up to see dreadlocked guy standing on her reception desk.

I turn back to Lilly and open my mouth to say something, but what? There are no words.

'You know what,' she says. 'Go! Go put your job before everything else again! But you'll be a lonely fucking old woman. And I...' her voice begins to break again 'I was such a good friend.'

I put my hand out to her, but she knocks it away and pushes the protestors out of her way. I reach out for her, but I'm being swarmed by the crowds and she's gone.

'What do we want?' Dreadlocks guy shouts at his audience.

'ANIMALS RIGHTS!'

'When do we want them?'

'NOW!'

'Please!' I shout, my voice breaking from emotion. 'Just go away!'

Victor is going to be here any minute. In fact, I already think I can smell his over powering Old Spice after shave.

'Shut up murderer!' a girl with pink dreadlocks shouts before chucking something cold and wet over me.

I close my eyes, not sure of what it is. I open my eyes, wiping the liquid off my eyes and look down to see that the bitch has thrown red paint on me. All fucking over me! My hair, my face, my clothes!

'You fucking bitch!' I shout, tears already at my eyes.

'Come on then, murderer!' she challenges. 'How do you feel with those animals blood on you?'

'POPPY!'

Everyone seems to turn round to stare at Victor walking down the stairs, his face like thunder. I run up the stairs to him, the paint dripping after me.

He puts his hand up to his brow, his hands shaking in anger.

'Poppy, what the fuck are these people doing here?' he whispers, furious.

'They're animal rights protestors.'

'I can fucking SEE that! And why the *hell* are you covered in paint?'

'Isn't it obvious? They've covered me in it,' I say losing my temper.

408

'Isn't it obvious?' he scoffs. 'Are you taking the piss out of me Poppy?'

'Oh, no! Of course not.'

'Really? Because it sounds like you're calling me a fucking moron? Is that what you're calling me Poppy?' His eyes grow black and he suddenly looks like he could kill all of these people in one swift movement.

'No,' I say, traitor tears escaping. 'I'm sorry. I didn't mean anything.'

'Well, maybe you should think before you speak next time. Now get cleaned up for Christ's sake and get us some drinks.'

He pushes past me and begins pushing the protestors out of the way. How the fuck can he speak to me like this? How can he stand there, with me crying, and just treat me like a piece of shit. What the fuck am I doing here? I didn't go to Uni just so I could photocopy for some prick. I wasn't born to be made to feel like shit every day and even if I was – that was my mother's job. The only person in the world that can tell me what to do is me. Me and my mother.

'No!' I shout after him.

The protestors quieten their jeers and turn to stare at me. Victor turns, his jaw tight, exposing his teeth like a dog ready to attack.

'No?' he says, glaring at me.

'Yes. No.'

God, that really doesn't make sense.

'What the hell do you mean, no?' Victor says, horrified.

'I mean...' deep breath Poppy, deep breath. 'That you can stick this lousy job up your fucking arse.'

'EXCUSE ME!?'

'You heard me. I quit. I'm not gonna stay here one more fucking minute and allow myself to be treated like a piece of shit. I'm too good for this place. I'm too good for you!'

I realise I probably don't look too good for this place covered in red paint.

'Well good luck ever getting a job in London again,' he scoffs, before turning on his heel and heading into the meeting room.

Oh my God. That's it. I've quit. He'll contact everyone he knows and bad mouth me.

No. No, he won't. This is the right thing. Either way it's too fucking late now. I ignore Suzanne's horrified face and run upstairs. I walk past the repelled stares as I go to my desk to get my bag.

'Oh my goodness Poppy. What happened?' Cheryl asks, stood up and offering me a tissue.

'I'm OK,' I say taking it and wiping my face.

'Pops, why are you covered in paint?' Neville asks running over. 'What happened?'

'What happened is that I'm out of here! I'm going.'

I turn round to face the whole office, everyone already staring, jaws practically touching the floor.

'Do you hear that everyone? I'm fucking out of here! I've quit! I'm not taking Victor's shit anymore. He can go fuck himself!' I scream.

I stop my rant, out of breath, to hear the clapping. Everyone crowds around me and claps.

'Well done Poppy,' they cheer.

'He's a right dick – good on ya,' they shout.

'Pops? What?' Neville asks, completely bewildered.

'I've gotta go,' I say pushing past him.

I storm out of the office, past the protestors, covered in paint head to toe. I don't have a job, but my God I have my own self-respect. I might not have the love of my life but I can no longer live in fear of thrown staplers hitting my head. This is the right thing. I'm almost sure. Either that or I'm having a nervous breakdown.

$$*\qquad\qquad*\qquad\qquad*$$

'I still can't believe you quit,' Jazz says, laying on the sofa, throwing Maltesers in her mouth.

'Don't,' I say sighing as I towel dry my hair. 'It's too early to talk about it.'

'Really?' She grins widely. 'Too early to talk about your journey home covered in paint?'

'Shut up,' I snap, shooting her a warning look. 'I've just scrubbed the last bit of paint off me.'

'I'm sorry, it's just too funny.' She covers her mouth to try and stop the giggles escaping.

'Really?' I snap. 'What's funny? How I've completely messed up my life? How I've made Ryan hate me and how I've quit my job? How I'll probably have to move back in with my parents because I won't be able to pay my Dad his rent? How Lilly will probably never speak to me again? Tell me! What the hell is so funny about that?'

She stares back at me, alarmed by my rant. I try to catch my breath but I can't. It's like all of the stress is sitting on top of my chest, like a giant fat man eating another Big Mac. One tear falls down my face, followed by another, before I collapse into inconsolable sobs.

'Oh babe,' Jazz says, putting her arm around me and squeezing my shoulder.

'It's just that....everything's just so....kind of....'

'Floopy?'

'Yeah,' I sniff, choosing to ignore her made up word.

She strokes my hair out of my eyes. 'You've just gotta have faith that one day it's all going to come together. It's all just going to be...'

'Unfloopy?'

'Yeah,' she scoffs. 'Like that's a word.'

A knock at the door startles both of us.

'I'll get it,' Jazz says, jumping up.

I pick up my tea and stare into it while she answers it. I just need to find another job. Quickly. Very quickly.

'Poppy, it's for you,' Jazz calls from the door.

'Me?'

I get up and walk towards the door. Please don't say it's my Mum. I seriously cannot deal with her today. I've managed to avoid her calls up until now, but what if she's taken matters into her own hands and decided to come tell me off? When I get to the door Jazz is stood with her arms crossed defensively, staring at Stuart.

'Poppy! I'm so sorry. Will you ever forgive me?' he cries.

411

'What the hell are you talking about? And what the hell are you doing here?'

'I'll leave you both to it,' Jazz says, shooting me a look which I know means 'any trouble – call me.'

'Poppy. I've made a terrible mistake. Please forgive me. Take me back,' he says, taking my hands.

'Stuart, get off me.' I throw his hands off me.

'Please!'

'Look, let's go outside for a minute,' I say, noticing Jazz staring at us from the sitting room door.

I practically drag him outside by his jacket.

'Stuart,' I take a big breath. 'You have two minutes to tell me what you're doing here.'

'OK,' he says, holding his hands up. 'Poppy, I heard that you've broken up with Ryan and I got your letter. And seeing you the other week, well it made me realise what a massive mistake I made leaving you. I've been regretting it ever since and I'm desperate for you to give me another chance. Please Poppy, give me another chance and I'll spend the rest of our lives making it up to you.'

A nervous laugh comes out of my mouth; then another, until full hysterical laughter takes hold of me.

'What is so funny?' he asks, hurt all over his face.

'Sorry, but are you serious? Am I on a hidden camera show? Is someone going to jump out of the bushes in a minute or something?' I actually look around.

'No, of course not,' he says. I suddenly realise his eyes are red and blood shot.

'Well, what about Claudia?'

'We broke up. She was never right for me Pops. It's always been you,' he says, his big dark blue eyes boring into me.

'So, basically she broke up with you and you thought you could go running back to poor old Poppy.'

'No! I never felt like her the same way I feel about you.'

'Really? Is that why you left me for her? Is that why you've been happily dating her for the past year?'

'Poppy, please! I'll do anything,' he begs, clasping hold of my hands again.

'Oh, why don't you just fuck off Stuart? I'm not interested.'

I throw his hands off me and turn to walk away.

'But...I need you. Please!' He grabs hold of my arm.

'Get off me Stuart!' I push him off me and fight the urge to punch him square in the mouth.

'Look, I'll be waiting for you, whenever you're ready to admit your feelings.'

'Just fuck off,' I shout, pushing him hard, letting out all of my frustration from the last week out on him.

*   *   *

'Hey Po Po,' Ollie says from the kitchen.

'Ollie, have you heard anything about Richard and Annabel?' I ask quickly, before Mum and Dad know I'm here.

'Nah. I keep trying to call him but he's not returned any of my calls.'

'Shit. Do you think he'll come to the wedding without her?'

'Who knows,' he shrugs.

My brother and his words of wisdom.

When I walk into the new Moroccan sitting room I find Mum and Dad watching The Apprentice.

'I'm telling you, I'm so like this man. We're just so similar,' she says.

'Alan Sugar?' Dad says, in disbelief. 'Don't be ridiculous Meryl.'

'Yes. We've both got the same ruthless business mind.'

'Hiya,' I say dropping my bag on the floor and perching on the edge of the sofa.

'Hi darling. How are you? Do you want some wine?' She holds up a half empty bottle.

'No. I'm fine thanks.'

I get the feeling that if I start drinking at the moment I won't be able to stop.

'You OK love?' Dad asks. 'You look a bit upset?'

'No I'm fine,' I say sadly, wishing I could just tell him all my problems and have them go away. Since when did life get so hard? 'Although....Well, I've had a rough couple of days.'

'Really? What's happened?' he asks, turning down the volume and sitting up in his chair.

'Shush Douglas! He's just about to fire someone,' Mum says, grabbing the remote control off him, her eyes glued to the TV.

'Well, I quit my job.'

'Quit your job?' he asks alarmed, his jaw falling open. Mum doesn't even look up from the TV.

'Yeah, but it's for the best. I've just got to find something quickly. I'll be fine,' I lie. 'Then Stuart had the cheek to turn up at the flat today.'

'Stuart?' Mum shrieks, looking up and muting the TV. 'What did he say?'

'Oh, some crap about him wanting me back, but I told him where to shove it.'

'Too right love,' Dad nods.

'Why on earth did you tell him that?' Mum says, almost out of breath. 'Douglas! Pause the TV or something will you? I thought we had that Sky add thing?'

'Sky plus,' Dad says, shaking his head and reaching for the remote.

'Err...because he treated me like crap and then left me,' I say, pissed off that she seems to have forgotten all the times I'd cried on her sofa.

'Yes, but Poppy, maybe you should give him another chance. I mean, he was always lovely.'

'Maybe to you! But he was a bastard to me. And I'm over him anyway.'

'Are you darling? Because you're not getting any younger, and it would be lovely for you to go to the wedding together. You know how much he and Henry think of each other.'

'I'm not just going to bring him to the wedding because Henry likes him!'

'Well...then maybe do it for me, hmm?'

'Why would I do it for you?'

'Just...just to make me happy, that's all,' she says, avoiding my gaze.

'Mum, why are you being so secretive? What are you hiding?' I demand.

'Well...you have to understand darling that I was put in a very bad position.'

Oh God, this must be bad. Mum never apologises.

'What did you do?' I say slowly, bracing myself.

'I...well, I suppose I...let people think...that you and Stuart are still together.'

'What?' I ask, too shocked to understand. 'WHAT?' I scream as it settles in. 'Why the hell would you lie to everyone!?'

'Well I didn't exactly lie darling. Everyone just assumed that you were still going out and I just didn't say anything. It's not really lying.'

'Yes it is! Dad, did you know about this?'

'I told her not to, love. She just wouldn't listen.'

'I'm so sorry darling, but I just assumed that you'd get back together. And then more time went on and I didn't know how to tell them and then all of a sudden it was the wedding.'

'Mum, we broke up a year ago.' I hold my temples in frustration.

'I'm sorry. But don't worry...I'll tell them,' she says sadly.

'Yes, make sure that you do!' I shout.

'I will. Of course....it will be hard on Henry and Abbey to have this bad news over shadow their wedding, but of course I'll tell them. And they'll all be pestering you at the wedding, feeling sorry for you. And Madge is so busy showing off about her daughter Rachel getting engaged. It will be hard, but...I suppose I'll get through it. I just hope the stress doesn't make me ill so soon before the wedding.'

Dear God, why does she do this to me!? Richard's relationship is the one she should be worrying about, not me.

'OK!' I scream. 'God I hate you guys! I will take him to the wedding but that is it. The minute the wedding is over you have to tell everyone it's over, OK?'

'Of course darling! Thank you, sweetheart. I really appreciate it,' she says, pouring herself a congratulation glass of wine.

'And you will tell them straight away after?'

415

'Let's not jump the gun, shall we? I mean, you may end up having a fabulous evening with Stuart and then...well, let's just see shall we.'

Chapter 31

'Poppy, it's Neville.'

'Oh hi Neville! I've actually been meaning to call you. I hear the temps are fighting over you,' I giggle.

'Yeah. You can't imagine how grateful I am to you.'

'Like I said – it's just good PR.'

'Well, thanks. So anyway, how are you? Have you found any work?'

'No. It seems Victor has blacklisted me from the entirety of London. Recruitment agencies aren't even taking me on. He must be really pissed.'

'Oh, he is. You should have seen him! It was hilarious!'

'Oh God. Oh well. Anyway, how are you getting on with the dating thing?'

'Great actually. I've met someone.'

'You're joking!'

Great. So I'm officially the only single person left in the world.

'I know, it's great isn't it! It's actually Megan in accounts.'

Megan? Oh yes, mouse hair lady with glasses that wears broaches.

'Oh Megan! That's great,' I say, trying to sound enthusiastic.

God, I'm going to die alone. Neville was my safety net. Now I'll have to go and buy ten cats and live up to the stereotype of an old spinster.

'Yeah, we've got so much in common! Anyway, I'm rabbiting on. I actually called for a reason.'

'OK?'

'My sister's a PA and is about to give birth to her second baby. They've been looking for someone to replace her and I thought of you. Would you be interested?'

'Would I be interested? Of course I would be! What company is it?' I ask quickly, intrigued.

'She's a PA to Michael Schorsky.'

'Oh, and what company does he work for?'

'He's Michael Schorsky. You know...the famous film director?' he says, speaking to me as if I'm clinically insane.

'Oh. No I don't think I've heard of him.'

He's obviously not that famous.

'Oh, that's strange. Anyway, it's only for a year and there's nothing guaranteed at the end of it, but it's a great opportunity. Not something to be sniffed at.'

'Oh right. Well, I'd definitely be interested' I say, already planning my interview outfit. 'But...well maybe you should offer it to Lilly first.'

I still feel so awful at how we've left things. I've tried to call her but she won't take my calls.

'I did offer it to her first.'

'Oh.' I can't help but feel a little upset. Neville was supposed to be in love with me, but he went to Lilly first?

'Apparently she's already got plans of her own.'

'Really?'

'Yep, but that's all she said. Right, it's settled then. I'll call Charlotte and get it organised.'

'OK great.'

See. Things are looking up. The universe is finally repaying me for my kind actions.

*   *   *

'Well, it's been lovely meeting you Poppy,' Charlotte says to me. 'In fact, I'd actually like you to meet Michael if you have some more time.'

'Oh...yes of course.' I get up and straighten down my suit.

'Just bear with me,' she says, struggling to get up from her seat, her enormous bump crowding her thin frame.

'So are you excited then?' I ask as she leads me through some double doors, into a long corridor.

'Excited about what?' she asks turning to me confused.

'You know...the baby,' I say pointing to her bump.

418

'Of course! Sorry, sometimes I forget! Well, it's my second, so I can't fool myself this time round and tell myself that it won't hurt and it won't be that hard. Plus, I don't think my vagina will ever be the same again, but you know. Sacrifices and all that,' she laughs.

'Oh...yeah.'

She leads me through onto what looks like a movie set. There's a sitting room set up, and people milling around reading scripts. I almost trip over a train set which seems to have a camera at the end of it.

'Wait here,' she says, smiling before she disappears.

I watch her walk over and start chatting to a man in his 40's sitting on one of those wooden camping chairs. He looks over at me, a suspicious look on his face as he looks me up and down.

She runs back over to me, excited and out of breath.

'Poppy – he's got about five minutes to meet you quickly. Follow me.'

I follow her into a small dingy room and sit down, trying not to sweat profusely with nerves.

'Hi,' he says, swinging the door open arrogantly. He stares at me, a bit like a rabbit in headlights, and picks up a chair. He drags it to the farthest part of the room and sits down, still seeming on edge. Is it me or is he acting a bit scared of me?

'Hi – I'm Poppy.' I extend my hand to him.

He flinches and looks to Charlotte for reassurance. She nods and he nervously takes my hand and then slowly shakes it.

This guy is mental.

'So Poppy, Charlotte says that you've got all the right skills, so I just want to get to know you a bit.'

'OK.' I smile nervously, wondering if I actually want to work for a freak. Not that I have a lot of options.

'So Poppy, are you a big fan of my work?'

'Um...yeah...I love your films,' I say lying through my teeth.

Let me think. When I googled him earlier I tried to remember a few of the film titles he'd made.

'I loved Dog's Life.'

419

'Really?' he says smiling, a little unsure still. 'What did you think of it?'

'Really...good,' I say as positively as I can.

'And what did you think about the story?'

'Oh, fab...really...emotional.'

'Emotional?'

Crap.

'Yeah...but in a funny way,' I say desperately trying to think of what a film with a dog in it could be about. 'I love dogs.'

He leans back in his chair and stares at me some more, as if he's trying to figure me out.

'You haven't seen one of my films have you Poppy?' he asks smirking.

'Yes I have!' I squeal.

'No you haven't,' he laughs. 'Do you even know who I am?'

'Um...OK, no I don't. Look, I'm really sorry I wasted your time.'

I get up and head for the door.

'Why? You're hired.' He leans back in his chair smiling widely.

'Sorry? What?'

'You're hired. I've had about six women interview for the position, but the minute they meet me they go all crazy ass on me.'

'It's true,' Charlotte says nodding, 'we've had some right stalkers in here.'

'So...you're not bothered that I don't know who you are?' I try to clarify.

'No – I think it's fantastic. Anyway, I must go get back, but unless we see anyone else today up to the job, it's yours. Charlotte will ring you to confirm soon. See you very soon Poppy.'

Wow – I can't believe it. I'm walking out of here with a new job. And the money – my God the money! I don't want to brag, I really don't. But...well, let's just say that it's £7,000 more than what I'm on at the moment. Can you believe it!? And they want me to start right away. Plus, the new job is going to be at different locations all of the time – depending on where the films are. They even said I'd have to occasionally travel with him to America and other film locations. I

420

know I'm not really the travelling type. I mean, I'm terrified of flying and with my luck it would either crash or get held up by terrorists, but still.

My name is Poppy Windsor and although I am single and pathetic I have a brilliant job working for a movie director.

*   *   *

Cheryl's number flashes up on my phone.

'Hey Cheryl. How are you?' It's amazing how being away from even the most annoying people can make you miss them.

'I'm fine thank you Poppy.' she says formally. 'I'm ringing to invite you to the leaving drinks this Friday.'

'Leaving drinks?'

'Yes. For the people made redundant. We're having drinks at Harry's Bar. Nothing that special, but I think you should come.'

'I don't know...' I can imagine Lilly as she bottles me with her beer bottle.

'Yes Lilly will be there, but for goodness sakes, you two need to make up. Lilly's miserable about it.'

'Really? You've heard from her?'

'Oh yes, we've talked almost every day.'

What?

'Promise me you'll come?'

'I don't know. Maybe.'

'Promise me Poppy. Swear on Matilda's life.'

'Cheryl! I can't swear on her life!'

'You can if you promise.'

'OK! Jesus, I'll be there.'

'Amazing. I have to give you back your tea cup anyway. Now, I've got an idea.'

*   *   *

When I arrive at the bar that Friday night, goodbye banners greet me. Even though Cheryl had promised that it would just be a few people there must be thirty people here. How embarrassing. Probably came to laugh at what a nut case I am.

'Hi Poppy,' Cheryl says, before I've even taken my coat off. 'Are you all set?'

'Yep,' I say, taking yet another deep breath. 'You got the CD and everything OK?'

'Yep. All organised with Phil in IT. Ready to go.'

'Oh thanks.' I smile as I realise she's already pretty pissed.

'I'm really jealous of you Poppy. Going to work for a famous movie director – travelling all over the place. Being free and single. You don't have a sham marriage like me.'

'You'll work it out,' I say hopefully, scanning the room nervously for Lilly.

'Will I?' she says, suddenly seeming sad. 'I confronted him about the affair and he says it's over, but how can I ever trust him again? He hasn't bothered with me since Matilda's been born.'

'I'm sorry Cheryl.' I don't know what else to say.

'Yeah I know. I'm fine, I'm just being silly.' She quickly wipes away a tear. 'Just make sure you appreciate all that you do have while you can.'

'OK thanks,' I say as she heads off to the toilet.

I order myself a wine and almost down it. I really need as much courage as I can get. I scan the room but this time I spot Lilly. She looks as fabulous as ever, her hair freshly blow dried. She's wearing a skin tight black dress which shows far too much of her boobs.

Cheryl signals to me from the other side of the room as the projector is turned on. She gives me the thumbs up and I smile. I walk as calmly as I can towards her, but my stomach's a mess. It's shaking so violently I'm sure I'm going to shit myself at any given moment. My throat is even trembling. Why the hell did I agree to do this? It's not even going to work. She's going to laugh in my face, call me chubby again and walk out.

'Ladies and gentleman,' Cheryl announces on the microphone. 'We're all here today not to feel sad about the few of us that are leaving, but to celebrate the time we had together.'

This is actually the most upbeat I've ever heard Cheryl. She should be a motivational speaker.

'I'd like to hand you over to someone everyone here knows and who has also recently left: Poppy Windsor.'

Even though I'm expecting it I still start in shock. I take the microphone from her and stare back at all of the familiar faces; all of them waiting silently for me to do something. They probably think I'm just going to entertain them. Maybe I should. Maybe I should do the can-can or start the Mexican wave or something.

'Hi,' I say into the microphone, it seeming to echo all the louder. Lilly is staring at me, her eyes full of contempt. 'So, I found this old photo the other day.'

Phil nods at me and a picture of most of us here from five years ago appears on the projector. Everyone instantly laughs. We all look ridiculous and young.

'So, most of us think this is funny. We're all so young and have such ridiculous hair styles. A lot of things have probably changed since then. A lot of you have gone on and got married and had babies. Well...obviously not me.'

Cheryl laughs politely. She's the only one.

'Anyway. I remember my first day here. I'd barely arrived in reception when this big breasted red head came barging past me, telling me to 'watch it'. I thought to myself, who on earth is that bitch?'

A few people giggle and look at Lilly.

'Little did I know she would turn out to be one of my best friends.' I stop myself, as I feel the emotion rising inside me.

'Well most of you will have heard that Lilly and I had a big argument and she decided she didn't want to be my friend anymore.'

I realise I'm speaking like a child, but I continue.

'Well, I don't think that's acceptable. I think most of you married people agree that in marriage people make mistakes all the time and you forgive each other, right?'

I avoid looking at Cheryl. Whoops, I didn't realise I'd upset her with this bit.

'Anyway,' I turn to Lilly. 'Lilly, I'm so sorry for everything that I did to hurt you. I honestly didn't mean it. So I thought I'd re-jog your memory of the past five years and if you still don't want to be my friend then fine.'

A photo of us doing shots at the first year's Christmas do appears on screen. A photo of Lilly holding up a broken heel and me crying hysterically next to it. A photo of us at Cheryl's hen night, dressed in pink tutu's, singing Grease on karaoke. Lilly and I on the floor after fighting over Cheryl's wedding bouquet. A photo of us drinking a fish bowl at a posh bank do Lilly got us into. Lilly dancing on the table at that do while I'm getting chucked out by the manager. Me asleep on the pavement and Lilly dragging me home with a traffic cone on her head. Us at a fancy dress party as Thelma and Louise. Me getting sick on her carpet. Her chucking a drink over a guy's head because he dared say he didn't like my dress.

I watch Lilly throughout all of the images, as everyone around her laughs. I don't know if I imagine it, but I swear she looks slightly touched underneath all of that stubborn aggression on the outside. The last photo flashes up. It's us squeezing each other in a tight hug, our eyes shut with the force. The projector turns off and people turn back to me.

I stare at Lilly and take another deep breath. I slowly get down onto my knees.

'I knew you'd make me beg.'

Everyone laughs and looks expectantly at Lilly, who still hasn't raised a smile. Is she seriously going to leave me hanging here?

'You're a real stupid bitch, you know that?' Lilly says, loud enough for everyone to hear.

I gulp, not sure if this is good. 'Um...yes?'

'Well, as long as you know,' she says, breaking into a massive smile.
She runs up to me and hugs me tightly, so tightly that I think I might
burst. Everyone around us applauds and honestly, it's just like a
movie. I got my friend back.

'You OK, Pops?' Lilly asks giving me a glass of wine.

'Yeah, just a bit emotional, you know,' I say wiping away a tear.

I really am going to miss everyone here. Not Victor or the actual job
part; but definitely the people. Even though I've made up with Lilly I
wonder if I'll see her as much. It's going to be hard with us both at
different jobs.

'I'm so sorry Lilly. I really am.'

'Pops, let's not talk about it again, OK? Anyway, I haven't told you
my great news.'

'What?'

'Me and Cheryl are going into business together,' she smiles.

'What? And you think that's a good idea? You've called her a twat in
the past.'

'Pops, it's all decided. We're doing a freelance PA service.'

'Oh my God, that's great. I've got a job working for some director
guy.'

'Really? Who?'

'Um....Michael Schorky?'

'Shut your fucking mouth! That's fucking amazing!'

'You know him too? God, I'm the only one in the dark.'

'Come on, let's get shit faced,' she grins.

This is why she'll always be in my life.

'I can't get too bad. I've got the wedding tomorrow.'

Chapter 32

'How do I look?' Abbey says to her friend who I think is called Tracey.

It's hard to keep up to be honest. It was mayhem when I arrived here this morning. The whole suite was filled with relatives, photographers, make-up artists, hair dressers. I briefly got introduced to them all but I'm still struggling to remember anyone's names.

'Fine. Does my dress look OK?' she asks back, fiddling with her hair.

'Forget about you – how do I look?' Mum says, pushing them both out of the way of the mirror and examining her cream and brown dress and enormous hat.

That's exactly what she needs – the poor cow looks like she's going to vomit from nerves.

I walk closer to her and place my hand on her shoulder.

'You look gorgeous Abbey. Really stunning,' I say adjusting her veil and trying not to stare at her giant pale breasts threatening to escape from her corset. 'And just remember – at least she didn't wear white.'

'Thanks Pops,' she says, laughing and taking a deep breath. 'Your hands are really cold. Quick – help me.' She grabs both my hands and puts them up to her forehead. 'I'm boiling.'

And she's not lying. Her forehead is heating up.

'I'm just so frigging nervous and with the rain and everything! I mean, what if it's a sign?'

'I've actually heard that rain on your wedding day is good luck,' I say, smiling convincingly.

'I'm just so nervous! What if I trip?' she says, her forehead creasing under my hand.

'Then you trip. Who cares? The main thing is that you and Henry love each other – this really is just a day – the main thing is that you're going to be together for the rest of your life.'

'You're right.' She starts to relax her shoulders.

'Can someone help me with my dress?' Abbey's Mum says, wandering round in a fluster.

'I'll try.' I try the side zip, but there's no way the zips going to go up. The dress is miles too small.

'Sorry, but I can't seem to do it.'

'Why not? It goes up – I know it does! I've worn this dress before!' She's getting more flustered by the minute.

'Let me try,' Abbey says, also seeming to struggle with the zip.

'Oh my God! There's a fly in here!' I hear my Mum shout from the bathroom. 'Quickly! Someone kill it!'

'I've got my own problems!' Abbey's Mum shouts back. 'This bloody dress!'

In a second she whips the dress up over her head and continues to struggle with the zip in her underwear.

'The fly! It's back! Quickly!' I can hear my Mum calling again.

Everyone tries to ignore her, concentrating on their own problems.

'I can't hear anyone coming!' she screams.

I'm going to have to deal with this. She's my mental mother.

'Mum,' I say, walking into the bathroom. 'Stop being a drama queen. Abbey's worried enough.'

'Get the fly swatter! Aaah!' She runs around the bathroom at a fly which I really can't see.

'I can't see any fly,' I say looking round the entire bathroom.

Tracey joins me in the bathroom.

'Everything OK?' she asks, looking at Mum as if she's a huge liability.

'No! There's a fly in here. He's hiding! I won't be able to rest until I know he's dead.' She seems genuinely terrified.

'Come out fly,' Tracey sings 'let's call him Harry. Come out Harry,' she giggles, clearly half cut from the champagne being passed round.

'That's not helping,' Mum says disapprovingly.

'Well, I'm sure he's gone,' I say, all too aware of the time.

'No! He's like a little clever person – he's waiting!'

'It's just a fucking fly!' I scream while Tracey backs out of the room.

'Don't use that language Poppy! And he was like a little spy.'

'A fly that's a spy?' I ask, weary. It's going to be a long day.

'Yes! It was like he had a little camera attached to him! Plus he's hidden so well,' she says, eyeing every corner of the room.

'Mum, how much have you had to drink?'

*   *   *

Before we know it we're all at the back of the church. Mum's stopped thinking a fly is out to get her and Abbey's mum is safely in her dress, even if it is threatening to pop at any moment.

The sound of the organ blasts through our ear drums and we follow her down the aisle, the entire packed church staring at us. I walk as slowly as possible in my dress the colour of poo, trying to ignore the attention and instead focus on the beautiful details. Candles fill the church, emitting a tender romantic light which reflects of the garlands of roses which scent the church. It's beautiful.

I find myself tearing up when the priest talks about the bond of love. They seem to gaze so lovingly into each other's eyes, as if they were the only two people in the world. It's actually made me see my brother in a better light. I know we've never gotten on, but when I see him through Abbey's eyes I see a genuine adoring man. I wonder if I'll ever be that happy.

Is it me or is the priest ogling her breasts?

'I breast you in the name of the father, son and the holy spirit.'

Breast you? Oh my God. Abbey goes bright red and Henry looks like he might punch the priest in the face.

'Bless you! Sorry – bless you,' he corrects himself.

Awkward giggles fill the church. Why can't we just have one family occasion without it ending in shambles?

*   *   *

I'm smiling for photos at the back of the church when I see her. Annabel. What the hell is going on with those two? Are they back together? You wouldn't know from how normally they're behaving.

A hand on my waist pulls me out of my daydream.

'Hey sexy,' Stuart says into my ear. 'You look gorgeous.'

I flinch away from him, his hot breath repulsing me.

'Thanks,' I say trying to ignore him and gaze in the other direction.

'So, are you ready for our date?' He takes my hand.

'It's not a date,' I say throwing his hand away. 'Like I said on the phone – this is just for my family. There's no possibility of us getting back together.'

'OK sweet, whatever you say,' he says, arrogantly guiding me towards his car.

We drive in silence and I'm glad for the quiet. All morning I've had to deal with the constant chatter coming from Mum, Abbey, her Mum, her sister, her friends. I think about how close I was to marrying Stuart before he left. How I'd thought he was going to propose when he said he wanted to talk and instead broke my heart. Would I be happy with him now if he had proposed and we'd instead got married? When I look at him now we just seem like totally different people and it shocks me to think I ever thought we were compatible. And then I think of Ryan. My feelings for him are so overwhelmingly strong, they make any previous feelings seem ridiculously inadequate.

Once we're inside the reception I grab two glasses of champagne of one of the many waiters milling around and down one immediately.

'Thanks,' Stuart says, going to take the other glass from me.

'Sorry – did you think this was for you?' I laugh cruelly, before starting to drink the other one.

'Oh, maybe you should slow down a bit, hey?' he says, looking anxious.

'I don't think so,' I snort. 'If I have to play happy couple I'm going to have to get very, *very* drunk.'

'Poppy!' I hear Aunt Margaret call.

I swivel round and smile at her as she skips over, already looking half cut.

'Hi Aunt Margaret,' I say politely while swigging heavily on the champagne. I can already feel the calming effect of the alcohol.

'Poppy darling! How are you? Oh, Stuart! How are you Stuart?' she asks, hugging him tightly.

'I'm fine thanks Aunt Mags,' he smiles.

Aunt Mags. Who does he think he is? He only met her a few times when we were going out.

'You two still going strong then?' she asks joyfully.

'Oh yes, better than ever,' he says, wrapping his arm round my waist. I want to beat him off with a stick, but instead I plaster on a fake smile and clamp my lips shut. Say nothing.

'Your cousin Sarah is here somewhere with a lovely new man of hers.' She stands on her tip toes to scan the room.

Great. As if I didn't feel shit enough, being here in a dress the colour of dog shit, pretending to be happy with my utter creep of an ex. Now I have to see my supermodel cousin Sarah and her spindly spider legs. God, I hope she's got fat.

'Well, I'm sure we'll bump into her – must mingle,' I say walking away quickly.

I bump right into the happy couple, and Abbey grabs me, plastering a kiss on my cheek, her boob almost falling out in the process.

'Thank you so much for calming me down earlier,' she says, smiling from ear to ear.

'No probs.'

'Yeah, thanks Poppy. Abbey told me what you did – with mum and everything and...well, thanks,' Henry says, smiling awkwardly.

That's probably the nicest thing he's ever said to me.

'Hey Hen!' Stuart blasts running over to us. 'Can't believe you went through with it,' he laughs.

'Someone had to tie me down eventually,' Henry says, smiling lovingly at Abbey.

They launch into a long boring conversation about Rugby as Abbey waits patiently for them to finish.

I excuse myself and walk over towards another waiter, getting another two glasses. I just wish they were giving out free bottles of beer – I hate champagne. But hey, whatever gets me through today.

'Don't be drinking too much sweetheart – you don't want to get drunk and embarrass your brother on his day,' Mum says to me, appearing from nowhere.

'Thanks Mum – I'll keep that in mind,' I say knocking it back.

'Where's Stuart?' she asks looking around for him.

'Off catching up with Henry.'

'I hope he's behaving himself,' my Dad says, clearing disapproving of his presence here.

At least I have one person on my side.

'I've just seen Aunt Margaret. She looks well,' I say, trying to take the attention from me.

'I bet she does,' Mum snorts. 'If I had a bag load of poison injected into my face I'd look fantastic too, but some of us like to grow old with some dignity.'

'I just can't wait for this day to be over already.' I smile sympathetically to my Dad, who I can see is itching to get out of his suit and into his pyjamas.

I weave through what seems like hundreds of people, trying desperately to lose Stuart, who seems to be searching for me whenever I spot him. Why can't he just leave me alone!?

'Ah Poppy, over here,' Aunt Margaret calls to me.

I begrudgingly walk over to her, through the crowds of pretentious idiots and drunken family.

I see her standing next to Sarah and unfortunately she's still the spindly spider legged freak I remembered. Her long blonde hair dangles down towards her bum and her face has the same sucking a wasp expression as ever. But her boobs seem massive. Has she had a boob job?

'Poppy, obviously you remember Sarah and...Where has that new man of yours got off to?' she says, seeming annoyed.

'Oh, he's around here somewhere. Oh, there he is!' She begins waving like crazy at someone over my shoulder.

'Ryan!'

I turn round in what seems like slow motion to face Ryan, my Ryan, walking towards us. His smiling expression quickly changes to match mine. A sickening feeling creeps over me and I feel the colour drain from my face as I remember the last few words he spoke to me.

How can he be here!? How!? Does God hate me that much? Did I murder someone in a previous life!?

'There you are,' Aunt Margaret says. 'Ryan, this is Poppy.'

I freeze, wanting to evaporate; to be anywhere in the world but here. I avoid his gaze and look down at the floor, wanting to die. Hoping he doesn't punch me immediately in the face.

'Actually, we already know each other,' he says, in the same silky voice that I've missed so badly.

I feel the same familiar ache begin in my chest, the same longing and depression that I've felt for the past few weeks. This is torture.

'Oh really? How do you know each other?' Sarah asks seeming rattled.

I glance up at him for a second and feel myself flush when I catch his brooding eyes. Tingles run up my spine. This is unbearable.

'It's a bit of a long story actually,' he says, seeming relaxed. How can he be so relaxed?

'Hi Ryan,' Stuart says, appearing from nowhere and wrapping his hand possessively round my waist.

Oh my God. This is my worst nightmare.

'Hey,' he smiles back, looking confused as he stares at Stuart's hand on my waist.

'Oh, you know Stuart as well?' Sarah asks.

'Yeah, small world,' Ryan says. He stares at me, his eyes cutting through me.

I want to shout out that I haven't got back together with Stuart – that it's all just an act, but then my Aunt Margaret would tell everyone and my Mum would kill me. So instead we all just stand there staring awkwardly at each other. Ryan and Stuart seem to be glaring at each other. Sarah seems to be glaring at me. Aunt Margaret seems to be trying to work out why there is such a weird atmosphere. I almost do my awkward turtle tongue, but stop myself just in time.

'Well, I'm gonna go to the toilet,' I say, desperate to leave.

I practically run in there, sitting on the toilet taking deep breaths and trying to stop my body shaking. How can this be happening? London is a massive fucking place. How can we all be in the same wedding in St Albans?

When I realise I've been in there for about ten minutes I decide I have to go out and face the music. I can't stay in the bathroom all night, can I? No. Mum would only come looking for me.

I walk back into the giant reception room, trying to blend in and act natural as I walk to the bar and start queuing.

'Hey,' Ryan says, appearing next to me, his gaze accusing.

'Hi.' I smile and look down at my hands resting on the bar. I'm too ashamed to look at him.

'So...you're back together with Stuart?' he asks scathingly.

'No actually,' I retort, my back immediately up.

'Huh?'

I look up to see him studying me with curious eyes. His magnetic brown eyes.

'It's a long story,' I sigh.

'Doing stuff to please other people again are you?' he asks smirking.

I glare back at him.

'I'll take that as a yes then.' He gazes at me with probing intensity. There's no question of me looking away. My hands start to shake.

'Look – '

'I'm – '

We both speak at the same time and then laugh nervously.

'Sorry, you go,' he says, his eyes smouldering.

'I was just gonna say I'm really sorry, you know...about...everything.' I trail off, realising there's nothing I can say to change things.

'Don't worry. I was going to say I'm sorry.'

'You're sorry? Why? I'm the one that spread a vicious rumour about you!' I say, surprise showing in my voice.

'You didn't exactly mean to start a rumour. You just made one mistake and it escalated. I see that now. I know how you get yourself in these messes. I just totally overreacted and I'm sorry.'

Wow. This is a turn up for the books.

'That's OK. Although...'

'What?' he asks seeming intrigued.

'No, I was just gonna say that you did scare me a little.' I laugh nervously.

'Did I? Well, sorry. I honestly didn't mean to. To be honest I thought I'd be able to apologise when I came home that night, but...'

'But I'd already gone.'

'Yeah.'

'You could have called me though.'

I wonder if I hadn't bumped into him whether we ever would have seen each other again. I get the barman's attention and order us two beers.

'I know. But you could have too,' he says, his tone making it sound like he was confessing to a humiliating weakness.

'That's because I thought you hated me.'

His face turns sad and serious.

'Poppy, I could never hate you.'

I stare at his honest eyes and wonder if he has any idea of the effect he has on me. How I ache to taste those lips again.

'Ladies and gentlemen, if you could please make your way into the dining room – dinner is now served' the toastmaster shouts.

'Well, I guess I better get going,' I say, not wanting to leave him at all.

'Yeah, me too.' He smiles, but stays put.

'Oh and congrats for getting with Sarah. I'm really happy for you.'

Then before he can react I run into the dining room.

*   *   *

When I sit down at our table I take a swig of my beer and revel in the cool bubbly feeling that fills my mouth.

'Poppy, that's not very lady like,' Stuart says patronisingly.

'What?' I ask him, my back instantly up.

'Drinking beer at a wedding. Here, have some wine.' He starts pouring it for me.

'I'll have whatever the fuck I want, thanks,' I snarl.

Was he always this controlling? I just want to punch him so bad.

'OK, hunny, whatever you want.'

The meal seems to last forever. The food is yummy, especially the chocolate cheesecake, but all I can think about is how much longer I

have to wait until I can punch Stuart in the face. And Ryan. Will I
ever be able to kiss him again? Have I missed my chance forever?
The speeches begin and I hear the usual crap about thanking everyone
for coming and tune out, imagining Ryan naked.

That is until I see Stuart stand up. Why is he standing up in the middle
of the speeches? Everyone's looking at him smiling as he walks up to
the top table and takes the microphone. What the fuck is he doing?
Everyone's acting like this is the most normal thing in the world.

'Hi,' he says into the microphone. 'For those of you who don't know
me, I'm Stuart. First of all I want to say congratulations to Henry and
Abbey and thank you for such a beautiful day.'

The crowd swoons to him and I fight the urge not to vomit.

'Poppy,' he says, turning to look at me.

What the fuck?

'Poppy, I want to take this opportunity to say that I'm sorry for
everything that we've been through over the past year. It's all my fault
and you deserve better. That's why I'm willing to spend the rest of my
life making it up to you. So...' He takes a deep breath.

OH FUCKING GOD. NO. PLEASE NO. PLEASE PLEASE
PLEASE NO.

'Poppy, will you marry me?'

Chapter 33

The words echo around my head. I look around at everyone hoping they'll all be laughing hysterically. Like this is some big joke that everyone's in on, but all I get back is excited grins. Is he serious?

'So, what do you say?' he says.

All I can do is sweat profusely. Why is he doing this to me? Can I tell him to fuck off and die, or will that ruin the entire wedding? Will everyone say, remember Henry and Abbey's wedding when Stuart proposed to Poppy and she turned him down like a bitch?

'She seems speechless,' he says, still smiling at me, like he expects me to be the happiest girl in the world.

'It's a yes!' my Mum yells from the top table. 'Of course it's a yes!' The crowd goes mad clapping and whistling as Stuart runs over to me and kisses me on the lips. I'm frozen. It's like I'm watching this from the ceiling, having some kind of out of body experience. Like this isn't really my life, but a crazy dream. I discreetly pinch myself and wince from the pain.

Everyone around me is beaming.

'Congrats Poppy!'

'About bloody time!'

'When's the big day going to be?'

'You'll make a beautiful bride.'

'Aren't you a lucky girl?'

I still can't speak. I physically can't speak.

Abbey and Henry start their first dance and everyone enthusiastically starts to join in. Mum rushes over to me, grabbing and squeezing us both.

'Poppy, darling! I'm so happy for you both.'

Dad is behind her, looking worried as Mum starts waffling on to Stuart about weddings. My wedding. If I don't start speaking soon, it's going to be my wedding day. I'll be married to Stuart.

'Love,' Dad says, pulling me to one side. 'Are you sure this is what you want?'

I still can't manage to speak, but my eyes start pricking with tears. I have to get out of here. I have to get some fresh air.

I break through the crowds, pushing them away with my hands, and head towards the patio door. I push it open and shiver from the cold air. The rain is still pouring as heavily as this morning and the night is dark. I look around and run over to a small cover a little distance away where some people are smoking, getting half drenched in the process. I look around and take some deep breaths to try and calm myself. What a shame about the weather. The grounds of this hotel would have been gorgeous on a lovely day. There's a view across the town, each lit house seeming like a tiny tea light in the distance.

I step back, leaning against the wall. I close my eyes, trying to hear through the ringing in my ears. I put my cheek against the cold wall and try to hold onto my consciousness. I take my shoes off and stand there considering my options.

Option one – I run. I run until I'm in Scotland. I change my name, dye my hair and pretend none of this mess ever happened.

Option two – Say no to Stuart. Break my Mum's heart and possibly ruin Abbey and Henry's wedding.

Option three – Marry Stuart.

Option four – Keep quiet tonight and then break it to everyone tomorrow that of course I'm not going to marry that two timing creep.

Yes, option four. I just have to keep out of the way from everyone tonight. I wonder if I could get back to my room without anyone noticing I'm gone. I look towards the door and see Stuart coming out, asking people if they've seen me. Crap.

I run round the corner of the garage and straight into someone smoking.

'Oh shit, sorry.' I look up to them apologetically, still panicked and prepared to run. 'Ryan?'

He stares back at me, inhaling heavily on a cigarette.

'What the hell are you doing smoking?'

'I smoke when I'm stressed,' he says, with contempt.

'Why are you stressed?' I ask, almost drooling from how he looks; his hair wet and shaggy.

'Why do you think?' he asks eyeing me suspiciously.

'I don't know. That's why I asked.'

'Maybe because you're making a massive mistake marrying him,' he spits. He takes another drag from the cigarette.

'Who says I'm marrying him?' I ask, annoyed. How could he accept that I'd marry him so easily?

'Err, everyone. And you were hardly protesting,' he snorts.

Even in the dark I can make out his ticked off expression. He probably can't see me fuming.

'I couldn't speak for shock! I'm going to tell him as soon as the weddings over that of course I'm not going to marry him.'

'Why not tell him now?' he says, his voice hostile.

'Because I can't ruin the wedding,' I protest, picturing my Mum's face as my Aunt Margaret tells her she never saw me as the marrying type.

'Whatever,' he scoffs.

'Oh fuck off Ryan. Why don't you go and boss around your girlfriend Sarah?' I fume.

'She's not my girlfriend. We've been on like two dates.' He shakes his head, as if I'm crazy to believe anything else.

'That's not what she's telling everyone. Aunt Margaret's practically planning your wedding.'

'Well, she's a crazy old bag. I should have known she was related to you,' he scoffs, shooting daggers with his eyes. He takes another puff of his cigarette.

'Give me that!' I grab the cigarette out of his hand and throw it into the rain.

'Poppy, what the fuck are you doing?' he shouts outraged.

'I don't like you smoking!'

'Well guess what!? You can't tell me what to do anymore!' His face is tight with anger.

'Anymore? When the fuck could I?'

'Before...' he starts but then stops, looking away into the rain.

'Before what? I can't keep up with your games!' I shriek, tears filling my eyes.

'My games? What about your games!'

'I don't play any games,' I say as tears escape. 'Look,' I try to swallow the tears. 'I won't let you close enough to hurt me again. It's too painful. I think we should just say goodbye.' My voice breaks from the drama.

'Look,' he says, grabbing both my shoulders forcibly. 'Are you seriously going to get back together with Stuart?'

'No! How many times do I have to tell you!?' I sob.

'Well, you told me that before you got engaged to the guy! And like I said, I didn't hear you protesting. And you'll probably be too concerned about hurting people's feelings to ever tell them, and have four kids and a dog before you admit it to anyone.'

'Well, it's not like I've got any better options anyway,' I say, attempting a laugh but it instead coming out as a snort.

'Yes you do Poppy,' he says seriously. He takes my hands and wipes a tear from my face. 'Don't settle for him.'

His eyes envelope me and my legs turn to jelly.

'Sorry, don't settle for who?' Stuart asks appearing from round the corner.

Shit. I immediately drop his hands, feeling like I'm a cheating girlfriend, which I know is ridiculous.

'Actually, I said don't settle for you,' Ryan says to him, his face like thunder.

Their eyes lock and I begin to panic. Ryan's looking at Stuart with so much loathing I think Stuart might actually burst into flames.

'I told you to stay away from her,' Stuart says, his eyes not flickering from him once.

'What? You told him to stay away from me? What?' I ask, completely dazed.

'It's nothing. Come on, let's go,' Stuart says, pulling on my arm. 'Your Aunt Melinda wants to congratulate us.'

'No! I want to know what you meant!' I shout. 'When did you warn him to stay away from me?'

'No, come on we're going.' He pulls me away roughly, hurting my arm.

'She doesn't want to go,' Ryan says, taking hold of my other hand.

439

'What?' Stuart scoffs. 'And she's going to stay here with you? You dumped her the minute you found out about the baby. What kind of man does that make you?' he spits.

Baby? Oh fuck my life!

'I didn't know about the baby then!' Ryan shouts.

Didn't then? Please God, does he think I'm pregnant?

'Well I don't care that she's carrying your bastard child. I still want to marry her,' Stuart says.

'It's not my baby! How many times, it's not my baby!' Ryan shouts.

'It's not!' I shout. 'It's not true!' I shout.

'I don't care whose baby it is Poppy,' Ryan says, not moving his gaze from Stuart. 'It honestly doesn't matter to me.'

'She's still coming with me. Come on Poppy.' Stuart starts tugging me the other way, glaring at Ryan with revulsion.

'She said she doesn't want to go with you,' Ryan says, tugging me his way, his eyes back with fury.

'Both of you just get off me!' I shout, releasing myself from their grasp.

'Just go and see Melinda,' Stuart says, throwing me back angrily.

I lose my footing and fall back onto the wet grass. I look up in shock through the rain just in time to see Ryan's infuriated face.

'Poppy! Are you OK?' He rushes over to pick me up. His hands are trembling from what I think is rage.

'Yeah, I...I...'

Bam! Ryan turns and smacks Stuart straight in the mouth sending him flying backwards. Stuart looks up in shock but his face quickly turns monstrous. He runs at him, his face contorted and tries to punch him, but Ryan ducks and plunges towards him, throwing him onto the grass. Stuart manages to punch him back. They take turns rolling around in the mud punching and kicking each other.

'Stop!' I all I can shout, feeling completely helpless. They ignore me and carry on.

Oh my God. They're going to kill each other and it's all my fault. I run into the hall and grab Ollie and Richard who are on their way out for a cigarette.

'Po Po, what the hell happened to you?' Ollie laughs, taking in my muddy back side.

'Quick, they're fighting!' I shout, dragging them outside.

By the time we get back there's blood coming from Ryan's nose and Stuart's eyebrow is busted open. Ollie and Richard try to jump in, but they just seem to get involved in it, making the fighting group bigger. Elbows are thrust into faces, shins are kicked, arms and legs everywhere. Within a few seconds the fight seems to somehow spill into the hall and onto the dance floor.

People jump out of the way as they all scuffle, skidding to the centre of the dance floor. People stare, horror and shock on their faces. Richard and Ollie don't seem to be getting anywhere, just pushed further apart as the brawling continues.

I stare at them helplessly. How on earth can this be happening?

Ryan and Stuart lock onto each other and fall sideways, heading for the...oh shit, the buffet table. The table collapses as they plunge into it, smoked salmon and cucumber sandwiches falling to the floor. You'd think this would stop them, but they're too busy trying to get the other into a head lock to even seem to notice.

'Stop fucking filming!' I scream at the videographer who's turned his attention from the happy couple to the brawl.

Richard and Ollie finally manage to drag Stuart off Ryan and begin trying to reason with them.

'Calm down Stu, it's not worth it!' Richard says, looking at Ryan.

'I'm cool. I'm fine,' he says, as they relax their grip.

Stuart runs in a split second towards Ryan, pushing him into a table containing glasses of champagne. They smash into what seems like a million pieces, with them both rolling in the glass, wanting to fight to the death.

'For God's sake – stop them!' I shout to Ollie and Richard.

They run over and with the help of my Dad and Henry, manage to hold them back from each other.

'What the fuck is going on!?' Henry shouts over the music which is still playing.

441

'It's him,' Stuart shouts from Richard's grip. 'He's been trying it on with my fiancée.'

'I'm not your fiancée!' I scream, anger bulging through my veins. Gasps fill the room. I turn to see a mix of started and confused faces. Abbey's relatives whisper amongst themselves, already branding us white trash.

'What?' Stuart shouts his face red with fury. 'Don't tell me it's because of *him*!'

'You heard her. She doesn't want you!' Ryan snarls, blood dripping from his nose.

'Just shut up! Of course I'm not your fiancée, you idiot!' I shout, so sick of him and this whole act.

'Poppy! You don't know what you're saying,' my Mum says, suddenly by my side, clutching onto my arm.

'Yes I do Mum! Just stay out of this.'

'I will NOT! I will not let you ruin your life,' she shouts, her face panic-stricken.

'What!? So you think that by taking back a mean, controlling twat like him...I'll be helping myself?'

'Mind your language young lady!' she shouts before turning her attention to Ollie. 'I'm not going to let you be a screw up like your brother! You can't just go around bringing bastard babies into the world.'

Wow Mum. Wow.

Ollie goes to stand up for himself but then sighs heavily as he realises he can't be bothered.

'Why can't you both just be like Richard and Henry!?' she exclaims, her face getting redder by the second.

'Really?' Richard says. 'You think she should be happily married like me?' He looks at Annabel who is quietly trying to back out of the room. 'I'm not happily married! Annabel and I are getting a divorce.'

'W...what?' she stammers, looking around at the crowd, hot humiliation showing on her cheeks.

'A DIVORCE!' he screams back, his cheeks pink. 'We only played happily families today because I knew you'd cause a scene. Like you

442

always do. But fuck it, Poppy caused the scene, so why shouldn't I join in? Maybe I should try living a bit more like Poppy and Ollie. They seem happier than I am! They don't bow to your pressure!'

'But…but…it's only because I love you all,' she sniffs. 'I just want you to be happy.'

'We are happy,' I say quietly. 'You just need to let us get on with it.'

For a second I think she's thinking it through, wondering if she has been an interfering mother. Then she turns to Ryan.

'He's ruined everything! Just get him the hell out of here!' she screams.

What was I thinking? My mother, admit that she might have been wrong? Obviously not.

'Gladly!' I scream. I walk over to him and release him from Ollie's clutches.

'Come on.'

I take his arm and pull him away towards the reception area. I turn around to face the crowd and decide to put the record straight once and for all.

'Oh and just so everyone knows. I'm NOT pregnant! And I'm NOT marrying Stuart.'

Ryan and I walk in silence as I guide him towards the reception desk.

'Excuse me, but can I have the key for my room. I seem to have mislaid it. I think its room thirty five.'

I just hope someone picks my handbag up for me. The immaculate reception clerk looks us both up and down judgementally.

'Do you require any assistance?' she asks narrowing her eyes at me.

'No thanks. I just want my key. It's in the name of Poppy Windsor.'

She stares for a moment longer and then clicks onto her keyboard.

'Here we are. See you at breakfast Miss Windsor.' She takes one more disapproving look at both of us and then turns back to her computer screen.

'Come on,' I say, dangling the key in front of him. 'I'll get you cleaned up.'

He smiles weakly but I can tell he's in pain, the blood still dripping from his nose. I press the lift button.

'So, you're definitely not pregnant?' he asks, his face serious.

'Definitely not. It was a misunderstanding that got a bit out of control.'

He smiles as if he's thinking 'of course, it's Poppy – there's always a drama.'

The lift opens, presenting an old grey haired couple who instantly look alarmed.

'You kids look like you've been having fun,' the lady says, smiling warmly as they walk past us.

We both look at each other and smile.

'We used to have fun, didn't we dear,' the old man says to her, kissing her on her hand romantically.

The lift doors close and I catch our reflection in the mirrored door.

We look a right state. I thought Ryan looked bad, but I look equally rough. I'm drenched from the rain, my hair already starting to frizz and my dress is covered in mud from where I fell. Not that you could really tell, the difference in colour of the mud and the dress not being much.

'Well, we look like a sexy pair,' I say laughing as I turn to him.

His expression is deadly serious.

'What's wrong?'

'Pops, I'm so sorry,' he says, looking pained.

'What for?' I ask, desperate to make him feel better.

'I think it's pretty obvious.' He wipes blood from his nose with his sleeve.

'Don't be sorry. I enjoyed seeing you knock the crap out of him.'

He smiles briefly before the tortured look on his face returns.

'I doubt I'll be invited to their wedding anniversary party.'

The doors ping open and I help him out of the lift, putting his arm round my shoulders, even though I doubt he needs it. I just want to touch him.

I fiddle around with the electric fob in the door. The damn thing won't turn green. I keep trying, but the light stays red.

'Here,' he says, taking it from me, the heat from his touch sending me into a panic.

He swipes the card once and the door instantly opens. I walk in and turn on a lamp.

'Here, sit down and I'll get some towels.' I place him on the edge of the bed.

I run to the bathroom and grab a towel, running it under the tap. I clock myself in the mirror and remove the smudged mascara from under my eyes. I take a deep breath, suddenly nervous, and walk back out to him.

He's turned the TV on to a murder mystery, random dim screams filling the room. He smiles at me, still tortured. I walk up to the end of the bed, throwing my shoes in the corner.

'Still can't seem to wear a pair of shoes, then?' he grins.

I smile and stand in between his legs, patting the wet towel to his bloody nose.

'It seems to have stopped bleeding now anyway.'

I run my hand through his wet hair, his curly waves completely wild from the rain. His big brown eyes lock mine. Breathe, I have to remind myself. I've a sinking feeling that it's a wasted attempt.

'Let me see if you're cut anywhere else,' I say breaking away from his stare. I slowly take off his suit jacket.

'Sorry,' I say, as he winces from the pain.

'I'm OK,' he says, his breathing quickening.

'Shit, there's some blood through your shirt.'

The sight of the blood makes me feel nauseous. I slowly begin to take off his shirt, my fingers fumbling with the buttons. I try to ignore him watching me intently. He makes me so nervous. When I finish unbuttoning I carefully peel it off him to reveal his perfect olive skin and taught muscles. I trace my fingertips over the outline of his bullet wound scar on his shoulder.

'It's healed nicely,' I say, panting. He looks up at me and I struggle to breathe. 'I should check your back for cuts.'

I lean over his shoulder, letting my hands trace slowly down his muscular back, tracing his spine on the way back up. The silky feel of his skin is the stuff fantasies are made of. I dab the towel to a few small cuts, but nothing to worry about. I'm about to lean back when I

445

feel his fingertips gently touch the back of my knees, circling in opposite directions. It's so gentle at first I wonder if it was an accident. Tingles begin to go up my spine, but I try to ignore them. I lean back slowly and he catches me with his gaze, his deep brown eyes inviting me in. I swallow the lump that rises in my throat.

'Anyway,' I break away from it. 'We should probably get you out of your wet clothes before you catch a cold.'

'Yeah.' He puts his hands on my hips. 'You too...before you catch a cold.' His voice is like melting honey.

A mischievous, devastating smile rearranges his features. I stare into those amazing deep brown eyes, desire filling my body.

He reaches round to my back, his touch sending an electric current through my body. He finds the zip of my dress and slowly unzips it, all the time with his eyes locked on mine. I begin to shake uncontrollably. Get a hold of yourself Poppy.

He reaches up to my shoulders and releases the straps, letting the dress fall to the floor. I'm left standing there exposed, in my white strapless bra and black knickers, which I now notice have a hole on the side. But he's not even looking at my body, his eyes are still locked with mine, penetrating me, freezing me in place.

He puts his hands on my hips, pulling me closer to him. I squirm from his touch and hope he doesn't notice. He puts a finger into the hole on the side of my knickers as I try to remember how to breathe.

'Not expecting company tonight then?' he says, smiling amused.

I hit him on the chest, glad he's lightened the mood. He winces slightly, making me feel terrible.

'Oh God, sorry.'

'No, I'm sorry,' he says, serious again. 'But I just can't leave you alone anymore.'

I open my mouth, struggling to think of something to say. I search for the words, but I can't speak. I'm too mesmerised by his beauty. His sad, pained face is all the more beautiful and my body pulsates from the wanting. But I'm scared I'm dreaming this. God knows I've imagined it enough times.

He grabs hold of my hands and looks up at me. He stands up. He's so close, completely towering over me. I look up at him and feel every fibre in my body want to reach out for him, but my rational mind holds me back.

His hand strokes slowly from my hips up my back, making it curl with pleasure, until his hands are at my face. He grabs my face with both hands and leans in to me. His lips touch mine, engulfing me. I melt and almost feel my body go floppy from shock. His hands move from my face into my hair, then down to my back, wrapping me up in pleasure.

I hang my arms around his neck, diving in for more, determined not to let his lips get away from mine. I need more. I let my hands travel down his back, urging him closer, making him shiver.

He lifts me up and my legs instinctively wrap round his waist. He carries me the few steps back to the bed and places me down on it. He leans over me, kissing the insides of my thighs, then my stomach, making me squirm and whimper some more.

I shudder from the intensity of sensations as his hand glides over my thigh. He groans, a sound that makes my pulse leap. Makes me squirm to be closer still. He pulls away and I moan from misery.

'Promise not to hurt me?' he asks seriously, his face guarded.

I look at his defined arms and broad chest. Is he serious? Is this what's wrong with him? He's scared I'll hurt him in sex? Does he think I'm a massive big fat whale that's going to sit on him and break his bones?

'Um...yeah, of course,' I smile, slightly confused. 'I'll be gentle with you...and try not to touch your cuts.'

A wide smile breaks over his face.

'No, I don't mean it like that,' he laughs. 'I mean...promise not to hurt me.' His face is full of raw vulnerability.

I smile to myself. How could he think little old me could hurt a complete sexual being like him.

'As long as you promise not to hurt me,' I say, still half joking. But the truth is I'm already protecting my heart. I'm already scared of how he makes me feel.

'Of course not,' he smiles, drawing me in and kissing me softly on the lips.

I'm desperate to give in to him; to let my body take over. But he's too gorgeous to truly love me.

I pull away, ignoring the agony of being away from him.

'Promise you won't fuck me over? I don't think I could handle you breaking my heart.'

As soon as I've said it I feel stupid. Why can't I just go with it and see what happens? It's my stupid romantic side taking over again.

'Pops,' he exhales deeply, seeming annoyed.

'No, I mean it,' I interrupt. 'If we're going to do this we're going to do it properly.'

He straightens up, pretending to be serious, but not managing to hide his smile.

'I'm serious. No more mind games. No more mixed signals. No more kissing other girls. I'm not going to be a doormat anymore. If we're together we're together.'

'Glad to hear it,' he nods. He tucks some hair behind my ear and smiles. 'I agree to the terms. I could never hurt you. I'm completely crazy about you.'

'Thank God.' And then I pounce on him.

Chapter 34

When I wake up I'm sure that it was all a beautiful dream. I lie completely still, hoping that I can still at least remember it. I want to savour all of the dreamy details. Maybe I'll write it in a dream book. The kissing, his warm touch, the way his body felt, made completely for mine.

But then I feel his arms wrap round me and his breath on my neck.

'Morning,' he breaths, kissing my cheek.

I turn around completely shocked and gaze into his deep brown eyes as I wrap my hands possessively over his shoulders.

'I thought it was a dream,' I say as he slips his arms around me and starts kissing me on the mouth.

'Let's re-jog your memory then,' he says, grinning and leaning in to kiss me. 'Unless…you want some breakfast first?'

My tummy grumbles, betraying me.

'I'll take that as a yes,' he chuckles as he flicks through the room service menu.

'Yeah, OK. Just get me whatever.'

He picks up the phone with his back to me.

'Hello. Yep, were in room thirty-five. I'd like to order some food. I'll have a full English and my girlfriend will have the same, some pancakes and a tea. It has to be in a china cup, preferably a pretty one. Bring lots of sugar.'

Oh my God. He called me his girlfriend.

He turns back to me, completely unaware of how much I adore him.

'What?' he says, looking at me quizzically.

'You called me your girlfriend,' I say, flushing from saying it out loud like a teenager.

'Yep,' he says, kissing me on the nose. 'I'm gonna have a shower.'

He kisses me again and finally tears himself away.

'OK. Don't be long,' I say as seductively as I can.

I lay there thinking I must be the luckiest girl in the world and pinch myself one more time to check that it still isn't a dream. The room phone starts ringing. It must be room service asking a question about the food.

'Hello?'

'Pops, it's me,' Jazz says. 'You lose your mobile?'

'Hey Jazz. Oh my God – you are never gonna guess what happened last night.'

'Really?' she says, sounding completely uninterested.

'You OK?'

'Yeah...I think so. It's just. Something's happened. I need to tell you something.'

'OK, but let me tell you mine first,' I say excitedly.

'OK,' she says, seeming brighter.

'Guess who's in the shower right now?'

'Pops, anyone could be in the shower right now!'

'I know that! I mean. OK, who did I spend the whole night having sex with?'

'Oh no Pops! You're back together with Stuart? I knew this was going to happen!'

'No! No! It's Ryan!'

'Oh my God! Really? How?'

'It's a long story. Anyway, we had a long chat last night. Well, you know, in between. And he's amazing. He's even said I'm his girlfriend! Can you believe it?'

'Yeah that's great babe,' she says, sounding distant again.

'What's up?'

'Just promise you will be calm and not panic?'

'Oh God! What's happened?'

She's broken something. Or she's set the flat on fire! That's it! She's ringing me right now from the street, covered in one of those silver blankets that look like baking foil.

'Have you burned the flat down?'

'No! God, thanks for the confidence.'

'Oh,' I say sighing with relief. 'OK, well if it's not that what is it? Just tell me!'

'OK...I'm pregnant.'

450

THE END

Lightning Source UK Ltd.
Milton Keynes UK
UKOW04f1949100815

256709UK00001B/2/P